# ANNA SAYBURN LANE

# The Peacock Room

First edition

ISBN: 978-1-9164208-2-3

This book was professionally typeset on Reedsy.
Find out more at reedsy.com

*To Brenda and David, with love*

# Prologue

He weighed the weapon in his gloved hand, the heft of it reassuring. A proper gun, a man's gun. No questions, he'd been told by the guy in the south London pub. You don't want to know where it came from. He could guess, though. It smelled of grease and sweating hands, drugs gangs securing their turf and swaggering kids trying to impress each other.

He examined the black casing, then arranged on the table a bottle of isopropyl alcohol, a toothbrush and a soft cloth. He wanted it properly clean, a fitting tool for the work he had planned. He didn't want its history in here, stinking the place out with desperation and petty crime. Disgusting. He frowned at the particles of grit gumming up the trigger mechanism, the dirt embedded in the grip. If he could, he would have bought a new gun, box fresh and shining with a gleaming mahogany stock.

Bring me my bow of burning gold.

It would have to do. He put down the cloth, peeled off the plastic gloves and threw them in the trash, reached automatically for his bottle of hand sanitiser. The clean, cool scent soothed him.

It had been surprisingly difficult to get hold of a gun. He

was used to the US, where you could pick up a semi-automatic and enough ammunition to take out a junior high along with a quart of milk. Guns were harder to come by in England. But not impossible, if you had cash and connections and knew your way around the Dark Web.

He needed to practise. Eight rounds in the magazine, and he didn't know if he'd have time to reload. They all had to count. His face relaxed into a smile as he ran through the targets. Who to take out first? There would be so much choice. Personal, or political? He could pick them off, one by one.

Would she be there? She had to be. She'd be first. Like the feminists said, the personal is political. Well, she'd asked for it. His jaw tightened, remembering her face as she refused him. She'd had the gall to say no. After everything she'd done, she should be happy he'd even considered her.

He picked up the gun.

There was a shooting club along the coast, where guys in grubby khaki T-shirts with beer bellies blasted away at clays. He'd been down a couple of times, used the range and had some beers in the grim little bar. It had been useful. And on Sunday mornings, the noise from the range was good cover for his own practice. He could hear them now, the crack of shotguns echoing over the marshes.

He loaded the pistol and stashed it in his inside jacket pocket. He hated to think where it had been kept before. Stuffed down a pair of sweatpants, probably, nestling against pimpled buttocks.

Then he took a walk along the seashore, to the clump of scrub and bushes where he'd set up his targets. No-one came down this end of the beach, except a few lonely fishermen when the tide was high. He arranged the cardboard figures with painted faces. He'd taken more time on them than perhaps was necessary, considering what he was about to do.

He stood with his back to the trees, lifted the pistol and lined up the sights. He squeezed, firm but gentle, like he'd been taught. He had a good eye, a steady hand. By the time he'd finished, eight cardboard heads hung in tatters.

He walked forward to collect them, satisfied. At the top of the shingle shelf, he saw what he first thought was a body, prone on the beach. Shit. He broke into a run. Had he hit someone?

As he approached, it leapt up, a bundle of ragged clothes and a wild head of hair. The guy looked terrified, his eye fixed on the gun.

Rags flapping, the figure turned and hared along the beach, scrambling up the bank and disappearing into the distance. The gunman stood and watched him go. A tramp, maybe. A hobo. Nothing to worry about. He gathered up the cardboard figures and carried them back to the caravan.

# Chapter 1

H elen Oddfellow clutched her mug of tea, her eyes resting on the rooftops visible from the balcony of her tiny flat.

It was hot already, a beautiful May morning. The sky shimmered high and blue over London, a haze of pollution smudging the horizon like a dirty thumbprint. Tiredness was baked into her bones.

Sleep no longer came easily. When it did come, it brought a freight of unresolved troubles that her mind turned over constantly, like pebbles in her pocket. Last night she'd given up trying to sleep sometime after midnight and pulled on her walking boots. She'd traced the curve of the river Thames east from her home in Deptford, walking herself into exhaustion along the waterfront. In the grey pre-dawn, she'd returned home, slept for a while, and the alarm had rung all too soon.

She had a powerful urge to leave the flat again, stride out into the city or up onto Blackheath, stretching her limbs and quieting the mental chatter until her mind could rest. Or if not rest, be still enough to sit with pen and paper, to try to capture some of the images in her head. A day of walking and writing, that's what she needed.

But there was marking to do. Always, she'd learned, there

4

was marking to do.

When Helen started work as junior lecturer in English Literature at Russell University, she'd been looking for a fresh start, a peaceful life. She'd hoped the challenge and stimulation of a new job would help her move on from the trauma of the past few years, and the schedule would provide a comforting structure to her days. The post paid enough – just – to cover her modest outgoings.

Since September, she'd learned a lot. She'd discovered she enjoyed teaching undergraduates, seeing their fresh reaction to texts she had studied for years. She was expected to research and publish alongside the teaching, but that was no problem; she loved research. She was able to continue the work she'd started for her doctorate; her discovery of a play by Elizabethan playwright Christopher Marlowe had given her more than enough material. But it all took time. Which was why she'd planned to spend a couple of hours of Sunday morning getting her marking done.

Her phone rang.

'Helen? It's Nick. How're you doing?'

Nick Wilson. Her face flushed with pleasure. She hadn't seen the journalist for ages.

'I'm fine, thanks. What about you? How's work?'

Helen knew he'd moved on from the local newspaper where he'd been working when they first met. Life had been busy since then for both of them, but she missed his lively company.

'I'm good. Sorry for calling so early. I wanted to ask you about something I'm working on. It's a bit weird, but I thought it might be up your street. Fancy a coffee?'

Helen looked at the papers covering the desk in front of her.

'I'd love to. But I have a heap of work to do. And I promised Crispin I'd go down and have coffee with him later. Can you tell me over the phone?'

Her elderly neighbour relied on her for company these days, and she'd seen little of him in the past week. Sunday mornings were a regular date for a catch-up in his basement flat.

'It probably won't make sense. I need to show you some stuff.'

'Then why don't you join us? Crispin won't mind. He'll be pleased to see you. Come at about eleven.'

Something weird and up her street. She smiled. Life was never dull when Nick was around. Although, after the past few years, a dull life was pretty much what she'd been hoping for.

# Chapter 2

As predicted, Crispin was pleased to see Nick, especially when he handed over a box of patisserie. 'Maison Bertaux! How splendid. I haven't been for years.'

Crispin manoeuvred his wheelchair around to the big old coffee machine and started making cappuccino. Helen had helped him fix his yellow cravat and tie his shoelaces. The carers who got him out of bed and dressed him each morning didn't have time to make him look presentable, he'd grumbled. They kept telling him to get shoes that fastened with Velcro.

'Can you imagine?' he said, shuddering. For Crispin, looking dapper for visitors was a matter of pride. Now he was in his element, grinding beans and frothing milk while Helen piled eclairs, fruit tartlets and chocolate squares on a plate.

'Just like old times,' he said, beaming. 'Coffee, cakes and a handsome man for breakfast.'

Nick laughed and took a seat at the kitchen counter. He'd have blushed, a couple of years ago, thought Helen. But he seemed to have gained in confidence and urbanity.

'Don't tease him,' she told Crispin. 'He won't come again.'

He was right, though, she thought. Nick was looking rather

handsome. He'd gained muscle, his shoulders broad in his fresh white T-shirt. He was no longer the skinny kid with the cheeky banter, pushing his luck and more often than not finding he'd pushed too far.

'You do look well,' she said, feeling absurdly shy.

'Weights and kickboxing,' he said. 'I need to look after myself.' He didn't just mean his looks, Helen thought. He'd taken a bad beating during their previous investigation together, and needed three operations to fix his broken wrist.

He'd grown up in other ways, too; his dreadlocks were now cropped short, his clothes better-fitting, smarter. He still rode a motorbike, although the shiny model parked outside looked newer than the second-hand two-stroke he'd once ridden. His jacket was new, too, expensive-looking brown leather. Life seemed to be treating him well.

'So how's the new job?'

He shrugged. 'Pays the rent.'

'Are you still living with your brother in Lewisham?'

'Nah. Got a place in Soho now. I'm sharing with a mate from work. Handy for the office.'

Helen and Nick had met two years ago, when Helen's hunt for a hidden play had brought her to the attention of the same far-right activists Nick was investigating. After the success of his scoop, Nick had been in demand. He'd moved to a news and entertainment website, *Noize*. It clearly paid a lot better than the local paper.

He pulled a shiny silver laptop from the courier bag over his shoulder. 'To be honest, most of the work is really boring. I'm social media correspondent, which basically means I have to write about whatever some lame celebrity is saying on Twitter or Instagram. Last week's big story was a beef between a grime artist from Tottenham and a white rapper from LA. Anything with a racial edge, they chuck my way. Like it's a hand grenade, and only a mixed-race bro can defuse it.'

His grin was rueful, but Helen could see he was angry. He was a good reporter, tenacious and brave. He deserved better.

'So I've been doing my own research on the side. I'm hoping they'll let me work on it full-time, once I've got something to show them.' He opened a browser on his laptop. 'You got wi-fi, mate?'

Crispin snorted. 'I am not a complete dinosaur.' He snaffled a miniature chocolate eclair. 'These are so delicious.'

Nick keyed in a string of digits. 'Hope this doesn't bring MI5 round to investigate your IP address. I'm going in via Tor.' He grinned at Crispin. 'Don't worry, it's not illegal. You're practically untraceable. But of course, it's pretty heavily monitored these days, especially the buying and selling sites.'

'OK, so I am a complete dinosaur,' said Helen. 'What are you talking about?'

Nick paused, showed her a page that looked like it came from the early dial-up days of the internet: a black background with green glowing letters.

'The Dark Web. The sort of websites that you can't find on search engines. I've been investigating the way it's used by the far right. I wanted to see if there was anything online about Gary Paxton's trial. Turns out there's quite a lot. They're calling him a martyr; saying he was fighting to save the white race from an Islamic takeover. The great replacement. Heard of that?'

'I think so.'

'I have,' said Crispin. 'It was in *The Guardian*. A whole lot of straight white men who think they're oppressed.'

'That's the one,' said Nick. 'I've been digging around in these chatrooms and blogs, looking at the links between them. They all hook up: the ones that hate people of colour with the ones that hate gays; the ones that hate women with the ones that hate Muslims and Jews.'

'So basically anyone who isn't one of them,' said Crispin. 'Goodness knows how they think they can reproduce.'

'Haters gonna hate,' agreed Nick. 'But believe me, they've thought of that.'

Helen sipped her coffee and wondered what any of this had to do with her. 'It's interesting,' she said. 'I can see why you're doing it. But you said there was something you wanted to ask me about?'

'I found a really bizarre blog; an online comic, very graphic and violent. At first it looks like your basic misogynistic rubbish. But there's more to it.'

He moved the computer round to show a graphic cartoon image of a naked blonde woman, lying across a bed. Standing above her, holding a sword with its tip in the woman's open mouth, was a green and gold monster.

Helen screwed up her face. 'That's horrible.'

'Yeah, but look again. Look at the title,' said Nick.

Helen looked. 'Rintrah the Reprobate. So what?'

Crispin swivelled his chair around to get a better look at the picture. He reached for his reading glasses.

'There's something familiar about that monster,' he said. 'What is it?'

'There's more,' said Nick. 'The whole blog is about this character Rintrah. He's an evil superhero, carrying out acts of vengeance, mostly against women. It's crude, but kind of well-drawn, don't you think?'

Helen shrugged. 'Yeah, but...'

'So I looked him up,' Nick continued. 'Rintrah. There are two main sources. The first is a minor cartoon character in the Marvel Universe. The other source is the writings of the poet William Blake, which were apparently an inspiration for many of the Marvel Comics characters. I found a whole load of stuff about Rintrah online, written by one of your colleagues.'

'You're kidding?' said Helen.

'Nope. Petrarch Greenwood, Professor of Poetry at Russell University. Don't you work with him? He wrote all this stuff about Rintrah the Reprobate in Blake's mythology. He calls him the spirit of rebellion: a despised outsider, angry and destructive, but necessary, like the French Revolution.'

'Isn't he the one who was on the telly? Not the monster, I mean. Petrarch Greenwood.' Crispin was peering over Helen's shoulder.

Professor Greenwood was one of Helen's most senior colleagues, and a genuine celebrity. His television series on Blake and Wordsworth, *Romantics in the Age of Revolution*, had made him a public intellectual. Helen and Crispin had watched the series together, amused by Greenwood's flamboyant waistcoats, waxed moustache and booming voice. Crispin had called him a terrible ham as he strode through the streets of Soho, declaiming Blake's verse in front of sex shops and coffee bars.

She'd been slightly in awe of the man when she finally met him. But he'd been more friendly than many of the other academics, greeting her with a rather discomfiting bear-hug when they were introduced. And he was popular with the students, a gaggle of them trailing after him as he processed across the campus.

Helen stared at the monster. It stood on two feet, a hulking beast with heavy shoulders, covered in a shimmer of green and gold scales. Add a moustache, and it would look not unlike Petrarch Greenwood in his silk waistcoat, she thought. Predatory, nasty, but somehow magnificent.

'*The Ghost of a Flea!*' said Crispin, suddenly. 'That's what it looks like.' He turned to Nick. 'May I?'

He searched online for a moment, then showed them an image of a painting by William Blake: a bug-eyed monster with a protruding curled tongue.

'That thing scares me half to death. It's in the Tate. My mother took me to see it when I was a child. I've not been the same since.'

'There are similarities,' Helen agreed, peering at the sinister figure. 'Let's see if we can find a Blake image of Rintrah.'

They found another image, more human this time, but covered in scaly armour and holding a sword.

'This one on the blog is like a mash-up,' observed Nick. 'Like he's taken the two images and made something in between.' They flicked back to the blog. The similarities were striking. Whoever drew the images on the comic strip had borrowed Blake's iconography.

'Hang on,' said Helen, reaching for a strawberry tart. 'You're not suggesting that Petrarch Greenwood draws this blog?'

'Nah, that's not it. I wanted to know more about where this stuff all came from. Because whoever drew this is planning something. Look.'

Nick opened up the comments section of the blog.

'This takes us to the chatroom where they discuss all this

shit. They call it Rintrah Roars. It's mostly pathetic fantasies, sad guys mouthing off about what they'd like to do to women, if they ever left their parents' houses. But I found this.'

He clicked on a topic. '"Channel the spirit of Rintrah". Bear with me. It's pretty horrible, but there might be something here.'

Helen read through the discussion, pressing her lips together at the violence and hatred of the words. Her strawberry tart no longer tasted so delicious. Rape threats. Death threats. Enthusiastic discussions about using sexual violence to subdue uppity women, feminists who had apparently taken over the world.

'I don't see...' Then she saw. Someone had posted a flyer for a conference due to be held at Russell University in a couple of weeks' time. *Out of the Silence: A Celebration of Women's Words*, organised in her own department by Helen's boss.

'All the feminazis in one room,' said the text beneath it. 'What do you think? Do we pay them a visit?' Below was a list of vicious suggestions about what that visit should entail.

Helen went cold. 'This is a threat. Have you told the police?'

Nick looked annoyed. 'Nah. It's too vague. They'd laugh at me.' He wasn't a fan of the police, Helen knew. 'They're just chatting shit. I mean, it's a bit of a jump from commenting on an online comic to actually turning up at a conference. But I thought maybe you should know about it. And I wondered if you could get me a ticket? Might as well go along in case it does kick off.'

Helen sighed. What was she supposed to do with that information? 'I'll talk to the department head. I'm sure I can get you a press pass. Leave it to me.'

'Great. One more thing. I want to find out who's behind

the blog, who the author is. I'm going to set up an avatar, join the forum and start commenting. I thought it might impress the author if I could make the avatar Blake-related in some way. You know, try to get into his confidence. Maybe meet up sometime. I hoped you could help.'

'I really don't know enough about Blake. And it sounds dangerous.'

He grinned. 'Don't worry about me. I'll be careful. This is all online at the moment, anyway.'

Helen pushed away the half-eaten tart. She did worry. Nick's curiosity had almost got him killed before now.

'I'm not the expert. Maybe you should see if Petrarch Greenwood can help. Although he's busy writing his new book at the moment. But... hang on.'

Helen did know another Blake expert, she realised. And one far more approachable than the celebrated professor. Until she'd taken up the post at the university, Helen had worked as a walking tour guide, leading historical tours through London. The guides network was packed with expertise on all sorts of surprising subjects.

'I've got a friend who does William Blake walking tours around London,' she said. 'Barbara Jackson. Anything you need to know about Blake, she's your woman.'

She reached for her phone and looked up Barbara's email address. 'I really ought to get in touch with her. It's been too long.'

# Chapter 3

Something hit Nick on the side of the head. He opened his eyes, retrieved the scrunched-up ball of paper from his desk and lobbed it back.

A message pinged on his laptop. 'Have you finished that story yet?'

He shut his eyes again. His headphones delivered a blanket of noise, masking the tiresome banter of his colleagues. He'd written the story, but couldn't bring himself to read it over. Three hundred words about a footballer's wife who'd posted a series of cryptic but insulting messages about a pop singer who had been photographed with the footballer in a nightclub. His job was to decode the insults for the readers too thick to understand them without help.

Nick was so bored. He'd not admit it to anyone, but he missed his days on the local paper, getting out and about on his patch. This was not how he had envisaged life as a national journalist. He'd dreamed of joining the ranks of overseas war correspondents, dodging bullets and shrapnel for glory. Or working undercover, getting in with criminals and dodgy politicians, then exposing them in a blaze of publicity.

The music stopped. He opened his eyes. Toby, his news editor, was sitting on his desk, the headphone jack in his hand.

'What is your problem, Wilson? Where is my story?'

'It's done,' he admitted. 'Just checking it over.' He nudged the screen into life. An image of William Blake's *Ghost of a Flea* looked shiftily out at them.

'What the fuck is that?'

'Sorry. Nothing. Just something I found online,' said Nick. He'd been reading Blake's poems, none of which seemed to make a great deal of sense. He could get on board with *The Tyger*, vaguely remembered it from school. And some of Blake's paintings were brilliantly weird. But Nick wasn't really a poetry kind of guy.

'Here.' He found the story, trying not to wince at its banality.

'Send it over, then.'

Nick clicked his mouse.

'There, that wasn't so difficult, was it?'

Nick got to his feet. 'I need a coffee.'

To his annoyance, Toby followed him out to the office kitchen and leaned against the table football machine.

'Do you like this job?' Toby asked. 'Do you like the nice shiny office and the nice shiny salary and the nice shiny things you can buy with it?'

Nick sighed. 'Of course I do. But...'

'Of course you do. So why do you give me such a pain in the arse the whole time?'

Nick viewed his boss dispassionately. A middle-aged white man, trying to hang on to his youth with expensive jeans, brand T-shirts that stretched over his gut, and ridiculous puffy trainers. Worse, he tried to be matey with his young team, mangling street slang and attempting high fives. He made Nick tired.

'I'd like to work on something a bit more relevant,' he said.

'Social media is relevant. It's the only thing with any relevance these days. You want to go back to the bad old days of print?' Toby had worked for a tabloid newspaper before joining *Noize* and liked to affect a world-weary cynicism.

'OK.' Nick blew out his cheeks. Maybe it was time. He couldn't bear any more celebrity rubbish. 'How about this? I've been looking at some of the stuff that gets published out on the fringes. Forget Insta and Snapchat. I'm talking about the wild west of the web.'

Toby nodded. 'Wild West Web. That's good.' Nick knew he liked a snappy soundbite.

'I want to follow up something I found on the Dark Web. It's a sort of online comic. Quite violent, misogynistic, but very well-drawn. It's getting a lot of attention among the far-right bloggers and chatrooms.'

'Show me.'

Nick picked up his phone. 'Here.' He opened the blog at a post where Rintrah rampaged through a nightclub, overturning tables and smashing bottles, decapitating a man on the dance floor and dragging a woman out by the hair.

Toby sucked his breath in sharply. Then he started to chuckle. 'He's got something, this guy. Like you said, it's good, it's well-drawn. So what do you want to do – feature some of the comics? Get him to do some stuff for us?'

'No!' Nick couldn't believe it. Did Toby think this malice deserved a wider audience? 'I mean, I don't know who he is yet. I want to earn his trust, find out more. Try to meet him. There could be a story there.'

Toby looked again at the image, grinned. 'Yeah. Yeah, go for it. It's nasty, but it's edgy. I like it. See what you can find out.'

Back at his desk, Nick swallowed down his coffee, thankful to be allowed to focus on something that actually engaged his brain. He needed to make this work.

He went deeper into the forum. None of the commenters seemed to recognise the Blake references. It must be frustrating, he thought, to do all this stuff and then just have a bunch of idiots responding to it. Surely the author would be happy if someone actually got what he was doing?

He set up a new email account, linked it to a burner phone he'd bought at the weekend and created a profile on the forum. After some thought, he picked the user name Flea, and used a detail from the Blake painting as his icon. But how to respond to the posts? Helen was right, he thought. He didn't know enough.

He tapped out an email to Barbara, the woman she'd suggested he get in touch with. If he was going to sound convincing as another Blake fanatic, he needed help from someone who knew Blake inside out.

It had been good to see Helen again. She'd looked tired, and she was too thin. But she'd seemed a bit more at ease, more sociable than when he'd seen her last. He still cherished the memory of their earlier adventures, Helen shinning down a drainpipe in a slinky red dress, jumping on the back of his motorbike to escape from their attackers. Those were the days. In the last couple of years, she'd hidden herself away, seeming happy only when shut up safely in a library.

He remembered her complimenting him the day before, and found himself grinning like a fool. Don't be an idiot, he told himself sternly. She's just a friend.

# Chapter 4

Helen fidgeted in the low chair Caroline had waved her towards, her long legs folded awkwardly. She'd barely arrived at her tiny windowless office in the heart of Bloomsbury when Jessica, the departmental administrator, had tapped on the door.

'Caroline wants to see you urgently,' she'd said. The girl had looked thrilled. There was nothing she liked more than a bit of drama, especially if she could relay it around the department.

'OK...' Professor Caroline Winter, head of the English Literature department at Russell, was not someone you could say no to. 'Do you know what it's about?'

'Sorry!' trilled Jessica. 'No idea. But she had a long conversation with Petrarch Greenwood yesterday, and she's been in a right mood ever since. I can always tell. She's swiped the chocolate biscuits from the kitchen.'

Caroline was on the phone, one hand running through her frizzy mop of hair. She'd recently swapped her floral smocks for neutral trouser suits with statement jewellery. Her face was pink with heat, clashing with the orange blouse that had come untucked from her beige trousers.

What had Helen done wrong? Her students seemed to like

her. She'd submitted her research proposal on time. A few months ago, she had tentatively suggested a speaker on the Restoration playwright, Aphra Behn, for the conference on women's writing that Caroline was organising. Perhaps it was about that.

The event was going to be high profile, with big names from the academic, political and literary worlds. Jessica said it was Caroline's opening bid in her campaign to become vice chancellor of the university, a post likely to become free within the next couple of years. Presumably her change of wardrobe was an attempt to look more managerial. Helen didn't think it was really working.

The wall above the woman's head was dominated by a huge wall planner, the words *Out of the Silence* scrawled over it in wonky capital letters. Helen strained her eyes to see the headings. 'Two inches wide: women novelists and the domestic sphere,' read one. 'Daughters of Africa: celebrating the diaspora,' said another. The names beneath were of world-class scholars and authors. She couldn't see anything about Aphra Behn.

Most of the office shelves were crammed with texts about the eighteenth century, including Caroline's own best-selling *Marriage and Marketability: The Economics of Jane Austen*. The book was a classic, admired for its incisive analysis of the novelist and her times, and had cemented her position as the foremost Austen scholar of her day. Less well-known was her ruthless efficiency as an administrator and department head. Anyone who underestimated Caroline Winter based on her scruffy appearance was likely to regret it.

Caroline had kicked off her court shoes. She listened intently for another moment, then sighed deeply.

'If there's anything specific, report it to the police,' she said, her voice crisp. 'If it's just anonymous nonsense, ignore it. We'll have security. I'm sure it's nothing they can't handle.'

She switched off the phone and fixed Helen with her astute grey eyes.

'Death threats,' she said, fanning herself with a tatty cardboard folder. 'Who would have thought a conference on women's writing would bring the maggots out of the cheese?'

'I saw something online,' said Helen. 'I was going to tell you about it. There was a flyer for the conference, and a lot of horrible comments.'

'Oh, it's all nonsense,' said Caroline. 'Although some of the speakers are getting jumpy. I have at least one slot still to fill. I need something new; someone that hasn't already been done to death. Ideally an unknown or newly discovered writer. Any ideas?'

Aphra Behn wasn't going to cut it. Helen tried to dig names out of her memory. Before she could suggest anything, Caroline was off again.

'Now, what do you know about the Romantic poets?'

Helen's mind emptied. Her world was that of the sixteenth-century playhouse, where Shakespeare and Marlowe created the golden age of English theatre. Lakeland poets rambling the hills rhapsodising about daffodils meant little to her.

'Not much,' she admitted. 'I mean, I studied them as an undergraduate. But that was ages ago.'

'Pity,' said Caroline. 'You'd better start mugging up. I need you to take over Petrarch Greenwood's first-year poetry class.' She slapped the cardboard folder down on the desk between them.

'What?' Helen stared at her, horrified.

'He needs time out to work on his book. It's vital to keep the department's publication pipeline healthy. This is the curriculum.' She delved into the folder and pulled out a sheaf of paper. 'Here's the reading list. It's not too bad. You start with William Blake, *Songs of Innocence and Experience*. I expect you remember that one.'

Blake, again. 'Tyger, tyger, burning bright.' 'Little lamb, who made thee?' Fragments of verse danced in Helen's head, along with the monstrous images from the blog Nick had shown her on Sunday. But this was madness. Helen didn't know anything like enough about Blake to teach him.

'Here's the timetable.' Caroline was relentless, thrusting a paper into her hands before Helen could muster a coherent protest. 'There's a seminar on Thursday afternoon.' She smiled, blandly.

'But that's only two days' time.' Helen could hear her voice rising in pitch. 'How do you expect me to teach something I hardly know anything about?'

Caroline leaned back. 'I know you think of yourself as a specialist, Helen,' she said. 'But we need all-rounders, not one-trick ponies. Everyone should be able to teach any of the undergraduate modules. I'm sure you're up to it.'

Helen hesitated. A one-trick pony? Was that how they thought of her at the university? She'd thought Caroline respected her for the work she'd done on Marlowe. Yet it sounded as if she just wanted another pair of hands.

Caroline gestured to the folder on the desk. 'Petrarch is happy to help you. His phone number is in the file. Everything you need to know is there.'

Defeated, Helen picked it up. 'I'll do my best,' she said, trying not to sound grudging. She felt the security of her role, her comfortable niche, fall away.

'And I am of course enormously grateful,' said Caroline, her smile broad. 'Your contribution will be kept in mind when we consider the ongoing funding of your post next year.'

She looked back down at her papers. The interview was over.

# Chapter 5

Helen clutched the folder tight as she walked back to her office. All the things she should have said to Caroline flooded into her head, now that it was too late.

'All right?' called Jessica from behind her desk. 'Want a coffee?' Helen shook her head and kept walking.

The implied threat to the funding of her post was a shock. When Caroline had recruited her, she'd been full of praise for Helen's work and painted a bright future for her at Russell University. Helen had known it was a one-year contract, but Caroline had told her that was just a formality. They'd soon been talking about multi-year publishing schedules, and Helen had forgotten about the potential insecurity. Now she felt stupid, as if Caroline had somehow tricked her into accepting the role. Was the threat to her funding real, or just a bluff to force her into accepting the extra work? Because the workload would be substantial. She'd have to squeeze in four extra teaching hours a week, plus preparation and marking. And getting on top of the subject would take her ages.

Her Marlowe research had been on track for a September submission to a prestigious journal. But now that would be hard to manage. She could work evenings and weekends, she supposed, as she had while working on her PhD. But when would she find time for walking and writing? She thought sadly of the notebook shoved into her desk drawer at home. It could be a while before she took it out again.

There was a tap on the door. Jessica, of course, with a mug of coffee.

'Here. I thought you might change your mind. What did Caroline want?'

Helen sighed and took the mug. The coffee was black and unsweetened, the way she liked it. No doubt everyone in the department would know soon enough, and telling Jessica would save time.

'She's asked me to take on Petrarch Greenwood's first-year Romantic poetry module. Apparently he needs study leave for his book.' The unfairness was bitter. Why was she asked to sacrifice her work for his?

'Ah.' Jessica peered theatrically up and down the corridor, then closed the door. 'That's the reason they're giving, is it?'

'What do you mean?' asked Helen.

'There's been a complaint, over the weekend. Something about a student party. Caroline was furious with him in the meeting yesterday. I didn't catch much, but she was banging on about the reputation of the university and how he couldn't behave like that in this day and age. Thrilling stuff. Have you heard anything?'

That was even more annoying, thought Helen. If he'd been taken off the course because of misbehaviour, then why was she being punished for it?

She shrugged. 'I don't know anything about that. But I do know I've got a hell of a lot of work to do before Thursday.'

Jessica looked disappointed. 'Well, do tell if the students let anything slip.' She waited. Helen put down the coffee and picked up the papers again.

'I'll leave you to it, then. Ciao.' Reluctantly, Jessica departed.

A hell of a lot of work. Because it wasn't just any old colleague she was being asked to cover for, thought Helen. Those English literature students who didn't come to Russell to study Austen with Caroline Winter came to study Blake with the famous Professor Greenwood. She imagined their disappointment to be faced instead with a stammering woman who could barely recite *The Tyger*. She supposed she should call him, as Caroline had suggested. She shivered, imagining his horror at her ignorance.

Two days was nothing like enough time to read everything on the list, but she could make a start before talking to him. She could hardly ask Petrarch Greenwood which of the basic texts on William Blake she should read first. Especially as he'd written half of them.

Helen had been charmed by Blake's *Songs of Innocence and Experience* when she first read them as an undergraduate. The songs were short lyrics with an almost nursery-rhyme style, simple in language but big in concept. Then, like many students before and since, she'd been floored by his epic prophetic books, lengthy tomes in which Blake forged his own complex mythology. She thought she might just about manage to talk to the students about the *Songs*. But anything beyond that would require someone who had not been put off by Blake's difficulty.

Of course. She'd suggested Barbara to Nick just a couple of days ago. She reached for her mobile phone.

'Hello?' The voice was mistrustful. She smiled, picturing

her friend frowning on the other end of the line. Barbara didn't like being taken by surprise.

'Sorry to pounce on you like this. It's Helen. I know it's been ages. But are you in town today? I wonder if I could pick your brains over lunch?'

# Chapter 6

The café of the British Library was packed with students revising furiously for their final exams. They had the feverish look of people running purely on caffeine, pounding away on their laptops with empty mugs at their elbows.

'God, it's heaving. Maybe we should try outside,' said Helen. 'It's warm enough.'

The women wove their way through the tables, balancing trays of food. On the terrace they found a free spot, partly hidden behind a big concrete planter. They sat and attacked mushroom quiche. Barbara ate with the relish of a woman who didn't eat out often.

'I needed that. Thank you.' She pushed away her empty plate, extracted a mirror from her handbag and repaired her red lipstick. The older woman looked almost exactly the same as when Helen had met her a decade ago, at the horrible secondary school where they had both attempted to teach English. Barbara's shiny black hair was still neatly bobbed. Black eye-liner flicked up at the corners of her warm hazel eyes. She wore a striped Breton shirt, tucked into blue jeans, and a spotted neckerchief around her throat. Helen suspected she'd been wearing the same style since she was a teenager.

'But rising academic stars don't call old friends out of the blue just to buy them lunch, more's the pity. What's going on?' Barbara looked expectant. 'I had an email from a man who said he's a friend of yours. Nick Wilson. A journalist?'

'That's right. He's working on a story, something to do with William Blake and his character Rintrah? He's a nice chap. I hope you don't mind.'

'Sounds intriguing. He's invited me to lunch, too, so that's two free lunches I'm getting out of you.' She grinned. 'I hope I'm worth it.'

'Always.' Helen laughed. 'And I'm sorry it's been so long since I was in touch.'

At one time, Barbara had been the closest Helen had to a best friend. Indeed, it was at Barbara's suggestion that she'd become a walking tour guide. She had been one of the few people to realise how unhappy Helen had been as a school teacher, struggling with undisciplined teenagers and cynical colleagues.

Barbara herself had balanced tour guiding with supply teaching. 'I'm the one the kids try to make cry,' she'd told Helen cheerfully, when they'd first met. 'It's good practice for dealing with the public.'

Despite their closeness, Helen had not been in touch after the traumatic events that had led to her discovery of the Marlowe play.

'I should have called you before. But so much happened, I didn't know where to start. Then I stopped guiding, and this new job came up...'

And some things were too painful to talk about, even with a friend as understanding as Barbara. And if they had talked, Helen couldn't have kept up the pretence that she was managing just fine.

Barbara smiled at her reflection, checked her teeth for spinach, and put the mirror away.

'Don't be daft. I know you've been busy. Tell me about it.'

Helen sighed and explained Caroline's unexpected demand that she become an instant expert on Romantic poetry.

'We start with Blake. On Thursday. So obviously I thought of you.' She pulled the reading list from her bag. 'I've ordered everything, but I need help. Where do I start?'

'Blimey. Where does this fit in with your friend, and Rintrah the Reprobate?'

'It doesn't, really. Although Nick showed me some pretty nasty stuff online about a women's writing conference at the university in a couple of weeks' time. I'm a bit worried about it.'

Barbara took the list and Helen's proffered red pen. She leafed through, ticking some titles and underlining others.

'You should see the abuse I get online when I write about Blake from a feminist perspective. Academia doesn't seem to civilise people. As I expect you're finding out. Don't worry about it. Now. Start with *Innocence and Experience*. If you don't get those, there's no hope.'

'I did get them, once. But it's been so long.'

'Don't worry,' said Barbara. 'He never leaves you.'

Helen had last encountered Blake while studying English Literature at Manchester University, fifteen years ago.

'It was fine at first. But I got lost when we had to study the epic poems. It all seemed so wilfully obscure.'

Barbara grinned. 'That's what I love about him,' she said. 'Nothing's ever straightforward. There are always surprises.' She hesitated. 'In fact... but no, that might confuse you. I'll tell you later.'

'What?'

Her friend's smile was mischievous. 'Something I've been working on, about Blake's wife Catherine. I've always wondered about her. They had no children, and she's supposed to have devoted her life to her husband.'

'So?'

'So I thought I'd try to find out more. There's been more interest in her in recent years, despite the protests of the old fossils who want to dismiss her as an illiterate help-meet. We know she helped with the printing, for example, and coloured some of Blake's images. But I think there might be more to it than that.'

'Go on.'

'It's early days. But I'm wondering how much of a hand she had in some of the poems. The *Songs*, especially. Songs to children, songs from mothers to babies. Lullabies. Not the usual poetry for a man to write.'

'I suppose not.' Helen was sceptical. Little about Blake seemed typical. 'What are you basing this on, then?'

'There are theories that the Blakes lost a pregnancy, or maybe more than one. A miscarriage, or perhaps a stillbirth. It's all a bit tenuous, based on textual analysis of the poems. But I was digging around in the archive of one of Blake's circle, and I found a letter that might back it up. So I'm working on an article for the Blake Study Group journal, which will no doubt be shot down in flames. Anything newly discovered gets ripped to shreds by a pack of ravening dons, especially if it's by a woman and about Catherine Blake.'

Newly discovered. An unknown woman writer. Helen beamed.

'You should talk to my head of department. She's looking for an undiscovered writer for her women's writing conference. She'd love this. I'll suggest it to her, if you like?'

Barbara bit her lip. 'God, would you really? But it's not ready yet. I've got so much work still to do on it.'

'Why don't I ask her and see?' If nothing else, thought Helen, it would be a way of showing Caroline that she was a useful person to have in the department. But, she reminded herself, she also still had much work to do.

'I mustn't get side-tracked, though. You were saying about the reading list?'

Barbara gave her a level look over her reading glasses. 'You did ask. All right. I'll show you the letter when you've done your homework.'

She showed Helen the list.

'Look, these are the texts you really must read. I'll suggest a couple of critiques to help you get your head around the mythology.' She frowned. 'A lot of books by Petrarch Greenwood,' she said.

Helen laughed. 'Well, there would be. It's him I'm standing in for. He wrote the reading list.'

Barbara dropped the pen. 'You didn't tell me that,' she said. Her voice sounded strange. The colour had gone from her face, her red lipstick vivid as blood on snow.

'No, I don't suppose I did,' said Helen, surprised. 'Why? Do you know him?'

Barbara looked away. 'He taught me at Cambridge,' she said, her voice brusque. 'A million years ago.' She scrabbled under the table for the biro. 'He's involved with the Blake Study Group. He was the president, a few years ago. He's not a fan of Catherine Blake. Anyway. That should do to get you started.'

She thrust the pen and papers back at Helen, and slung her handbag over her shoulder.

'You've got a lot to do. I'd better leave you to it.'

'Barbara...' Helen hesitated. Whatever nerve had been touched, her friend clearly didn't want to talk about it. 'Thanks so much. Are you sure you don't want a coffee or something?' But Barbara was already shaking her head.

'Well, look. I really owe you. And I'll definitely talk to Caroline about the conference. But how about helping me out again at the weekend? Are you doing a Blake tour on Saturday? Could I bring some students along? I promise I'll keep them under control.' Barbara's tours were rarely oversubscribed, she knew. This would be a way of boosting her friend's income, improving her own knowledge and giving the students something that Petrarch would never have suggested.

Barbara bit her lip, then nodded. 'Why not? Meet me at St James's Church, Piccadilly, eleven o'clock.' And she was gone.

Why on earth, wondered Helen, had the mention of Petrarch Greenwood so upset her friend? Barbara had looked as if she might faint. Helen thought for a moment. Caroline had suggested she get in touch with him. She had the afternoon and most of Wednesday to spend in the library, speed-reading through Barbara's proposed list. That would give her at least the basics. And putting it off for longer would only make her more nervous.

She pulled out her phone.

'Professor Greenwood? It's Helen Oddfellow. Would it be convenient to call around tomorrow evening to talk about your classes?'

# Chapter 7

The man sat in the corner of a café in a Bloomsbury back street. Most of the tables were taken by students, Chinese and American, British and Indian, making a coffee last all afternoon so they could use the wi-fi. He blended in just fine.

Before he opened his laptop, he took out a bottle of hand sanitiser and cleaned his fingers in a practised motion. Then he ran over the keyboard with an antiseptic wipe. Most personal computers were filthy. People didn't think about how dirty they got. He looked around the café, saw a student cram carrot cake into his mouth and immediately return his greasy fingers to the keyboard. Disgusting.

There were too many people using the café wi-fi for a useful trace on the ISP router, should anyone be looking for one. He wasn't paranoid, just taking sensible precautions. He opened the Tor browser and typed in the web address he knew by heart.

He'd posted a new episode of his comic strip at the weekend, before he drove back to London. His eyes went first to the clicker at the bottom of the screen. More than 2,000 likes, and hundreds of comments. It had pleased his audience.

He had begun Rintrah the Reprobate as an outlet for his

frustration, a way of expressing his despair at the state of the world. Rintrah was his own agent of retribution, his avatar of rage. What would you do, he asked, if there were no repercussions?

The blog had a following – a big one – among a certain type of young white man. He'd started it not long after moving to the UK, inspired by Blake the fearless truth-teller, painstakingly publishing his visions and sending them out into an indifferent, unworthy world. Like Blake, he drew his images precisely, with flowing lines and colours more delicate than were usually found in comic books. But then this was not your usual comic. Like Blake, he was an artist. If the internet had existed in the eighteenth century, Blake would have published his work online. And, as he had discovered with Rintrah the Reprobate, he would have found his audience, out there in the world.

It was a world that no longer had a place for nice guys, people who played by the rules. Maybe once, the world had rewarded guys like him. But now, with affirmative action and feminism and all that crap, they were stuck at the back of the queue, accepting scraps. Rintrah the Reprobate showed them how to fight back.

In the final frame of the comic strip, a lush blonde lay spread-eagled across a bed. Her pimp lay dead next to her. He was particularly pleased with the detailed depiction of the guts spilling out on to the floor, glistening red and black. Above them stood Rintrah, the avenging monster, holding a massive sword in the girl's mouth.

'What do you think, dudes? Does she get a second chance? Your choice.' The scales shimmered green and gold, the tongue protruding. He wondered how many of the comic strip's readers would recognise the source.

The man clicked on to the comments.

'Awesome, bro. Skewer that bitch!'

'Run her through, man.'

'Make her swallow that sword.'

He wrinkled his nose. They were kind of disgusting, his followers. He lifted his gaze from the screen, surveyed the room. Which of the men in this café would agree with them? The quiet group of Chinese students, intent on their phones? The eastern European guy behind the counter, wiping down the coffee machine? He'd put money on the pasty-looking group in cheap suits who'd just been in on their lunch break. Office workers were the most frustrated, the most put-upon of all the emasculated sad cases he met.

But the question was, would the guys who indulged in this fantasy in the safety of an anonymous chatroom follow him offline? They needed to be ready. He had to move them on from fictional characters. There was a risk to that, but it was time to take the step. The next strip he posted would be real people, real world. Let's see if they could cope.

He opened a new topic on the Rintrah Roars forum, checking the stats. A few thousand users were online, a hundred or so logged in.

Topic: 'Let's take this offline.'

He thought for a moment, then began to write.

'Brothers. We've found each other here, we've got to know one another. We share a vision of the world, one where Rintrah the Reprobate tears down the femocracy that's been forced on us. We want a return to the natural order. But that won't happen without a fight. So I'm asking this seriously: are you ready? Are you with me? Because I'm going to take this offline. I have a target in mind. If what I plan comes to fruition, you'll hear about it. I promise you that. Everyone will hear about it. It will be big, it will be London, it will be soon.

'But I need to know. Am I a voice crying in the wilderness? Is Rintrah doomed to be a prophet before his time? Or will you rise up with me, on my command, find your own targets, fight your battles wherever you are in the world? Because this movement will require martyrs. I am prepared to be first. But I need to know I'm not the last. Over to you.'

He sat back and waited. The comments started to roll in.

'I'm with you, bro.'

'Just tell us what to do.'

'Ready to rock'n'roll.'

'Let's do this. I'm with you.'

But were they? he wondered, as the replies ticked up. Fifty, one hundred, two hundred. Were they really ready? He thought of the gun, the weight of it in his hand. Would they have the guts to pull that trigger?

One comment caught his eye: 'Sooner murder an infant in its cradle than nurse unacted desires.' A Blake quote, he recognised, from his book of subversive proverbs. One of these meat-heads knew who Rintrah was inspired by. He clicked on the guy's profile. Flea, he called himself. The man smiled. Maybe this was a kindred spirit. A Blake fan who might actually appreciate what he was trying to do. Maybe there was at least one person out there he could work with.

# Chapter 8

The doorbell rang. Petrarch Greenwood smoothed the paisley silk dressing gown over his ample stomach.

'Can you get that, Ronnie?' he called to his wife. He checked his reflection in the Regency looking glass. The spotted silvering softened the image it offered back, and he was content. He could still carry it off, the generous bulk of decades of good living. His height allowed him a little extra weight, so long as he dressed well. And he always dressed well.

He arranged himself beside the handsome mahogany desk in the window. His books were piled up artfully, his name clearly visible as the author.

Veronica entered the room soundlessly, hostess smile painted on her egg-smooth face, ahead of a tall, gangling woman with cropped blonde hair.

'Helen, dear girl, how good of you to come and see me!' he exclaimed. 'I see you've met my wife, Veronica. Ronnie, this is Dr Helen Oddfellow, who will be shouldering the burden of teaching my first-year students.'

He watched the girl take in the beautiful room for the first time.

'Oh, how lovely.' She stopped, delighted, in the centre. He adored seeing the impression this room made on people, with its generous bay windows framed in turquoise silk curtains, thick Persian rugs and peacock print wallpaper. It was his riposte to an ugly quotidian world. See what you can do, if you care enough about beauty?

Helen crossed to the window and looked down into the busy street. 'Amazing view.' The portico of the British Museum was immediately opposite, the pale stone softened by early-evening sunlight. Petrarch felt proprietorial towards the institution, with its seething crowds of tourists.

'It's rather something, isn't it?' He was by her side, his height affording him a tantalising glimpse of surprisingly ample breasts beneath a plain white button-through shirt.

'Shall I get us some drinks?' asked Veronica.

'Good idea! Why don't you open a bottle of fizz? Helen and I have lots to discuss.' He sensed the young woman edging away from him.

Not so fast.

He grasped her shoulders, noticing her flinch. 'So good of you to help in my hour of need, Helen.' He planted a kiss firmly on each high cheekbone, above her clenched jaw. 'I really can't thank you enough.'

She stepped back, almost stumbling over a low leather footstool. Doesn't like being touched, Petrarch noted. Claustrophobic, perhaps?

'Well, Caroline asked me to,' she said, retreating to the other side of the desk. 'She said you needed time off for your book.'

She didn't have the confidence to protest, though. Good. She deferred to his seniority, his celebrity. She didn't want to make a fuss. Her eyes went to the door, hoping perhaps for

Veronica's reappearance. Petrarch was pleased. He liked to have the upper hand.

He had been surprised, and a little alarmed, when Caroline told him she'd asked Helen Oddfellow to take on his under-graduate class. He'd expected her to find a postgrad student, or perhaps to take the class herself. Even Caroline had to admit that Helen knew nothing of his subject.

'The others are flat out,' she'd said, during their long and uncomfortable meeting on Monday. 'And I have *Out of the Silence* to organise. If you think I'm covering for you again, when I've already warned you I don't know how many times, you can forget it. Helen's the only one with any spare teaching capacity.'

Helen's appointment the previous September had set the older academics clucking like the hens they were. She was an unknown quantity, her former PhD supervisor had protested. She had diverged completely from her original doctoral thesis, ignored his advice and gone her own way. Even if the result was an astonishing piece of work, she had no previous academic experience, and had only taught schoolchildren.

Caroline had managed the affair smoothly, securing the publication of the newly discovered Marlowe play for the university press alongside Helen's appointment. The uni-versity's great and good had been delighted. Petrarch had watched the whole kerfuffle with amusement, secure in his own position and never expecting to have much to do with her himself.

But it wasn't Helen's reputation for research brilliance that concerned Petrarch. She'd solved a long-hidden mystery, outwitted a killer and brought down a dodgy religious organisation in the process. She was a meddler, unable to let something go when it didn't seem right. A dangerous person to have around, especially at the moment.

Things were a bit ticklish, as he'd admitted to Caroline. But he'd cool it a bit, let things die down. So long as no-one tried to stir them up.

'Can I ask you something, professor?' Her chin was up and her gaze was steady.

'Call me Petrarch, please.'

'Have I called too late in the evening?' She was smiling slightly. 'I didn't realise you got ready for bed so early.'

Damn it, she was taking the mickey out of his evening attire. He often appeared in pyjamas and dressing gown – and very fine examples they were too – to unnerve students and junior colleagues. He didn't expect them to call him out on it.

'No, of course not.' He tried to keep the annoyance out of his voice. 'I like to be comfortable once I am home for the evening.' It was barely eight o'clock, for heaven's sake. Of course he wasn't going to bed.

She nodded, solemnly. 'I see. I usually feel more comfortable fully dressed,' she said. 'Although no doubt William Blake would disagree.'

'Ah.' He smiled, settled himself into the leather sofa and patted the cushion next to him. 'Do take a seat, Helen. You're referring to the story of William and Catherine reading *Paradise Lost*, naked as Adam and Eve in their garden. Possibly apocryphal, but so delicious. I think we must allow it, don't you?'

She perched on the edge of an upright chair. 'I'd need to know more about the source. Was it reliable?'

He sighed. The woman was impossible to charm. He might as well get down to business.

'Tell me, how much do you know about William Blake?' He sat back, expecting a stammered attempt to disguise her ignorance.

She returned his gaze. 'Next to nothing,' she said firmly. 'I've not studied him since I was an undergraduate myself. I'm working on it.'

She delved into the hefty rucksack she'd been lugging around since she entered the room and extracted a notebook.

'You'll have to tell me what I need to do. What stage are the students at, and what should we discuss at the seminar?'

Her honesty impressed him as bluster would not have done. And he always enjoyed being deferred to. He began to fill her in. The students were coming to the end of their first year as undergraduates. Some she would know already, as they had taken the introductory Shakespeare module she'd taught in the first term. He'd been teaching them poetry since the autumn, a whistle-stop overview starting with Chaucer and medieval romance.

'We've been focused on the Romantics since January,' he said. 'We did *Lyrical Ballads* at the start of the year, so Coleridge and Wordsworth are covered for now. For Blake, we start with *Innocence and Experience*. They have essays to deliver this week, so they might want to discuss any questions or difficulties. Don't give them extensions, no matter what excuses they offer. They've had plenty of time.'

Helen scribbled in her notepad. 'What are the essay themes?'

'The usual. "Shewing two contrary states of the human soul". How does Blake use language and imagery to delineate the states of innocence and experience, and the possibility of their co-existence?'

42

'Interesting.'

'I suppose so. Although it does rather lose its allure when you've heard it a thousand times before. Lambs and tigers, the pastoral and the urban, sexual freedom and sexual jealousy.'

Petrarch thought of all the essays he'd read over the years, all the excited outpourings of ink, as young minds started to open to the infinite possibilities of the poet's mantra that everything that lives is holy. Something he'd tried to show them himself, although he felt he'd almost exhausted his exploration of infinity. He'd drained himself by infusing his enthusiasm for the grandeur of Blake's mind into these waiting receptacles. Some were grateful, some were fertile ground. Others were not.

He sighed. 'But that is the lot of a teaching academic, as no doubt you are discovering for yourself.'

'Actually,' said Helen, 'I'm really enjoying it. The freshness of the students helps me to see things differently.' She smiled. 'Of course, I've been doing it less than a year. I'm sure it's different when you've been at it as long as you have.'

He'd felt like that once, he remembered. A melancholy reflection. She was making him feel old; an unforgivable insult.

'They'll be on to the meaty stuff next,' he warned. '*Vala, or the Four Zoas. Visions of the Daughters of Albion* – particularly important to understand his very modern attitude to sexuality. And then *America* and *Europe*, to understand the revolutionary aspect. I'm sure you've read my book. Or, at the very least, watched the television series.'

She flushed, and he saw at once that she had.

He turned the screw. 'You'll probably want to save *Milton* and *Jerusalem* for next year. Assuming you're still with us then?'

Helen put down her notepad. 'I certainly hope to be,' she said, her voice steady. 'But perhaps by then your book will be finished, and you'll find you enjoy teaching undergraduates again.'

Veronica arrived with a tinkle of champagne flutes and a companion. For once, Petrarch was relieved to see her.

'Look, here's Brett come to join us,' she said. About time, thought Petrarch irritably. He had dispatched his assistant to the British Library that afternoon with a list of references to check out. He'd assumed he had sloped off home early.

'I wanted to drop off those papers, in case you needed them tonight,' the young man explained. 'I've put them on your desk in the study.'

Brett carried a silver tray with glasses and a bottle of Perrier Jouët Belle Epoque, beaded with condensation. Petrarch surreptitiously wiped the sweat from his forehead. He really needed this.

Brett poured the wine carefully and handed the first glass to Helen.

'It's so good to meet you, Dr Oddfellow. I've been reading all about your Marlowe play. Every research student dreams of making such a discovery,' he said.

She smiled. 'Thank you. I'm sure you'll have every success working with Petrarch.'

Had he heard a hint of mockery in her words, or indeed in Brett's answering smile? Maybe he was imagining things. Helen couldn't know the true state of his research, even if Brett was all too aware of the mire in which he had become immersed.

He took a brimming glass and downed it, enjoying the

delicious buttery taste.

'To our joint success,' he said. 'Ronnie, do we have any foie gras? All this work has made me rather hungry.'

'Not for me, thanks,' said Helen, reaching into her rucksack again. 'Could I ask one more thing? Caroline gave me the reading list, but I can't read everything before tomorrow's tutorial. Could you take a look and let me know what you'd prioritise?'

He took the list, trying to see it without putting on his reading glasses. It was covered in red pen. Someone had already given it a ferocious edit. He noticed two of his later works had been crossed out, while some by his academic rivals were starred. Particularly those by the feminist critics.

'You've made a start, I see. Who made these suggestions – was it Caroline?' Damn her for her cheek, if so.

Helen smiled. 'No, actually. It was one of your former students. She's still very much a Blake enthusiast. Barbara Jackson. Do you remember her? It must have been sometime in the eighties, I suppose. At Cambridge.'

He hated being asked questions like that. 'I'm sorry. There have been so many students, over the years.' He spread his hands regretfully. 'Maybe I'd recognise her face.'

If it had been particularly pretty. But then there had been a lot of pretty faces at Cambridge. A lot of drugs too, which made memory difficult. Whole terms had passed in a haze of marijuana and copulation. Happy days.

'Well, you certainly made an impression on her,' said Helen. 'She's still researching Blake. Catherine, in particular. Her role in his work.'

Petrarch snorted. 'Not another one. It's accepted that she helped with the printing. But the feminists have her role out of perspective. They'll be suggesting she wrote the poems, next.'

The name rang a bell. Jackson. Was she one of those witches who kept banging on about misogyny at Blake Study Group meetings?

'Is that so unlikely?' asked Helen. 'I mean, that she might have contributed?'

Petrarch took a cracker loaded with pate, and crunched it down. 'My dear girl, Catherine was illiterate. As you would know if you'd read my biography of the great man.' He swigged the last drop of champagne from his glass and glared at Helen. She was young and clever, but he was rich and famous. That meant he won.

# Chapter 9

Helen shaded her eyes and scanned the groups of young people sitting on the grass of Gordon Square Gardens. She'd barely left the library in the past two days, cramming her mind with Blake's poetry, critiques of his works and biographies of his life, trying to prepare for this seminar. She didn't feel anything like ready to fill Petrarch Greenwood's sizeable velvet slippers. She'd proposed they hold their first session outside in celebration of the spring, hoping it would put the students in a forgiving mood.

She spotted her group near the centre, lounging on the lawns under a big copper beech tree. She already knew three of them from the course she'd taught in the autumn. Nothing to worry about, she told herself, ignoring an impulse to flee.

As she approached, a girl kicked up into a handstand and came down in a backbend, pink and orange hair brushing the grass. Rose O'Dowd, eighteen years old, relishing her escape from small-town Northern Ireland. Helen remembered her well, a warm-hearted girl with a zest for life.

'How do you do that?' she asked, sitting cross-legged next to her. 'Hello, everyone.'

'Hiya, Helen.' Rose extracted herself from her backbend, face flushed. 'How's it going?' She shook out her rainbow curls and looked around, as if hoping for applause.

Habib Sherazi, a shy young man from Iran whose essays revealed the soul of a poet, looked up from the book he was reading and gave Helen a quick smile. The book's script was unfamiliar, Helen saw, maybe Persian, the cover beautiful with gold lettering on a turquoise background.

Helen didn't know the third member of the tutorial group, Liz Streeter. Petrarch had described her, perhaps unfairly, as a dull but conscientious girl, with a face as square as her character. She took a pen and notebook from her oversized tote bag and sat up, back straight with expectation. Uh-oh, thought Helen. She won't let me get away with anything.

Oona Sinclair sat a little aside from the others, knees hunched under her chin and her pale auburn hair shielding her face. She looked up quickly when Helen arrived, then dropped her head again, as if disappointed.

At the end of the autumn term, the girl had played Ophelia with a dangerous, delicate beauty in the university theatre company's production of *Hamlet*. She'd had many conversations with Helen about the play, revealing a mature understanding of Ophelia's impossible position, caught between her roles as daughter and lover in a court that allowed women no independence outside the walls of a nunnery. She'd talked about applying for a place at the Royal Academy for Dramatic Arts, excited by the possibilities of a career in the theatre. She'd even gone to an open day at RADA and come back bubbling with enthusiasm.

'Hello, Oona,' said Helen. The girl looked up, her light blue eyes rimmed with red. 'How are you? Are you involved with any plays at the moment?'

Oona shook her head and pulled her cardigan closer around

her bony shoulders. She looked as if she'd lost weight.

'Not really,' she said, turning her attention back to her phone.

Oh God, thought Helen. What had happened? Maybe some love affair gone wrong. She hoped the girl would emerge from it before exam time. She would have a proper talk with her later.

'OK. Who else are we waiting for?' There should be five of them, she remembered.

Rose shaded her eyes and looked around the park. 'I can't see him,' she said, her earlier bounce deflating. 'Maybe he's not coming.' For a moment, she looked as miserable as Oona.

'Deepak's always late,' said Liz. 'We usually start without him.'

'How rude of you,' said a patrician voice. A tall, lithe boy in white linen trousers and a designer logo T-shirt rounded the tree and ruffled Rose's hair. He sank to the ground and sat with his back against the tree trunk. He was wearing expensive-looking mirrored sunglasses.

'Apologies for my lateness, Dr Oddfellow,' he said. 'Deepak Sinha. As Liz has pointed out, punctuality is not my strong point.' He leaned back and drew on a cigarette, posing like a movie star.

'Please put that out,' said Helen. The smell of cigarettes made her nauseous.

He looked in surprise at the cigarette, as if he hadn't noticed it.

'Sorry, I thought as we were outside…'

'No.' Helen watched as he flushed dark red, then extinguished it in the soil beneath the tree.

She surveyed the little group. Habib was putting his book

away, busily rummaging in his rucksack for a notebook and pen. He turned away from the other students, as if he didn't want to look at them. Rose was fiddling with her hair, watching Deepak from under her fringe. Oona had shrunk into herself. The atmosphere, already edgy, felt more tense. Only Liz seemed impervious to Deepak's entrance.

'Right, shall we begin?' Maybe they'd loosen up once they started talking. 'Some of you have already met me. I'm Helen Oddfellow, and I usually teach Elizabethan poetry and drama. I'll be taking over the poetry module you've been doing with Professor Greenwood. I'm not an expert on the Romantics. But I've been working with Professor Greenwood to understand what you need to get you through the rest of the term. I'll be doing my best to make sure you don't suffer from his absence.'

Petrarch had suggested she keep her ignorance hidden, but Helen didn't like secrets. They had a nasty habit of coming back to bite you.

Oona looked up. 'Can I ask a question?' she asked, her soft Scottish brogue barely audible. 'When will Petrarch... when will Professor Greenwood be back?'

'I don't know.' Helen was surprised by the anxiety in the girl's tone. 'He's working on his book, which I understand has to be finished by the summer. So I expect you will have to make do with me until the end of the year.'

Oona's head dropped, the curtains of hair closing over her unhappy face. She looked as if she was trying not to cry.

'I thought this was just for a week or two,' said Liz, frowning. 'It's not what I signed up for. We pay our fees, you know.'

Deepak gazed into the distance, a cynical smile twisting his handsome mouth. But Habib's face brightened, and Rose too seemed more cheerful.

'That's great,' she said, her voice buoyant with relief. 'Can we talk about the essays? Cos I could really use a little bit more time on mine, Helen.'

'Good idea,' said Helen. 'But there won't be any extensions. Let's talk about the essay theme, Rose, and see if we can help you get it finished on time.'

The discussion moved on. Rose's thoughts, as Petrarch had predicted, were standard musings on childhood as a state of pastoral innocence among woolly lambs and shepherds, while industry and cities brought misery to the chimney sweeps and shackled prisoners of experience. She talked with one eye on Deepak, Helen noticed, as if checking to see whether he approved. She was more nervy than Helen remembered, less sure of herself.

By contrast, Deepak was full of self-confidence. He threw the occasional observation into the discussion, intelligent but flippant, as if he was more interested in sounding sophisticated than engaging with the subject. Helen got a feeling he was used to operating on the surface, with clever words a substitute for real ideas or feelings.

Petrarch had said Deepak was bright, but lazy. 'He's coasted through life so far,' he'd told her. 'His father's a rich politician in Mumbai, mother a socialite. He's been to exclusive schools, had all the privileges of his class. He's used to getting through life on connections, charm and looks.'

Helen vowed to subject his essay to a forensic examination.

Habib made the most interesting contributions. He had a good feel for the language, pointing out the contrast between the lullaby sing-song of the *Innocence* poems and the clanging, insistent rhythms of *Experience*. His shyness seemed to fall away when he was talking about poetry.

'You can hear the hammer blows,' he said, his eyes shining. '*The Tyger* is the sound of the industrial revolution, drowning out the birdsong and the calls of the lambs. The sound of experience shouting down the softer pastoral voice that Blake associated with childhood.'

'Blake didn't grow up in the countryside,' Deepak objected. 'He was a Londoner, wasn't he? He grew up in Soho. Hanging out round Old Compton Street.' He raised an eyebrow at Habib, who reddened and looked away.

'Ah, but that's where you're wrong,' said Helen. Thank goodness for Barbara, she thought. Her friend had emailed her the notes for her Blake walks, explaining how the young poet roved south to the village of Newington Butts, down into Peckham Rye, past the village of Dulwich, even walking as far as the pleasant market town of Croydon. 'He grew up in Soho, yes. But London was smaller in those days. South of the river it was pretty much market gardens and farmland. Blake walked a lot and he would have had plenty of opportunities to see shepherds and lambs in the fields, or hear birdsong and rippling streams. And the contrasts between the noisy, dirty city and the peace of the countryside would have been that much more stark, without the acres of suburbs we see today.'

'That makes sense,' said Rose. 'I like towns with edges. Where you're in the town on one side of the road, and in the country on the other.'

Helen smiled. 'In fact,' she said, 'I've a proposal for you all. Saturday morning. My friend Barbara, a walking tour guide, has kindly offered to give us a tour of the places where Blake lived and worked. It will give you a sense of how different London was in Blake's time.'

'Is this obligatory?' grumbled Deepak. 'I mean, Saturday morning... Some of us have other plans.'

'Only if you want to deepen your understanding of Blake, learn about London in the eighteenth century and trace the topography of the later prophetic books,' she told him. 'Of course, if you'd rather have a lie-in, that's up to you.'

'I think it sounds great!'

Bless Rose for her enthusiasm, thought Helen.

'Come on, Deepak. It'll be a laugh.' Rose's voice had an edge of pleading.

'I'll come,' said Habib. 'Sounds good.'

'Excellent. Eleven o'clock, in the churchyard of St James's, Piccadilly. It should take a couple of hours,' said Helen. Liz wrote down the details in her notebook.

'Oona? Are you free to join us?' asked Helen.

She looked up at her name, as if her thoughts had been elsewhere, offered Helen a watery half-smile.

'Maybe,' she said, pulling the long sleeves of her cardigan over her hands. Helen got a glimpse of the silvery scars on her arms. She knew that Oona had endured a difficult childhood. Her tutors had been warned that she had a history of self-harming, and they should be alert to signs of mental-health problems. Was she hurting herself again? Helen wondered.

'I'd really like it if you came along,' she told her, and was rewarded with another half-smile.

As the seminar drew to a close, Helen reminded them about the essays. 'If anybody wants to discuss their essay – or anything else – do come and find me. I'll be in the library for the rest of the afternoon,' she said.

Oona was on her feet and halfway across the park before she had time to catch her. But they had a one-to-one tutorial scheduled for the following day, Helen remembered. She'd speak to her then.

The others were still packing their things away and chatting. Helen walked slowly back to the library, her relief at having got through the first seminar on Blake tinged with concern. What had happened to the students she'd known since the autumn? Rose's enthusiasm and freshness of response had become a little desperate, as if she was performing for an audience. Habib was quieter than before. And Oona – lovely, passionate Oona – seemed sunk in despair.

Helen wondered if she should ask Petrarch Greenwood about them. But the thought didn't appeal. She'd found her encounter with the great man disturbing. He seemed to have treated their meeting as a sparring match, as if needing to prove his superiority. Helen didn't like games. She preferred people who said plainly what they wanted.

Remembering his vulpine smile as he called for foie gras pate, she got the impression that Petrarch thought suffering was justified, if it satisfied his appetite. She was glad not to be the research student working with Petrarch on his book.

# Chapter 10

Petrarch was hiding in his study. Supposedly he was working, or at least overseeing the work as Brett tapped away on his laptop on the big Arts and Crafts desk, transferring notes on Blake's correspondence from hundreds of dusty index cards on to a computer spreadsheet. Rearranging the seating plan for the captain's table on the *Titanic*, thought Petrarch.

In the hall, the iceberg that was Oona had breached the outer hull. He could hear her sobbing. Earlier that day, in a fit of optimism, he'd told Veronica that he and Brett were not to be disturbed. Somewhere, he'd convinced himself, in that pile of cards was the missing heart of his new book, already months behind schedule. He just had to find it.

Veronica was taking her duties as a gatekeeper seriously. This was bad news. A confrontation between Oona and his wife could have horrible repercussions, after the promises he'd made Veronica. But he didn't want to see Oona, not in this state. She'd been increasingly difficult lately. And this invasion of his home was inexcusable.

He heard his wife's soothing tones, Oona's voice, rising in pitch.

'I just want to see him for a minute,' she wailed. 'Why isn't he teaching us anymore?'

Why did he always pick the fragile ones? She'd been so delectable as Ophelia, fresh from the salt-sharp winds of the far north, eyes wide and full of stormy seas. He'd invited the *Hamlet* cast to his Christmas party and sought her out.

He remembered that first time, grasping her thin wrists in his big hands, turning them over and caressing the silvery lines that criss-crossed the pale skin. She'd tried to pull away, but he'd held on, kissed them, listened while she'd haltingly laid out the bones of her wretched childhood. The much-loved father, killed in an offshore accident when she was thirteen; her unstable, grief-stricken mother, lashing out at Oona in a drunken rage. The isolated cottage, miles from anywhere on the rocky shore of Hoy. Her battle to get educated, to find an escape route, as far from her mother as she could get. He'd been moved by the story, truly saddened. But perhaps that should have been his cue to withdraw.

Instead, he'd made her promise not to hurt herself again; called her his mermaid, his selkie. Made more promises: help with her RADA application, maybe a little flat somewhere south of the river when her degree was finished. He'd look after her. And in return, she would be his.

And he would have looked after her, only things had got difficult. Caroline had heard about the summer party, somehow. He'd love to know which of the students had betrayed him. Not Oona, that was certain. She'd been calling and texting constantly. But she hadn't seemed herself on Friday night; had cried for hours afterwards, although nothing had happened she had not participated in before.

Veronica, back from her visit to their son in Oxford, had arranged a busy weekend of social activities, and Petrarch had been unable to slip away as he usually did. And Caroline had made it clear on Monday that the less he had to do with his students, the better. He'd reluctantly agreed, staying away from the department and not answering Oona's text messages.

Which, he assumed, was why she was here. He wished he hadn't given her the security code for the building. That had been a strategic error, and no doubt one that Veronica would notice.

He heard her smooth tones now, ringing with false concern.

'But, my dear, Petrarch can't drop his important work every time a student wants to see him. Don't you have a personal tutor you can go to?' Veronica asked. 'A student counsellor or something?'

'He said I should come to him if I needed anything,' sobbed Oona. 'I can't believe he wouldn't see me, if he knew I was here.'

Petrarch squirmed. The tapping of the computer keys ceased for a moment. Brett looked up from the screen.

'I can give her a message, if you want,' he said. His voice was flat, indifferent; his clean-shaven jaw set hard. If Petrarch sent Brett, she would know he meant it. It would be harsh. But he needed his space. How could he work, with all this emotion swirling around?

'OK,' he said. He felt the meanness of the gesture. 'Tell her I'll call her later tonight.' He hesitated. 'It would be best if she didn't talk too much to Veronica. She gets suspicious.'

Brett pushed back his chair, scraping it noisily on the parquet floor, and left the room.

Petrarch eyed the pile of index cards beside the laptop. He could remember when the dusty old cards had actually meant something; when he'd scribbled the notes with mounting excitement, back in the nineteen-eighties. Then only nerds had computers and only typists typed. He had been working in the library of his parents' house in Chichester, while his mother died quietly upstairs. He'd come home to nurse her, his beautiful and beloved mama, and to get away from some unpleasantness that had erupted at Cambridge.

He'd taken the kernel of an idea, a thought about the impact of the wars in France and America, and Blake's own trial for sedition, and developed it into a barnstorming theory, the book that had made his name. Each index card, each notation in his flowing black ink, had once represented a new possibility, a new way of thinking about Blake's poetry. He'd been full of certainty, seeing more clearly than he'd done since childhood.

'If the Sun and Moon should Doubt, they'd immediately Go Out.' He'd taken Blake's words as his motto, and they were inscribed above his desk. They seemed now less an inspiration, more a jibe.

He wanted to Go Out himself, to wander the streets or shut himself in a quiet cinema, away from the world. He went to the window and looked down at the busy pavement, pleating the silk curtains between nervous fingers.

He listened.

'Calm down, Oona.' Brett's voice was sharp, sharper than he'd like. 'Petrarch's working. He doesn't have time for this. He told me to tell you he's busy. He'll call you when he's free.'

'Fuck you, Brett.' Petrarch jumped. Her voice was scornful, angry. 'Do you do all his dirty work for him? What else – do you hold his dick when he pisses?'

He was amazed. That wasn't the Oona he knew. He noticed

how carefully she was articulating her words. Was she drunk, perhaps? She'd always been cautious around booze, accepting only one glass of wine in an evening. But this seemed out of character.

'There's no need for that sort of language,' purred Veronica. She sounded like she was enjoying this hugely. No doubt planning the humiliating revenge she'd serve up to him later. 'I can see you're upset. But I'm going to call the police if you don't leave now. And make a complaint to the university about harassment.'

Shit, thought Petrarch. Don't do that.

'Come on,' said Brett. Oona yelped. Petrarch guessed he'd taken hold of her. He heard the front door open. 'Out you go. Back to wherever you came from.'

Like putting out a stray cat, thought Petrarch, a little shocked.

The door slammed. Petrarch heard a few half-hearted thumps and a shouted curse, then silence. He ventured into the hall. Veronica was peering through the spyglass in the front door. She straightened and turned with a contemptuous smile.

'You can come out now. The scary little girl's gone.'

He took a deep breath. 'Ronnie, I'm sorry. She shouldn't have come here. I don't know how she got into the building...'

His wife laughed, a short bark that was completely without mirth. 'I expect you told her the code. Please stop insulting my intelligence. And inform your grubby little slut that my home is off limits.'

Brett was backing away, looking embarrassed.

'Now, Brett, I think it's time for a drink. You've been hard at it all day. Come on. You can tell me what progress my husband is really making with his book.'

Brett shrugged and followed her into the living room. Petrarch could do with a whisky. But the invitation had clearly not included him. He retreated to the study, sat at the desk and put his head in his hands. It was all getting a bit out of control.

# Chapter 11

'Oona...'

Helen hesitated. She couldn't force the girl to open up to her. But Oona was so clearly miserable, and Helen hated to see her unhappiness.

'Look, you don't have to tell me anything you don't want to. But what's happened? Back in December, you were doing so well – *Hamlet*, plans for RADA, and your essays on Shakespeare were brilliant. But now you seem completely uninterested in your work.'

The girl was staring at the floor in Helen's office, twisting her hair. Her eyes brimmed with tears, the pale lashes making her face look naked.

'I'm just a bit tired,' she said, her voice breaking as the tears started to spill. Helen handed her a tissue. 'I'm not sleeping very well,' the girl admitted. 'I was...' She broke off and blew her nose. 'I was seeing someone. And now he doesn't want to see me anymore.'

She looked sideways at Helen, an appraising look, as if trying to work out whether Helen knew. Who was it? Helen thought of Deepak, suave and self-assured. He was undeniably handsome. And, Helen remembered, he'd also been in the production of *Hamlet* in the autumn, playing

Ophelia's brother, Laertes.   Had they started going out together then?

'I'm sorry about that. Break-ups are miserable,' said Helen. She felt old, trying to remember the last time she'd been dumped by a boy. It was the worst feeling in the world, at the time.

'Yeah. Well, I suppose it happens. It's kind of pathetic, isn't it? I mean, there are worse things. It's embarrassing, really. Getting this upset about it.'

Oona had lost her father as a child, Helen remembered. She knew herself how devastating the death of a father could be.

'Sure. But it's a horrible feeling. You have to make sure it doesn't damage your work, though. You've done so well. It would be a real shame to let this bring down your grades.'

Bloody Deepak, she thought darkly. Why did it have to happen in the summer term, just before the first-year exams? She remembered Rose in the tutorial, looking at Deepak for approval every time she spoke. The boy was a menace.

Oona blew her nose again and stuffed the tissue up her sleeve.

'I know. I'm sorry about the essay. I will try to get it done over the weekend.' She offered a wobbly smile. 'I thought it would be Petrarch marking it, you see. He said not to worry about it.'

Helen frowned. 'What do you mean?'

'Nothing. Just that it didn't matter if it was late.  Not to worry about my grades.'

Helen was annoyed. What was the man doing, telling her not to give the students extensions to their essay deadlines, but telling Oona it didn't matter if she submitted late? Was he trying to undermine her?

'I see. When did he say that?'

Oona was looking at the floor again. 'Before the... last week, when I last saw him. We met up. I don't think he knew then that he wouldn't be marking them.'

Helen looked at her sharply. Was she wrong about the culprit for Oona's distress? Before what? she wondered.

'You got on well with Professor Greenwood, didn't you?' she asked, trying to keep her voice gentle. 'I saw how disappointed you were when you heard he wouldn't be back this year.'

Oona shrugged. Helen passed her the box of tissues again.

'He was nice to me,' she said, her voice rising. 'He said he'd help me. With RADA and everything. And to make sure I got the grades I needed. But now he won't even see me.' She started to sob into a tissue.

Helen felt somewhat out of her depth. Did Oona mean that Petrarch was the man she'd broken up with? It had been drummed into her – somewhat embarrassingly – that staff who engaged in what Caroline had called 'inappropriate relations' with students risked disciplinary action. Although Jessica had claimed later that everyone was at it.

Awkwardly, she patted Oona's arm, wondering what she should do about this unexpected turn of the conversation.

'Oona, I'll help you as much as I can, with your RADA application and with staying on track with your work. Really, from what I saw in the autumn term, I think you have every chance of getting good grades. There's nothing to worry about.'

Should she ask directly about Petrarch Greenwood? Or would that be opening a can of worms that perhaps would be better left shut? Especially if the relationship was over.

'You can come and see me any time,' she said. 'Anything you'd like to talk about.' Maybe it was best to leave it at that. Oona could decide for herself whether she wanted to confide further.

Helen thought about Petrarch, his bulk and his greed as he devoured foie gras and champagne. She shuddered at the thought of him pawing this fragile, damaged young woman. Maybe she'd misunderstood. Perhaps Oona simply saw him as a father figure, someone who would temporarily fill the gap left by her own father's death.

'All right.' Helen smiled, hoping to move the conversation back on to more stable ground. 'Let's talk about the theme for your essay. How are you planning to approach it?'

The girl drew herself up, dried her eyes and attempted a brave smile. 'Flowers,' she said, unexpectedly. 'Blake's use of flowers to contrast innocence and experience. The lily and the rose.'

They read over the flower poems together, Helen noticing with unease Blake's sexualisation of the undefended lily. She thought again of Professor Greenwood, whose book on Blake and sexuality had made much of the metaphor. A girl could do with a few thorns to defend herself, she thought, glancing at Oona's guileless face.

# Chapter 12

Nick sat at the breakfast bar in the Soho flat he shared with Dom, the music editor at *Noize*. He'd heard him come in sometime in the early hours, crashing around the kitchen making a fry-up, the remains of which were now congealing in the sink. Nick had pulled a pillow over his head and managed to get back to sleep, before his alarm woke him at seven.

It was tempting to get his revenge on Dom with some pumping music to shatter the early-morning quiet, but he didn't want company. He had things to do before joining Barbara and Helen for the Blake guided walk at eleven.

Midweek, Nick had taken Barbara for lunch at a smart Soho restaurant to pick her brains. They'd liked each other immediately. As Helen had promised, she knew everything there was to know about Blake, and he'd started to put her suggestions into action.

He had bought a massive volume of Blake's illustrated work, along with a couple of books written by the graphic novel author Alan Moore. Barbara had taken one look at the Rintrah blog and spotted influences from Moore's superheroes in *The Watchmen* and *V for Vendetta*.

'Moore was hugely influenced by Blake, not least in his

depiction of London,' she'd said. 'Bet you anything this Rintrah bloke is an Alan Moore fan too.'

Together, Nick and Barbara had scanned through Rintrah's previous posts, with Barbara pointing out Blake references. Nick had started to drop in appreciative comments, under the name of Flea, making it clear he got the references. At Barbara's suggestion, he used Blake's alternative proverbs from his satire *The Marriage of Heaven and Hell* as a source. Flipping through the book, he found himself smiling. He was starting to enjoy Blake's humour.

On his laptop, a recently published blog showed Rintrah poised to have sex with a pale ginger-haired woman who lay compliant in the centre of a circle of watching monkeys, their faces leering.

'Brace yourself!' read the caption coming from the monster, depicted this time with a huge phallus. The comments posted underneath were the usual mixture of infantile innuendo and graphic violence. Nick thought for a moment and checked his Blake volume.

'Damn braces; bless relaxes,' he typed. It was a typical Blake line: both absurd and inventive, upturning the meaning of the words. He took a mouthful of coffee, and waited.

But not for long. 'Heh.' It might be short, but it was a reaction, and the first he'd had from Rintrah, supposed author of the blog. And it meant the guy was online.

Nick thought quickly. 'Great post, Rintrah. Did you get the monkeys from *The Marriage of Heaven & Hell?*' The book included a startling passage about monkeys and baboons coupling together then devouring each other, part of Blake's vision of hell.

Another short pause, then the answer appeared below.

'Yeah. You know Blake.'

Nick waited. He didn't want to seem too keen, for fear of arousing suspicion. His patience was rewarded a moment later.

'Still there?'

Nick grinned. Rintrah the Reprobate sounded needy, anxious. An artist wanting acknowledgement, or maybe just a connection with someone who wasn't an idiot.

'Yeah, just grabbed a coffee. Blake blows my mind. I studied him at uni. But you are the first guy I've seen who gets him properly,' he wrote.

'Thanks. Good to know.' The answer was prompt.

Where are you? wondered Nick. Here, in London? The backdrops to some of the stories suggested as much. He glanced out of the window, glimpsing a pale and cloudless azure sky between the tall buildings. Trucks were crawling up the narrow streets, making deliveries to the cafés and bars that lined this stretch of Soho. It was almost half-past eight; Dom would be up soon, grumbling about his hangover.

'Great to talk to you. It would be cool to hear more,' he wrote. 'Maybe off the forum?' He held his breath. But surely Rintrah would want to talk to someone who really understood, who got Blake when most of his followers saw only nude women or bloodthirsty violence.

A comment flashed up. 'OK. Be in touch.'

Nick grinned again. He was reeling him in. As the webmaster, Rintrah would have the email address of anyone who commented on the posts – in his case, the new account he'd set up using his burner phone.

He wondered again who the artist was in real life. Despite the puerile level of some of the posts, he didn't think Rintrah was a kid. The pop culture references, the influence of 1980s graphic novels, suggested a man in middle age, perhaps older. And the accomplishment of the drawing made Nick wonder if he had art-school training.

Nick pictured a white man – it had to be a white man – getting on a bit, but desperate to stay relevant, sitting behind his screen sending his bile out into a world that didn't appreciate him as he thought it should. Someone whose time had been and gone, whose resentment and bitterness had built up over the years, curdled into cynicism. He realised he was picturing Toby, his news editor. Someone with culture, he reminded himself, and education. Not Toby.

He unplugged his laptop and shoved it into his bag. There was no way he was going to clean up the remains of Dom's midnight feast before making himself breakfast. He'd get something to eat at a café on his way to Piccadilly. As he grabbed his phone, he saw an email had popped up on his newly created account.

'So, Flea. Are you just audience, or do you want to be part of this revolution?'

Nick punched the air. He had direct contact with Rintrah – and the guy wanted him on board.

'I'm in,' he replied. 'Let's get this thing on the road.'

# Chapter 13

Helen sat in the paved courtyard of elegant St James's Church, enjoying the warmth reflected back from the stone flags. The place was busy with market stalls selling handicrafts and antiques. The red brick and pale stone façade of the church loomed behind her.

She hoped enough of the students would join them for it to be worthwhile. She'd persuaded Caroline to pay for a private tour, arguing that it would benefit them to get a better understanding of London's history and its relation to Blake. Also, she was keen to hear what Barbara made of the students. Her friend had a quick instinct for people, and had experience of being taught by Petrarch Greenwood. Perhaps she could shed some light on the odd atmosphere that Helen had noticed during the tutorial. And Nick was coming too. Helen was pleased; she hadn't really expected him to join them. She had taken a little more care than usual with her appearance that morning, swiping on a slick of mascara and rubbing gel through her short hair. She was trying to pretend this was in no way connected to seeing Nick again.

Barbara arrived, wreathed in cigarette smoke. Despite the warmth, her make-up was immaculate.

'You make me feel so ungroomed,' teased Helen. It usually

took her seconds to slick back her hair in the mornings and wash her face.

'You're young,' said Barbara, gloomily. 'You can get away with the fresh-faced look.' She extinguished her cigarette. 'Is Nick coming? He's really sharp, isn't he? And funny. I liked him a lot.'

To Helen's surprise, Barbara was not particularly shocked by the Rintrah blog, or the threats to the conference.

'You can find a whole bunch of weird stuff relating to William Blake online. There are some seriously strange people out there.' She shrugged. 'Just ignore it. No point in worrying unnecessarily.'

'That's what Caroline says.' Helen wondered if they were dismissing it too easily. 'But this comic thing is a bit strange, isn't it?'

'Not really. Blake has inspired more popular culture than any poet apart from Shakespeare. The Marvel Comics thing is huge. A fan adopting one of his characters for a superhero is far from the strangest thing that's happened to William Blake. And the chances of any of those idiots being able to find their way out of their bedrooms and on to the street is pretty low, if you ask me. Forget about it.'

Out in the sunshine, surrounded by tourists, Helen's fears seemed out of place. She looked around the churchyard to see if any of the others had arrived.

'There's Habib.' The young man emerged from the church and raised a hand. Helen liked him for his quiet intelligence and love of language. His grasp of English was so good, she almost felt it was a pity to correct his occasional grammatical errors. But he insisted that he wanted her to be exact, to tell him of every tiny mistake. Only with perfect English, he explained, could he hope for a good job in Britain or America when he finished his degree. Helen had not asked him why he did not wish to return to Iran.

'It is so peaceful inside,' he said, smiling. 'I like it very much.'

He'd handed in his essay the day before, as had Liz. Oona had promised to write hers over the weekend, but said that would mean she couldn't join the walk. Helen wondered if she should have given her more time.

And now here was Rose, swinging along in a short cotton frock the colour of egg yolk, which clashed cheerfully with the pink streaks in her hair. She wriggled out of her backpack and delved into it, emerging triumphantly with a sheaf of paper.

'See, I said I'd do it.'

'Well done,' said Helen, pleased. She'd not really expected the girl to meet the deadline.

'Hiya, Habib.' Rose hugged him, looking over his shoulder. 'Anyone else here?'

'Not yet,' said Helen. She introduced the two students to Barbara and scanned the street. She spotted Liz, standing outside the gates, frowning at her phone, as if uncertain she'd found the right place, and waved her over.

'No Deepak, then,' Liz said bluntly. 'There's a surprise.'

Helen saw Rose flinch.

'Not yet.' The girl was pretending to be interested in the jewellery displayed on one of the stalls. 'Look, this is pretty. Anyway, it's only just eleven.'

As if to underline her point, the church bells began to chime. As the last notes fell away, Deepak sauntered through the gates, with Nick close behind. Helen saw Rose's face brighten, and felt her own spirits lift.

71

Barbara led them to the cool interior of the church, the white and gilt ceiling curving away above their heads.

'Take a look at the font,' she said.

The students gazed at it dutifully. The marble bowl was intricately carved with Biblical scenes, the stand as a tree trunk, amazingly life-like with roots growing into the base and branches curving up to support the bowl. Two figures stood either side of the trunk, foliage growing over their naked bodies.

'William Blake was baptised in this font in November 1757, as a new-born baby,' said Barbara. 'It's thought to be by the Dutch carver and sculptor Grinling Gibbons.'

Helen saw Rose swallow a yawn, although she was listening politely. Deepak stood impassive, mirrored sunglasses still on. He probably couldn't see anything. Silly boy, Helen thought. She glanced at Nick, who was crouching to get a better view of the stand.

'It's really good,' he said. 'Are these two figures Adam and Eve?'

'That's right.' Barbara said. 'It's interesting that Blake was so obsessed with the themes of good and evil, innocence and experience, and this font where he was baptised shows the moment of choice. Eve taking the fruit of the Tree of Knowledge of Good and Evil from the serpent.'

Helen looked again. The snake was coiled around the tree, holding the apple in its mouth, right in front of Eve's face. Eve was gazing at the snake with longing. Helen wrinkled her nose. She didn't much like snakes.

'Do you think Blake was thinking about this when he wrote about innocence and experience, then?' asked Rose.

'Well, it's possible,' said Barbara. 'Although he'd have been only a few days old when he first saw it. But look up his illustrations to *Paradise Lost*. There's a strikingly similar image there.'

Liz scribbled it down in her ever-present notebook. Deepak yawned openly, his tongue pink behind white teeth.

'Why don't you take off your sunglasses, Deepak?' Helen asked. 'Maybe you could see what Barbara's telling us about.'

'We're going out again now,' said Barbara, quickly. They emerged into the sunshine and waited to cross Piccadilly.

'The Blakes didn't have far to come from their home in Broad Street. Regent Street hadn't been built yet, so we're taking the side streets that were – more or less – in existence in Blake's time. Watch out for the traffic.'

They slipped up narrow Swallow Street, over Regent Street and into the symmetrical calm of Golden Square. Helen saw Rose stop to drop a coin into a cup held by one of the many homeless men who slept in the park, their sleeping bags claiming the benches that surrounded the square.

'Why did you do that?' Deepak asked, falling into step with her. 'You can't help everyone.'

Rose shrugged. 'I can help one person. There but for the grace of God, as my ma would say.'

'The homeless charities say you should donate directly to them, not to beggars,' said Liz. 'It doesn't really help them.'

Nick laughed. 'I think if you asked any of the guys here, they'd say giving them a quid helps them.' He dropped a coin in another man's cup and grinned at Rose. 'You do what feels right to you, girl.'

They moved on, weaving their way through narrow streets lined with small, old-looking brick buildings, mostly shops and restaurants. Barbara paused at the end of the road, opposite a stark concrete building with a café built into the base of a high-rise tower block.

'I'm afraid this is all that remains of the birthplace of William Blake,' she said. 'This tower block is built on what used to be 28 Broad Street.'

She gestured around them.

'Back in the eighteenth century, you'd have found prosperous and respectable merchants living here, where the film companies and advertising agencies are today. Blake's family home was a hosiery business, with the shop on the ground floor. They lived above it, like most of their neighbours. Engravers and printers, hat-makers and tailors – these little businesses made up the Blakes' world.'

Liz was taking photographs of the surrounding streets with her phone; Habib was listening intently. Nick waved at a guy lugging crates of pastries into a café.

'They do the best flat white in there,' he told Helen. 'My office is round the corner.'

'Come on, Rose.' Helen's sharp ears picked up Deepak's whisper. 'I've had enough of this. Let's go and get a coffee.'

Helen swung around in outrage, but Rose was too quick.

'We can't,' she hissed. 'It'd be rude. Anyway, this is interesting.'

Good girl, thought Helen.

# Chapter 14

Helen strode off ahead of the group, past the independent businesses of Broadwick Street – a fabric shop selling lengths of silk; a quirky record shop with vintage vinyl and posters of punk bands from years gone by. Rose and Nick caught her up.

'I like this part of London,' said Rose. 'There's so much to see.'

Helen smiled. 'Me too. It's where I used to come when I was a kid. Hanging out at the Soho pubs with my friends, all dressed in black and trying to look cool. That scruffy-looking pub across the road used to be a music venue. We went there all the time.'

Rose laughed. 'I can't imagine you as a Goth.'

'I can,' teased Nick. 'Listening to terrible music and drinking cheap cider.'

'Too true,' Helen admitted. 'But it was a very long time ago.'

They turned the corner into Old Compton Street, which always made her think of Crispin. 'The Catwalk,' he called it. Not everything had changed – it was still the boys' street.

Helen turned her head, noticed Habib's eyes were wide. Deepak, next to him, gestured towards a couple embracing in a doorway, made some comment. Whatever it was, it made Habib uncomfortable. He shook his head, blushed, and turned away.

Why can't he leave people alone? wondered Helen.

The group caught up with them, and together they crossed the busy Cambridge Circus junction, made their way past shoppers in Covent Garden and Long Acre. Finally they stopped in front of the grand stone edifice of Freemasons' Hall.

'Here we are,' said Barbara.

Across the road was a line of well-preserved small shops in the now-familiar style: narrow, built of red brick, with two or three rows of tall windows in the upper storeys. A smart florist, a tailor's shop and a milliners displaying hats that looked like contemporary art.

'This row of shops is very similar to the engraver's shop run by James Basire, where Blake was apprenticed for seven years. It was number thirty-one, which as you can see is now that grand pillared building. But the shops and houses to either side…'

'Oh, come on. This is bullshit.'

Rose gasped. Barbara paused, and everyone stared at Deepak.

'I mean, everywhere we go, you tell us what we're looking for is no longer here, but we can imagine what it might have been like. What's the point of coming here, then?'

'Deepak,' Helen began, sharply.

'No.' Barbara held up her hand. 'He's right. London changes constantly, and it would be amazing if all the places we'd like to see still existed. It's frustrating. Our predecessors didn't preserve the houses we'd have liked them to. But then, the city isn't a museum.'

'So why are we doing this?' asked Deepak. 'Why not just look at old drawings, or read about it? Blake wrote about a different London, one that doesn't exist anymore. Why pretend it does?'

Barbara raised an eyebrow. 'Anyone? Why do we come and look at old buildings, and try to imagine how it would have been?'

'Because... because it is still here, in bits,' began Rose, hesitantly. 'And it is the same city, but layered over. Some bits are on top of other bits, but if you dig down, or look carefully in the gaps, you can get a glimpse of what's survived.' She was blushing, the heat mounting in her cheeks.

'And that's what was happening when Blake was alive too,' said Liz. 'You said that church was only a hundred years old then, and Golden Square was newly built. So the London that Blake's parents knew was already changing and getting covered up.'

For once, Helen was relieved to hear Liz's voice.

'Whose feet are sore?' asked Helen.

Rose raised her hand, her smile rueful.

'Then you know how it feels to walk a mile in London, from Blake's home to his workplace. And Liz is right, those walks would have changed drastically in Blake's lifetime. Lambeth, where he lived for ten years, industrialised during his time there. His poems about dark Satanic mills, or the chartered streets of London, were reactions to the changes he saw about him. London doesn't stand still. Understanding that helps us understand his poetry.'

Deepak shrugged. He wasn't going to apologise, Helen saw. He drew a little apart from the others, stuck his hands in his pockets.

'One final stop,' said Barbara. 'No-one has to come.' She eyed Deepak. 'But as we started with the church where Blake was christened, I'd like to show you the place where he died. I warn you now, the building is no longer there.' She smiled. 'But the view down to the river is. And it's still satisfyingly atmospheric.'

She led them through the narrow streets around Covent Garden and up into The Strand.

'Can we go down there?' Rose peered into the narrow alleyway, which was not inviting. 'It looks private.'

A stone archway led to a dark passage through a building and down a dingy stairwell. A scrolled plaque on the arch announced that this was where the Fountain Tavern stood in the eighteenth century, and that the little alley, now Savoy Buildings, had once been Fountain Court.

'We can. Come on through.' Barbara led them through the archway into the narrow passage, its walls covered with grubby white tiles, pressed in on all sides by tall buildings. It was a gloomy place. They paused at the top of some steps.

'We're underneath the Savoy hotel,' said Barbara. 'Above us are the kitchens, gearing up to provide food for the wealthy guests staying in this famous luxury hotel. But before it was built, we'd have been standing in the barely respectable Fountain Court, last resort for those out of money and luck.'

She dug in her handbag and brought out a photocopy. 'Look. This drawing was made after Blake's death, by one of the pre-Raphaelite artists who were influenced by him. It shows the small first-floor room in which William and Catherine lived in Fountain Court, until Blake's death. He died in this room.'

She smiled at the impassive Deepak. 'It's gone, of course. But this underground passageway gives you an idea of the gloom and darkness of the room, contrasted with the light from the river.'

Helen looked at the paper Barbara held out. The pencil sketch showed a bare room with a bed, a chair and a cupboard. But light streamed through one window with a view of the river, an impression of boats and movement.

'I'd swap his room for mine,' said Rose,. 'Imagine being able to sit up in bed and look at the river.'

Barbara led them down the stairs and out into a quiet maze of streets. They crossed into a tranquil garden.

'We'll end here,' Barbara said. 'If you want to explore Blake's London further, keep walking west and you'll come to Westminster Abbey. Blake spent a lot of time there when he was an apprentice, sketching the tombs. You can see the influence of the effigies on Blake's figures. And if you're still feeling energetic, head over Westminster Bridge into Lambeth. The Blakes lived there for ten years, in Hercules Buildings.' She grinned. 'Unfortunately the house has been knocked down and replaced with a housing estate. But there are some interesting mosaics under the railway arches.'

'That was useful,' said Liz, packing away her notebook and pen. 'But I'm heading back to college. I've got work to do.'

'I'm going to Westminster Abbey,' said Habib, his eyes shining. 'Anyone want to come?'

Rose hesitated. 'I think I might have had enough looking at things for one day,' she said. 'I'm ready for some lunch.' She crouched down, rummaging in her bag as if looking for something, clearly waiting. When she looked up, Deepak was laughing at her.

'Come on then, let's get you fed.' He held out his hand and pulled her up. 'I think we deserve a decent restaurant after all that walking.'

Rose looked as if all her birthdays had come at once.

Helen rolled her eyes at Barbara. 'Come on. Let's leave them to it.'

Barbara turned to Nick. 'Helen and I are going back to my flat for lunch. Do you want to join us?'

'That's a nice idea, but I've got stuff to do.' He looked up from his mobile phone. 'I've got his email address,' he told them. 'Rintrah. He responded to one of the comments I made on the blog. All down to your advice, Barbara. I'm reeling him in.'

He grinned, and Helen saw triumph on his face. She recognised that look: Nick was on the trail and would not let up until he got there. She felt a prickle of answering excitement.

'Look.' He showed them the email exchange. 'I'm going to set up a meeting. Find out who this bastard is.'

'Be careful,' warned Helen. 'He could be dangerous.'

Barbara laughed. 'Not in my experience of Blake obsessives. He'll be some pot-bellied old guy with a long beard and a head fried by too much acid in the sixties.'

'You worry too much,' said Nick, fondly. He hugged them briefly and walked away.

# Chapter 15

Sweat ran down his back, sticking his T-shirt to his skin. The trailer's flimsy curtains were closed tight, taped to the walls at the bottoms and sides, but the sun baked the thin-walled box as if he was in an oven. His fingers slipped on the tiny screwdriver.

He put it down, grabbed a towel and wiped the sweat from his forehead, upper lip and neck. He crossed to the sink and washed his hands in cold water. He couldn't afford to mess this up.

He dried his hands, applied sanitiser and waited for it to cool him. He was making progress, but it was slow work. He needed longer; ideally a few practice runs. But the conference was such a perfect opportunity. If he wasn't prepared to go over the top now, then when? He'd be just another keyboard warrior, whining about his fate, refusing to do anything about it.

He checked the instructions. His hands steady and cool now, he reached again for the wires, checked the polarity and twisted them together. It was intricate work, but doing it this way would leave all the power with him. He'd be able to control it from his phone, trip it early if he needed to.

It was always good to have a back-up plan. Who knew how

quickly he'd be taken down, once he started shooting? The lack of armed police in Britain, the general slow-wittedness of the security forces, suggested he'd have plenty of time. But you never knew. This way, the explosion would wipe out the emergency services and police, as well as finishing off whoever was left in the auditorium.

He let his mind linger for a moment over the carnage: body parts flying; blood running down the walls, pooling on the floor and soaking the seats. It would be a charnel house. He imagined himself in the centre of it: the screams and the panic, the pleading and the dying. Waiting, arms spread wide like a sacrament, for the blast.

He tied off the wires with a neat knot. He'd seen the documentaries, learned about the way that forensic scientists pored over the remains of an explosive device, looking for a signature. He liked that idea; imagined them noticing with grudging admiration the neatness, the fearful symmetry of his construction.

'This is not just any bomb,' he murmured to himself. 'This is the most beautiful bomb anyone has ever made.' He wanted it to be perfect.

There was a thump on the door. He set down the intricate construction, heart leaping. What to do? The light was on, but that didn't mean he was home. If he ignored it, would whoever it was go away?

'Open up!' It was a woman's voice, rough and accustomed to shouting. He heard a dog, growling low. He hated dogs, vicious, unhygienic creatures. What if she forced the door? She sounded like she might, and the lock was feeble.

'Wait,' he yelled. He took the equipment into the tiny bathroom, placed it carefully in the cupboard under the sink.

He closed down the Tor browser on his laptop, opened Google and logged on to a porn site, angling it to leave the screen visible. He washed his hands again, unlocked the door and opened it, wiping his hands on a towel.

'What do you want?' It was the woman who owned the campsite and stables, a hard-faced bitch with dyed blonde hair and smoker's wrinkles around her pink-painted lips.

'You're using too much power. I've been checking your meter.' She peered past him into the gloomy room. 'Why do you have the curtains closed all the time?' He saw her lip curl into a sneer as she saw the flicker of the laptop screen, pumped-up bodies automatically going through their paces, women's mouths rounded into O shapes as they gasped and writhed. He wished he'd turned the sound on.

'I'm watching a movie,' he said, matching her sneer with his own. 'The light obscures the screen.'

'Dirty git,' she said. She looked at the towel in his hands. 'Interrupting you, am I?'

'You are,' he said smoothly, making to shut the door.

'I'm putting up your rent,' she yelled. 'All that extra electricity you're using. You're supposed to sleep here at night, then bugger off and look at the sea during the day. It's a holiday centre for families. Not perverts.'

He reached into his briefcase, took out his calfskin wallet and extracted three twenty pound notes.

'If I had a family, I wouldn't let them within a mile of your crappy trailer park,' he told her. 'Don't ask for more. You won't get it.'

He closed the door, locked it and stood with his back to it, breathing hard. He'd chosen the place because it didn't look like anyone here cared about anyone else's business. And for the location, of course. But it seemed there was nowhere you could go without some woman barging in, wanting to give you a hard time.

He went into the bedroom, raised a corner of the curtain and saw her trudging back up the track, stopping to give the dog a handful of biscuits from her anorak pocket. He wiped the sweat from his forehead again.

His phone buzzed. He checked it: an email from the guy calling himself Flea.

'Hey, buddy. You in London? Want to meet up?'

He put the phone down on the bed. Did he want this? On the one hand, it was cool to be appreciated. In all the months he'd been writing Rintrah, this was the first time he'd felt someone actually understood what he was doing. But did he want to be understood? It was safer to be the only one who knew, to play to a gallery of idiots who laughed at the violence and got off on the sex. If this guy Flea recognised that he was forging an ideology, fomenting a revolution – then what? He'd take him seriously, in a way the others would not.

And he might have his own ideas about the way forward. Rintrah needed imitators, not critics. His experiences of working with others in the past had not been happy. You thought you were all working towards the same goal, that you were the leader, then suddenly you discovered the others were meeting up without you, making plans behind your back and taking the project in another direction altogether.

Or – and this was always a possibility, he reminded himself – what if Flea was a counter-revolutionary, a secret service plant from MI5? He'd heard of that happening in the US. Guys who had a spectacular all planned, only to discover their co-conspirators were actually CIA. He needed to be cleverer than that.

He picked up the phone. 'I'm out of town,' he wrote. 'Business to attend to. Where are you?'

A fuzzy photo appeared. He frowned, waited for it to resolve into a sharper image. He saw an ornate marble plaque, scrolled and garlanded. Lettering within the garland proclaimed that this was once the location of Fountain Court, a dingy alleyway near the Thames. Blake's last home, and the place where he'd died, although the plaque made no mention of that.

'Paying my respects,' said the text that accompanied the image.

If this was MI5, they were doing remarkably thorough research. Maybe he should arrange a meeting. It couldn't hurt to check Flea out.

'Cool,' he responded. 'I'll be in touch.'

# Chapter 16

Helen and Barbara walked along the riverside in companionable silence. Despite their disparity in height, they walked well together, Barbara's brisk steps keeping pace with her own strides. Usually she had to remind herself to slow down, to let her puffing companions catch up. The sense of ease she remembered from her early friendship with Barbara was returning. Only one other person had been this comfortable to walk with, she thought, remembering Richard's loping gait, his long legs almost outpacing her.

'Thank you,' she said, breaking the silence as they paused to cross the road on to Westminster Bridge. The scaffold-shrouded tower of Big Ben showed it was one o'clock. 'That was really good. I think they got a lot out of it. I certainly did.'

They crossed the river at Westminster Bridge, dodging tourists taking selfies against the golden stones of the Houses of Parliament. Barbara led the way past St Thomas's Hospital and across the busy Lambeth Palace Road.

They rounded a corner into a quiet residential street, with a pleasant low-rise block of flats stretching along one side of the road.

'Hercules Road, Lambeth. Ring any bells?'

'The William Blake Housing Estate,' read the sign. On one side, a blue plaque.

Helen laughed, delighted. 'You're living in Blake's old house!'

'Well, as your handsome young student would have pointed out, I'm living in the completely different block of flats that replaced the Blakes' house. I couldn't believe it when I saw this flat for sale, though.'

'I'm sorry about Deepak. There's always one,' Helen said.

Barbara shrugged. 'I've had worse, believe me. One last thing. Then we'll go and eat, I promise.'

She led them into the gloom of the railway arches that looped along the street. A train roared overhead. Helen's eyes gradually adjusted to the darkness.

'Oh!' She stopped in front of a panel of mosaic work, turquoise and red glowing unexpectedly against the yellow London brickwork. 'How amazing.'

The panel depicted a seated figure hunched over, face buried in its knees as if in despair. The massively modelled limbs, strong and clear, were clearly from a William Blake painting. 'There is a Grain of Sand in Lambeth that Satan cannot find,' read the text across the top.

'There are loads more,' said Barbara, gleefully. 'Look! This underpass is full of them. And there are mosaics on all of the railway underpasses here.'

Lambeth artists and craftspeople had created an outdoor art gallery of finely wrought mosaic panels in tribute to William Blake, Barbara explained. As well as reproductions of Blake's paintings, there were pages from *Songs of Innocence and Experience*, Blake's curly handwriting as carefully reproduced as his images, making the harmonious whole that he strove for. Helen stopped before a depiction of a shackled old man, his eyes closed and his long beard flowing down to his knees.

'This is amazing. Look at the way they've done his eyelashes, and the hairs of his beard.'

Barbara was smiling. 'I knew you'd like them. And I think Blake would have loved them, too. To have his work preserved so beautifully, and so publicly. So that everyone can enjoy them.'

Barbara pointed out a pair of fine reproductions of portraits of Blake and his wife Catherine, the latter taken from Blake's own tender pencil sketch. The delicate mosaic used white and grey tesserae to delineate Catherine's face, and larger pieces of broken crockery for the background. It was a sweet image hinting at domesticity and duty.

Catherine's eyes were demurely cast down, a few curls of hair escaping her linen cap. The portrait fitted with the traditional depiction of a submissive wife. Helen looked again at the portrait of Blake, shining eyes gazing intently under his fine, large forehead, the very image of an inspired poet.

'Don't you wonder what Catherine's eyes would be like, if she looked up?' asked Barbara. 'There are a couple of portraits from her later life, not very flattering. But she had big eyes, very expressive.'

'Actually,' said Helen, 'I was wondering what she was looking at. At first I thought sewing, or reading, but Petrarch Greenwood says she was illiterate...'

'She signed her marriage certificate with an X, and some letters supposedly from her are mostly in William Blake's handwriting. So it seems likely she learned writing later, probably from her husband. But illiterate doesn't mean stupid. Nor does it mean, because your handwriting is poor, that you have no facility with words.' She looked shrewdly at Helen. 'Go on. What were you thinking, then?'

'Well, that she might be drawing, or colouring. You said she helped colour Blake's designs. Or, I suppose, writing. Practising her letters, maybe.'

Barbara turned away from the portrait and found another mosaic. A scarlet blossom bloomed against the sooty old brick.

'*Infant Joy*. It was the first of Blake's poems I knew. I love the way it defers to the child, the new-born infant. And the assertiveness of the baby, who knows its own name.'

Helen read the words, familiar again now that she'd re-read the *Songs of Innocence*.

'I hadn't thought of that before,' she admitted. 'It's unusual. A dialogue between the mother and baby, and the baby naming itself, claiming its two-day experience of the world as joyful.'

*I have no name*
*I am but two days old.*
*−What shall I call thee?*
*I happy am*
*Joy is my name.*
*−Sweet joy befall thee!*

It seemed so simple, thought Helen, with the repetition of the short, plain words, the lullaby rhythm.

'Like something a mother might sing to her child.' Or a father, she supposed. 'But they didn't have any children.'

'Lots of people don't have children,' said Barbara.

Neither Helen nor her friend, for a start. She wondered whether that was something Barbara regretted. Helen was conscious of the passing years, but the idea of motherhood seemed remote, something that happened to other people. She wasn't sure she was the maternal type.

Barbara turned back to the poem. 'So. Like you said, it makes you think of something a mother would sing to her baby, a lullaby or something. And yet it was written by a thirty-year old man with no children.'

'True enough.'

'The child says he or she is two days old, and has no name. People have wondered about the two days thing. Why not a day old, or a week? Why two days?

'Then I found out that there used to be a tradition that a child was baptised on the third day after birth. So a two-day-old child is literally a child that has no name, that is free and joyful and can name its own essence. It only exists for its mother and father – and itself, of course. There are no records, until the christening. A two-day child does not officially exist.'

'Go on.' Helen leaned forward.

'So it's not impossible, is all I'm saying. That the Blakes could have had a child – a two-day child that didn't live until the christening. And that *Infant Joy* was a record of that child, otherwise unrecognised, unwritten in history.'

'Would there not be some record, though? Family letters, birth certificates?'

Barbara shook her head. 'Birth certificates weren't introduced until the mid-nineteenth century. There are no surviving letters to or from Blake before 1795. Also, so many children died as babies, or were stillborn. Perhaps it wasn't something Blake wanted to talk about. It's not exactly dinner party conversation, even now, is it?'

Her voice was uncharacteristically harsh.

'But come inside. I've got something to show you.'

They crossed the road. Barbara unlocked the door into the communal hallway and led them up the stairs into a neat first-floor flat with a view of the railway arches, and beside them a little row of houses.

'Have a seat. I won't be a minute.'

Helen sat at the counter which divided the kitchen from the rest of the living room. Barbara's old house in Camden had been dark and rather gloomy, dominated by her mother's old-fashioned tastes. This place was bright and modern, more colourful than Helen had expected.

'I chucked everything out, basically. I'd been living with that furniture since I was a kid. When Mum died, I sold the house and bought this place. I wanted a fresh start.'

Helen admired a yellow and blue abstract print on the wall and looked for the signature.

'I didn't know you liked Barbara Hepworth.'

'Didn't you?' Barbara smiled, placing blue bistro-style cutlery and big orange bowls filled with green pea soup on the table. Helen began to feel as if she was in a still life painting, colours carefully chosen for maximum impact.

They ate for a while in silence.

'You said you wanted to show me something else,' Helen said, scraping away the last of the delicious soup.

'I did. You said there'd be a record of a baby's death or stillbirth. Well, maybe there is.'

Barbara grabbed her battered laptop and pulled up a folder.

'Here. Most of the archival work that's been done around Blake has focused on correspondence to and from his male friends. So I thought I'd take a look at the women.'

Early in his career, when the Blakes were living in Soho, she explained, William Blake had been part of a literary and artistic circle organised by a Mrs Harriet Mathew, wife of a clergyman, in Soho's Rathbone Place.

'Mrs Mathew was one of the first bluestockings,' said Barbara. 'Lots of artists used to come – Angelica Kaufman, for one, and Blake's friend, the sculptor John Flaxman. There's a lovely description by one of the attendees of Blake singing his poems to the company, and them all sitting in silence afterward. Which I suppose might be appreciation, or perhaps bafflement.

'Anyway, I discovered that some of Harriet Mathew's papers are preserved in the Women's Library. I admit, I was hoping for a journal, with lots of description of the meetings, ideally with Blake's lyrics and songs. But there isn't much – she doesn't seem to have kept a journal. There are a few letters. Including one from Anne Flaxman, John's wife.'

Barbara pulled up an image of a letter, bold black handwriting still clear after three centuries.

'Here. It's not dated, unfortunately, but the letters seemed to have been kept in order. It's placed after April 1784 and before January 1786.'

Helen read it aloud.

'My dear Mrs Mathew,

'Hoping this finds you well as it leaves me and may I beg to thank you for your very pleasant entertainment of myself and Mr Flaxman. We have seldom enjoyed a happier evening.

'As I promised to do, I have been to visit our poor afflicted Mrs B. She bears her trouble hard poor soul and laments much. Mr F says B works hard and says nothing. I beg you to visit Poland Street, as Mrs B was much raised up by company.

'Your affectionate friend,

'Anne Flaxman.'

She grinned at Barbara. 'This is great! It doesn't name Blake specifically, though...'

Barbara shrugged. 'Doesn't matter. It mentions Poland Street, which is where the Blakes moved in 1785, just round the corner from Broad Street. We went past it this morning. And can't you just imagine Blake, working hard and saying nothing after a personal tragedy?'

She handed Helen a cup of coffee.

'Now. Have you ever heard of *An Island in the Moon*?'

# Chapter 17

The William Blake manuscript generally known as *An Island in the Moon*, Barbara explained, was an unpublished hand-written collection of satirical sketches, poems and songs. It fell somewhere between the traditions of London's scurrilous chapbooks and scandal sheets, and the satirical flights of Jonathan Swift, whose *Gulliver's Travels* was published in the early part of the eighteenth century.

'It satirises a literary salon, not unlike the Rathbone Place set. Blake stopped being invited after a while, because he offended people with his strongly expressed opinions. So perhaps this was his revenge.'

The manuscript described gatherings of men and women representing different philosophies of life, talking nonsense to each other, stuffed with in-jokes and contemporary references.

'It's actually very funny. Quite rude, in parts.' But it was mainly notable today, Barbara said, for its inclusion of the first drafts of several poems later published in *Songs of Innocence*.

'Including *Infant Joy*?' asked Helen.

'Unfortunately not. *Holy Thursday*, *Nurse's Song*, and *The Little Boy Lost*. Blake describes the poems being sung to the company, in the way that we know he sang them to Mrs Mathew's gatherings in Rathbone Place.'

'Where's it kept?' asked Helen. 'Have you seen it?'

'Not yet. It's in the Fitzwilliam Museum, in Cambridge. I'd love to go, but I'm a bit low on funds.' She looked embarrassed. 'It doesn't pay as well as you might imagine, offering freelance walking tours about minority-interest dead poets. But as soon as I can get the money together, I will. Maybe we could go together?'

Helen's smile faded. Cambridge to her meant the Parker Library in Corpus Christi College, where Christopher Marlowe had studied. It meant the research trip she'd undertaken with the historian Richard Watson, on a golden spring day more than two years ago. She'd shown him the old court where Marlowe had lived, and he'd looked at her as if he was falling in love. She'd tried to play it cool. Neither of them had any idea on that sunny, happy day that Richard had less than a week to live.

Despite various opportunities and invitations, Helen had resisted going to Cambridge ever since. She'd wanted to keep it pristine in her memory. But she couldn't live like that forever. And Barbara's idea had caught her imagination in a way that little had since the discovery of the Marlowe play.

'That's crazy. We need to get you some funding,' she said, firmly. Barbara, with no academic post, was reliant on her own earnings and any one-off grants she could garner to fund her research.

And Helen needed to find her own way into Blake's world, she realised. Petrarch Greenwood was the authorised version, the signposted route. She wanted to discover Blake for herself, to slip in through an unmarked side door or follow a

disused corridor, which might be a dead end or might lead…
somewhere new. Perhaps, with Barbara as her guide, she'd
get a fresh view of this maddening poet. And it would be good
to be working with someone again. She'd been too much on
her own.

'I'll talk to Caroline Winter. I bet she could find the
money, especially for an undiscovered woman writer,' said
Helen. Considering the amount of money the department
was spending on the *Out of the Silence* conference, the cost
of two train fares to Cambridge would hardly be noticed.
She'd been intending to talk to Caroline about Barbara's work
anyhow, and this would be a good way in.

'God, that would be brilliant. I haven't been for years.'

Barbara started to wash up. Helen picked up a bright orange
tea-towel.

'I'd forgotten you studied at Cambridge,' she said. 'I guess
you have lots of memories of your time there.'

Barbara nodded. 'Yeah. It doesn't change.'

'And that was when you met Petrarch Greenwood?' Helen
could just imagine him swaggering down Kings Parade in his
fancy outfits.

'It was.' Barbara frowned into the sink full of dishes.

'He must have been a good teacher. To have sparked such a
strong interest in Blake, I mean.'

'Yes, I suppose so.' Her voice was flat. Helen thought with
unease about her tutorial with Oona.

'Barbara, is there something I should know about him?' she
asked. 'About the way he treats students? It doesn't seem to
be a happy memory for you. And his students – my students
now – don't seem very happy either.'

The older woman's jaw was taut.

'I'm sorry to hear that.' She pulled off her washing-up gloves and picked up her cigarette packet. 'He was a lecherous bastard, Helen. He seemed to think the students were included in his salary. Perks of the job.'

'You mean he had sex with them?'

'Well, obviously. This was the eighties. But he was greedy. Even for those days. He got pushed out.'

'Pushed out?'

'They called it study leave. But everyone knew what it was. He just disappeared one day. We didn't see him again. Next thing I heard, he had published his book and been snapped up by Russell.' She lit a cigarette and leaned out of the window, waving the smoke away from the room.

Helen was unsurprised by the revelation, but disturbed nonetheless. Had he had sex with Barbara? She was being uncharacteristically evasive. Maybe Barbara had been in love with him, and been rejected. Perhaps that was where her hostility to the man had come from.

Was he still sleeping with his students? Helen wondered. Surely not, at his age. She thought of Oona's tears, Rose's relief when she'd told her the professor would not be teaching them again that term. Study leave, she thought, uneasily. Again. If he was harassing the female students these days, he'd be on very shaky ground, celebrity or not.

'I'm worried about the girls in my group,' she said. 'There's something wrong. Do you think that might be it?'

'It might be,' said Barbara. 'Maybe you should ask them. Nobody ever asked me.'

# Chapter 18

'Sorry, Petrarch, she's busy all morning. Do you want to wait?'

Petrarch Greenwood was not used to needing an appointment. Grumpily, he took a mug of bad coffee from the impertinent girl who guarded Caroline's office and sat on the grubby orange sofa, knees creaking as he lowered himself down.

'It's this *Out of the Silence* thing,' the girl said, perching on the arm of the sofa. 'It's taking up all her time. It's going to be massive. Are you excited about it?'

'Eh?' He looked at her in disbelief. Why would he be excited about another attempt to glorify a few minor female writers, deservedly ignored in their own day, now dragged out as evidence of undiscovered genius? She was still sitting there, apparently waiting for an answer, swishing her blonde hair about to attract his attention. Pretty, but obvious. Not his type.

'Not particularly.' He reached into his bag for the *Times Literary Supplement*. He wasn't going to spend his morning gossiping to the admin assistant about women's literature. 'It's not something that concerns me.'

She slipped down on to the seat next to him. 'That's not

what I heard,' she said, her silly voice full of portent. She even tapped him on the knee, for heaven's sake. She didn't seem to have any respect for his status.

'I'm a Romantic Poetry specialist,' he informed her, icily. 'There aren't any female Romantic poets.'

'What about Catherine Blake, though?'

'What?' He threw down his paper. The girl – what was her name? Janet, Jessica, something like that – was goggling at him with her baby-blue eyes. 'She wasn't a poet. What nonsense have you been reading?'

The girl was smiling, a cat-like smile that was infuriating in its pert air of superiority. 'Caroline is very excited about her. She's asked me to buy train tickets so that Helen Oddfellow and her friend can go to Cambridge to do some research. They're going to present a paper about Catherine Blake at the conference.'

Petrarch was momentarily speechless. What on earth were the women doing now? Helen Oddfellow knew nothing about Blake – nothing at all! She'd admitted as much. He'd agreed to her taking over his first-year student group, under duress. But she was supposed to stick to the curriculum, walk them through the work they needed to do for the exams, and then go back to her precious Christopher Marlowe. What the hell was she doing messing around with Catherine Blake?

The door opened, and Helen walked out of Caroline's office. Her cropped hair was scruffy, her plain white T-shirt and black jeans made her look more like an undergraduate than a lecturer. Yet she dared aspire to his territory.

'Helen!' He struggled out of the low sofa, heaving himself up.

'Are you all right?' She paused. She didn't smile.

'What do you think you're doing? How dare you suggest a presentation on Blake, without talking to me first?' he hissed.

Her eyebrows shot up. 'Not William Blake, Petrarch. Catherine. And I'm not presenting. It'll be my friend, Barbara Jackson. The one I told you about – your old student. Remember? You should do.'

'Petrarch, are you coming in? Or do you want to come back tomorrow?' Caroline's voice, sharp, from the office.

'You had no right,' he snapped at Helen, sweeping past her and through the door. He closed it with more force than he'd intended.

'What is it, Petrarch? I'm rather occupied.' Caroline was a complete mess, her unflattering blouse crumpled, hair frizzing everywhere in the heat. Any make-up she might have worn had slid down her face, leaving dark mascara marks under her eyes. God, thought Petrarch, this department is unravelling. Was he the only one who cared about keeping up standards?

'Is it true?' he demanded.

'Is what true?' Caroline regarded him wearily.

'Are you really running a session on Catherine Blake at the conference? And if so, why didn't you ask me first? You'll turn the department into a laughing stock.'

Caroline took off her reading glasses and massaged her eyes. 'It's a new proposal. I'm considering it. I understand there is more work to be done to support the theory.'

'What theory?' Petrarch felt heat mount in his face, and wished he had tied his bowtie more loosely that morning. 'There is no theory. It's just a bunch of crackpot feminists. We get them all the time in the Blake Study Group. You have to be firm.'

100

Caroline leaned forward and pressed the intercom on her desk. 'Jessica? Is my next appointment here yet? Good. I won't be a minute.'

She pushed her hair back and stood, all of five foot in her bare feet.

'Petrarch, I agreed to see you because Jessica said it was urgent. Frankly it is none of your business who I invite to speak. Especially as you have given me no help with the conference at all. Now, do you have anything else to say before you leave?'

Petrarch felt his confidence deflate like a punctured balloon. Damn. He'd come to tell Caroline about Oona, in case Veronica did as she'd threatened and made a complaint of harassment. And now all he'd done was rile her, when he was already on shaky ground.

'Um. Yes. Sorry, there was something.'

He reached for his handkerchief, pressed it against his forehead. It really was very hot in the little office.

'One of the students came to my flat last week. Concerned that I wasn't taking the class anymore, you see. I... she had been to visit once or twice before. Anyway. It's all dealt with, but my wife – Veronica – might mention it. And I thought you should know. There's absolutely nothing to worry about. It won't happen again. And should Ronnie talk about making a complaint – well, I thought it was best you knew. No need to take it further.'

He looked up from his hands, twisting his handkerchief into knots. Caroline's expression had shifted beyond weariness towards contempt.

'Is that it?'

He nodded.

'Off you go, then.' She flicked the intercom again. 'Send them in, Jessica.'

# Chapter 19

Nick sat on a bench under the huge glass roof. The sun beat down on the atrium, heating the place up like a greenhouse. It was humid, the air moist with the smell of hundreds of hot people and a whiff of grilled cheese from the snack bar. He checked his phone; he was dead on time. The question was, would Rintrah show?

He was taking a risk, he knew. It was one thing setting up a hard-to-trace anonymous profile online. But a meeting risked blowing his cover completely. Nick didn't have a particularly high profile as a journalist, though – he'd never worked in television and his byline photo was years old. He didn't do social media for personal stuff, and he used a *Noize* avatar for work. Anyway, like Barbara had said, Rintrah was probably some middle-aged guy with a laptop and an obsession. He wasn't the sort of violent thug Nick had dealt with before.

And nothing beat meeting a contact face-to-face. He'd have to do it sometime, to get a decent story. Toby was pushing for progress, and the women's writing conference was less than a fortnight away. If there was a story to uncover, he needed to move fast.

The blogger had been the one to suggest the meeting place.

Nick had never been inside the British Museum before. He'd arrived half an hour early to check it out. It didn't seem to contain much that was actually British, he noticed. It was full of stuff from all over the world, no doubt nicked by freebooting colonial exploiters. And there weren't many British people inside either, except for the crocodiles of over-excited primary school kids in their high-vis jackets, toddling past the Egyptian mummies. The visitors came from all over the world, too, bused in to see the priceless artefacts taken from their own countries.

He looked around the busy atrium, conscious of the sweat dampening his armpits. The place was enormous, with a staircase winding up around the central column of the Reading Room. Rintrah could be anywhere, anyone. Nick felt uncomfortable, wondered if he was being watched from somewhere. He squinted against the light, looking up at silhouettes of people on the upper floors.

There was a tall man standing at the top of the central staircase. He was gazing down into the room, but Nick couldn't see whether he was looking at him specifically. On the other side of the atrium, another man checked his phone, then looked around as if trying to find someone. Was that him? A white guy, middle aged, wearing a dapper linen suit. Nick half-rose, then sat again as a woman greeted the man and they headed towards the galleries together. He looked back to the man standing on the stairs; he was gone.

He should be wearing a red rose or carrying a rolled-up copy of *The Times*, thought Nick. Rintrah had specified where he should wait: a bench near a marble statue of a bloke on a horse. Whoever he was, Rintrah knew the museum well.

He'd run the venue past Barbara, who had told him that

the British Museum had some Blake drawings and prints on display on the top floor. She'd been amused by the cloak and dagger aspect; had even advised him on what to wear to look like a Blake enthusiast.

'Ideally, you should grow a beard and long hair, and wear a trilby,' she'd told him. 'They all latch on to this drawing of Blake with a slouchy hat and scarf. Romantic, I suppose.'

Nick had informed her he would rather die than wear a trilby.

'You're too young, anyway. And not white enough. Could you bear to dress all in black? Maybe with a Doors T-shirt?'

The Doors were a step too far, but Nick was wearing jeans and a black T-shirt and thought he looked pretty anonymous. He checked his phone again. No message, and it was now fifteen minutes after the meeting time. Damn. Looked like Rintrah was going to blow him out. Maybe he should send him a message.

He looked up to scan the crowd one more time. A couple of police officers were striding across the atrium, accompanied by a security guard. Nick looked around for any sign of trouble. There was none. And they were heading his way.

Uh-oh. He'd had too many experiences of stop and search on the streets not to recognise one in the making. Although being picked up in the middle of a museum was new.

He stood as the officers approached, arms carefully out to his side, hands in full view.

'Would you mind telling us what you're doing, sir?' asked one of the police officers. She was young, polite, perky. Her colleague, a big guy sweating through his shirt sleeves under the heavy stab vest, looked immovable. Not the sort you would want to try to get past in a hurry.

'Always happy to help, officer.' He tried to keep the weariness out of his voice. 'Would you mind telling me what this is about?'

The security guard was standing to one side, carefully not looking his way. Which made a change from the crowds of tourists in the atrium, who were all staring at him.

'We've had a report from a member of the public of a man fitting your description, carrying a knife,' said the woman. 'Are you armed in any way?'

Nick exhaled, noisily. 'Of course not. I'm waiting for a friend; we were going to look at the William Blake prints, but he's been held up. Come on, you can see I don't have anywhere to keep a knife.' He held his arms out, let them see for themselves the tight T-shirt and slim-fitting jeans. His trainers were standard, old-school, his ankles bare.

The police officers exchanged looks. Bet you don't even know who William Blake is, thought Nick, forgetting for a moment that he'd been in the same position just over a week ago.

'May I take your name and address, sir?'

Nick sighed and complied. At least they weren't giving him the full pat-down; that would be too humiliating. As he always did, he asked for a written record of the encounter. He had a pile of the forms at home; fewer since he'd moved out of Lewisham, but still more than enough. He liked to show them to colleagues who questioned his assertion that they lived in an institutionally racist society. He'd yet to meet a white guy his age who'd been stopped and searched even once.

He waited while she scribbled down the details, then stuffed the paper in his back pocket.

'Can I go now?' he asked, sick of the whole business.

'Not going to see the Blake prints?' she asked, raising an eyebrow. 'They're very good.'

He stared her down. 'I've gone off the idea.' He gave the security guard a filthy look, stomped across the atrium, through the grandiose entrance hall and out into the sun. Who had reported him? One of the tourists, alarmed by the sight of something out of Africa that wasn't in a glass case? He sat on the stone steps and dug out his phone.

One message.

'Sorry about that. You're not what I expected. I needed to see how you would react.'

The bastard. Nick clenched the phone in fury. So Rintrah had reported him, because he wasn't the white guy he'd expected to meet. He jumped to his feet and swivelled around, trying to spot whoever had sent the message. He'd show him how it felt to be grabbed off the street while minding his own business.

But then... He breathed deeply, getting his pounding heart back under control. His kickboxing coach had taught him never to react in anger.

'Your anger is energy; store it and control it. Use it when it's needed.'

Nick had to get this guy's trust. For whatever sick reason, Rintrah had decided to test Nick. So he needed to pass the test, whatever it was.

'I conserve my energy for the real fight,' he wrote. The real fight being against racist dicks like you.

'Good,' came the reply. 'I will send for you again.'

# Chapter 20

Helen and Barbara sat on the steps that led up to the grand classical portico of the Fitzwilliam Museum. They were early. The fast train from Kings Cross had deposited them in the ancient university city just after nine o'clock, and the museum did not open until ten.

The good weather had held; they basked in morning sunshine which turned the bone-white stone to pale gold. Cyclists whizzed past in the street, students and academics heading for the colleges. The first groups of tourists were disgorged from coaches and herded in the same direction, down Trumpington Street to the city centre.

Five minutes' walk would bring them to Corpus Christi, Christopher Marlowe's old college, with its imposing Victorian frontage and library masking the medieval buildings that Marlowe would have known. Helen's head was full of images from her last visit there with Richard. His delight at the treasures in the library. Their excitement at the evidence they unearthed together in the archive. And most of all, how they had stood together in Old Court and he'd put his hand over hers, resting on the ancient, warm flints. The knowledge that she would never see him again still hurt, still felt unreal, more than two years after his death.

'You're very pensive.' Barbara stubbed out her cigarette. 'Penny for them.'

Helen tried to laugh it off. This was no time for a meltdown.

'Sorry. This place – Cambridge – makes me think of Richard Watson. We did some research here together. It sort of feels like his natural home. Where he should have lived. He'd have been happy here.'

Helen had told her friend a little of her relationship with the historian.

'You miss him.' Barbara's voice was kind. 'More than you let anyone know.'

'Mostly I'm busy. It's OK. But there are places where I just feel like I see him. I can imagine him here so easily. Then every time I see a tall man walking or cycling past, I get this crazy hope it might be him. Stupid.'

A warm hand covered hers, against the stone of the steps.

'Not stupid at all,' Barbara said.

Behind them, a clanking of locks announced the imminent opening of the museum. On cue, dozens of church bells started to chime the hour, the notes rising above the city, sweetly discordant. Ten o'clock.

Helen scrambled to her feet, glad to be doing something to chase away the ghosts. 'Let's go in.'

The magnificent entrance hall took her breath away. Light streamed through the high domed lantern, pooling on to rich mosaic floors. Marble pillars, a dark algae green at ground level, dried-blood red above, supported the sweeping staircase.

'Wow. This is quite something.' Helen stopped, stared upwards at the gilded and arched ceiling, the white marble statues frozen in their niches.

'Isn't it just? I could spend weeks in here. Those Victorians really wanted to make an impression.'

Barbara led the way through the entrance hall, down a flight of shallow marble stairs and presented herself at a closed oak door, where she rang the bell. The Founders Library, not open to the general public.

A white-haired woman in a cardigan admitted them to an airy room with a high coffered ceiling. Every wall was stacked with leather-bound books, their gilt lettering gleaming. Wooden panelling surrounded tall windows that gave out on to lawns at the front of the building. A big mirror between the windows reflected back yet more shelves of books, as if the entire room was built of them.

'Great, isn't it?' Barbara said. 'I've been here before – unfortunately, hardly any of the works by William Blake are on general display. They have several of the illuminated books, including copies of *Songs of Innocence and Experience* and *The Marriage of Heaven and Hell*. But you have to make an appointment to look at them. I can't see the point of amassing all this material and then hiding it away so only academics can look at it.'

'I suppose they have to think about conservation,' said Helen. 'But it seems a shame.'

They presented their credentials and sat at a long table covered with red baize while the librarian brought out the precious manuscript of *An Island in the Moon*. Barbara immediately began taking photographs of each page, blank or otherwise.

'I want to go over them later,' she said. 'See if there's anything I've missed.'

The manuscript gave a strong impression of Blake's lively mind. Black ink closely scribbled over each folio, with smudges and scratched-out words where the poet had changed his mind. Helen had read a transcript on the train, amused by the witty banter of the dialogue and songs. It blew a raspberry at anyone who thought Blake had no sense of humour.

'Here.' Barbara turned to page fifteen of the manuscript. '*Holy Thursday*, one of the poems from *Songs of Innocence*. As you can see, he revised it heavily as he went along. Isn't it amazing to see his mind at work?'

Helen leaned over the page. Knitted loops of black ink obscured several lines, with their revisions underneath. It gave an impression of having been written at great speed, Blake's imagination leaping from line to line, replacing and improving his words with stronger rhythms and clearer images.

Barbara pointed further down the page. 'And that one is *Nurse's Song*.' She turned the page. 'Then we have *The Little Boy Lost*. A short poem; just two stanzas.'

Helen read it through. Blake's handwriting was clear, even with its vigorous loops and scrolls. After the melancholy little poem, he'd inserted a moment of contemplation: 'Here nobody could sing any longer.'

There were another two folios of gossip, songs and non-sense, then Barbara turned the page, turned it back again, and frowned. The next page began mid-way through a sentence.

Barbara traced the curly letters. 'He's writing about en-graving and letter-press printing,' she said. 'Something of an obsession of his. But it looks like there's a page missing.' She took a photograph, then switched her attention to the final page. It had been turned sideways and used as a sketch pad, with pen-and-ink drawings of horses' heads, dogs, lions and men's profiles.

'The descriptions I've read of the manuscript say the sketches might have been done by Robert, Blake's brother, who was his pupil at the time. They're a bit clumsy, although goodness knows, Blake's own drawings of animals are less than successful,' Barbara said. 'Every school kid I've taught has laughed their head off at his picture of the tiger.'

'True enough.' Helen leaned back in her chair, musing. 'But what about the missing page?'

They asked the librarian, who smiled, a little superciliously. 'Yes, that's been established for many years. There are at least two pages missing,' she said. Her tone implied that any real scholar would have known that already.

'How did the museum come by the manuscript?' asked Helen.

The woman tapped a label on the front of the box where the manuscript was stored. 'Donated by Charles Fairfax Murray, 1905. He was a very generous benefactor to the museum.'

'And the pages were missing when he donated the manuscript?' Helen was taking notes.

'Yes, of course. Although it was mounted differently. We carried out some conservation work. There's a note from the conservator saying that the pages were missing. It should be in the box.'

So, Helen thought, either the pages were missing when the donor acquired the document, or he detached the pages and kept them separate, sold them, or destroyed them for some reason.

'We need to know about Charles Fairfax Murray,' she said

to Barbara. 'Who was he?'

Barbara regarded her friend with a mischievous smile. 'You're getting quite into this, for someone who wasn't that interested in Blake a few weeks ago. Why don't you see if you can find out?'

Helen went online. Ten minutes later, she reported back.

'Murray was a minor pre-Raphaelite painter, who worked in the studios of Burne-Jones and Rossetti, then moved to Italy. He became an art collector and dealer, with an amazing art collection. He was quite close to the Rossetti family, which explains the manuscripts and paintings he acquired from them.'

'Interesting.' Barbara pushed back her chair. 'Dante Gabriel Rossetti was one of the earliest and most prominent champions of William Blake, after Blake's death. He bought Blake's notebook at auction, and worked with his first biographer. But that could be the link between Blake and Charles Fairfax Murray, I suppose. Maybe that was how Murray got hold of the *Island in the Moon* manuscript.'

Helen delved into the museum's catalogue, with the help of the librarian. There was no record, she said, of how Charles Fairfax Murray had acquired the Blake manuscript, or when. But he'd definitely had it by 1893, when it was listed in a catalogue of Blake's works. A long list of entries showed that Murray had indeed been a generous patron to the Fitzwilliam Museum, with donations including a Titian painting, Japanese ceramics and literary manuscripts from William Morris, Dante Gabriel Rossetti and his sister Christina, as well as William Blake. Helen focused on the manuscripts, all donated in 1905 and – apart from the Blake – all connected to the pre-Raphaelites.

'There are usually some on display upstairs,' said the librarian, who seemed to have decided to be helpful. 'Room three, at the top of the main staircase, British art of the sixteenth to nineteenth century. I'm not sure what's on display at the moment, but they'll be in the cabinets.'

Barbara was still poring over the *Island in the Moon* manuscript. 'You go,' she told Helen. 'I'll get on here.'

# Chapter 21

Helen passed through the splendour of the marble entrance hall and walked up the wide, shallow steps. Room three was a double-height gallery, hung with oil paintings by Van Dyke and Gainsborough. She wasn't keen on this type of art: swaggering aristocrats and their vapid-looking wives, swathed in satin and velvet, staring down at the plebs with cold hauteur. Stopping below a Van Dyke portrait of a lord in a magnificent embroidered waistcoat, she thought again of Petrarch Greenwood. His sneer, as well as his taste in clothes, was echoed in the painting before her.

Two glass cases covered in green baize stood against the wall, below a pair of saucy Hogarth paintings. *Before* and *After* showed a young couple flirting in woodland, and then lying in post-coital disarray, the woman's face pink and her legs on display. Not subtle, but Helen preferred them to the domineering poses of the aristocrats.

She drew back the baize on one of the cabinets. A book lay open, vigorous black handwriting looping across the page. She read the legend beside the book. Rossetti's poem on the death of John Keats, given to the museum by Charles Fairfax Murray in 1905. She stooped low to read Rossetti's words, trying to follow the text amid the many crossings-out and revisions.

A crash, and the glass shattered.

Helen screamed as shards flew up to her face. She covered her eyes with her hands, feeling a sharp pain at her temple. An alarm bell started to clang.

Helen's hand was wet, blood trickling between her fingers. Shocked, she felt for the source. A sliver of glass was embedded just above her right eyebrow.

*What the hell just happened?*

A great lump of white plaster lay on the Rossetti manuscript, amid the shattered glass of the display case. God, thought Helen. It almost hit me. She stared at it, imagining the mess it would have made of her head.

She looked up at the ornate white plaster ceiling. Had a piece of the mouldings come loose and fallen? Movement caught her eye. A dark-clad figure was running around the far side of the high-level gallery that circled the room, just below the ceiling.

'Hey!' Helen shouted.

A thunder of footsteps announced a puffing museum attendant. The woman grabbed her arm.

'What happened? What did you do? Are you hurt?'

'Nothing! Look, there's someone up there.' She tried to shake off the woman's hand, pointing. But the figure had disappeared.

The attendant was talking into her radio, calling for a first aider and security staff. Helen scanned the gallery wildly. She'd not imagined the figure, she was sure. But she couldn't see a door into or out of it. She dug in her pockets for a tissue to stem the blood coming from her temple.

'Do you want to sit down? You must have had a shock. Let

me have a look at your head.' The attendant looked shaken herself. Helen sat in the chair she proffered, still trying to figure out what had happened.

'There was someone up there,' she repeated. 'How do you get into the upper gallery?'

'Hold still.' The attendant held a folded handkerchief against Helen's head. She winced as the glass dug into her flesh. 'The gallery? There's a spiral staircase. But it's been closed for months.'

Helen craned to look around the woman, bulky in her uniform.

On the other side of the room, a figure wearing dark clothes, hood up, emerged from behind a curtained-off alcove.

Helen sprang to her feet. 'There!'

The man vaulted a red rope and sprinted towards the exit. Helen shook off the attendant and gave chase. She paused at the top of the main stairs. A pair of security guards stood at the bottom, but she could not see the man. She pivoted, went right into the next room along, ignoring the stares of the other visitors and the blood running down her face. She caught a glimpse of a dark figure disappearing through the door at the far end.

She wasn't sure what she was going to do when she caught him, but Helen's heart was pumping. No-one chucked lumps of masonry at her and got away with it. She swung through the next room, then left into a long gallery. She ran past gilded altarpieces and the sweet faces of endless Madonnas, swerving around marble statues and startled visitors. A gallery attendant called out, tried to block her path. She dodged around a display case, too quick for him. She could hear the man's running footsteps ahead of her.

At the end of the gallery, a left turn took her towards another staircase leading down. She ran to the top of the stairs and paused for a second, trying to catch her breath. But he must have gone down; the staircase was signed to the exit.

She started to clatter down the steps. She'd been so close; she didn't want to lose him now.

Something shoved her in the middle of her back, and then she was falling. She plunged, headfirst, down the hard marble stairs.

# Chapter 22

Helen's head hurt. A siren was rising and falling, very close, the noise drilling into her brain. She tried to turn her head and found she could not move. She opened her eyes, frowning against the light.

'What's going on?' she muttered, her mouth dry.

Someone took her hand. 'It's all right, Helen,' said a reassuringly professional voice. 'You're on your way to hospital. You fell down some stairs.'

'Thank God you've come round,' said Barbara, her voice wobbly. 'I thought you were dead. What happened?'

Helen thought. 'Not sure. I think I fell…' She remembered falling, the shock of tumbling headfirst down stairs. And before that, running. And before that… something had fallen on her. Was that right?

'Hold still, and don't try to talk,' said the paramedic. He moved into her eye line, a young black man with dyed blonde hair. 'I'm going to check your pupils. I'll shine a light into them, just briefly. Is that OK?'

She tried to nod, but couldn't.

'Don't move your head. We've got you on a back board, in case there's any damage to your spine,' he told her.

Shit. She hadn't thought of that. Images rose in her

mind: a wheelchair, confinement, the struggle to walk again. Horrible.

'Is that likely?' she asked, swallowing down dread.

'Let's hope not. Can you move your toes?' he asked.

Helen wiggled them, felt a wash of relief at their response. 'Yeah.' That meant she'd be all right, didn't it?

'That's good. Try not to close your eyes.'

She winced at the bright light.

'Great. That looks normal. But you were out for...' he paused, checked a clipboard. 'Almost five minutes. There's a chance of concussion, so the hospital will probably keep you in for a bit to monitor you. We're almost there.'

Something was nagging at Helen. 'I went to look at something,' she said. 'Barbara, did anyone tell you what happened?'

'I wish I knew,' her friend replied. 'An alarm went off, and there was lots of crashing about upstairs. I went out of the library to see what was happening. When I got to the main entrance, they were herding everyone down the stairs and out of the building. I went round to the other exit to see if I could find you in the crowds, and then an ambulance pulled up. The next thing I knew, they were carrying you out, looking like a bloody corpse. Literally. You were completely white and there was blood all over your face.'

'There was a guy... someone in the gallery,' said Helen. She remembered running, a figure in black ahead of her. 'I didn't see his face.'

'There were lots of people in the gallery,' said Barbara.

'No, I mean... at the top. The gallery around the room I was in.' Helen gave up, her head pounding now. The siren screeched again as the vehicle swung right and pulled up.

She was fast-tracked through on the ambulance trolley, despite her protests. The paramedic stood by her side until she'd been handed on to a nurse, stern-looking in her emergency scrubs.

'We'll get you looked at. Are you the one the police want to talk to?'

'I don't know.' Why would the police want her? wondered Helen, bewildered.

'What have you been doing?' asked Barbara, despair in her voice. 'I thought we were having a nice, calm research trip to a museum library.'

So did I, thought Helen.

For the next half hour, she was prodded, examined and tested, until the staff were confident her spinal cord had not been injured by the fall. She was finally allowed to sit up while the grumpy nurse deftly removed the shard of glass from her temple and applied a dressing.

'It doesn't need stitching,' she said. 'We use superglue. It works the same and doesn't hurt. Now, because of the bang on your head, we're going to need to keep an eye on you. Which means you'll be taking up that bed for a few hours yet, unless we can get you on to a ward.'

The nurse huffed off, clearly annoyed that Helen was hogging her resources. Before she had time to draw breath, a uniformed police officer put his head around the door.

'All right if I come in? We've got a few questions about what happened.'

Yeah, thought Helen. Me too.

# Chapter 23

Rose was late for their one-to-one tutorial. Helen drummed her fingers on the desk. She was still confused about her frightening experience in Cambridge the previous day, and not in a patient mood.

With the help of the police and gallery staff, she'd pieced together what had happened, but she still had no idea why. She'd been lucky not to have been killed by the falling lump of plaster, the police had told her. The museum was trying to work out where it had come from, and seemed more worried about the possibility she might sue them than anything else. In the panic after her fall, the man she'd been chasing had escaped the museum. The police had not found any witnesses who saw him push her down the stairs. They were examining the museum's CCTV, they said, but Helen had heard a note of scepticism in their voices.

Had she imagined seeing him up on the balcony? Had she really been pushed, or simply fallen? Her own memory was now so confused that she found it hard to be sure.

She'd made it home late on Tuesday night, refusing the hospital's advice that she should stay overnight for observation. Barbara had pressed her to come back to her flat in Lambeth, but Helen was longing for the solitude of her own bed. She'd spent the morning catching up on work, and was in no mood for dilettante students.

Finally, the door swung open and Rose drifted in, murmuring apologies for lateness.

She was transformed since Saturday's walk. Glowing with wellbeing, her cheeks flushed and her green eyes witchy bright, she dropped down into the low chair opposite Helen, a blissed-out smile on her face, and stretched out her bare legs. Helen noticed the unusually subdued grey sweater she wore over her yellow sundress. It was fine cashmere, with too-long sleeves rolled up over the wrists. A man's sweater.

Ah, Helen thought. Deepak's sweater.

'Shall we talk about your essay?' She passed it over the table. 'You did a good job. It reads like those poems really resonated with you. Tell me a bit about how you approached the question.'

'Um. I sort of read the poems, and thought about what you said about nature, and Blake going on walks.'

Rose had managed to bring her body along to the tutorial, but her mind was clearly elsewhere. In vain, Helen pressed her to be more specific, explain her thinking. The students had exams in just a few weeks' time. If Rose was to do herself justice, she needed to emerge from her love-sick fog and focus.

'Come on, Rose. You wrote a good essay! What's up with you today?'

'Sorry.' She yawned. 'I'm a bit sleepy. Late night.' She stretched and smiled, almost insolent in her satisfaction. She glanced at Helen, noticed for the first time the dressing on her forehead. 'What happened to you?'

Helen sighed, feeling old. Her own late nights were caused

by insomnia, guilt and worry, not young love.

'Nothing. I fell down some stairs. Look, I know you don't want to hear this. But this is your chance. You're a bright girl, you've got a good brain and this is your best opportunity to use it. Don't mess your exams up just because you've decided you'd rather have a good time than work hard.'

Rose's eyes snapped open. 'That's not fair. I do work hard. I wrote the essay, didn't I? Anyway, Petrarch says I'll pass...'

She stopped.

Helen frowned. What did the girl mean? Had Petrarch Greenwood promised them good grades for... for something? She remembered Oona, telling her that Petrarch had said not to worry about her essay.

'Rose... do you mean Professor Greenwood? He won't be marking the exams. I will.'

'But he said...' She stopped again, bit her lip. 'Nothing. Doesn't matter.'

Helen watched her for a moment in silence. A furious blush mounted from Rose's chest in the V-necked jumper, mottled her neck pink and suffused her face. She looked away, then down at her hands.

'What?' She sounded younger, a stroppy schoolgirl caught out in a lie. But Rose was pretty much incapable of deception, Helen was sure.

'I'm trying to understand what you just said. Did you mean that Professor Greenwood told you he'd make sure you passed the exam?'

'He said I shouldn't worry about it.'

'That's not quite the same, is it?'

'He said... he said that he'd make sure we did all right.' Her voice was barely a whisper.

124

'OK.' Helen kept her voice gentle. 'Who's "we", Rose?'

She bit her lip. 'Me and – the others. The ones who went to his party.'

'What party? Who else was there?' Helen thought of the opulent flat on Great Russell Street, Petrarch's glacial wife Veronica handing round champagne and canapés. She couldn't quite see how this fitted.

'Just – just a few of us. People he'd taught. Some of the older students, as well. Second and third years.'

'Oona?'

Rose nodded.

'What about university staff, or Petrarch's wife? Were there other lecturers or tutors there?'

Rose blushed again. 'No – yeah, actually. One or two. Not his wife, though. I didn't know he was married.'

Helen pressed on. 'Why did he say you'd do all right, if you went to his party? What happened at the party?'

She looked down, hiding her hands in the sleeves of her borrowed sweater. 'I don't know. Nothing?'

Helen didn't believe her. But Rose would answer no more questions, and her distress was so evident, in contrast to her happiness when she'd entered the room, that Helen decided not to ask any more. She'd heard enough. Time to talk to Petrarch himself.

# Chapter 24

H elen didn't want to give him any warning. As
soon as her day's work was done, she marched
across Russell Square and pressed the buzzer for
Petrarch's flat. She hoped Veronica wouldn't be in. She didn't
want to have to make small talk.

'Hello?' It was Petrarch himself, sounding older than she
remembered. His voice was hesitant, as if he was worried
about who might be calling.

'It's Helen Oddfellow. Can I come in? I want to ask about
the examinations.'

She bounded up the stairs. At least he was fully clothed this
time, dressed in traditional professorial garb of bottle-green
corduroy trousers and a rumpled linen shirt. He looked older,
too. His hair needed cutting and his beard could have done
with a trim. Interesting. Maybe the dandy look was only for
public consumption. She took confidence from his lack of
preparedness.

'I thought I should know about the exam papers, as I'll be
marking them,' she said. She strolled into the drawing room
and leaned against the back of a chair. 'Have they been set
yet? Or do you use a standard paper?'

'They follow a format. I vary the questions, of course.' He

looked distracted, moving objects around his big mahogany desk. Several of his books were piled on it in order of size, spines carefully facing into the room. A stack of Moleskin notebooks was lined up on a leather blotter, a beautiful fountain pen next to an open book. On the wall, against the shimmering peacock wallpaper, hung a good reproduction of one of Blake's most striking images: a naked figure standing within a rainbow-coloured sunburst, arms spread wide. The print was exultant, the very image of freedom.

'The 1794 print,' said Petrarch, seeing her gaze. '"Albion rose from where he laboured at the mill with slaves." I find it inspirational.'

Helen thought of her little Ikea desk at home, spiral-bound notebooks fighting for space with her laptop, text books piled on the floor, uncapped biros shoved into a mug without a handle. Petrarch Greenwood didn't actually work at this desk, she realised. It was just for show, as if he had imagined reverential visitors being shown around a Petrarch Greenwood museum, pausing to admire the place where he wrote his books.

'Can I see a past examination paper? And the marking scheme?'

'There's one in my study.' He glanced towards the door. 'My assistant is busy at the moment...'

Helen didn't want the conversation to be interrupted. 'Perhaps you could let me have it before I go, then. No need to disturb him now.'

'Of course, if you would find it helpful. The thing is, I plan to mark the papers myself. It's sweet of you to offer, but there's really no need. It seems more appropriate for me to assign the final marks.' He perched on the edge of the desk, placing his hand on top of the pile of books. I wrote these, he seemed to be saying. You are no threat.

'Rubbish,' said Helen, firmly. 'Caroline asked me to take on the class, and that includes marking. Study leave means study leave, after all. I'm sure you're making good use of it.'

She strolled to the windows and looked down at the street. Now or never.

'Rose told me this morning you'd promised some of the girls good grades. You'd better tell me why you think they deserve that.'

He laughed, a harsh, incredulous bark which had an edge of shock. Helen turned to see him drawing himself up to his full height, his eyes narrowing.

'I've no idea what she means. I probably said they were all capable of good grades. If they worked hard.'

'Was that here? At one of your parties? They must have been impressed with the flat. It's quite a big deal, for a teenager from an Irish village or a small Scottish island.'

He put his hands in his pockets and returned her gaze.

'Yes, I expect it is. I like to have my students over for a drink at the start of the summer term. I don't think it hurts to let them see the sort of life you can aspire to as an academic.' He swept his gaze over her old jeans and T-shirt. 'If you are good enough, and understand how the system works.'

Helen frowned. Was he threatening her? She wasn't having that.

'Rose isn't the first of the students to say that you told them not to worry about their grades. That you'd make sure they did OK. And I'm wondering why that is. Especially given the circumstances in which you left Cambridge.'

He raised his eyebrows and walked closer to her. Too close;

she felt the threat of his bulk, the heat of him, inches away. He smelled faintly of alcohol, sour booze from the night before.

'Be very careful, Helen. I left Cambridge because I was offered a professorship at Russell. I don't know what you are insinuating, but it sounds like vicious gossip. There's nothing improper about an academic hosting a party for undergraduates.

'I know you're used to teaching schoolchildren,' he said, his tone scornful. 'But these are adults. And I resent your tone. You've been teaching my students for – what – two weeks? And you've barged in without an appointment, interrupting my study leave, alleging I promised them good grades for personal reasons.'

'Well, I wanted to understand...' Helen wondered if she should have been on firmer ground before coming to see him.

'Not to mention your attempts to move in on my turf with this nonsense about Catherine Blake. Give you an inch and you take a mile. The other academics were right to warn me about you. It rather looks, Helen, as if you are trying to smear me for your own professional gain.'

Helen gasped. 'Of course I'm not. But I had to ask the question.'

'And I've answered it. I'll get you a copy of last year's exam paper. I'll mark it this year, as usual.' He crossed the room, his thick lips curled into a self-satisfied smile, and disappeared into the hall.

Shit. She'd made a complete mess of that. And what did he mean about being warned about her by the other academics? Helen thought with anxiety of her colleagues, wondered who had been bad-mouthing her. Jeremy, she supposed. who had supervised her PhD. He'd made little secret of his dislike for her. But the others?

Petrarch had admitted he'd invited students to his flat, which was unorthodox, if not actually evidence of misconduct. But he was known for being unorthodox, in his dress and his views and his work. Was she misreading all this, she wondered, affected by Barbara's revelations about the man? Helen didn't want to make enemies at the department, especially not ones as influential as the professor.

The door re-opened and his assistant, the young man who'd been there on her first visit, came through with a plastic folder.

'Professor Greenwood asked me to give you this, Helen. He says he needs to get on, if you'll forgive him. Lots more to do before we pack up for the day.'

She smiled, trying to remember the man's name. 'Thank you. I'm sorry, I…'

'Brett Albion. I'm helping with the new book. Just chasing up references and so on.'

'Great.' She guessed that the professor wasn't much fun to work for. 'He must rely on you a lot.'

'I don't know about that. But it's really a privilege. I've been a Blake fan since I was a kid. I remember watching the TV programme Petrarch did, when I was still at school. It blew my mind. I never thought I'd actually be here in London, working with him.'

Helen checked the folder, which contained the previous year's exam paper, as promised, and the marking scheme.

'I guess it must have its compensations, then.' She thought for a moment. 'Do you get to go to his famous parties?'

The man's face closed down. 'I'm staff. I just do my job. No partying.'

Helen wished she hadn't mentioned the subject.

'How are you getting on, Helen? Any more progress with that work about Catherine Blake? Or – wait, that was your friend, wasn't it?'

'Actually, I've been working on it with her. Caroline Winter has asked her to speak at the *Out of the Silence* conference. We're making good progress.'

'How exciting.' He paused and looked at her more closely. 'You've injured your face. What happened?'

She sighed. Petrarch Greenwood hadn't even noticed, she realised. 'Nothing. Well, something, obviously. It's weird. I was at the Fitzwilliam Museum yesterday. We wanted to see the *Island in the Moon* manuscript. And someone chucked a lump of plaster. It hit the display case I was looking at.'

'That's terrible! Are you OK? Did they catch him?'

'Unfortunately not. The police seem to think I imagined him.' She picked up her bag and headed for the hall. 'I didn't imagine this, though.' She touched her fingers to her forehead, which was starting to hurt again.

She had planned to call on Oona, see how she was getting on and rearrange their tutorial. Oona's essay had arrived, and wasn't bad, to Helen's relief. But she felt suddenly exhausted, the events of the last couple of days catching up with her. Maybe she'd go home, get an early night and try again in the morning.

# Chapter 25

Despite her setback with Petrarch, Helen wanted to check with Caroline Winter about the exam marking. She decided to tackle the head of department early, before anyone else arrived.

Caroline was already at her desk. At eight in the morning, Jessica had yet to arrive to keep the gates, so Helen made two coffees and carried them in.

'Oh, bless you.' Caroline took one with a grateful smile. Her desk was covered with spreadsheets and sticky notes in different colours.

'No problem. How's it going?'

Caroline sighed. 'A bit of a nightmare. I suppose these things always are. A couple of people have dropped out. I'd hoped to get Cherys Caldwell, but the trans lobby said they'd call for a boycott and protest. Which I was prepared to risk, but Cherys has decided it's not worth the hassle.'

Cherys Caldwell was a fiercely feminist American literary critic, whose rigorous work on gender and literature had brought her to prominence in the 1990s. However, her uncompromising stance on the concept of women's literature had brought her into conflict with transgender activists. The previous year, she'd refused to accept the work of transgender women for contention in the prestigious all-women literary prize she chaired. The decision had caused outrage. She'd been sacked from her position with the prize, and her university had been urged to end her tenure. Since then, she'd been met with protests everywhere she appeared.

'She's just fed up,' confided Caroline. 'She says she's spent her whole life fighting against people trying to shut her up, and she's damned if she's going to let them win this time. But she's tired and needs a break. I'm still hoping she might change her mind, but I don't think it's very likely. I can't remember the last time she changed her mind about anything.'

'Who else have you got?' asked Helen. Caroline talked her through the timetable. The final day of the conference – at which Caldwell had been scheduled to appear – was intended to highlight the work of women writers who had been unrecognised, unpublished, unheard or uncredited.

'There are so many examples of women whose work was claimed by men,' said Caroline, her eyes gleaming. 'Dorothy Wordsworth, to name an obvious example. Even when William published her account of her ascent of Scafell Pike, he didn't attribute it to her. Percy Bysshe Shelley, trying to re-write Frankenstein so that people would think it was his work, not Mary's.'

She pushed up her reading glasses. 'In fact, it would be the perfect slot for your friend Barbara's work on Catherine Blake. How did you get on in Cambridge?'

'We made some progress. We saw the *Island in the Moon* manuscript. There are missing pages, and we're looking into where they might be. The donor's archive is in Manchester, at the John Rylands Library.'

Helen paused, wondering if she was pushing it too far.

'We really need to visit the archive. But it's a more expensive trip than Cambridge. I was wondering...'

Caroline tapped her teeth with her pen. 'Can you do it before the conference? It starts a week today, remember?'

Helen swallowed. 'Early next week. I have tutorials on Monday, but maybe Tuesday?'

Caroline nodded decisively. She jumped to her feet, marker pen in hand, and scribbled on the big whiteboard.

'Are you presenting together? I'll put you both down. Friday, 2pm. Straight after lunch, which is a bit of a graveyard shift, but this would wake them up. We could really make a splash with it. Press interviews, maybe even TV? They all love a bit of controversy.'

God, thought Helen. How would Barbara feel about that? She was already anxious that her theory was too thin to stand up to scrutiny. What if they didn't find anything in Manchester?

'It's still quite early days,' she ventured.

'Nonsense. Nothing like a bit of publicity. And it'd get people checking their own work, looking in archives you don't even know exist yet. There might be a clue out there somewhere, waiting for someone to find it. And you never will, unless people know you're looking. Decide when you want to go to Manchester, and tell Jessica. She'll book trains. Any problems, let me know.'

She dug around her desk and found a battered business card, which she pressed on Helen.

'Here. Ring my mobile if you need me. I'm relying on you.'

Helen took the card, feeling rather sick. Once Caroline had an idea, like Cherys Caldwell, she rarely changed her mind. And she had a way of making people go along with her.

'Thanks for the coffee. I'd better get on,' said Caroline, settling back down at her desk.

Helen had come in with the intention of raising Petrarch Greenwood's relationships with his students, she remembered. How had she allowed herself to get so side-tracked?

'I wanted to ask you something else. It's Professor Greenwood,' she said. 'He wants to mark the students' end of year papers. I thought that might be inappropriate.'

'What?' Caroline frowned. 'Why? If he wants to do them, that's up to him. He always has.'

Helen hesitated. 'One of the students suggested… maybe I misunderstood, but she seemed to say she'd been promised a good mark if she attended a party at Petrarch's flat. And… I heard that there were concerns previously, about relationships with students. When he was at Cambridge.'

Caroline pushed her glasses up her nose and fixed Helen with eyes that were suddenly as grey and opaque as sea ice.

'If this student is making an allegation, she should come to see me in person. I'm sure I don't need to tell you how dangerous it can be to make unsubstantiated accusations. Especially on the say-so of undergraduates, especially if you may have misunderstood them. I will not have gossip undermining the reputation of this department. I had thought better of you, Helen.'

She looked down again and started writing. Helen was dismissed.

# Chapter 26

The man stretched, looked up from his laptop and ordered another skinny latte. His work that morning had been fruitful. Nobody took Rintrah for a fool and got away with it.

He'd been suspicious as soon as he'd seen the guy strut over to the bench in the museum on Monday. Without giving it any thought, he'd assumed that Flea was white. He assumed that all of the guys who posted in the Rintrah Roars forum were white.

Not that Rintrah was a white thing, exactly. But black guys – they didn't fit. They had their own places, their own stuff. Drill music and grime, videos and gangs. It was a different culture. Sure, they had problems, mostly self-inflicted, if you asked him. Drugs and knife crime. But that was part of the threat, part of the takeover. All he knew was, a black guy on Rintrah Roars was suspicious.

So he'd made the phone call, watched as the cops came, observed how Flea reacted. Standing up on the balcony overlooking the atrium, he'd had plenty of time to take photos of the man.

This morning, he'd run the clearest photo through image search until he found him.

It hadn't been easy. Facial recognition technology was notoriously bad at recognising black faces. The usual sites where people tagged photos, Facebook and so on, had drawn a blank – which was suspicious in itself. Eventually he'd found a couple of news photographs taken outside a court building, almost two years ago. Flea looked different – younger, skinnier, with short dreadlocks – but the man was almost sure the face was the same. He cross-checked with the name in the caption and eventually found Flea's photograph attached to some articles on a new media website.

Got him.

Nick Wilson. A fucking journalist. And not just any toe-rag hack, but one who'd been responsible for sending a race defender to jail, who had undermined a political organisation set up to protect Britain from foreign influences. The reports of the court case related how the man had worked with Helen Oddfellow, the female academic who was now threatening to undermine William Blake. This was too much of a coincidence. It had to be a conspiracy.

What did the journalist want? Presumably he intended to write some kind of exposé, a take-down of Rintrah's plans. Wilson had nothing yet, he was sure of that. All his questions, trying to find out what he was working on. Well, he'd find out. He'd be involved, all right. Rintrah would make sure of that. And as for Helen Oddfellow – well, she'd already begun to see what he was capable of.

He was in a café just across the street from the *Noize* offices. He'd watched Wilson saunter in just after nine, wearing a big pair of expensive headphones. He clearly did all right for himself. The man would be back in the evening, follow Wilson discreetly and find out where he lived. No doubt there were plenty of guys online who'd like that information. He wondered what it would be worth. But he didn't need the money. He, Rintrah, would decide Nick Wilson's fate himself.

He closed his laptop and turned to his phone. Maybe it was time to give another tug on the leash.

'Hey, Flea. Are you keeping yourself in readiness? I have something big planned. I'd like you to be a part of it. There is more I need to do to prepare. But we should meet, next week, to discuss it.'

He sent it off, sipped his coffee and waited for the message to make its way twenty feet across the road to Wilson's mobile.

Seconds later, the reply came back. 'Sure thing. What are you planning?'

He smiled. 'All in good time.' He switched off the phone. Meditatively, he rolled his shoulders and smoothed sanitiser over his hands. It had been a busy week, what with one thing and another. He felt good. He'd taken risks, and gotten away with them. He'd started to act in the real world.

He relived the heart-shattering smash of the display cabinet, the mad dash through the galleries. Helen Oddfellow was a worthy opponent. He admired her, despite himself. She was fierce, and determined. But he had beaten her, fooled her and everyone in the museum. He had proved he could act decisively, daringly, and win. He was starting to enjoy himself. And with luck she too would be there at the grand finale. In the crosshairs. It couldn't be more perfect.

But first he had another score to settle, another woman to take down. The memory that gnawed at him, poured acid into his guts and would not leave him in peace. He'd changed his mind about the girl's fate. He didn't want her to be there, mocking, at the end of his story. He wouldn't waste a bullet on her. He wanted her gone, dismissed. He wanted her to know her shame, die with him watching, in full knowledge of what she had done to deserve it.

The café was almost empty, the staff gossiping at the till. He pulled out his sketch pad and turned to an empty page, grabbed a pencil and sketched an outline. A girl, thin and delicate, a cloud of hair that reached to the base of her spine, her head thrown back. Kneeling, her thighs spread wide to straddle an old man, puffy and bloated. Around her, he quickly drew faces watching, laughing or turning away, their expressions by turns eager and disgusted.

He thought for a moment. What else? He drew the next scene, a vicious pleasure taking over. And the next, excavating the images from his memory, spewing them on to the paper. He couldn't unsee them. She should be made to see them too, to witness the ugliness, the shame that he'd felt.

He reached for his pastels, began tinting the drawings. Pale auburn for her hair, cream for her flesh. Tones of grey and putrid green for the man, then gold for Rintrah's scales. Rintrah the Reprobate, standing above her, masterful, waiting for his due. Holding his sword, and his cup, to receive her blood.

# Chapter 27

The phone buzzed again. Petrarch had set it to silent, unable to bear the constant ringing and the pings of messages that had been coming since the early morning. Now it vibrated near-constantly on the table, the itch of a bad conscience.

He'd checked the messages. She said she'd been sent something he needed to see. Not a pregnancy, then; that was good. There had been a few of those, over the years. Silly girls who thought that somehow he'd be overawed by the idea of creating new life. As if he and Veronica hadn't been through it all before with David, now thankfully off their hands. But it was always unpleasant, the persuasion and the tears; the pleas and the slightly sordid money transfers; the assurances that they must look to their own futures, not throw their careers away before they had even begun.

He'd have to do something, though. His neighbours in the British Library Humanities Reading Room were looking increasingly tetchy. Only the serious researchers made it to the reading rooms before ten o'clock on a Saturday, and they didn't appreciate any sort of disturbance, no matter how minimal.

He'd fled the flat when it became clear that the messages

were not going to stop. He couldn't bear Ronnie's sarcasm. He wondered, without caring much, if she was having an affair with Brett. They had been talking behind his back, he was sure, since they jointly ejected Oona from the flat a week ago.

But an affair seemed unlikely. Ronnie had never been a particularly carnal creature, and he wasn't sure that Brett had it in him. Petrarch had required all his powers of imagination to engender his one son, a boy who resembled his mother in almost all particulars, and now worked for his uncle's venture capital fund. If there was one thing Veronica and her family were good at, it was making money.

After David bought his flat in Oxford, Ronnie speedily redecorated his room and claimed it as her own. Petrarch still asserted his conjugal rights from time to time, for the sake of his pride as much as anything. But recently she'd been less and less willing. Her face reminded him of one of Monet's courtesans, bored and contemptuous above her well-preserved body. She could hardly claim she hadn't given him reason to look elsewhere. He'd stopped worrying that she would divorce him. She enjoyed the prestige of being the professor's wife, the kudos of every television appearance. And the thought of managing without her money was impossible. He simply couldn't afford a divorce.

He sighed as the phone buzzed again. He picked up the device and looked. Twenty-three messages this morning. This was ridiculous. He opened one at random. It had an attachment, an image of some sort. He squinted, trying to make it out on the small screen.

Christ. It was a photo – no, not a photograph, a photo of a drawing. But there was no mistaking what it depicted. Oona, her auburn hair streaming down her back, her slim torso twisted to show her full breasts. And – oh God – was that meant to be him, Petrarch? His bare belly swelling obscenely, like a parody of pregnancy. He drew himself up in his seat, pulling his jacket defensively closed over his paunch.

What was this hellish thing? He checked the message's text.

'There are more. They're disgusting. And whoever sent it says he has videos. He says he'll put them on the internet. Petrarch, that would ruin my career. Who would accept me at drama school? Who would employ me, except as a porn actress? You've got to find out who did this. Please, please call me back.'

Petrarch was sweating through his shirt. He pushed back his chair, left the books he'd selected more or less at random piled up on the table. He had to get out. He stumbled towards the door, thinking only that he needed air, some place he could think.

He turned and walked down the stairs, out into the sharp sunshine of the red brick courtyard. He took his phone out again and tried to look at the picture, but the sun was too bright. It vibrated again. A call this time. Taking a deep breath, he answered.

'Petrarch, thank goodness, why aren't you answering?'

'I just did answer. Oona, calm down. I've been busy. I was in the British Library. I can't answer my phone in there.'

'Are you there now?' Her voice was eager. 'I can come over.'

'No!' His eyes darted around the courtyard, as if she might be lurking behind the sculpture. 'I'm just leaving. I have to go somewhere.'

Quick, think of something. The gothic towers of St Pancras railway station, looming above the library, caught his eye.

'Paris. I'm getting the Eurostar. There's a conference.'

'But did you see the drawings?' she wailed.

Christ, this was a nightmare. 'I saw. Obviously there's someone very sick out there. When did they send them? What's the email address?'

'It wasn't an email. It's a letter. A letter with these horrible drawings. It was left in my pigeonhole, sometime last night. I found it this morning. I don't know what to do.'

He reached for his handkerchief, wiped the back of his neck. 'What does it say?'

'It's weird. "Bromion rent her with his thunders on his stormy bed."'

'Bromion? Are you sure that's what it says?'

'Yeah. Then it goes on: "Behold the harlot here on Bromion's bed."'

'This harlot,' said Petrarch, automatically. There was a pause.

'How did you know that?'

Because it's from Blake, Petrarch wanted to say. *Visions of the Daughters of Albion*, Blake's key text for understanding the relations between the sexes. As you'd know, if you put as much energy into study as you do into having hysterics.

'Never mind.' His brain was churning. Who? Someone at the party; someone who had watched as he and Oona were joined, male and female in one person. The same bastard who told Caroline about the party? A student, then. But who?

'What else?'

'It says Oona – no, not Oona...'

'Oothoon?'

'Yeah. I think so. It says Oothoon will be chained to the rocks and rent by eagles.' She sobbed. 'That all wives should

143

be held in common. That I must face the wrath of Rintrah.'

Lord. Whoever it was, they had imbibed their Blake pretty much indiscriminately.

'Sweetheart, it's clearly a nutcase. Ignore it.'

'But he says he has videos. And that he'll put them on the internet. What am I going to do?'

Petrarch had no idea. Could someone really have filmed them? He had a strict no-phones policy at parties. Maybe it was just a threat. Of course, he filmed them himself, for his own records. But no-one else knew about the hidden cameras.

'They're bluffing. Let me think about it. I have to go now. But I think it's best we keep our distance, Oona. Don't you? Whoever drew this feels threatened by our relationship. Perhaps we should accept that we have had our time.'

'What?'

'We have celebrated the divine in each other, Oona. We have caught the joy as it flies. We can't tie it down, or capture the essence of what made it so beautiful. This is a warning. It's over. I want to remember you as the glorious goddess you are, Oona, soaring on the wings of Eros. Don't let's spoil that image with tears.'

He was on comfortable ground now; he'd said those words many times before. Whoever sent the letter – he'd find out; he'd pay them off, somehow. It would not be the first time a jealous student had tried to make trouble for him.

'I can't believe you're doing this to me. You bastard,' she said, voice rising.

'Be brave, darling. You have so much life ahead of you. I am an old man...' he laughed, self-deprecating. This usually worked better in person, him holding the girl's chin and wiping her tears with a handkerchief. 'And you are a glorious nymph, with the whole of the world to explore. It has been an honour to be your guide, but it's time for me to let you go.'

She was silent. 'Goodbye, my Oona,' he said. 'Goodbye.' He ended the call and put the phone back in his pocket, with some relief. He felt better, now it was over. But the letter. That was troubling. Although surely, if he had been the target, he would have had one too.

His stomach lurched. Oona said hers had arrived that morning. What if there was one in the post, waiting for him? Veronica usually went through the mail first, weeding out the charitable requests and offers of appearances or talks. Forgetting about his books upstairs, he turned quickly for home.

# Chapter 28

I t was late. Helen yawned so wide her jaw clicked, and closed her laptop. She'd worked all weekend to make time for the Manchester trip on Tuesday.

Barbara had been on the phone constantly since Helen had broken the news about the conference. She was in a major panic about the presentation. Eventually Helen had promised to present it with her, just to calm her down. Now she was trying to get her to focus on what they needed from the John Rylands Library, a vast Victorian repository of knowledge.

'There are more than a thousand letters in the Charles Fairfax Murray archive,' Barbara had reported, her voice rising. 'I've asked them to get out anything that mentions the pre-Raphaelites. But they said it was all boxed up together and we'd have to do our best.'

Helen fought off irritation that this now seemed to be her problem. She couldn't keep working at this rate, she thought. It would be all right if she was sleeping properly, but brain work didn't tire her body enough for it to relinquish its hold on consciousness.

She checked the time on her phone and groaned. Fewer than eight hours until she had to get up for Monday morning tutorials. Please, she prayed, let me sleep tonight.

The phone informed her she had six new emails. She sighed. Three from Barbara. She'd look at them in the morning. One from her sister: a photograph of her niece and nephew, and a reminder that her niece's birthday was the week after next. Helen smiled for a moment at their grins, gappy with missing milk teeth. She'd not seen them for months.

Two messages from Oona. They'd had a tutorial on Friday, when they had unpacked Oona's clever but disturbing essay about Blake's use of flowers to demonstrate innocence and experience. Jealous roses with thorns, naked lilies delighting in love. Oona had seemed almost back to her earlier self. She was still pale, still looked tired, but she was engaging again with her studies.

Helen opened the first message. 'Can I talk to you? I don't know what to do.' It had been sent that evening, four hours ago. A second one, sent an hour later: 'Sorry. Forget it. Doesn't matter.'

Helen looked at the messages, dubious. She wished she'd checked her phone earlier, but she'd been flat out preparing for this week's Romantic Poetry lectures and tutorials, trying to keep one step ahead of the students' knowledge, while catching up with the marking for her Elizabethan Drama second years.

It was past eleven. Oona had said that whatever it was didn't matter. She'd presumably decided how to deal with it herself. Helen would drop her a line in the morning, check that everything was all right.

She gave her teeth a cursory brush and fell into bed. Thoughts of the presentation, Barbara's fears, her own workload and now Oona's messages tumbled through her head. She'd need to get a birthday present for her niece, too. What did seven-year-old girls like? Helen had only wanted books at that age, desperate to escape into a more colourful and exciting world. Maybe she should make a list of everything she needed to do in the morning, she thought, rolling over in bed. But before she could reach for the light, she was asleep.

\* \* \*

Something was ringing, right by her head. Helen struggled awake. It wasn't her alarm clock, not yet. She grabbed her phone, noticed the time. Six forty-five.

'Hello?' she croaked.

'It's Rose. I'm scared. I went to her room, but I can't go in there on my own. I've just got back, I've been away all weekend. I came back early to get changed, and I found this thing. And something's happened, I know it has.' The girl's voice was high, gabbling so fast Helen could barely keep up with her words.

She sat up, rubbed her face.

'Rose... slow down a bit. I've just woken up. What's the matter? What's happened?'

A slow, wobbly intake of breath. 'It's Oona. I think something bad has happened to Oona.'

# Chapter 29

Rose jumped up from her seat the moment Helen walked into the reception area of the halls of residence. She wore Deepak's grey sweater over a denim mini skirt. Judging by the dark circles under her eyes, she had not had much sleep. She was clutching a piece of paper.

'Look.' She thrust it at Helen.

Helen took it and read the scribbled words. 'I can't deal with this, Rose. We used to be friends. Maybe you'll understand.'

'What's this about?' she asked.

'Turn it over.'

The paper was thick, as if torn from an expensive sketch pad. The other side was a dense mass of writing and drawing. With a shock, Helen recognised the style. She looked more closely at the drawings, sexually explicit depictions of men and women, conjoined in various ways. Around the edges, faces watching. Expressions of lust, curiosity, disgust and laughter. These pictures were more detailed, skilled and true to life than the cartoon images from the blog. But the style was clear. This, Helen thought, was Rintrah's hand.

And there was no question, either, who the drawings depicted. The central figure was Oona, her thin body and clouds of red hair unmistakeable. And the figure coupling with her – at least in most of the images – was the bloated body of Petrarch Greenwood. Helen felt sick.

'Where did you get this, Rose?'

'It's horrible, isn't it? I haven't talked to Oona for ages, but she sent me a text over the weekend, asking if I was free.' The girl looked ashamed. 'I ignored it. I was away all weekend. When I got home, I found this pushed under my door. I tried her phone, but she didn't answer.'

Oh God, thought Helen, remembering the emails she herself had ignored.

'Where is she? Have you been to her room?'

'I...' Rose's voice tailed off. 'I knocked on the door. She's just down the corridor from me. But there was no answer.'

'Maybe she was asleep?'

Rose wrung her hands. 'I turned the handle. The door was unlocked. But I didn't dare go in.'

'Why not, Rose?'

She fixed Helen with her green eyes. 'Because something very bad has happened. Don't ask me how I know. I felt it, when I touched the handle.'

The dread that had accompanied Helen all the way into London rose to her throat. Something in Rose's face told her that the girl was right. Helen wasn't superstitious, though. She tried to be practical.

'Right. Well, let's go and find out, then.'

She bounded up the stairs, too impatient to wait for the lift. Rose scrambled along behind her, out of breath.

'Which door?'

'Number eight, at the end of the corridor. I'm number five.'

Helen took hold of the chrome handle. She felt nothing but

cold metal. She rapped firmly on the pale wooden door.

'Oona? It's Helen Oddfellow. Can I come in?' She turned the handle and pushed the door open.

The smell hit her first. Coppery, metallic. The smell of a butcher's shop. Her throat thickened. She swallowed hard.

She switched the light on, illuminating a mass of clothing and paper, as if someone had upended all the cupboards and drawers on to the floor. She picked up a crumpled pile of paper: an essay on Coleridge's *Kubla Khan*, marked by Petrarch Greenwood. He'd given her a B minus. A mug lay on the bed, the remains of the contents spreading a tea stain across the rumpled sheets.

A door was ajar on the opposite side of the room. Helen could see white tiles, a light pull hanging in the corner. The light was on.

'Rose?'

'Yeah?'

'Stay where you are. Don't let anyone in.'

Helen crossed the room in a couple of strides and pushed open the bathroom door.

Oona lay like a waxwork, her skin white as bone and her lips bruise blue. The water in the bath was crimson. Her arms floated on the surface, shreds of skin flapping loose at one wrist.

Helen stopped, her brain stalling as she tried to process what she was seeing. She forced her legs to carry her forward, knelt by the side of the bath, damp where the water had sloshed on to the floor. Droplets of red spattered the white tiles. They had run down the wall, pooled in the seal by the edge of the bath. The room was cold; no steam rose from the bathwater.

She put clumsy fingers to Oona's icy neck, tried to find a pulse. The girl's jaw was rigid, her eyes open, as if startled. Helen looked for a long moment into her pale blue eyes; saw the same blankness she had once seen in Richard's face. Time telescoped to that moment; stood still.

She heard a strangulated cry, looked up to see Rose at the bathroom door.

'Is she dead?'

Helen tried to speak, found she had no voice. The smell of blood in the water hit her again, and her stomach contracted. She covered her mouth, looked away, closed her eyes for a second. Breathe, she told herself. She began to shake.

'Get back outside.' She met Rose's eyes, wide with horror. 'Go down to reception. Get them to call an ambulance.' She could hear her voice beginning to rise in panic. This wouldn't do. She needed to be strong, for Rose.

She struggled to her feet, took the girl by her shoulders and gently pushed her back out of the room.

'Now, Rose. Ambulance and police. Go.'

Rose turned and fled.

Helen closed the door behind her and sat heavily on the unmade bed. No. Not again. She couldn't bear it. Too late. Not again. She folded over the pain in her chest, fought the urge to scream. Not again.

She still had the paper in her hand, scrunched up in her fist.

Her hands shook as she spread it on her knee. The images were horrible, the juxtaposition of the painted girl's vulnerable body with the pitiful corpse in the next room almost too much to bear. Who had done this? She felt sure this was the same person who drew the Rintrah blog. Hounding Oona to her death.

If Oona had received this – when had it arrived? Before she emailed her, Helen supposed. Was this what she wanted to talk about? Helen thought in torment of the messages. If only she'd picked them up earlier. If only she'd called when she did see them. What time had Oona died? She remembered checking her phone, just before she rolled into bed, past eleven o'clock. Was she still alive then?

She looked at the images, trying to understand. Oona with Petrarch Greenwood, enclosed in a sort of sickly looking flower. Oona with other men, faceless. People watching...

Helen looked again, realisation dawning. A girl's face, laughing, with rainbow-coloured hair. A dark-haired boy, with something of a look of Habib. Habib! What on earth was he doing there? A man standing with him, embracing him tightly from behind. And was that Deepak, his lip contorted into a sneer, standing bare-chested above Oona's body?

Was this a record of Petrarch's dodgy parties? Helen tried to follow the text. The words underneath were semi-familiar, had a Blakean ring to them, but told her little.

'Behold this harlot here on Bromion's bed,' said the text underneath the picture of Oona and Petrarch.

The final frames were different. In one, Oona was alone. She knelt on a rock, holding a huge knife, its tip pressed to her breast. In the final frame, she lay stretched out on the rock, an enormous bird hovering over her, pecking at her chest.

'Rend away this defiled bosom,' read the text.

Helen spread the paper out on the bed and photographed it with her phone.

# Chapter 30

Caroline was grey-faced, slumped against her desk. Helen paced around the office, tripping over boxes and piles of paper as she tried to explain what had happened.

'Helen, please just sit down.' Caroline's voice was strained.

'Sorry.' She sat on the edge of the desk. It was barely nine o'clock and she felt as if she'd been awake for days.

She'd waited with Oona's body until the police arrived, Rose trailing behind them. Helen had showed them the bathroom. Swiftly a policewoman had taken Helen and Rose to wait downstairs in the reception area. She had been kind, making small talk and arranging cups of tea, keeping them calm. She'd given Helen her card, PC Maggie Lambert.

'Call me anytime,' she'd said. 'Anything you remember that could be useful.'

The paramedics had arrived with their bags. Helen had felt stupidly guilty that she was wasting their time. There was nothing any paramedic could do for Oona now.

The reception area was soon full of students, wide-eyed and chattering, some close to hysterical. Oona's room had been sealed off with police tape and an officer stood outside, answering no questions.

The police were asking for the rooms nearest to Oona's to be vacated temporarily, Caroline said, while they did a thorough investigation of the scene.

'I wonder if it would be best for them to be rehoused until the end of term. They're bound to be upset. The welfare service will arrange it.'

She slapped the desk, making Helen jump.

'Damn it to hell. How did we not see this coming? She had a history of self-harm. The university medical service knew. Her aunt had asked her tutors to be informed, in case there was any deterioration. I have to speak to her mother this morning, after the police in Orkney have broken the news.'

Helen shivered. She couldn't get warm, despite the growing warmth of the day.

'God. That's going to be tough.'

'Yeah. It's the worst.' Caroline's voice was hollow. She'd done it before, Helen realised. 'But I thought she was doing all right?' Caroline's voice rose to a wail. 'She started so well in the first term, with *Hamlet* and everything.'

Helen felt wretched. 'I thought so too. I noticed that she was unhappy when I took over the group this summer. But we talked, and she said it was a relationship break-up. She was quite calm about it, and when I saw her on Friday, she'd done her essay and she seemed much better. There was no sign she was planning to hurt herself.'

The unanswered emails from Sunday dug at her conscience. But then there had been nothing particularly alarming about their tone at the time. She'd re-read them several times: 'Can I talk to you?' and then, an hour later: 'Doesn't matter.' What had happened during that hour? she wondered. What had changed, what had led to this tragedy?

Helen had given a statement, in which she'd told the two police officers questioning her about the emails and the phone call from Rose. She had handed over the paper that Rose had given her, although she'd refrained from telling them about her suspicion that it depicted not just Oona, but several of the other students. After all, she could be wrong. She didn't want to get anyone dragged into this unnecessarily.

Asked about the man in the drawing, she had hesitated, then said it looked as if it was intended to be one of the professors at Russell University, albeit in a very crude and unflattering depiction. She'd been asked if Oona had been in a sexual relationship with the professor and told them, truthfully, that she didn't know.

'I think I recognise the style of the drawing,' she'd told a sceptical-looking policeman. 'There's an online blog, Rintrah the Reprobate. Very misogynist and violent, and related to the poet William Blake. I think this could be drawn by the same person. He seems to have targeted poor Oona.' He'd politely noted down the blog's name. Helen wondered if he'd do anything with the information.

Now Rose was being interviewed by the police in Helen's office. Helen worried about the impact the sight of Oona's body might have had.

'I think it would be a good idea to move Rose out of her room for a few days,' she told Caroline. 'She was really upset.' The girl had begun to hyperventilate while she and Helen were waiting for the police in the reception area. Then she'd started to cry, and had barely stopped since.

'OK. Do you know if she has friends here she could stay with? She probably shouldn't be left on her own.'

'I think she's going out with one of the boys in my tutorial group. Deepak Sinha?'

Caroline rolled her eyes. 'Marvellous. Why do the girls you like always fall for the boys you don't?' She was frowning. 'Didn't Deepak have some sort of relationship with Oona? Do you think this is anything to do with that? Assuming the police confirm it was suicide. No sign of a note, I suppose?'

Helen paused. She had yet to tell the department head about the letter Oona had received. 'I don't think so. There were papers all over her bedroom, though. There might have been something. I didn't look.'

After Caroline's warnings about her concerns over Petrarch Greenwood, Helen had not relished the thought of bringing him up again. But perhaps it was better to tell her sooner rather than later about the letter Rose had given her.

'The thing is,' she began, fiddling with her phone to find the photograph she'd taken.

A quick knock on the door, and Jessica stuck her head in.

'Helen? The police have finished with Rose. She'd like to see you.'

# Chapter 31

Rose huddled into the low armchair in Helen's office, pulling the grey sweater over her hands.

'Are you cold?'

The girl nodded.

'Me too. I think it's the shock. Do you want coffee? I'm going to make some.' Helen flicked on the kettle.

'What did you do with the letter?' Rose asked.

Helen spooned instant coffee into mugs. She hated the stuff, but it would do. She didn't fancy a grilling from Jessica in the departmental kitchen.

'I gave it to the police.'

'No! What for?' The girl's face was anguished.

'I had to, Rose. They need to know what happened.' She poured the boiling water into the mugs and handed one to the girl. 'Come on. Tell me why you're so worried about it.'

Rose let her breath out. 'Because – did you look at it properly?'

'I did.' Helen wanted to hear it from Rose.

'I think… there was a picture that could have been me. And one of Deepak. And Habib.'

Helen nodded. 'Yes, I thought so too. But I wasn't sure.'

'And now the police will know we were there. And then

everyone will find out – my family, and everyone at home, and Deepak's family…' She buried her face in her hands. 'I can't believe you gave it to them.'

Helen sighed. 'There was nothing else I could do. Oona's dead, Rose. This is serious.' She waited a second or two, thinking. 'You said you were there. Where's "there"? What do you mean? And why would anyone need to know about it?'

Rose looked up, her face angry red. 'Petrarch's bloody party, of course. What did you think it was?'

So Helen had been right. 'Rose… can you tell me about Petrarch's party? What happened there? Because if it could have affected Oona, and what happened to her, we need to know.'

Rose stood up. 'No.' She wiped away tears, streaking mascara across her face. 'You wouldn't understand.' She pulled out her phone. 'I need to make a call. In private.'

You're not a police officer, Helen reminded herself. You're supposed to be looking after her, not upsetting her more.

'I'm sorry, Rose. I'll wait outside.'

She stepped into the corridor and leaned against the door, watching the faces of students and staff passing to and fro. Who else knew about this? Who had been at the party? Rose, Deepak, Oona, Habib. Petrarch, of course. When she'd asked about the party before, Rose had said there were some older students, and a couple of staff members. She thought of her colleagues, nose wrinkling. Would any of them really have gone along with this?

And Rintrah. Rintrah the Reprobate, with his vicious drawings and his threats. He must have been at the party with them. Who was he? She watched the passers-by: the students

159

from all over the world; the middle-aged staff with their set ways and their caution. Which of them might have been there? Watching poor Oona being degraded and humiliated. Helen tried to imagine what it must feel like, to have been exposed in that way, and to have to carry on, seeing the other students at classes and seminars. She remembered the girl sitting under the tree in Gordon Square, her loose hair shrouding her like a veil.

A yell from the behind the door made her jump. 'Bastard!'

Then she heard a thump, felt something slam into the door. Quickly she opened it. Rose's phone lay on the ground at her feet, pink plastic shattered.

'Are you all right?'

'Not really.' She stared at the phone. 'I can't believe it. I thought I'd go back to Deepak's place. He's got a bloody enormous flat. I didn't want to stay in my room. But he says he doesn't want me there. That he's got to work, and I distract him. And I thought maybe he didn't know about Oona, so I told him and he said everyone knew about it. And then he said we should cool it a bit, and that he was worried because they used to go out together and he didn't want anyone blaming him.'

She sat down, abruptly. 'He's dumped me. This is the worst day of my life.' She began to cry, again.

Helen awkwardly patted Rose's back as she sobbed. She wasn't good with overt emotion. Tears had been something to get a grip on in her upbringing. Even while dying from breast cancer, her mother had discouraged 'all that soap-opera stuff', slipping away from her daughters determinedly dry-eyed. Rose cried unrestrainedly, like a child who'd fallen over and hurt herself. Helen felt her pain, and wished she would stop.

She tried to find a way to help.

'The university will find you somewhere to stay temporarily,' she began. She felt another lurch of guilt. 'But let me know if you need company. My flat is tiny, but I've got a sofa bed you could sleep on. For a night or two, anyway.'

Helen hoped she would say no.

Rose sniffed a bit longer, accepted a tissue. 'Thank you. That'd be really nice. Sorry I shouted earlier. I really don't want to be on my own tonight.'

I do, thought Helen. But she had already failed one student. She wasn't going to let another one down.

# Chapter 32

He turned off his phone and slipped it back into his pocket. The news was out. And, as he'd planned, everyone had assumed it was suicide.

It had been easier than he'd expected. Oona had let him in without a fuss, told him about the letter. She'd been surprisingly calm, worried only that it would harm her reputation as an actress if there were videos of the parties. She seemed to have gotten over Petrarch Greenwood remarkably quickly, for someone who claimed to be in love. Frailty, thy name is woman.

He'd asked to see the letter. Annoyingly, she said she had got rid of it. He'd checked the room later; found nothing. She must have thrown it away. He felt hurt, wondered if she knew how much care and work had gone into making those images, for her alone. That, more than anything, had sealed her fate.

She deserved it. He felt again the humiliation of her rejection, her face ugly with contempt. He'd earned her, worked for her. She should have complied with gratitude. William Blake believed women completed men, were necessary counterparts to them, but could never dominate them. All the crap about independence had to go. Without women, men became sterile, in thought as in deed. The world would wither and die.

And so he'd approached her, confident of his right to her. And she'd held him with her pale blue eyes, and said no.

So this time, he'd taken no chances. He'd comforted her, reassured her that everything would be done to track down the author of the letter. He'd said he personally would ensure that any videos were found and destroyed. Finally, he had persuaded her to run a bath and get into her bathrobe, while he made her a cup of tea. She'd drunk the tea, and after that everything had been easy. She would never say no again.

Oona Sinclair had been the last in a long line of women who had said no. His mother, snatching cookies from his hand, warning him that fat people didn't succeed in life. Girls at high school, laughing at the weirdo chubby kid with the passion for comics and gaming. And when he'd complied, when he'd won a prestigious college place and joined the gym, worked out and lost the flab, cut his hair and turned himself into the type of guy he'd thought they wanted – still it was a big, fat no.

He remembered asking his college room-mate if he had BO or something, some really obvious thing he could fix.

'No, dude,' the guy had said, once he'd finished laughing like a hyena. 'They just think you're weird.'

He'd thought that coming to London would fix it. London – rainy grey-skied London, the medieval European city with its gothic history. Surely he'd fit in here. He'd find his place, as so many outsiders had done before.

His introduction to London had come through the graphic novels of Alan Moore, dark sagas of vengeance and blood-letting against the backdrop of abandoned Tube stations, blitz-destroyed churches and murky alleyways where Jack the Ripper had hunted his victims. He'd fallen in love with Moore's visions of the city, the spires of the churches and the grand, crumbling architecture. Peopled by pale wraith-like figures muffled up in dark clothes, with soulful eyes. His people.

He crossed to the window, gazed out at the brand-new multi-coloured towers rising from building sites, bathed in bright sunshine. A line of men in high-vis clothing trooped past, black, brown, every race you could imagine. This was not what he'd expected when he crossed the ocean.

But he'd done it. He'd taken his first victim. He was Jack at the start of his killing spree, V launching his vendetta. He'd given this city fair warning.

He took a protein shake from the refrigerator. The battle was on, and he'd drawn first blood.

He turned the news over in his mind. How did it feel? He'd enjoyed playing to the gallery, ridiculing women online, encouraging his followers to pile into feminist discussions with rape threats, death threats. But none of it had been real. It was shadow-boxing, a bit of a laugh. This, however, was personal. And she was really, shockingly dead. Because of what he had done.

What do you call a dead feminist? A start.

On Friday, he would don the mask that hung on his wall, the Guy Fawkes face that had been adopted by protesters worldwide in recent years. He would be taking it back to its roots. Forget the virtue-signallers and the social justice warriors. V was a vigilante, a fighter for a better future. He was prepared to lose his life, along with his identity, in that mask.

Anonymity was strength when you were going into battle.

In a few days' time, of course, it wouldn't matter. Everyone would know his name, his face. He'd be the man, both martyr and hero.

He took the mask from the wall, placed it over his face and looked in the mirror. The grinning moustachioed face that looked back at him seemed innocuous, a Halloween costume. He opened the desk drawer, took out the gun and unwrapped it. With the weapon in his hands, the mask took on a new menace. Unlike V, he did not plan to blow up Parliament. He would fight, single-handed, against the feminist conspiracy that was driving the world apart.

Where better to begin than this ludicrous celebration of women writers? A sham, a plot to diminish the great writers of the past. Caroline Winter, the harridan who ran the department and pussy-whipped even the most senior male academics. The sheep-like hordes of women students, eager to learn the myth of female superiority. And Helen Oddfellow, determined to drag down the towering genius of William Blake.

*Out of the Silence*? He'd leave them with nothing but their own horrified screams.

He levelled the gun to his shoulder, aimed at the mirror. This would be the last thing many of them ever saw. A laughing mask and a loaded gun, dispensing death.

# Chapter 33

Helen dished up spaghetti and tomato sauce, wishing her culinary repertoire was a bit more extensive. She didn't often cook for other people.

'Here. It's a bit basic,' she admitted, putting the bowls down on the desk, swept clean of her usual papers and books. Barbara and Rose sat around it on mis-matched chairs.

'It looks lovely,' said Rose, politely. She started picking at the food.

'Pasta is great,' said Barbara. 'I'm starving.'

Barbara had turned up at Helen's flat shortly after Helen and Rose had arrived home. She'd been full of the work they needed to do in the Charles Fairfax Murray archive in Manchester. In all the horror of Oona's death, Helen had forgotten their planned trip.

Heart heavy, she'd told Barbara about the tragedy.

'God, how awful. I'm so sorry.'

'Rose was with me when we found her,' Helen had explained. 'She's staying here tonight. She needs some company.'

Rose's grief-stricken presence had suggested a long evening ahead, and Helen had been secretly relieved to see her friend. Barbara opened the bottle of red wine she'd brought with her and talked through the challenge of how to approach the research they needed to do in the archive. Helen wondered whether she'd be able to go to Manchester in the morning. It seemed a bit callous, to abandon Rose.

'I'm convinced the key to this will be the Rossetti connection,' Barbara said, twisting spaghetti around her fork. 'Murray was part of the Pre-Raphaelite Brotherhood. The Rossetti brothers, Gabriel and William, helped produce the first biography of Blake, and they were both keen collectors of literary manuscripts. Gabriel bought Blake's notebook when it came up for auction. They would definitely have been interested in an unpublished manuscript like *An Island in the Moon*.'

'Rossetti as in the poet Christina Rossetti?' asked Rose, looking up from her plate. She was shifting the food around, not eating. Helen wished she'd say if she didn't like it.

'That's the one. There were four Rossetti siblings, two boys and two girls. Christina and Gabriel were the poets. William and Maria earned the money, kept the households running. Do you like Christina Rossetti?'

Rose nodded. 'We did *Goblin Market* at school. It was a bit weird, but I liked the descriptions. The teacher said it was mostly about sex, though. I don't think she approved of it.'

Barbara laughed. 'Pretty much everything can be read as about sex, if you put your mind to it. But your teacher was probably right. It's also about friendship and sisterhood.'

'Yeah. That's what I liked. I didn't know she was from a big family, too.'

Helen looked at Rose again, noticing the spark seemed to be back in her eyes. 'Have you got lots of brothers and sisters?' She realised she knew hardly anything about the girl's background.

'There are five of us. I'm in the middle. My two big brothers work with my dad in the milk-processing plant. Ma works part-time in the village shop, and I've two younger sisters still at school. They're bright; they should go to university too. Not that my brothers aren't bright. But they just wanted to get out and start bringing home the money.'

'Five. Wow. There was just one of me,' said Barbara, topping up her glass. 'I can't imagine what that's like.'

Rose's smile transformed her face, then vanished as quickly as it had come. 'I miss them,' she said. 'It's like there's a gang of you, and now it's just me. You fight with them all the time, but you're on the same side.'

Helen thought briefly of her own sister, who rarely seemed on the same planet, never mind the same side. She lived with her husband and kids just ten miles away, but Helen only saw them at Christmas and birthdays, always awkward occasions. She needed a birthday present for her niece, she reminded herself. Maybe Rose could suggest something suitable.

'You know, you've reminded me of something,' said Barbara, pausing with her fork part-way to her mouth. 'Helen, do you have any poetry by Christina Rossetti?'

Helen got up and searched the heaving bookshelves. Eventually she unearthed an old paperback copy of *Poetical Works*, the pages splayed with use.

'I think I bought it second-hand. I don't actually remember reading it much.'

Barbara took it and scanned the index.

'Here we go. *Sing-Song*, her collection of poems for children. And very odd some of them are too. Rather a lot about death, for a children's book.'

Helen and Rose leant over her shoulder, reading the index

of first lines. 'A baby's cradle with no baby in it.' 'Baby lies so fast asleep that we cannot wake her.' 'Why did baby die?'

'Wow. She didn't hold back, did she? How come she was so obsessed with babies and death?' asked Helen.

Barbara shrugged. 'I think Victorians generally were obsessed with death. And babies died all the time. But it seems odd now, especially in a children's book. I was wondering if she'd read Blake's *Songs of Innocence and Experience*. There are some similarities in the style.'

'And she wrote about roses and lilies, like Blake did in the *Songs*,' observed Rose.

So she did, realised Helen, flipping the pages to the poems themselves. 'The rose that blushes rosy red, she must hang her head. The lily that blows spotless white, she may stand upright.' It was almost a gloss on Blake's *The Lilly*.

Helen was reminded powerfully of Oona's essay on flowers in Blake. She felt a stab of sadness that the essay counted for nothing now; that Oona's clever analysis would not go towards her degree, would never be developed further, would not be filed away at the end of three years' study as a record of Oona's academic achievements. No-one else, Helen thought, would even read it. Oona should be here with them, making new discoveries, her curious mind turned to the future. Not lying cold somewhere, being examined by a pathologist.

'Barbara, I don't know if I can go to Manchester,' she said. 'I feel like I should be here. And I don't want to leave Rose on her own.'

'I'll be all right,' said Rose. But her tone was unconvincing.

Helen looked from the student to her friend. She saw disappointment in Barbara's eyes, and a hint of panic. Rose was trying to look brave, and failing. They both needed her.

But she couldn't be in two places at once.

She thought about her bank balance. Would it cover a train fare to Manchester? Maybe Caroline would reimburse it.

'Rose, why don't you come with us? It might be interesting for you, and you can carry on with your college work in the library. We're getting an early train tomorrow.'

The girl hesitated a moment, then her face brightened. 'I'd like that. I've never been to Manchester.'

'We'll be in the library,' Barbara warned. 'We're not going shopping or clubbing.'

'That's OK. I'd like to help, if I can.'

Helen smiled. 'You're getting quite interested in this, aren't you?'

Rose nodded. 'When you two are talking about it – well, it's not just reading about what someone else says you should think about a poem, or a novel. It's finding stuff out. Thinking about history, about real people and why they wrote what they wrote. It's interesting.

'I didn't really get it before. I'd say something about a poem I liked, and then Deepak or someone would laugh. Then Professor Greenwood would say I should read his book about it, and Liz would ask if it was on the reading list, and I'd sort of give up. I mean, it doesn't matter what I think about a poem, does it? To anyone apart from me.'

It was the most coherent expression Helen had ever heard of why she loved researching literature, and how students were put off the subject.

'If you respond to a poem, then it matters. Even if it only matters to you, you've learned something. And you have no idea how that might change your life.'

'I suppose so.' Rose sounded sad again. 'Although my life

has already changed, hasn't it? Everyone's life. Oona's life.'

# Chapter 34

Rose insisted on doing the washing up while Helen and Barbara finished the wine. Quietly, Helen told Barbara what she'd seen that morning in Oona's room.

'I can't get it out of my mind. That poor girl. And Rose was with me; she saw it too. I hope you didn't mind me suggesting she came with us.'

She picked up her phone.

'There's something I want to show you. Oona had been sent a letter. I've given it to the police, but I took a photograph first. Tell me I'm not imagining things.'

She opened the photograph and handed the screen to Barbara, who sucked in her breath.

'Rintrah.'

'Yeah. That's what I thought.'

Barbara enlarged the image, zoomed in on particular sections, read the text. 'It's from *Visons of the Daughters of Albion*. The text, I mean. A Blake poem about sexual jealousy, and how it enslaves us. Some of the images are echoes of that, too.'

She pulled back out, looked at the image as a whole.

'It's Petrarch Greenwood,' she said, flatly. 'Who's that with him?'

'Oona. The student who died. Rose said it shows one of his parties. There's a picture that could be Rose, too. And the other students.'

'Christ.' Barbara stood and thrust the phone away, screwing up her face. 'It's still going on.'

'You know about it?' Rose was in the doorway, a dishcloth in her hand. 'You bloody know about it, don't you?'

'Yeah.' Barbara stared at the floor. 'He was my tutor, when I was at Cambridge. 1988.'

'Tell her about him, then,' said Rose, her face fierce. 'Tell her what he does.'

Barbara sank on to a tapestry footstool and sighed, a long exhalation that ended in silence. Helen perched on the arm of the red leather armchair, watching her friend. All her bright poise, her polished, neat exterior, was cracking. She rubbed her face and her lipstick smeared. Her pale skin looked chalky against her dyed black hair. She lifted her head, looked at Rose. Her hazel eyes were rimmed with red.

'I'm sorry. I'm sorry your generation is still going through this, Rose. It's not your fault. It's a power thing.'

Rose shook her head. 'It's not just that, though, is it? It's because no-one talked about it before,' she said. 'People like you, who knew what he did, keeping it quiet. Letting him get away with it.'

'Hey,' said Helen. 'Rose, don't shout at my friend. Can one of you please tell me what Petrarch has done?'

Barbara stared into space. 'In Cambridge, he lived in this big old house. Bare floorboards, velvet cushions, rugs on the floors. Bohemian, we thought. He invited all the students to come over. Of course, he wasn't that much older than us then, so it seemed fun at first. There was lots of hash, everyone smoking and passing around joints. Lots of booze, too.'

She stopped, rubbed her eyes.

'Lots of girls. Petrarch picked the ones he liked best. We all sat around on the floor, like the bunch of hippies we were, and he'd read to us. Blake, mostly. Eastern philosophy, sometimes. Anything that justified what happened next.'

She broke off, looked at Rose.

'Does this sound familiar?'

Rose nodded. 'Kind of. Cocaine, pills, champagne. But he didn't bother much with poetry.'

'Then he'd have sex with the ones he wanted,' said Barbara. 'He'd make you stand in the middle of the circle and undress. Then he'd do what he wanted, in front of everyone. And then you got passed around the circle, everyone having a turn. All the men, anyway. He said it was a sacred ritual; sharing the wealth. Celebrating the divine female. He said we completed each other.' She was speaking in a monotone, her voice flat. Finally, it cracked. She buried her head in her hands.

Helen crouched beside her friend, a hand on her shoulder, feeling Barbara's struggle to regain control. Barbara had always been the stoic, the one who Helen relied on to be strong. It broke her heart to see her secrets dragged out of her, to see the pain she still carried around.

The older woman shrugged her away. 'It was bullshit, of course. We weren't being celebrated; we were being abused. Never mind. I expect you're wondering why on earth we went along with it.'

She dug in her handbag for a mirror, started to wipe away her smeared make-up.

'You kind of get pulled in. It seemed... rebellious. We were kids, you know? Away from our neat suburban homes, our careful parents. Throw off the mind-forged manacles, kiss the joy as it flies. That sort of thing. Not that there was much joy. Not for me, anyway.'

Helen could see the appeal, for a curious and adventurous teenager. But they were so vulnerable, so easily bruised and damaged.

'And he always had his favourites,' Barbara continued. 'I was one, for a while. He told me I was special. The one who completed him.' She barked a harsh laugh. 'His emanation. Ridiculous, I know. But I was nineteen, so I believed him. Then I got pregnant, and he dropped me from a great height.'

'Shit.' Rose drew close, her anger quickly fading. 'Poor you. What did you do?'

'Petrarch said he'd pay for the abortion,' said Barbara, her voice brittle. 'I didn't want to, at first. But he made it clear there'd be no support if I had the baby. And I couldn't take that situation home to my parents. They'd have been so disappointed. They were thrilled, when I got the place at Cambridge. So I agreed. I had to go to Norwich, to a nursing home. He said he'd come and collect me afterwards, but he didn't. I got the bus.'

She felt in her bag. 'Sorry. Do you mind if I smoke?'

Helen wasn't about to exile her to the balcony. 'Barbara, that's awful. I'm so sorry.' She turned to Rose. 'And he's still doing this?'

Rose took a deep breath. 'Yeah. Less of the poetry, more just sex. Oona – she was the one he liked best. His favourite. She'd been going to these things since Christmas. I only went once. A couple of weeks ago.'

She grimaced.

'I hated it. I thought… I thought I ought to go. That it would be uncool to say no. And he was really persuasive, Helen. Not just promising us good grades, but saying we'd never understand Blake properly unless we tried living by his philosophy. And I knew Deepak had been going, and I kind of hoped he'd start to take me more seriously…' She trailed off. 'That didn't work, obviously. Now he just thinks I'm a slag.'

Helen looked from Barbara, a fifty-year-old woman still carrying the pain of that early betrayal, to Rose, practically a child, her buoyant lust for life tarnished. What a mess. And they were just two of the dozens, maybe hundreds of students he'd preyed on, over the decades. How many lives blighted? And Oona. Surely this should be before the police. If Oona had been subjected to this abuse, that was a motive for her to have taken her life. Petrarch Greenwood needed to answer for her death.

'Show me the letter again.' Barbara stubbed out her cigarette. She picked up the phone. 'Have you got a copy of Blake's prophetic books?'

Helen found the copy of the illuminated books she'd borrowed from the library, a hefty tome with colour reproductions of the poet's work. She passed it to Barbara, who flicked through the index, then opened the book at a page showing an enormous bird swooping over a woman's body.

'Here you go.'

Rose gasped. 'That's the picture from the letter.'

Barbara turned back a few pages. 'Like I said. *Visions of the Daughters of Albion*. Petrarch's favourite text.' She showed them the title page, a nightmarish composition of fleeing, contorted bodies, dominated by a hovering figure, winged, his hand held up in judgement. Opposite, a claustrophobic study of three despairing figures, two shackled back to back, a blood-red sun behind them.

'God.' Helen felt the power of the image, even as she flinched away from it. 'What's it about?'

'Some people say it's about slavery. But on the face of it, it's about sexuality and jealousy. Oothoon is in love with Theotorman. She walks in the valley, looking for him, and picks a flower. She's raped by Bromion. Theotorman captures the pair of them, and binds them back to back. Oothoon tries to persuade Theotorman that she still loves him and her love is pure. She calls the eagles to rend her breast to prove her love. But Theotorman is overcome with jealousy and grief and doesn't listen.'

'Nice.' Helen wrinkled her nose.

'The interesting bits are Oothoon's pleas for love to be recognised as innocent, and modesty as hypocritical. She offers to bring girls to Theotorman, and says she will watch him copulating with them, taking delight in his pleasure. As you can imagine, that's catnip to someone like Petrarch.'

Helen frowned, turning the pages. 'Do you think Petrarch drew the images and wrote the letter? That he sent it to Oona?'

'No way,' said Rose. 'He wouldn't have drawn himself like that. He looks really horrible, like a sea monster or something.'

Helen sat back on her heels. Was there some other way of finding out who sent the letter? Rintrah, she remembered. Nick was in contact with Rintrah.

'I think I should talk to Nick,' she said.

# Chapter 35

'Hello, stranger.' Nick leaned back in his chair, happy to be distracted. Helen hardly ever called him. He'd hoped he would see more of her with this Rintrah business, but she'd disappeared back into her work.

'Can you hear me OK? I'm on a train to Manchester.'

He could hear the clacking of the track in the background.

'Loud and clear. What's happening?'

His smile faded as Helen explained about the student who'd killed herself. He grabbed his notebook and took the phone into the kitchen, away from his colleagues.

'Shit, man. That's awful.' He started taking notes, wrote down the girl's name.

'Was she one of the girls on the walk?' He remembered the kooky Irish one with the rainbow hair; the serious one who'd disapproved of everything.

'No, Oona didn't come. The thing is, she got a letter, before she died. Threatening, with horrible drawings of her and – and some other people from the university. It looks to me like it came from the same person who draws the Rintrah blog. The style, some of the images – and the text is from Blake.'

'Wow. Can you send me a photo?' This could be big, Nick

thought. If Rintrah was linked to the university, if he was hounding female students to their deaths, then this story was going places.

There was a slight pause. 'Sorry. The police have got it. But the text was from the *Visions of the Daughters of Albion*, if that means anything to you. And some of the images were taken from that, too.'

Nick noticed her hesitation. Did she really not have a photo of it? Why didn't she want him to see it?

'That's a pity. I'll look up the poem, though.'

'I wondered how far you'd got with contacting this guy? Barbara says you were going to meet him in the British Museum?'

'I was. But he bailed. I think I scared him off.' He wasn't going to admit to Helen that he'd been stopped and searched by the police, right in the heart of the British cultural establishment.

Now it was Helen's turn to sound disappointed. 'Damn. I was hoping you might have found out who this bastard really is.'

'Sorry. He said he'll be in touch again, though. He said he's planning something, and he wants me to be involved.' Maybe Nick could use this. Let Rintrah know he knew about Oona, knew about the letter. Perhaps it would give him some leverage.

'But you didn't see him? You don't know what this man looks like?'

'It was kind of busy in the museum,' said Nick. He thought back to the atrium, the teeming tourists and the people leaning against railings, looking down. He remembered the tall man standing on the stairs. Could that have been Rintrah?

He didn't know. Would he recognise him again if he saw him?

'I'll get the bastard, though. I'll have another try at setting up a meeting.' He didn't want Helen to think he was rubbish at his job. 'Maybe he just wanted to check me out.'

'Yeah.' She sounded unconvinced. 'Maybe you should tell the police what you've found out about him. I told them that I thought the letter was from was the same person as draws the Rintrah blog. But I don't think they took much notice.'

'I'll tell them when there's something to tell. No point in wasting their time.' Nick had absolutely no intention of involving the police.

He ended the call, frustrated not to have more progress to report. He needed to make contact with Rintrah again.

Back at his desk, he looked up *Visions of the Daughters of Albion*. He scrolled through the images of contorted naked figures. Which ones would Rintrah have used? He found a particularly gruesome picture, a girl lying on her back, a vulture or something pecking at her chest. That might appeal, he thought. The nudity, the sadism, the ritual sacrifice.

He took a screenshot, attached it to an email.

'I see you've made a start,' he wrote, and sent the message into the ether.

# Chapter 36

Manchester lived up to its reputation as the rainy city. The three women, fresh from the heatwave that was baking London, were unprepared for the grey skies and drizzle when they emerged from the train station. Helen remembered her first term at the northern university, when it had rained solidly for three months, and cursed herself for not bringing an umbrella.

They dashed through the rain-slicked streets, red brick buildings looming on either side. Helen led the way through the city centre, past the enormous neo-gothic Town Hall and the classical dome of the Central Reference Library, where she'd spent one summer working on her dissertation. They crossed the plaza, dodging puddles and the trams that sliced through the square.

'I'd almost forgotten about rain,' said Barbara, her face cheerful. 'It's quite refreshing.'

'I wish I could forget it,' grumbled Rose. Her hair stuck in streaks to her forehead. 'I'm soaked.'

They emerged on to Deansgate, busy with shoppers and office workers. The John Rylands Library was a huge Victorian construction of ornate red sandstone, fused with a new glass and steel extension. They entered into the modern atrium, shaking off the rain.

'We need the special collections reading room,' Barbara told the man at the desk. 'I've ordered some papers.'

'Second floor,' he told her, pointing to the lift.

A man in an orange cagoule with a friendly round face held the door for them. 'Special collections? Me too. I'll show you the way,' he said. He had a soft Lancastrian accent. Helen noticed he was wearing cycle clips around the bottoms of his jeans.

They crossed to a gloomy, low-lit stone corridor of gothic arches and carved ceiling bosses.

'It's like a castle,' said Rose, eyes wide.

'The special collections room used to be here,' said the man. 'They've moved it to the new building now, up at the other end of the corridor. The facilities are much better.'

Helen, Rose and Barbara put their belongings in lockers. Around them, scholars were scanning through papers, photographing them and making notes.

The librarian brought out five big cardboard boxes. Barbara rolled her eyes.

'We'll never get through all that lot,' she said.

Helen was thinking the same. It was a needle in a haystack, and they didn't even know what the needle looked like.

'We'll have to scan through them, then. And focus on the right period,' she said. 'There's three of us. That should help.'

'This one has most of the Rossetti correspondence,' said the librarian. 'But it's not all to Charles Fairfax Murray. He acquired other collections of letters, from dealers and artists. That box is quite late; mostly twentieth century, when he made his bequests to museums at the end of his life.'

'We can probably ignore that,' said Barbara. 'We know

he already had the *Island in the Moon* manuscript by the 1890s. Although it might be interesting if there's a record of the bequest to the Fitzwilliam Museum. It might confirm whether or not there were additional pages that went missing.'

'That shouldn't take long. Rose, can you do that?' asked Helen. 'Just scan through and look for anything to or from the Fitzwilliam Museum in Cambridge. Or anything that mentions *An Island in the Moon*.'

The girl nodded and took the lid off the box.

'Keep the papers in order,' Helen whispered. 'And be careful with them. Anything that looks useful, let me or Barbara know.'

She and Barbara divided the other boxes between them. Helen started opening the white envelopes in which the bundled letters were kept.

'My dear Howell...' began the first letter. Helen checked the signature. It was not from Murray, but someone signing himself Fred Sandys. Helen looked him up on her phone. Frederick Sandys was a pre-Raphaelite painter and close friend of the Rossetti family. But who was Howell?

She read the letter, interest quickening. 'I must ask you to let me have tomorrow either the picture – the money – or the address of the gentleman who has bought it. I suppose you are aware I have a County Court Summons for eighteen pounds?' Whoever Howell was, he seemed to be unreliable.

Further letters from Sandys sought money or an explanation in vain.

'I do so hope you will let me have some more money at once. I have had nothing, I can do nothing. What is to be done I know not,' she read.

'Who is Charles Howell?' she asked Barbara. 'He seems to

have run off with Fred Sandys's money.'

Barbara looked up and shrugged. 'Don't know. Try Wikipedia?'

'Look,' said Rose, in an excited whisper. 'A letter from Trinity Hall College in Cambridge to Charles Fairfax Murray. It mentions the donations to the Fitzwilliam Museum.'

'Oh, well done.' Helen leaned over to read the correspondence.

'You have given the Museum a gift which will become the nucleus of an Autograph Collection of literature, but a collection which is never likely to contain anything more profoundly interesting than your gifts of autograph remains of Blake, William Morris, DG Rossetti and Christina Rossetti.' The letter was dated 1905.

'Is it important?' asked Rose.

'It could be.' Barbara broke off to photograph the letter. 'It confirms that the manuscript was given along with other handwritten work by poets and writers of the time.' She smiled at Rose. 'And it shows that he was interested in Christina Rossetti, too.'

Nothing about the condition of the Blake manuscript, though, thought Helen. No mention of any missing pages.

She logged on to the library's wi-fi and looked up Howell, Charles Augustus.

The man was another art dealer in the pre-Raphaelite circle, but one with a reputation for shady dealing. He too had been a close friend of the Rossetti family, acting for a while as Gabriel Rossetti's agent, until they fell out over business. Howell even seemed to have encouraged his mistress to forge Rossetti paintings to sell as originals. Helen wondered if Fred Sandys ever got his money.

She read on, increasingly fascinated by the story. Howell had been charming and popular, with impeccable taste and an appetite for risk. He had arranged for the recovery of Dante Gabriel Rossetti's poems from the coffin of his wife, where Rossetti had thrown them in a fit of guilt on her death. Howell had been present when the coffin was opened, she read.

She dragged herself back to the work in hand: scanning through the dozens of letters sent to Howell. Most seemed to be about money, or about paintings or manuscripts he had promised to people, which did not always materialise.

'Any luck?' she asked Barbara, who was whizzing through her envelopes of correspondence to Fairfax Murray.

'Not so far. Lots of letters from people wanting to sell him stuff, or questioning the origin of various paintings. Not much about manuscripts, though.' She sighed. 'We need weeks, really, not a day.'

Helen updated her on the identity of Howell. 'He seems to have been a bit of a rogue, but charming. He was close to the Rossetti family, too. So I suppose it's possible he might have been interested in the Blake manuscript.'

'That's a thought,' said Barbara. 'I've found nothing in Murray's letters yet. I'm up to 1870; just before he went to live in Italy for ten years. I don't suppose he acquired it there.'

Helen returned to the white envelopes. A letter from the National Portrait Gallery about a portrait, complete with a pencil sketch. A note to effect an introduction to a Mr Charles Dickens, 'at the office of *All The Year Round*.' She smiled and showed Rose the reference to the prolific Victorian author.

She turned over another page and saw a small sheet of

writing paper, undated. The address at the top was Albany Street, near Regent's Park, where the Rossetti family had lived in the mid-1850s.

'My dear Mr Howell,' Helen read. 'Thank you very much for the really pretty paintings. I shall take them to the Superior just as they are and ask her for what they will be most suitable. I did not in the least expect anything so very delicate and beautiful. Pray remember us to Mrs Howell, and believe me yours sincerely, Maria J Rossetti.'

She looked up. 'A letter from Maria, Christina's sister. They must have been on good terms, if he was giving them pictures. I wonder what Superior they were talking about?'

'Mother Superior?' asked Rose. 'Were they Catholic?'

'That's a complicated question,' said Barbara. 'Anglo-Catholic, probably. Both sisters were very religious – and I think Maria actually joined an Anglican convent in London. Perhaps that's what she's referring to.'

Helen stretched, wondering if it was time to take a break. Neither she nor Rose had slept much after the horrors of the previous day, and they had left London before seven.

'Anyone else fancy some lunch? I need food. Not to mention coffee,' she said, setting aside the envelope.

# Chapter 37

Barbara and Rose sat at a round table while Helen bought sandwiches and coffee at the cafeteria. The man from the reading room was just ahead of her in the queue.

'Got to keep the caffeine levels up,' he said, smiling. 'Have you come far?'

'London,' said Helen. 'It was an early start.'

'Ouch. You deserve a double shot, then. It's just a ten-minute bike ride for me.' She glanced at his ankles and was pleased to see he'd removed the bicycle clips from his jeans.

'Lucky you,' she said. 'It's a lovely place to work.'

'What are you working on, if you don't mind me asking?' he said. 'I heard you mention Dickens.' He hurried to explain. 'I wasn't eavesdropping. But he's my specialist subject and I have this sort of internal alarm that goes off when anyone says his name.'

Helen laughed. 'I understand. It was just a letter that mentioned someone going to see him. An art dealer. We're looking at pre-Raphaelite artists and poets. Not really my area, but it's linked to some work my colleague is doing about William Blake.'

'Right. Everything's connected, when you look hard

enough. Dickens was involved with the pre-Raphaelites, too, so I know a bit about them.' He paid for his coffee. 'Do you mind if I join you?'

His name was Michael, he said, and he was a postgraduate student at Salford University, researching Dickens's attitude to religion. Helen explained a little about their work, careful to avoid telling him anything that could betray Barbara's big idea about Catherine Blake.

'From what I know, Blake and his family were decidedly non-conformist,' she said. 'And he was angry about the hypocrisy of the established church. Like Dickens, I suppose.'

Michael nodded vigorously. 'Yeah. He could be very critical of established religion.'

'What about the Rossettis?' asked Rose. 'Barbara said they were Anglo-Catholic. But I thought Catholicism used to be banned or something?'

'Not quite.' Michael smiled at her. 'Catholics were persecuted and discriminated against, but that started to ease in Victorian times. Do you know All Saints church? It's fantastic, a very ornate Victorian Gothic building on Margaret Street in the West End of London. Dickens lived close by at one point. I think the Rossetti family was involved with All Saints.'

Rose looked it up on her phone. 'Yep. The convent that Christina and Maria were involved with was attached to All Saints. All Saints' Sisters of the Poor. The sisters attended the church.' She looked excited. 'Maybe we should go there when we get back to London.'

Barbara looked at her watch. 'Maybe. But right now, we should get back to work. We've only got a few more hours before we need to leave for the train.' She smiled at Michael. 'Good luck with Dickens. Excuse us, please.'

They made their way back to the special collections room.

'OK,' said Barbara, after a few minutes. 'This could be something.' Her voice was brisk, but Helen could immediately hear the excitement in it.

She held up a letter.

'From William Rossetti – that's Gabriel and Christina's brother – to Murray, January 1871. "I have seen Howell, who says he has something new of Blake's. Gabriel is resolved to drop Howell, after much trouble over the sale of his miniatures. I am therefore not in a position to do business with him at present. It would nevertheless interest me to hear your opinion of his acquisition." A month later, Murray went to live in Italy.'

'That sounds interesting. Something new of Blake's.' Helen put down her own papers and rubbed her eyes. Her head had started to ache.

'If Murray did buy whatever it was from Howell, it might even have been the *Island in the Moon* manuscript itself,' said Barbara. 'Which would be exciting. Helen, can you find anything from William Rossetti or Murray to Howell, around 1871?' She laid the letter flat on the desk and photographed it.

Helen skimmed through the packets, head pounding now as she tried to decipher the signatures. She could see no letters from either man. She looked at the two unopened boxes. As Barbara had said, they needed weeks, not one day.

She pressed her fingers into her temples, feeling over-whelmed. What had they actually discovered? Everything seemed connected to everything else, but not in a way that proved anything.

As she often did when puzzled by research, she took out a

pad of paper and tried to think like Richard had. 'What do we know so far?' he'd ask. 'Write it all down.'

She picked up her pencil. At the top of the page, she set out what they knew of the *Island in the Moon* manuscript with the missing pages. It had been written in 1784, around the time that Catherine Blake might have lost a child. Blake died in 1827, his papers dispersed and sold. Fifty years later, Howell had acquired 'something new of Blake's' which he might have sold to Fairfax Murray. *An Island in the Moon* resurfaced in 1893, more than a hundred years after it was written, in Murray's possession. And in 1905, Murray gave it to the Fitzwilliam Museum, by which time at least two pages were missing. When had they been extracted?

She wrote down the daunting list of possibilities. During Blake's life, thrown away by him or Catherine. Assuming they kept the manuscript whole, the pages could have been removed by Howell or whoever owned it before Fairfax Murray, at any point up to the donation to the museum.

She looked again at the mass of papers before them. They needed to track down not just when and how Murray had got hold of the manuscript, but what happened to the missing pages. Which might or might not support Barbara's theory about Catherine Blake's contribution to the *Songs of Innocence* poems.

She pushed her chair aside and walked to the window. How had she let herself get side-tracked into this fool's errand? Just over two weeks ago, she had been working on her own research, tracing historical references in Marlowe's plays, secure in the questions she needed to ask and the sources she needed to consult. Now she was running around the country, working on a tenuous hunch of Barbara's, when back in London her students needed her.

The image of Oona's body surfaced again. She'd been trying to push it away, fill her mind with other things. Barbara's theory about Catherine Blake might or might not be true. But Oona's death was all too real. She thought of Petrarch Greenwood, and the revelations from Rose and Barbara about his treatment of female students. When she got back, she vowed, she'd confront the man. First thing tomorrow morning. And this time, she would not let him wriggle off the hook.

With a sigh, she returned to her seat. Only a few days, then the presentation would be over and she could get back to her own work. She checked her watch: four o'clock. More letters: a long correspondence about raising money for a memorial for a painter Helen had never heard of; promises of supplying a collector with literary autographs; enquiries after the health of Howell's wife. She skimmed them, piled them neatly to one side, and began to plan ahead. The train back to London left at six; she should be home by nine. Time to prepare for the morning's work, then an early night.

The envelope she'd been working through was empty. She gathered the papers to put them back before moving on to the next. But something stopped her from sliding them in.

She paused, put down the papers and looked again into the envelope. There was one more letter, folded small at the bottom. She shook it out and smoothed it flat, recognising Maria Rossetti's energetic script.

'5 Endsleigh Gardens, NW.

Wednesday.

My dear Mr Howell,

I write to thank you again for your many kindnesses. The

191

flowers for Christina are adorning her table and quite impress her by their remarkable beauty. She particularly wishes me to convey her thanks for the little poem & sketch which she answers with one of her own, on the reverse. She is much improved today & the doctor considers that this happy circumstance may continue and even increase.

With kind remembrances to Mrs Howell

Yours affectionately

Maria J Rossetti.'

Holding her breath, Helen turned the paper over. Her heart began to thump.

'Barbara,' she said, 'I think I've found a Christina Rossetti poem.'

# Chapter 38

'You've what?'

Quickly Barbara took a photograph of the letter from Maria, and the two stanzas of verse on the back.

'Where was it? Make a note of the envelope. Is it dated?'

Helen showed her. 'If the letters are in chronological order, it must be 1870 or 1871,' she said, looking at the dates on the surrounding correspondence. 'I was focusing on that period, because of your letter from Rossetti to Murray. Undated, though.'

'What is it?' asked Rose, picking up on their excitement. 'What have you found?'

Helen saw the librarian look up from her desk. They'd need to show her, check whether this was a new discovery or something that had been found and catalogued before. But first, Helen wanted to read the lines.

'It's a poem,' she told Rose. 'On the back of a letter from Maria Rossetti to Howell, the art dealer. Hush a minute and let me see if I can decipher it.'

The black ink handwriting was firm and distinctive, sloping to the right, and mercifully readable. The signature at the bottom – Christina G Rossetti – used a distinctive long s for the double s in the surname. Another point to check for authenticity.

Helen picked up her pencil and transcribed the words. The hairs on her neck began to prickle.

*'Little infant shining bright*
*Never lived to see the light.*
*Thorn-defended peeping rose,*
*Winter nips: the petals close.'*

She paused. Barbara stared at the words, emotion working in her face.

'Blake,' she blurted. 'Look, the first line – it echoes *The Tyger*. And infant – not baby, like the *Sing-Song* poems, but infant, like *Infant Joy*. This has to be linked to Blake, somehow.'

'And the flowers,' said Rose, leaning over the table to look. 'Thorns and roses.'

Helen gazed at the text. 'Never lived to see the light.' The suggestion of a miscarriage or stillbirth was clear. She turned back to Maria's letter. Christina 'wishes me to convey her thanks for the little poem & sketch, which she answers with one of her own.'

'She's answering a poem that Howell sent her,' she said. 'A verse, and a sketch.' She thought of the missing pages from the Blake manuscript. Who knew what they held? Verses and sketches, like the other pages? And where were they now? She turned to the second stanza of the poem.

*'Where shall I keep you? Where none look.*
*What keeps my soul safe? My prayer book.*
*Where does a bird sing? High on a perch.*
*Where should I seek you? Inside the church.'*

Barbara smiled. 'A riddle poem. She wrote lots of those, in *Sing-Song*. Helen, I've never seen this one before. I really think it might be new.'

'What's she talking about in the second verse?' asked Rose. 'The baby?'

Helen was wondering the same thing. 'I suppose so,' she said. 'Inside the church – perhaps Christina was thinking there would be a grave, or a plaque. Or maybe just the idea that she would pray for the baby in church. She talks about a prayer book.'

'There wouldn't have been a church grave,' said Barbara. 'Not for a stillborn or miscarried baby. I think she's talking about keeping the baby's soul safe, remembering it in prayers. The soul was often thought of as a bird.'

The women were silent for a moment. Helen wondered if Barbara was thinking about her own lost pregnancy, so many years ago. But there was another possibility, she thought. Was Christina referring to the verse and sketch that Howell had sent her?

The librarian arrived at their table.

'Have you found something interesting? May I see?'

Helen showed her the letter and the poem on the back. 'It was in one of the white envelopes, so I guess someone must have catalogued it. But maybe they missed the poem?' she suggested.

The woman checked the list appended to the cardboard box in which the letters were stored. 'You might be right. The collection hasn't been digitally scanned or catalogued, so I can't search it online. But I'll go through the written catalogue.' She broke into a smile. 'Well done. Don't put the documents back in the envelope yet. I should make a note to go with the letter. And I'll ask one of our experts to take a look.' She hurried back to her desk and made a phone call.

The excitement had begun to spread around the special collections room. Scholars at nearby tables looked up from their studies, raising their eyebrows. Whispers started to circulate. A new poem. They've found a new poem.

Helen sensed a presence by her side and looked up. Michael was standing beside her.

'What've you found?' he asked. 'Anything about Blake?'

His voice sounded slightly odd, his jollity a little false. Helen hesitated.

'A note from Maria Rossetti,' she said. 'It seems to have some verse attached.' She turned the page back so only the letter was showing.

'How exciting. I didn't know Maria Rossetti wrote poetry.'

'She didn't...' began Rose.

'As far as we know,' Barbara broke in. 'But maybe she did. Or maybe someone else added the lines at a later stage. Too early to say, really.' She smiled at him, blandly.

'Perhaps I can help? May I see?' He was avoiding her eyes, angling for a better view of the paper. Instinctively, Helen put her hand over the words. She was feeling protective of their find.

'That's OK. The librarian is going to ask someone to have a look. How are you getting on with Dickens?' she asked.

He held his hands up. 'OK, I get the message. I was just on my way out.'

He pushed through the door at the end of the room. Helen and Barbara exchanged looks.

'That was odd,' said Barbara.

'Yeah. I don't know. Maybe we're just getting paranoid.'

'Helen, last time we worked on this, someone chucked a lump of plaster at you and pushed you down the stairs. I think we're justified in being cautious.'

'What?' Rose stared at them, horrified.

'It might have been a coincidence,' said Helen. The words sounded feeble. And now she had brought Rose along with her, and another stranger was taking an unhealthy interest in their work. She felt a sudden grab of panic. Time to go home.

'Let's get packed up,' she said. 'The librarian can look after this. I think we should be getting back to London.'

# Chapter 39

I t was dark by the time she got home. To her relief, Rose
had opted to return to her student room. Helen needed
silence and solitude to process the day's findings.

She unlocked the heavy front door, her head still buzzing
with questions. What was the significance of the cryptic
Christina Rossetti verses?

She paused in the hall, leafed through the flyers from pizza
companies and junk mail to see if there was anything for her.
The house was quiet, apart from a gentle hum of television
from behind the door of the ground-floor flat and a rather
louder hum from the basement. Crispin preferred to turn
the television up rather than wear his hearing aid.

One envelope looked interesting – heavy paper, hand-
written in block capitals with her name and address. No
stamp, she noticed. Hand-delivered. She slid her finger under
the flap.

'Hello? Is someone there?'

The voice was faint, but the distressed tone was unmistakeable. Helen shoved the letter in her bag and clattered down
the steps to the basement.

'Crispin? Are you all right?' she shouted through the door.

'Oh, Helen.' He sounded like he was crying. 'Thank

goodness you're back. I fell out of my chair and I'm bloody stuck.'

'I'll get the key.' She raced up the stairs to her fourth-floor flat, dumped her bag and grabbed Crispin's door key. This wasn't the first time he'd needed emergency assistance.

He lay in the hall like a sad heap of old clothes. He turned his tearful face to her.

'I'm sorry to be such a nuisance. I was trying to get to the loo. I'm afraid I didn't make it.'

'Don't you worry.' Carefully Helen helped him into a sitting position. 'Are you hurt? Shouldn't your carers have been here by now?'

'They should. But they didn't come.'

They established that he'd broken no bones, although he was cold from lying on the floor in wet trousers. He refused her offer to call an ambulance, or at least a taxi to take him to hospital.

'It's only been a couple of hours. Maybe if you could get me into the bedroom?'

Helen carried him through to a chair, fetched a bowl of warm water and a flannel, and helped him undress.

'I'm so sorry. You shouldn't have to deal with this,' he said, distress in his voice. 'It's so bloody humiliating.'

She helped him into his pyjamas, and then into bed. 'Don't be daft. You'd do the same for me.'

They looked at each other and laughed.

'I don't think I could pick you up, darling. Although I'd be happy to put you to bed any time you need it.'

'I'll remember that. Now, can I get you anything? Water? Chamomile tea?'

He raised an eyebrow. 'Horlicks? I'm not dead yet. Get

me some water, if you could. And some whisky, to go with it. And pour a large one for yourself. You know where the bottle is.'

Shoes kicked off, Helen sat on the bed next to her friend, cradling her glass of single malt.

'You should get one of those alarm things,' she said.

'I know. They keep telling me. It's very boring, though. Tell me about your day. Where have you been?'

Helen explained about the trip to Manchester and their discovery of the poem.

'How exciting! Show me!'

'Here.' Helen opened the photo on her phone and read the text aloud.

He grimaced. 'It's rather maudlin, isn't it? Blighted rosebuds and all that. Very Victorian. Didn't Christina Rossetti die of tuberculosis or something?'

'No idea.' Helen yawned. 'But I tend to think of lady Victorian poets languishing away in white gowns, coughing up blood.' How weird to be surrounded by death, a regular household visitor carrying off children, brothers and sisters.

'The second verse is interesting, though,' Crispin continued. 'It sounds like a riddle, as if she's hiding something and telling us where it is.'

Helen read the lines again. 'That's what I thought. But I wondered if I was being too literal. She wrote it in response to something a friend had sent her, a verse and a sketch. I did wonder if it was referring to that. But Barbara thought she probably meant something about the memory or soul of the baby.'

'Pass me my specs.' Crispin studied the lines. '"Where shall I keep you? Where none look." I mean, it's got to be a hiding place, really.'

'Go on, then. What do you think?' she asked. Crispin was a crossword fiend, and his facility with cryptic clues had unlocked puzzles for her before.

'Well, it's not hard, is it? She's keeping something where no-one looks, which would fit with her prayer book, which only she would look inside. The book is kept – um – on a perch somewhere.'

He looked over his glasses at Helen's sceptical face.

'All right. Maybe that one's not so obvious. But wherever it is, it's inside a church. There you go.' He put the phone down, looked smug.

'Yeah, but which church?' asked Helen. As the words passed her lips, she knew. What had the man in the library said? A Victorian church in London, attached to the convent that Maria and Christina were involved with. She grabbed her phone and typed into the search engine.

'All Saints church on Margaret Street,' she said. 'It could be there.' She knew Margaret Street: a narrow thoroughfare near Oxford Street which she sometimes used as a cut-through on her way to the shops from the university. Maybe she could talk to the vicar, arrange a visit. Tomorrow. She'd do it tomorrow.

She finished up the whisky, yawned again and checked her watch. 'God, it's almost eleven. I got up ridiculously early. I'd better leave you to get some sleep, Crispin. Ring me in the morning and let me know how you are. Especially if the carers don't arrive.'

He grasped her hand tightly for a moment. 'Thank you for rescuing me, sweetheart. And let me know how you get on at All Saints.'

Wearily, she trudged back up the stairs to her own flat. Pushing through the door, she found her bag, with the envelope spilling out of it. She sank into the big leather armchair in the corner of the living room and opened the letter.

As soon as she saw the heavy sketchpad paper, she went cold. An illustrated letter. Like the one sent to Rose. She spread it on the arm of the chair.

A tree grew on one side of the paper, delicate branches drooping over the page, their leaves a diseased arsenic-green. A snake coiled around the tree trunk, an apple in its mouth. Hanging from the tree, wrists shackled, a naked woman. A woman with cropped blonde hair, a noose around her neck.

He'd drawn her. Dead.

She read the text alongside the image.

'In the morning, glad I see

My foe outstretched beneath the tree.'

*A Poison Tree*. William Blake's meditation on how hatred grows through pretended smiles and secret tears, until it produces lethal fruit. Rintrah had declared Helen his enemy. He'd been here, to her home, had put this warning missive through her door. He knew her, knew where she lived. And she still had no idea who he was.

# Chapter 40

Midnight. She'd have got it by now. He imagined her arriving home, tired after the trip to Manchester, finding it on the doormat. Opening the envelope, seeing with a shock her own image. How did it feel to know you were being targeted, watched, monitored? To see your death foretold? Your move, Helen Oddfellow.

His helper in the north had sent him a photo: Helen in the library, leaning over a desk with the other old witch, and the little Irish girl. Rose O'Dowd. His helper had been able to tell him little of what they were working on, though. Pre-Raphaelites, he'd said. A connection between Blake and the pre-Raphaelite brotherhood. And they'd found something, something they were excited about. A poem. But he'd been unable to find out more.

Rose was next, Rintrah decided, taking up his brush and dipping it in water. The girl with the soft curves and the sweet smile. He needed an accomplice, an ally. His helpers were too timid; he couldn't rely on them. Flea was a traitor, and would be dealt a traitor's fate. He had let the journalist get too close and find out too much.

He looked again at the photograph taken in the library. Rose was surrounded by the enemy, in mortal danger of corruption. But he could offer her salvation. She was good-hearted, he could see that in her. Sympathetic, kind, with a curiosity about the world. He just needed to get her away from the flint-faced crones who would feed her poison, destroy her capacity for love.

He remembered how Blake had chosen his wife, Catherine. She'd told him she pitied him. He'd replied: 'Then I love you.' And she'd been his uncomplaining helper for the rest of his life.

Women were not born to lead, or to create poetry or great art. As Blake had written, power warped their femininity, the gentle strength that fitted the domestic sphere. Female power was against nature, led only to misery. His mind rested for a moment on his mother, sharp-edged in her suits and heels, impatient with his childish fears. Detaching him, handing him over to his beloved Rosetta, the housekeeper who fed him forbidden cakes and doughnuts. Until his mother found out and sacked her.

They'd found a poem, possibly by Maria Rossetti. One for their pathetic conference, he supposed. Anyone reading women's poetry could see the awkwardness, the anger, the absence of harmony. They had no sense of grandeur, of the sweep of history and myth. Women were designed to help and comfort, not to compete. It was absurd to think that Blake's wife, his illiterate and sympathetic help-meet, could have written his poetry. It was doubtful if she could even understand it. The whole thing was a slur on Blake's reputation; yet another attempt to undermine great men, to push women out of their supporting role and on to centre stage.

Well, if they stood centre stage, they would have to take the risks that came with it. He smiled. He'd gained the trust of those in charge. His plans were almost complete. He would not just have entry to the conference – he'd be right in the middle of it, with everything he needed. It had been laughably easy, which just showed how unprepared women were for power. They needed men, people like him, to stage the simplest things. And that vulnerability would be ruthlessly exploited.

But he still needed a helper. Someone who would not be questioned, who would sit meekly, awaiting her fate at his hands. His silent instrument. She would see the beauty of it. Together, they would be immortalised. Their images all over the internet, on television and in newspapers, repeated a million times over. An inspiration to others. Their bodies would be shattered, dispersed into the ether. But their story would live on.

He lifted his brush from the paper and considered his work. It was painted with love. She would see that. He'd glorified Rose, the generous roundness of her body, the inviting sympathy of her smile. The rainbow hair, spread around her like a nimbus. He'd made her almost into a goddess, someone worthy to take her place by his side. Yet it served, too, as a warning of what was happening to her. The poison she was imbibing, the sickness that would invade her.

The letters to Oona and Helen had been harbingers of death. This would be an invitation to life, everlasting and immortal life as his consort. And he would offer her one chance, before their last day on earth. To join with him corporeally, to make one whole before they shattered into a thousand pieces. To be completed, and to complete him. And then, together, they would be ready to face their deaths.

# Chapter 41

I t was going to come out, he knew it. The police would find the letter, and someone would identify him from the pictures. Petrarch paced the study into the early hours of the morning, sweating through his silk pyjamas. Plausible deniability. It was a drawing, not a photograph. Someone's sick fantasy. Nothing to do with him.

He'd done his best to cover his tracks. What had he missed?

He'd been working on it since the phone call on Monday. Caroline had been brisk and careful. If she knew about his relationship with Oona – and he was pretty sure she suspected, at the very least – she wasn't going to give anyone a reason to think that she knew.

'Sad news, Petrarch. We've lost a student. One of your poetry undergraduates, Oona Sinclair. She was found dead this morning, possibly by suicide. I know how sorry you'll be. The police are investigating.'

Petrarch had deleted all the messages from his phone; everything from Oona, the horrible pictures she'd sent from the letter. But they'd be on her phone, wouldn't they? Was there a way to get hold of her phone? he wondered. That was the first thing the police would look for, wasn't it? He tried to remember if he'd replied to any of the messages. He hadn't

– he'd answered her call, but that was all.

He kept going though, deleting all the party invitations, the messages to and from other girls and boys. He'd spent half the night on his computer, getting rid of hundreds of videos from the hidden cameras around the flat, memories which had brought him so much pleasure over the years. Deleting the videos had been a wrench; he'd spent many hours reviewing past pleasures and felt them almost to be an insurance against his old age, a library of liberties to be revisited when he was no longer physically capable of such excess.

The videos went back decades. He'd digitised videotape which dated back to the early eighties, recorded in the house in Cambridge where it all began. He allowed himself a nostalgic moment; he'd loved Cambridge. His student years in the mid-seventies had probably been the highlight of his life: a blissful scene of music, poetry, newly liberated women and pretty boys. He'd rented the house with four other English students, all of them peacocking around the university city in crushed velvet and paisley print, putting together a band in a desultory way, spending hours playing guitars and sitars while sprawled on cushions on the floor. He'd deepened the love of William Blake that he'd discovered at school, quoting poetry to a houseful of beautiful boys and girls as they experimented with drugs, music and sex.

He'd felt like he'd discovered El Dorado, the place he'd been searching for all his life. It soothed away all the confusion and pain of his days at his cathedral school, where he'd been plucked for glory as a soloist by the predatory choir master. Here, he would not be dropped when his voice broke. He was surrounded by love and admiration, his every desire quickly met. When his bandmates moved on after university, he'd stayed, a graduate student, then a fellow. He'd bought the house, made it beautiful and opulent with silk and velvet, and the girls kept coming to the parties.

The Cambridge days had come to an end. A girl, of course, a blonde with a gloriously voluptuous body and cherubic face which had blinded him to her rapacious soul. She'd tried to blackmail him, then when the money ran out, she went to the university authorities. He'd been summoned to a meeting, told bluntly that no formal action would be taken, but it would be as well for him to absent himself for a while.

The Dean had him in for whisky afterwards.

'It won't do anymore, Petrarch. You're attracting too much attention. The college is awash with feminists, all waiting for a chance to bring us into disrepute. Take study leave. Go and write that book you keep talking about. Then have a look around. One of the newer universities, perhaps. They'd jump at the chance to employ you, and they don't get the media focus that we get here.'

So he'd gone home to Chichester and written the book that had made his name, working away at his mother's house, his intellectual rebirth coinciding with her death. And when she'd gone, he'd sold the Cambridge house and the Chichester rectory, pooled the money to buy the Great Russell Street flat. He'd remade himself, become respected and admired, eminent even. Television producers loved him; the university boasted of him; the girls kept coming to the parties.

And now, all of this was threatened again. It wasn't fair. He hadn't hurt anyone. He'd simply tried to live the best, the most beautiful and full life that he could. Where was the harm in that?

209

# Chapter 42

P etrarch was woken by rapping on the door. He jerked awake, head propped uncomfortably against the arm of the sofa in his study. He must have fallen asleep, exhausted by work and worry. Panic gripped his chest.

'Who is it?'

'Sorry, did I wake you?' It was only Brett. He'd been dreading Veronica, her sarcasm peeling away his defences. Yesterday she'd been full of false sympathy about Oona, cooing about the tragedy of it.

'No, it's fine.' He checked the time: nine o'clock. He hadn't been to bed, had worked on through the night. Had he done everything he needed to do? He thought he had.

'I suppose we should get on.' The thought of trying to engage with the book was impossible. But he had to do something. Pretend everything was normal, push on through.

'I heard about Oona. Ronnie rang me.'

Ronnie? When had Brett started calling Petrarch's wife by her pet name? And when had she started ringing him without Petrarch knowing?

'Very sad,' he snapped, forcing the words out. He didn't want to talk about Oona.

'Isn't it? She was so young. And really very beautiful. But

vulnerable. You could see that in her, couldn't you? That one day she would just... break.'

Brett mimed snapping a twig in his hands. Petrarch flinched.

'Anyway, there's someone to see you in the lounge. She arrived at the same time as me, so I let her in.'

Christ, not the police. Petrarch's heart began to thump harder.

'Who is it?' His voice sounded weird in his ears, as if he was listening to someone else.

'Your colleague, Helen Oddfellow. Shall I make coffee?'

Shit. Shit, shit, shit. But of course she'd be back, with her grubby suspicions. He'd seen her off last time, guessing that she had nothing definite from the students to incriminate him. Rose, he remembered. She'd been talking to Rose O'Dowd, the plump little Irish girl who'd been at the last party. He felt a prickle of fear. What did she know this time?

He pulled on his dressing gown, then decided to get dressed. He tried to pad silently from the study to his bedroom, but the door to the drawing room was open.

'There you are, Professor Greenwood. Sorry, is it a bit early for you?'

She was standing in the doorway, eyeing him coolly in a way that reminded him of Veronica. He felt at a disadvantage again.

'Not at all. I don't dress until I need to leave the house. I wasn't expecting anyone,' he said. He hoped his voice was cold enough to reassert his authority. This was his space, dammit. She shouldn't even be here. He'd have a word with Brett, make it clear that unexpected visitors were to be kept out until he'd vetted them.

211

'Well, don't dress on my account,' she said, moving back into the drawing room to let him enter. He sat at the desk, grounding himself with the rich mahogany, the pile of books with his name on.

'Is this about Oona?' he blurted, unable to keep the words in.

She raised an eyebrow. 'What do you think, Petrarch? Should it be?'

'I can't think why else you would be disturbing my study leave without an appointment, again. I'm extremely saddened by the news of her death. As I said to Caroline, I understand she had a history of self-harm and mental-health problems.'

'So any adult in a position of authority over her should have recognised her vulnerability, and taken extra care with her,' said Helen. Her voice was full of controlled fury. 'But instead, you took advantage of her, exploited her sexually and humiliated her. Like you've done to so many students, all your teaching career. Right back to your time in Cambridge, when you were pushed out. They called that study leave, too, didn't they?'

He sat very still. What did she know? Rose would not have known all this. More importantly, could she prove anything? Accusations were cheap.

'You are making slanderous accusations,' he said slowly, staring at the grain of the desk. 'If you repeat them to anyone else, I will sue you for defamation.'

He looked up, saw in her eyes that she was sure of herself this time.

'I don't believe you have a shred of evidence. Who's been telling you their sad little fantasies? It's an occupational hazard, and the more famous the academic, the more often it happens. Vulnerable young women, far from home, looking for a father figure...'

Helen laughed. 'Father figure? Come on, Petrarch. The women I've been talking to are not fantasists. Believe me, they took no pleasure in recounting what you'd done to them.'

So she'd dug up one or two students from his past. He boiled with fury. How dare she go snooping?

'So why are they not here with you?' he asked. 'Where are they, these brave women? Have they made official complaints to the university? Are they ready to accuse me to my face?'

Helen held his gaze. 'Is that all you have to say? No remorse, no regret for having driven a young woman to suicide? I found her body, you know. It's not something I can forget. Don't you feel any twinges of guilt about the young lives you blighted?'

Rage filled him. He'd enhanced their lives, not blighted them. He'd opened their eyes to the infinite possibilities that lay beyond the pathetic quotidian round. He'd seized them before the mental chains bit deep, given them a glimpse of the paradise of eternity. And this mealy-mouthed woman called that blight?

He rose to his feet, his bulk giving him a sense of power. He stepped towards Helen, saw her take half a step backwards.

'Don't come here threatening me!' he roared. He felt his heart pumping, his face reddening with blood. She was nothing. He shoved her shoulder and she staggered backwards, shock on her face.

'Get out. You have no right to be here. I'm calling my lawyer. I'll put a restraining order on you. And be very, very careful you don't spread your sordid gossip. I'll destroy you, Helen. You want a career in academia? Forget it. Back off, or you'll find your reputation so tarnished no university will touch you again.'

Out of the corner of his eye, he saw Brett edge into the room with a tray of coffee cups. Damn him and his timing.

Helen straightened and squared her shoulders.

'Do calm down.' Her voice was shaky, but she was keeping it together. She turned and smiled at Brett. 'Coffee would be lovely, thank you.' She took a delicate cup, tiny in her big hands. 'Petrarch, I've dealt with bullies before. Believe me, you're going to have to do a lot more than shout about lawyers to scare me off. What about the letter? Do you have a handy explanation for that?'

The letter. Damn it, so she did know about the letter. He struggled to control his breathing. She said she'd found Oona's body. Had she found the letter, too?

'What letter?'

'You know what letter. With the pictures of you and Oona. And others. Who sent it, Petrarch? You must know. You know who was there.'

He'd been going through the possibilities in his head since Oona had sent him the hateful images. He'd discounted the girls, and drawn a blank with the boys. The malevolence, the anger, was outside anything he'd experienced since his schooldays. He recognised jealousy when he saw it. But that was the point of the parties. Everyone had someone. No-one needed to be jealous of anyone else.

'I have no idea what you're talking about.' If Helen could be brazen, so could he. Every academic who'd confronted him over the years, who'd questioned his relationships with students, had backed down when he threatened their reputation. He wasn't above turning the accusations back on them.

214

At least one student had been prepared to make false claims against his colleagues. Usually, the mere hint of what he could do to them was enough. Helen was different. She seemed genuinely fearless. But was she? He watched her, wondered whether her self-confidence was really as impenetrable as it looked.

'I thought I'd see if you could help me work out who'd sent it,' she said. 'But if not, I guess I'll have to take what I've found to Caroline. Who will take it to the police.'

He took the coffee from Brett, who was staring studiously out of the window.

'Caroline, who has been my friend for more than twenty years, will ask the same questions I'm asking now. Where are these students accusing me of the things you say I've done? Who is drawing silly pictures and sending them to Oona?

'You've been on staff for less than a year. Why should she believe you? If you make these false accusations, legal action will follow.'

He swept his hand around the room, indicating the rich furnishings, the generous space.

'Can you really afford that, Helen? You've been building up a nice little life for yourself, haven't you? A comfortable job in academia, a cosy flat in the suburbs. Safe.' He smirked. 'But go ahead, chuck it all away. You'll lose the lot. And you might think you're young enough to start again – but are you really? You're halfway through your thirties, unmarried, with a temporary job that's up for review in two months' time. Your salary just about pays the mortgage, without much to spare. Your parents are dead. Do this, and you'll have no-one to turn to. No friends, no family to bail you out.'

He paused for breath. Her face was unreadable, but he

thought he detected a tremor in the hand that held the coffee cup.

'Oh, I have friends,' she said. 'I won't let them down. And they won't let me down, either. Perhaps you should come along to the *Celebration of Women's Words*. Caroline's asked Barbara and me to speak on Friday afternoon. We're presenting new findings about Catherine Blake, and her input into Blake's poetry. Yet another woman that men have tried to silence and pigeonhole over the years.'

Her colour was high and she was breathing fast, her eyes sparkling and combative. She really was most attractive, in her boyish way. But she was talking nonsense.

'Catherine Blake has been thoroughly researched over the years. She was illiterate. Blake taught her everything,' he said. 'I do hope you're not going to make a fool of yourself.'

She had the chutzpah to laugh. 'Actually, I think you hope I am. But you should come, anyway. You might recognise my co-presenter. She's not one to be cowed by threats, either.'

Brett cleared his throat. 'It sounds very interesting. Can you tell me more about your theory?'

For God's sake, thought Petrarch. The woman came round and accused me of sexual abuse. Now they're turning it into some kind of academic seminar.

'Helen's leaving,' he said, as firmly as he could. 'And we have work to do.'

The woman put her cup down. 'Last chance, Petrarch. I'm going to Caroline. Unless you want to do it yourself?'

'Get out.' She was unbearable, so smug and self-righteous. He couldn't believe he'd been finding her attractive a few minutes ago.

'I'll see you out,' said Brett, lunging for the door. The poor fool probably had a crush on her, Petrarch thought. He watched them go, his pyjama jacket clammy with cooling sweat. Plausible deniability, he repeated to himself like a mantra. Plausible deniability.

# Chapter 43

He sent Brett away after lunch, saying he had a headache and needed to rest. It wasn't much of a lie. He lay on his bed, pleating the velvet throw between his fingers, listening to the traffic outside the flat. If Helen really went to Caroline, he'd be on very sticky ground. He'd told her the parties had stopped, that Veronica wouldn't countenance them anymore. He wasn't sure that she believed him, but she'd needed to pretend she did. Caroline was good at hearing only what she wanted to hear and seeing what she wanted to see. Maybe he should call her. Maybe she'd call him. Maybe he should do nothing. Plausible deniability.

He heard Veronica's key turn in the lock, and a moment later her heels tapped across the parquet floor. Petrarch had a sudden longing for the comfort she used to offer him, the calm she once brought to the apartment. He'd found her so restful, after the hysterics and drama of many of the other students. She had moved in almost before he noticed, smoothing his daily life, protecting him from day-to-day annoyances. Getting married had been the logical step.

'Ronnie!' he called. 'I'm in here. Come and join me.'

She'd once lain by his side every night, stroking his hair and murmuring endearments, always there when he woke from nightmares, flashbacks to the cathedral school, soothing away his shouts of pain and fear. He heard her footsteps, padding more quietly this time. She'd kicked off her stilettos, was walking in her stockings down the hall.

The door opened. She wore a beige cashmere twinset, her hair softly curled on her shoulders, caramel and honey.

'Come here, Ronnie. Sit with me on the bed,' he said.

She leaned against the door, regarding him with a cool gaze. She'd been twenty-three when they'd married, with a soft smile and gentle voice. She still looked far younger than her forty-eight years. He wasn't sure how much of that was down to nature and how much to her regular cosmetic clinic appointments. Her style had changed little. Her hair was the same honeyed blonde and she'd barely put on weight, even after David was born. It was hard to put your finger on what had changed. It was as if she'd hardened into place, set like concrete in the image she had chosen.

'What's the matter?' She checked the slim watch on her wrist. 'Are you sick?'

'I'm… I'm just sad,' he said, the words taking him by surprise. 'Won't you sit with me?'

She sighed and picked her way across the room, avoiding the piles of laundry that she no longer removed for him. She perched on the edge of the bed.

'Really, Petrarch. This isn't good enough, you know. Hiding from the book won't make it go away.'

'It's not about the book.' And it wasn't, for once. The book had become an overarching shadow, an almost abstract threat, like nuclear war had been during the Cold War. He woke every morning to the knowledge it was there, and spelled disaster. But not necessarily today.

219

She tapped him briskly on the arm. 'Then what are you doing in bed?'

'I'm worried,' he said. 'About Oona. About what's going to come out.'

Haltingly, he explained about the cartoon images that Oona had sent him, about the letter she'd received.

'Helen Oddfellow has seen it. I suppose she'll give it to the police. And they'll come and ask about Oona, and my relationship with her.' He stumbled over the words, feeling ridiculous. Relationship. They didn't have a relationship. Hadn't had.

'I'll have to deny it all, of course. But I need your help. I need to know you'll back me up.'

He was unable to meet the merciless blue of Veronica's eyes. He felt ashamed. It was not an emotion he often allowed. He didn't like it.

She tutted. 'Stupid. Still making a fool of yourself over girls, Petrarch. At your age. Look at you. You have everything you could want: a beautiful apartment, a prestigious career. An intelligent and devoted wife.'

He looked up, surprised. Veronica had little sense of humour, but it sounded as if she was joking. There was no sign of it in her face. Her forehead remained egg-smooth, only the pinching of her nostrils demonstrated her contempt.

'Yes, I mean me.' She didn't smile. 'And still, you persist in these stupid games with these little girls. Risking everything you have. Everything we have.'

She slapped his hand, a surprisingly sharp sting. He struggled upright against the pillow.

'Don't do that.'

She slapped him again, harder, across his face. Tears sprang to his eyes.

'And now you expect sympathy?' she hissed. 'Because your stupid little whore decided to slit her wrists? You think I should feel sorry for you? For Christ's sake. You've humiliated me for years with your little girls, your sordid parties. You're a greedy pig.'

She stood, her face twitching.

'If you want me to support you, I expect to see you work. Is that clear? You get up, put some clothes on, write that fucking book, do that fucking TV series, and bring in some fucking money.'

Her words shocked him more than the slap. Veronica never swore, never raised her voice. And she never, ever spoke about money, despite being in full charge of all their financial affairs.

'You think this place runs itself, Petrarch? The service charge alone costs thousands of pounds a month. All your fine wines, all your books, the food, the heating, the housekeeper. Do you really think we can manage on the pittance you get from the university?'

They used to manage all right, he thought. But it was true, there used to be more book royalties and TV fees coming in. He knew that Veronica had some investments, some money of her own that she'd inherited after her father died. Her parents were rich, had paid off the mortgage on the flat as a wedding present, and her money had been a welcome addition, although not the primary incentive most of his friends had assumed.

'I thought we were managing,' he ventured.

'Because I manage,' she snapped. 'Because I take care of all the bills, juggle your salary and my investments, and ensure we can just about make ends meet every month. Don't think I do it because I like it. I do it because, if I didn't, we would be on the streets. We'd have to sell up, buy some horrible little flat out in the suburbs. Is that what you want?'

She stalked to the window and pulled open the curtains. Sunshine filtered through the plane tree outside.

'See? Daylight, Petrarch. Work time. Get up. Get dressed. You want my support? Earn it. Go to the library, write some books. Get up, now.'

He swung his legs over the side of the bed, pushed his feet into his slippers. He couldn't look at her. She reminded him, suddenly and unbearably, of his mother, forcing him back to school on a Monday morning.

'I'm sorry,' he muttered.

Veronica slammed the door behind her.

# Chapter 44

The police officers arrived in the evening. There were two of them: an Asian man, slightly overweight, and stern-looking young woman. Petrarch buzzed them in. He'd been in his study, scrolling through social media for mentions of himself, or of Oona's death, while pretending to work. Veronica was watching television in the living room. He could hear canned laughter through the wall, some idiotic comedy show.

'We have a few questions about the death of your student, Oona Sinclair.' The woman got straight to the point. Petrarch considered calling Veronica to offer them coffee, but decided this might go better without her. He was still reeling from their earlier confrontation.

'Of course. Terribly sad. Come through.' He took them into the drawing room with its impressive view of the museum.

'Very nice,' said the man, solemnly. He sat on the sofa, took out a notebook and waited with his pen poised.

'I'm PC Maggie Lambert,' said the female officer, 'and this is PC Vijay Patel. Can you tell us how well you knew Oona Sinclair?'

He took a deep breath, wondering belatedly if he should have asked for a lawyer to be present. But surely that would just make him look like he had something to hide?

'Not particularly well. She started on my poetry course in September. She was bright, enthusiastic. But I haven't taught her recently. Another tutor is taking the class while I'm on study leave.' Helen bloody Oddfellow. He wondered uneasily if they had interviewed her already. And if so, what she'd told them.

'And when did you last see her?'

Petrarch was ready for that. 'At the start of May, around three weeks ago. I gave a little drinks party for some of my students, to wish them well for their final term. I don't think I've seen her since.' It was true, strictly speaking. He'd not actually seen her when she came to the flat. It seemed safer to mention the party straight away, make light of it. With luck they'd go on to other things.

'Who else was at this party?'

'Mainly students, a few of my colleagues.' He named two of the English department academics who had attended. They had as much to lose as he did, if this got out. He thought he could rely on them for discretion.

'And what did you talk about, when she called you on the weekend before her death?'

Petrarch's heart jumped. They had her phone records, then.

'I'm not sure I remember a call...' he began.

The young woman cocked her head at her colleague. 'Vijay?'

PC Patel consulted his notebook. 'Forty-eight calls or text messages, between eight-thirty and eleven-twenty, Saturday 16 May.'

Petrarch swallowed. 'I – I only spoke to her once. I was busy; I don't answer my phone when I'm working. She was worried about an essay. Panicking. I asked her to stop calling me so often. It was inappropriate.'

'Inappropriate.' PC Patel echoed the word, writing it down slowly in his notebook. 'Right.'

'How would you characterise your relationship with Ms Sinclair?'

The questions went on. How often did he see Ms Sinclair outside of tutorial or lecture situations? Were they having a sexual relationship? Had Ms Sinclair spoken to him about emotional or mental-health conditions, and if so, had he reported them to the university? Was he aware of any attempts to threaten, coerce or blackmail Ms Sinclair? Had any such attempts been made on him?

By the time the officers left the flat, thanking him politely for his help, Petrarch had sweated right through his shirt. He'd stuck to his line that Oona was a nice girl, but rather anxious and needy. His offers to help her with extra tuition had been misinterpreted, and the approaching examinations seemed to have tipped her over the edge. He felt bad about her death, but wasn't sure what else he could have done.

It sounded plausible to him. But then he didn't know what else the police had. He assumed from the questions about blackmail that they had seen the letter, with the vile drawings. But if so, had they identified him? And would that have any weight? PC Lambert had told him they would make a report to the coroner, who would hold an inquest into the death in due course. He might be called as a witness, if the coroner thought it necessary.

He definitely needed that lawyer, he decided. Veronica had found him a good one when a student made a complaint eight or nine years ago. She had been expensive, efficient and made it all go away. But Petrarch was afraid to ask Ronnie for help again. He'd find the lawyer's number himself.

He opened the door to the living room a crack. Veronica was asleep, her brightly coiffed head nodding against a cushion while the television played nonsense. He retreated to her bedroom and ransacked the little French bureau for the lawyer's number.

He didn't find it. But he did find their bank statements, and the annual report from Veronica's accountant for the performance of her investments. He frowned, smoothed the paper out and looked in incomprehension at the numbers. He resorted to counting the noughts on his fingers, unable to believe what he saw.

They were incredibly rich. Or rather, Veronica was. He counted again. She had more than thirty million quid under management in various funds. Each quarter she transferred a small fraction of her profits to their joint bank account, which was rosy with health. And she'd been trying to keep him on a short leash, telling him they were about to run out of cash if he didn't get his book written.

He sat back on the chair, trying to take it in. No wonder Veronica had been able to afford expensive lawyers. He supposed that was one consolation. But his book – she knew how he loathed it. And she was still trying to guilt-trip him into working himself to death, with all that cash floating around. The absolute bitch.

He went back to the cabinet, continued rifling through the papers. Veronica didn't just pay the household bills; she paid Brett's salary directly from her own account. He'd always assumed it was paid by the English department. Caroline had certainly allowed him to think as much.

He flushed with anger. Brett was the one person who

truly knew how far from finished his book was. He'd seen Petrarch's despair over getting it done, the fear that all too often led to him declaring work over for the day at lunchtime, or even before then. Had he been reporting back to Veronica all the time? Petrarch wondered. No wonder she was so scathing about his progress. Had Brett tipped her off, when Petrarch had retired to his bed after lunch?

She hadn't hired an assistant for him, he realised. Veronica had hired a spy.

# Chapter 45

Helen hurried up the stairs to the seminar room. This would be the first time the students had come together since Oona's death, and she wanted to gather her thoughts before they arrived.

She was sleeping badly, troubled by visions of Oona dying alone and scared, her calls for help unanswered. The letter she'd received haunted her too. She no longer felt safe in her flat, wondering all the time if someone was watching it, whether they were outside, or making their way up the stairs. She'd contacted the police, but been met by scepticism. The letter didn't mention her specifically, didn't make an overt threat. They'd keep it on file, they told her.

The letter, Petrarch Greenwood's threats to her career – all sitting undigested among a pile of stuff she didn't know what to do with. She needed to tell Caroline about what Rose had divulged of Petrarch's parties. But Rose was too scared to make an official complaint, and Helen wanted more evidence before she put herself in the firing line again. Her head ached in the relentless heat, and she thought with longing of the Manchester rain.

She'd hoped to arrive first, but Liz was already in her seat. The girl was hunched over her laptop, short brown hair framing her square face in an uncompromising style.

'Hello, Liz. How're you getting on?' Helen realised how little she knew about her. Had she been friends with Oona? Was she upset about her death? Liz gave off an air of such self-sufficiency, it was hard to imagine her being upset about anything. But maybe that was unfair.

'OK, thanks.'

'How are you managing the workload? It's always difficult when the exams are coming up.'

Liz shrugged. 'I manage. I always have. No point in making a drama about it.'

Helen sat on the table and unpacked her bag. 'You work very hard.'

The girl laughed, a slight edge to her voice. 'When you look like this, you have to work hard. No-one is going to give you better marks because they fancy you. No-one's going to give you extra time for an essay because you're starring in a play, or whatever.' She looked down, stared at the table, as if worried she'd gone too far.

'Liz...' Helen wondered what on earth to say. 'You're doing really well. And there's nothing wrong with the way you look.'

She saw the girl's jaw clench. Nothing wrong was not enough, Helen knew. The world was harsh to women who didn't meet conventional beauty standards.

'It's difficult,' she said, sympathetically. 'The first year at university is always tough, when you're trying to find your place and keep on top of the work, too. You can always talk to me, if you'd like to.' She felt a flush of shame, remembering how she'd said the same to Oona. But then, when the girl had asked, she had not answered.

Rose arrived next, chatting with Habib. She was telling him about their trip to Manchester, bragging about the work she'd done in the archive.

'I found this letter from Cambridge University, which we were looking for. And Helen found a new poem,' she was saying. She'd recovered her usual bounce. Helen felt almost resentful at the girl's youthful resilience.

Caroline Winter, who had asked to speak to the students, bustled through the door. She looked surprisingly smart, bright blue shirt tucked neatly into her grey trouser suit, hair brushed and beige lipstick still in place. Of course, Helen remembered, it was Thursday already. The *Out of the Silence* conference started this morning. Caroline must be on her way there. There would be no chance to talk to her about Petrarch today.

'Right, is everyone here?' Caroline asked.

'One still to come,' said Helen. Deepak was late, as usual. She had sent them all a text message to ask them to attend the seminar and let them know the change of location from the park. He hadn't bothered to reply.

Caroline looked at her watch. 'I don't have much time. We should get started.' She took off her glasses and massaged the bridge of her nose. 'I wanted to talk to you today about Oona Sinclair,' she said, her voice brisk. 'I'm sure you will have heard the sad news about Oona's death earlier this week. She was a well-liked and hard-working student, with a bright future ahead of her, and showed great potential for her work in the theatre. I'm personally devastated by her death, and I'm sure that, as her friends, you are too.'

Rose blushed, and Liz looked away. Only Habib looked genuinely upset.

'There will be an inquest into the cause of her death, but at present, the police tell me there is no reason to think that anyone else was involved. I would ask you please to refrain from speculation about the causes.'

Caroline looked hard at them, her eyes resting a moment on Rose.

'We do not know what happened, or why. So let's not spread gossip. Meanwhile, if you have any information that you think relates to her death, talk to me or to Dr Oddfellow, and we will arrange for you to speak to the police.'

Helen raised a hand. 'Do we know about the funeral?'

'Oona's aunt is travelling from Scotland to make arrangements. I believe it will be held in Orkney,' Caroline said. 'As soon as we know more, I will let you know and try to help anyone who wishes to attend.'

Helen pictured a windswept island, a tiny stone church isolated in heather moorland. She'd never been to Orkney, was vaguely aware that it was far north of the Scottish mainland. A lonely place for a lonely grave.

'One last thing,' Caroline continued. 'I want all of you to know that the student counselling service is here for you, if you are finding life difficult or want to talk to someone. Please don't feel you have to face your difficulties alone.' She put down a handful of leaflets for the student welfare centre and the Samaritans charity, looked at her watch again and departed.

Helen surveyed the three bowed heads: Rose's multi-coloured curls, showing mouse at the roots now; Habib's dark waves; and Liz's brown bowl-cut. She felt as never before a responsibility for these young people, a desire to protect and comfort them, as she wished she had protected and comforted

231

Oona.

'Is there anything that you would like to say, or to ask about?' she said. 'It's tough, losing a friend. It can bring up all sorts of complicated feelings.'

Habib looked up. 'We should do something,' he said. 'Light a candle, or read a poem. Remember her. She should not have died like that.'

Helen nodded. 'That's a nice idea, Habib. Maybe in the gardens, where we used to meet?'

'Brilliant idea,' said Rose. 'I'll be there.' She looked relieved at the thought of doing something.

'OK,' said Liz, slowly. Then she looked up. 'But she shouldn't have done it. Committed suicide, I mean. It's so selfish. Think about her poor family.'

She thrust out her jaw, her face flushed.

'Everyone always thinks about the person themselves, how sad and tragic and all that. But it's just self-indulgent. Everyone has problems. We don't all go killing ourselves.'

'Wait,' called Helen, recovering from her initial shock. 'We don't know what happened, or why. Let's not jump to conclusions.'

'Rubbish,' said Liz. 'She cut her wrists, Rose told us. And she'd done it before. Attention-seeking. Typical of that sort.'

'Shut up,' shouted Rose. 'You don't know anything about her.'

'I know the type. She'd do anything for attention. She was shagging half the university, from what I heard.'

'You absolute bitch!' shrieked Rose.

Helen's head pounded. The girls' angry red faces shouted accusations. She didn't know what to do, how to make them stop. She was assaulted with a powerful vision of Oona, glassy eyes open and arms floating in her ghastly bath of blood. Squeezing her own eyes shut, Helen covered her ears with her hands.

'Stop it!' begged Habib, above the noise. 'This is horrible.'

The shouting stopped. Helen opened her eyes, saw them all staring at her. She opened her mouth, realised her throat was too tight to speak.

She turned and walked out the door. She kept walking, along the corridor and through the department, ignoring Jessica's questions, down the stairs and out into the street. She didn't stop till she reached Gordon Square, where she slumped on to a bench. Head in her hands, she began to weep.

# Chapter 46

'Helen?' It was Habib, his voice gentle. He crouched on the ground next to the bench, his dark eyes soft.

Helen was all cried out. Her face and hands were wet with tears. She knew she must look a complete state, her face blotched and eyelids puffy. She checked around the gardens. No-one else seemed to be taking any notice of her.

She wasn't cut out for this lecturing job, for being responsible for other people. She was barely in control of herself. Pathetic. She felt drained of energy, exhausted.

'Hi,' she managed. 'I'm really sorry.'

The boy sat next to her on the bench. 'You are sad. You cared about Oona. Crying is not a problem.'

She tried out a wobbly smile. 'Thank you. But I shouldn't have left the class like that. What happened?'

He sighed. 'I think you scared them a bit. They went quiet, and then Liz said she was going to the library. I think Rose went back to her room.'

Helen remembered Liz's angry red face, ugly with spite, shouting about Oona's selfishness.

'They were both upset,' she said. 'It's not easy.' She smiled at the boy. 'I liked your idea about doing something to mark

Oona's death. Or her life, I suppose.' Such a short life; just eighteen years.

'We need to do something. We owe it to Oona, to remember. It is our responsibility,' he said.

Helen nodded, heart full. If anyone was responsible, it was she.

'Can I ask you something?' His eyes were troubled, his dark brows drawn together.

'Sure.'

'What is an inquest? Caroline said there would be an inquest into her death. I don't understand what that is. Does it mean the police?'

'Yes, but don't worry.' Helen recognised fear in his face. She supposed the police in his country were not the impartial force she'd been brought up to believe in. 'The police will investigate the circumstances. They will look at how she died, and try to find out what might have caused her death. And then they'll give their evidence to the coroner, who hears from anyone else with information. The coroner decides what happened.'

'OK.' He didn't look happy. 'Will the police talk to me?'

'I don't know, Habib. I suppose it depends. How well did you know Oona?'

He spread his hands, sighed. 'Not well. I only saw her in class.' He smiled at Helen. 'I don't know much how to talk to girls. My mother did not like me talking to a woman not in my family. And I don't have any sisters. So it is hard. I think girls are different here.'

He'd lied, Helen realised, with a shock. He'd been at the party, which meant he'd seen Oona there. From what Rose said, and from the images on the blog, everyone had seen

235

Oona there.

'It must be difficult,' she said. 'I suppose it is very different. Do you find it strange, things like parties and nightclubs where everyone dances together?'

He looked away. 'I don't go to parties or clubs. I don't drink alcohol. Parties here mean everyone gets drunk and behaves badly. I promised my parents I would not go. It is better that way.'

Helen decided not to push it. There would be little to be gained from forcing him to tell her something he didn't want to admit. All the same, she would have dearly liked to hear his take on what had happened at Petrarch Greenwood's party – and what he, of all people, was doing there.

'Of course,' she said. 'Well, if you didn't know Oona well, and hadn't been to any parties with her, I don't suppose the police will need to talk to you.' She let her words settle.

'Why do you keep asking about parties?' he asked, frowning.

Helen got to her feet. 'Just something one of the other students mentioned,' she said. 'It's probably nothing. I should be getting back.' She wondered if she should go to Caroline, admit what had happened in the seminar. She was embarrassed, but perhaps it would be better for the head of department to hear from Helen directly, rather than getting the gossip second-hand.

'Wait.'

She waited. His face was working, his mouth twitching under his neatly trimmed beard and moustache.

'I went to one party,' he said. She sat back down.

'OK.'

'At Professor Greenwood's home.' He passed his hand across his eyes, as if trying to wipe memories from his brain.

'It was very bad,' he said. 'There were lots of people drinking too much wine, and taking drugs. I didn't... I did not want to be there. I did not think it would be like that. They were... they were behaving very badly. Taking clothes off and everything.' His voice was angry. 'I wanted to go home. But one of the students who was there... he made me drink some wine. And he said I should stay.'

'It's all right, Habib,' she said, her voice gentle. 'Everybody goes to parties they wish they hadn't when they're students.'

He shook his head. 'Not like that.'

'Habib, it's OK. You can tell me.'

'Oona was there,' he said. 'With Professor Greenwood. He... he made us watch them together. I didn't want to. It was horrible. Oona was crying.'

Helen's heart constricted. So Oona had not been a willing participant in the spectacle. She thought again, with revulsion, of Petrarch. His menacing bulk, his bullying manner.

'That's awful,' she said. 'It must have been very upsetting for you.' Not to mention for Oona, and Rose, and all the other women waiting for their turn to be abused and humiliated, she thought.

'I went away,' he said. 'Into another room. I could not watch anymore.'

But he had watched, for a while. So he had been there, in that room, with whoever had drawn the images. Should she show him the picture? she wondered. It might be too much for him. Helen didn't want another student driven to self-harm.

'All right, Habib. It's OK. No-one will judge you for going to that party. Like I said, we all make mistakes. All of us. And if anyone is to blame for what happened, it's the man who organised it.'

'Will I need to talk to the police?' he asked.

'I hope not. But if you do, it would be about what happened to Oona. Not anything that you did,' she said. 'If Oona was hurt and upset, it could be important for the coroner to know about it. But you were not the only person there.' She hesitated a moment. 'Who else was at the party, Habib? I'd like to talk to them.'

He shook his head. 'No. It is enough that you know I was there. I won't tell you about anyone else.' This time, she was sure he meant it.

# Chapter 47

Habib left her sitting on the bench. Helen got out her phone and looked again at the images from the letter. Rose. Oona. Petrarch. Habib. One more face she recognised.

Deepak hadn't turned up to the seminar. She hadn't seen him since he handed in his Blake essay a week previously. She'd marked it, disappointed to find a mediocre mix of regurgitated opinions from Petrarch Greenwood's book and Deepak's own rather superficial reactions. Helen got the impression that he didn't think much of Blake. She'd hoped he would bring a fresh perspective, as well as his keen intelligence, to this most un-English of English authors.

But that was before Oona's death, and the pictures. She looked at the drawing of his face, his sardonic smile. Deepak and Oona had been close in the first term, Helen remembered. Had it been hard for him, seeing her with Petrarch? Had he been jealous, hurt? And what had been his reaction to her death? She realised she owed a responsibility to this privileged young man, as much as to her other students. But he was not answering his phone.

Helen headed back to the department. Jessica was helpful, for once. She looked up his address in the filing cabinet without prying into the reasons. Helen had been amazed at first at how much of university life ran on bits of paper, instead of computer files.

'Here you go.' Jessica fished out a paper from a folder. 'It's a private address, not a university residence. Lots of the overseas students – the rich ones at least – have their own flats. Their parents buy them in the hope it will keep them out of trouble. And as an investment, of course.'

Helen scribbled down the address, just off Great Portland Street. His parents must be loaded, she thought. She remembered Petrarch Greenwood's description of Deepak's father: a senior politician in the Indian government.

'Very good of you to go to all this trouble to return his essay to him, Helen.' Jessica smirked. 'A little beyond the call of duty?'

'I'm worried,' said Helen, shortly. 'He didn't come to the seminar this morning.'

'Don't worry,' Jessica said, with a conspiratorial smile. 'He's gorgeous, isn't he? There's one in every year. He's a bit of a bastard, but you just know that, if he wasn't a student, you so would.'

'It's not that...' Helen spluttered.

'Course not. Don't worry, I won't tell anyone. You wouldn't be the first, that's all I'm saying.'

Helen handed back the paper. 'Believe me, I'm not interested in seducing students. Life's complicated enough.' She couldn't resist asking, though. 'What do you mean, I wouldn't be the first?'

Jessica winked. 'That'd be telling. But Professor Greenwood has had more than his fair share, from what I hear.'

She lowered her voice and leaned across the desk.

'She was in here the week before she died. Oona Sinclair. Desperate to talk to Petrarch; wanted me to go through his diary and tell her where he was. Poor girl – I mean, can you imagine? But then of course, he married a student, when he first moved here.'

Helen remembered the icy woman who'd ushered her into Petrarch's flat.

'Was she really a student? I've met her. What's her name again?'

'Veronica. Ronnie, he calls her. This was before my time, of course. But Caroline told me once. It was a bit of a scandal, but they were more relaxed about things in those days, and her parents were fine about her getting married, so that was all right. He needs to be careful, though. From what Brett tells me, he's not exactly calmed down with age.'

'Brett?'

'Brett Albion. Works with Petrarch.'

Ah yes, Helen remembered. His research assistant. 'What's he been saying?'

'Oh, nothing much. Just that Petrarch still has some pretty decadent parties. I don't think he approves. Caroline says it's nothing to worry about, though.'

'Caroline knows about them?'

Jessica looked over her shoulder and dropped her voice. 'Well, obviously. Nothing happens round here that she doesn't know about. But she'll forgive him anything, so long as he keeps pulling in the overseas students and the funding, through those telly documentaries.'

Helen hesitated. Even if what Jessica said was true, Caroline still needed to know what she'd learned. And she should tell her about the fiasco at the seminar, too.

241

'I need to make an appointment with Caroline, while I'm here. Can you find a slot for me to talk to her tomorrow?'

Jessica pulled out the departmental diary, while Helen marvelled again that it wasn't all online.

'Sorry. She's over at the conference again all day. You might catch her before it starts, though. She'll be there from eight.'

God, thought Helen, hoisting her rucksack on to her shoulder. Tomorrow afternoon, she and Barbara were due to give their joint presentation about Catherine Blake. She should be concentrating on that, not chasing down students all over the city.

She looked at her watch. In a final attempt to find out more about the Rossetti letter and poem, Helen had arranged to visit All Saints church. She didn't have much hope that she'd find anything, but thought it worth a shot. She'd promised to meet the priest at five. Well, she could go after talking to Deepak, she thought. It wasn't far from Great Portland Street.

She cut through the university buildings, crossed over busy Gower Street and headed down University Street towards Fitzrovia.

# Chapter 48

The glass and steel building looked out of place, slotted in among the Regency terraces. Helen double-checked the address and pushed through to the pale marble lobby.

'I'm looking for Deepak Sinha,' she told the uniformed man behind the desk, almost hidden by an enormous display of orchids. 'I'm Dr Oddfellow, his university tutor. I have some work for him.'

'One moment.' The man raised a telephone receiver. Helen heard the phone ring for a long time. Just as the man shrugged and was about to replace the handset, it was answered. He relayed the message, checking Helen's name as if he thought she might have made it up.

'He says to leave it here,' he told her.

'I need to talk to him about it,' said Helen, firmly. How dare this rich kid treat her as a lackey?

The man sighed and passed on her words. Eventually he pointed her to the lifts in the corner of the lobby.

'Seventh floor.'

The door opened on a dizzying view, the floor-to-ceiling windows of the hall flooding the room with light. More orchids were arranged tastefully on a low table by the front door. Deepak stood unsmiling in the entrance, shirtless and wearing loose linen trousers. He had his silly sunglasses on again. He was unshaven, Helen noticed, and a couple of pimples had erupted around his nose. A smell of tobacco smoke hung in the air.

'I brought your essay,' said Helen. 'I wanted to talk to you about it, given that the exams start in a few weeks' time.'

He motioned her inside.

'Would you mind putting a shirt on?' His bare chest made her uncomfortable, especially after her conversation with Jessica. He shrugged, disappeared into another room. Helen gazed around the white and beige room, with big windows looking out over the treetops of London. Huge squishy sofas were arranged with set-square precision around a glass-topped table. The glass was smeared with rings from drinks, and littered with ashtrays and cigarette butts. Despite the detritus, the space felt impersonal, like a hotel room. Helen got the feeling it had been bought fully furnished, or maybe furnished by his parents, without much input from Deepak himself.

There was a family photograph on the mantelpiece, formally posed: an elegant woman seated beside a severe-looking man in a dark business suit. On her lap sat a fat baby, a nervous-looking toddler standing between the man's legs. Helen wondered which child was Deepak.

He reappeared, clad in a white T-shirt and without his sunglasses. His eyes were bloodshot.

'Why did you come here?' he asked. His voice was truculent. Helen raised her eyebrows.

'Because you didn't come to the seminar this morning. And you didn't return my phone call, and you have only a short time before your examinations. I want all my students to have the best chance to do well,' she said. It wasn't the whole truth, but it was nothing but the truth, she told herself.

'Also,' she added, trying to make her voice kinder, 'I hadn't seen you since Oona's death. I was worried about you.'

He grunted and flung himself into an armchair. 'I've lost my phone,' he said. 'Or maybe it got stolen. I need to get another one. Anyway, I've been working.'

'Good.' Helen took the marked essay from her bag. 'I'm afraid you haven't done too well with this one, Deepak. It looks as if you spent more time reading Professor Greenwood's book than you did reading William Blake.'

He took it, his face flushing dark with annoyance. 'He told us to read his book. He said it would save time.'

'It's a good book. I've read it too. But I wanted to know what you thought about the poems. I already know what Professor Greenwood thinks.'

Deepak let his breath out in a noisy, exasperated sigh. 'What does it matter what I think?' he asked. 'I'm just not that interested in him. It's silly, most of it. Stupid nursery rhyme stuff. I'm here to study Shakespeare. Dickens. Proper authors, not this nonsense.'

Helen smiled. Finally, a genuine reaction. That gave her a starting point.

'Good. Write about why you think it's nonsense,' she said.

'What?' He looked confused.

'Tell me why you think he wrote nursery rhyme stuff. Explain why it reminds you of nursery rhymes. Why do you think it's silly?'

A smile cracked his face. 'Don't you like it, either? I thought I was the only one.'

245

She laughed. 'I found Blake hard to get into at first. You don't have to like your set texts, Deepak. But you do have to read them, and do your best to understand them, and the world in which they were written.'

He nodded, leaning forward. 'Everyone goes on about how amazing he is, how spiritual and revolutionary and all that. And all I can hear is this tum-te-tum-te-tum rhythm, and all this rubbish about lambs and flowers. You think that's spiritual? You should read some of the Hindi epics. They make Blake's world look mundane.'

'So tell me more about that in your essays. Compare the Hindi epic poems to Blake's mythical world. That's exactly the sort of insight you can bring to your study that the others can't,' said Helen. 'And think about that rhythm, and why he used it, and why he picked lambs and flowers to write about. Yes?'

'Yeah.' He grinned. 'Yeah, all right. If it'll help. I thought Petrarch would be marking it, so I should agree with what he said. He said...' Deepak broke off, suddenly.

'He said you'd get a good mark?' asked Helen, tentatively.

'Yeah.' He reached for his cigarette packet, then looked at Helen and let it drop. 'Look, do you want a coffee or something?' So he did have some manners, Helen thought.

'Coffee would be nice,' she said. She followed him into the sleek stainless-steel kitchen. Only the microwave and the coffee machine showed signs of use.

'What else did he say?' she asked, as he selected a pod and slotted it into the machine. 'About getting good marks, I mean. Did he say you should go to his parties?'

The boy froze. 'What?'

'Rose told me,' said Helen, trying to keep her voice gentle.

'She said Professor Greenwood had told her that she'd get a better mark if she went to his party. I wondered if he'd told you that, too.'

He turned slowly to face her. 'What else did Rose say about the party?' The colour had gone from his face; his dark brows drew together.

Helen waited a moment. 'Why don't you tell me about it?' she asked.

'I can't.' His voice was quiet, despairing.

'Why not?'

He turned away, leaned his arms on the gleaming work surface and buried his head in his hands.

'Deepak...' Helen hesitated. 'I think those parties had something to do with Oona's death. I've heard a little about them. I'm worried that students are being abused. That people are getting hurt. I know you were close to Oona at one point. Can you at least tell me if I'm right to be worried?'

He snatched the coffee cup from the machine and hurled it to the floor. Helen flinched as it smashed on the granite tiles.

'Why does everyone think it's my fault?' he yelled. 'I liked Oona. We had fun. But it's not like I have to marry a girl just because I sleep with her. We split up before the end of the autumn term. After the play was over, at Petrarch's Christmas party. When she first went off with him.'

He turned to Helen, his eyes flashing.

'Ask Petrarch, why don't you? If anyone fucked Oona up, it was him. Jesus. You should have seen him pawing her in front of everyone. You think I liked watching that?'

'It's OK, Deepak. I'm not blaming you for anything,' she said. Even so, she moved around the kitchen, putting the counter between herself and the angry young man.

'So Professor Greenwood started a relationship with Oona before Christmas? How many parties did you go to? Just that one, and the one with Rose?'

He slammed his hands on the counter. 'I don't care what Rose says. She went along because she wanted to. No-one made her do it. It was completely consensual.' He glared at Helen. 'I don't understand that girl. I like her, but why would she go to a party like that? She's a nice girl. But she says she wants to know what it's like, and then of course she has to take part, and then she wishes she hadn't. And now she's trying to blame me, pretending she only went along because I asked her to.'

Great, thought Helen. A different standard for nice girls and rich boys. She had no intention of staying while he shouted and threw crockery. She'd heard enough to corroborate what the others had told her.

She collected her things together from the living room. When she left, he was slumped on the sofa, lighting a cigarette. He turned as she got to the door.

'I'm sorry,' he said. 'I just don't know how to handle any of this. And I can't get involved. My parents would disown me.'

What a mess, thought Helen, descending to the ground floor so fast her stomach took a minute to catch up. What an absolute mess.

# Chapter 49

The first thing Helen noticed was the heavy scent of incense, which made her want to sneeze. The second was the explosion of colour and pattern: interweaving reds, blues and golds on the ceiling and floor; tiled murals of saints and bible scenes running the length of the walls. The Victorians who decorated All Saints had not held back.

Helen stepped inside and closed the door behind her. She was glad to shut out the bustle of nearby Oxford Street and the angry confrontations of the day. She sat near the front and gazed at the richly gilded altarpiece, the blue sky and golden stars of the heavens painted in the vault above. Just for a moment, she allowed herself to relax.

Despite the peace, the church was not completely silent. Behind her, at the rear of the nave, rhythmic breathing rose and fell, breaking into an occasional snuffle or snore. She twisted around in her seat. The back rows of chairs were occupied by comatose bodies in sleeping bags. Plastic bags stuffed with belongings served as pillows, kept protectively close. The church had become a sanctuary for people who needed a roof over their heads, not just for those in need of spiritual shelter.

Remembering Rose's generosity to the homeless man they had seen in Golden Square, Helen felt for her purse. Quietly, not wanting to wake anyone, she placed a couple of pounds beside each of the sleeping men. Not much, but enough for a cup of tea. I can't help everyone, she remembered Rose saying. But I can help one person.

One of the men opened his eyes.

'What's the matter?' he asked.

'Nothing.' Helen blushed. 'Don't worry.'

He sat up, saw the coins. 'Was that you?'

She nodded. 'I hope you don't mind…'

He laughed. 'I don't mind, love. But you shouldn't waste your money on those other bastards.' He took the coins in his fist, rolled on his side and went back to sleep.

'Hello!' An athletic-looking figure in jeans and flannel shirt stood at the altar rail, his smile wide. 'You've met our guests, then.' His voice had an east London rasp. Only his dog collar gave away his profession.

Surprised, Helen hurried to meet him.

'Father John? I'm Helen Oddfellow. Thank you for agreeing to see me.' She'd expected a middle-aged or even elderly priest, not this young man in his casual clothes.

He shook her hand, his grasp warm and firm. 'No worries. It's always good to meet someone with an interest in the church. Let's go through.'

They sat at a plain table in the parish room that adjoined the church, its whitewashed walls something of a relief after the visual overload of the church itself. Helen took from her bag a transcript of the Rossetti poem they had discovered in the Manchester archive.

'It was on the back of a letter from Maria Rossetti to the

art dealer Charles Howell,' Helen told him. 'It needs to be properly authenticated, but it seems to be by Christina Rossetti. And I wondered if it meant anything to you? Given their connection to All Saints.'

The priest took his glasses from his shirt pocket and read. '"Never lived to see the light." How sad. So many babies died at birth. And so many women, too.'

'It's the second stanza that I'd like your opinion about particularly,' said Helen. She leaned forward as he read the words.

*'Where shall I keep you? Where none look.*
*What keeps my soul safe? My prayer book.*
*Where does a bird sing? High on a perch.*
*Where should I seek you? Inside the church.'*

His eyes crinkled as he smiled and tipped back his chair. 'So you think that what you're seeking could be inside this church?'

Helen sighed. 'It's a long shot, I know. But this was the church that the Rossetti sisters attended. I thought it was at least worth asking if you knew of anything here associated with them. Anything hidden. I don't know.'

Crispin had been insistent she should visit, after seeing the poem. Barbara had been more sceptical. She'd suggested Helen take a quick trip while she went through the slides one last time before the presentation.

'They did, that's true,' said Father John. 'But the church was completely restored ten years ago. I'm pretty sure there was nothing hidden on perches or behind panels. Everything was taken apart and thoroughly investigated. And the convent moved to Oxford decades ago. I suppose you could get in touch with them. They might have something in the library.

That's where the convent records are held.'

'Of course. I'll do that. But thanks for taking the time to meet me. It's been lovely to see the church.' Helen was disappointed, but not surprised. She pushed back her chair.

'Wait a second.' The priest put his hand on her arm. 'I've been thinking, since you called yesterday. There is something it might be worth you taking a look at.'

He stood and walked to the back of the room.

'Now. There's a small cupboard at the back of the Lady Chapel. It was used to keep hymn books, orders of service, that sort of thing. A bit out of date, so we never used them. We emptied it out, during the restoration.'

He knelt beside a table covered with a green cloth.

'Here, help me with this.'

Together they pulled out a black-painted metal chest and lifted it on to the table. Father John took out a set of keys and unlocked it.

'This is the contents of that cupboard. I've had a quick look over the years. I was meaning to chuck most of it out, but I'm always so busy. I never quite got around to it. I did find one book, though, that you might like to see.'

The box was crammed full of faded copies of *Hymns Ancient and Modern*, their green and red cloth showing the use of many years. They lifted them out. At the bottom was a cardboard folder. Pencilled into the top corner, the word 'Rossetti?'.

Helen glanced at the priest. He nodded and smiled. 'Go ahead.'

She drew out a small book, covered in soft green leather. '*Book of Common Prayer*,' read the gilt letters on the front, with a cross above the words. The book was closed with an ornate clasp. Holding her breath, she opened it.

'C. G. Rossetti,' read the faded ink script in the top right-hand corner of the title page. Helen noted the use of the long s in Rossetti, the same as in Christina's signature on the poem.

'Wow,' she said. She smiled at the priest. 'I'm surprised you've not had it valued, or sold it. It's probably worth quite a lot to Rossetti scholars.'

'Ah, well.' He shrugged. 'That would be a shame, wouldn't it? To take it away from the church, where she left it.'

Helen's mind raced. This must be the prayer book that Christina wrote about in the poem. It had been kept inside the church, in the Lady Chapel. Carefully, she flipped through the pages. The book had been well-used; the paper was soft and the corners rounded and furred. She inhaled the soothing smell of old book: a rich, earthy scent that reminded her of chocolate. But no scraps of paper, no sketches or verses fell out of the leaves.

'Do you think it's what you were looking for?' asked Father John.

'Maybe. But there should be something else.'

She examined the binding at the front and back of the book. There were no signs that it had been tampered with.

She closed the book and turned it in her hands again. Engraved on the leather spine was a tiny gilt picture of a bird perched on a twig, its beak open.

'"Where does a bird sing? High on a perch." This has to be it. There has to be something here.'

There was a gentle rap on the door.

'Visitor for you, Father John,' said a matronly lady in an apron.

'Ah, that'll be your friend from Manchester,' said the priest.

Helen leaped to her feet, the book still in her hand. 'My

friend?'

Father John looked puzzled. 'Maybe I misunderstood. Michael something, from Salford University? He rang yesterday, said he'd been researching Christina Rossetti with you in Manchester. He asked if I knew when you were planning to visit, so he could come and help.'

A door at the end of the room opened and the red-haired man from the library walked through. Helen sprinted for the door back into the church.

'Wait!' he shouted. 'It's not what you think!'

She paused, looked from him to the priest. Was this a set-up?

'I wanted to warn you,' said Michael. 'I was worried about you.'

She paused, realised she was still clutching Christina Rossetti's prayer book. The priest stood between them. Could she trust him? Could she trust either of them?

'Helen, do you know about Rintrah the Reprobate?' asked Michael.

She turned her back to the door, fingers touching the handle. Was this him? The man who'd made vile drawings of Oona being abused, horrible cartoons of women being tortured? The one who'd drawn Helen herself, hanging from a tree? He looked so ordinary. Friendly. She'd liked him. Trust no-one, her gut told her. She'd been wrong about friendly men before.

'Who are you?' she asked. 'Are you Rintrah?'

# Chapter 50

'God, no. I promise you, I don't think like that.'

Michael sat on the edge of the table.

'I didn't mean to scare you. But if you've seen the blog, you'll know there are people out there who have it in for people like you.'

'Women,' said Helen, flatly. 'We're half the human race.'

'Helen…' The priest was looking nervously at the prayer book, she realised.

'Who is this man?' she asked him. 'Why did you tell him I was coming?'

He sighed. 'I thought you knew each other. He said he wanted to help with whatever you discovered. I'm sorry. I didn't know you'd be upset.'

Helen wondered. Not all priests were trustworthy.

Michael spoke again. 'Helen, this man, Rintrah… he has a lot of followers. There are hundreds of them. I was contacted. Asked to find out what you were doing. There's going to be something big, an attack of some sort.'

'Then you should talk to the police,' said Helen.

'I have. They said they were aware of the situation. But I was worried for you, so I contacted Father John here. I thought perhaps you'd come, after I told you about the church.

And I took a train down, to tell you myself. And to help you. You've found something, haven't you? It needs protecting.'

He glanced at the book in her hand. His smile was ever so slightly forced. She stared at him, his round face and his easy manner. He met her eye boldly, his expression earnest. No, she thought. You're lying.

'I think I should go,' she said. She looked uncertainly at the prayer book. Was it safe to leave it with Father John? Now that she'd found it, she really wanted to unpack its secrets.

She appealed to the priest. 'Look... you know who I am. You know where to find me. Will you let me borrow this book, just for a day or two? I promise it won't come to any harm. I'll bring it back as soon as I can.'

He looked unhappy. 'I would, Helen. But it's not really mine. I don't know...'

Helen's hand closed around the metal of the door handle. Slowly, she turned it. Then she pulled the door open and fled through the church.

Behind her, she heard Michael shout and start to run. She turned, saw Father John rugby-tackle him. The two men went crashing to the ground. She paused.

'Go!' The man she'd given money to was on his feet, running to help the priest. 'I'll deal with this. No-one hurts Father John when I'm around.'

Helen waited no longer, ran through the courtyard and into the street. She crossed, heedless of lorries beeping their horns, and swerved down a narrow passageway. If he tried to follow, she'd make it bloody difficult. She raced down the passage, emerged on an unfamiliar street and randomly turned right. At the next junction, she glimpsed crowds of people and busy shops, and ran towards them. She emerged on to Oxford Street as a bus was about to pull away from the kerb. Making one last effort, she lunged for the platform just as the doors closed.

Red-faced and breathless, she climbed to the top deck and sat down. She looked in some disbelief at the book she had purloined from the church. What was she thinking of? And where was she taking it?

She looked at the destination display of the bus: Kennington via Parliament Square. Right then, she thought. We're going to see Barbara.

# Chapter 51

'**B**limey. What happened to you?'

Helen was sweating, having run all the way from Westminster Bridge. She'd been terrified that the police milling around the Houses of Parliament might have been tipped off about a woman who had stolen a valuable antique book from a church.

She collapsed into an armchair and pulled the book from her rucksack.

'Never mind. I think I've got it. Christina Rossetti's prayer book. It was kept in the church.'

'Wow.' Barbara grabbed her reading glasses. 'They let you take it?'

'Um. Sort of.' She caught Barbara's disapproving glance and started to giggle. 'Sorry. It's not funny. I sort of... I sort of took it.'

She tried to explain how she'd panicked when the man from Manchester had appeared.

'I couldn't believe he'd followed me. And I'd just found the book, and I didn't want to leave it where he could see. So I legged it.'

Barbara groaned. 'You idiot. You'll get arrested.'

'I know,' said Helen. 'I'll phone the priest later. He was a bit busy when I left. But let's investigate it first. Here, look at this picture on the spine. I think it's the publisher's logo.'

'A bird, singing on a perch. Like in the poem?'

'Exactly.' Helen opened the book wide and squinted, looking into the narrow gap that opened up at the spine. 'There must be something in it. A message, or a paper or something.'

'Hang on a second.' Barbara brought her capacious make-up bag through from the bedroom and fished around in it, emerging triumphantly with a pair of eyebrow tweezers. 'Here you go.'

Helen took the implement, felt for a moment along the spine, then grasped an edge of folded paper. Gently, in case she was damaging part of the book, she started to pull.

The paper slid slowly out, folded in concertina fashion to fit into the space behind the binding of the spine. Holding her breath, she smoothed the page flat. She could see a sketch and some scribbled lines of verse. She hesitated a moment, then turned it around for Barbara to see.

'Go on. Tell me what it says.'

Barbara began to read.

'*I am not yet born*
*What shall I call thee?*
*I joyful am*
*Joy is my name*
*Sweet joy befall thee!*'

This was it, then. The first draft of *Infant Joy* – a few changes, but clearly the same poem.

'Amazing,' Helen said. 'Let me see.'

She gazed at the lettering. One thing was immediately apparent. The verse was written in two hands, the lines alternating between them. The handwriting of the first line she recognised – Blake's clear, confident script, familiar from his engraved poems. The other hand was more hesitant, the letters larger and a little shaky. The c of the word call in the second line was reversed. With a thrill, Helen remembered reading that Catherine had reversed the C in her name when signing a letter written by Blake on her behalf. A common mistake when people first learn to write.

'So you were half-right. They wrote it together,' said Helen. 'It's a joint production.' Question and answer, like Christina Rossetti's poem. Call and response. Two minds working closely together, William and Catherine Blake looking ahead to the joyful joint production of a child.

'Look at the drawing,' said Barbara, a catch in her voice.

Delicate pencil lines outlined a woman's arms, cradling a swaddled infant, the child's eyes closed and a tightly furled rosebud tucked into the clothing. The drawing was full of tenderness.

Helen's eyes were suddenly full of tears. '"I am not yet born". They were looking forward to the birth of a baby,' she said. 'To becoming parents. And that never happened. The baby died.' She felt the pain of it lance into her breast, down the centuries.

'Yeah,' said Barbara. 'Shit, isn't it?'

# Chapter 52

Nick was in the *Noize* news room, being wired up by the head of security. Toby was getting impatient for a story. He had told him about Oona's death, and the suspicions that it could be connected to the Rintrah blogger. Toby was keen on that angle, especially once he'd seen a photograph of Oona. Nick had managed to find a publicity shot that the university theatre company had taken when she played Ophelia in *Hamlet*. She looked suitably tragic in tattered clothing, a crown of weeds on her head.

'Bit of a looker, wasn't she? So this is the one who topped herself in the bath?' asked Toby.

Nick had persuaded him to hold back on running a story until he could firm up Helen's account of the poison-pen letter sent to Oona. It would have much more impact if they could reproduce the letter, and the drawings, at the same time. But Toby was pushing him hard.

'It's been more than two weeks,' he pointed out. 'You still don't know who he is.'

Nick wished Helen would be more forthcoming, but she'd been impossible to get hold of in the last couple of days. When she finally had answered her phone that morning, she'd sounded exhausted and despondent. As far as she knew, the police had made no progress in tracing whoever had sent Oona the letter.

'And nor have I, to be honest. I've spoken to everyone I can think of who might know about it. There was something dodgy going on with Greenwood and the students. But that's as far as I can get, and he's threatening to sue if I take it further. Have you made any progress your end?'

So he'd emailed the man calling himself Rintrah again, pushing for a proper meeting the same day.

'I want to hear more about Oona Sinclair,' he'd written. It was the first time he'd used her name. Risky, perhaps, but it showed he wasn't messing around. That he could join the dots, that he knew about the students and what happened at the university. He'd said that he was willing to help on future operations.

Toby had insisted he record the meeting, so they would have proof before they published their accusations of Rintrah's involvement in Oona's death. Nick hadn't worn a wire before and was secretly quite excited about it.

It was his second assignment of the day. Helen had sent him a press pass for the *Out of the Silence* conference, and he'd gone along for the opening ceremony. He'd seen no sign of the threatened visit by Rintrah Roars' keyboard warriors. The conference centre had been full of women; mostly cheerful-looking girls, some serious older women with short hair. Helen's boss had given the opening speech, turgid stuff about women needing not just a room of their own but a platform of their own. There had been security on the doors; not much, but they were doing bag searches, which was reassuring. He'd promised Helen to go back for her presentation with Barbara tomorrow.

'There you go. Start the recording when you're at the rendezvous, before the guy arrives. Press it once. It takes forty-eight hours of recording, so no worries about running out of space.' The head of security, a big New Zealander who had been a professional rugby player, grinned at him. 'Keep your jacket on. I've taped it to your back, so it shouldn't show under your shirt, but best that he doesn't find it, hey?'

Nick wondered what Rintrah would do if he found out he was being recorded by an undercover journalist. Call the police again? Send him a nasty drawing in the hope he'd top himself? He laughed. He wasn't expecting trouble. They were meeting in a public place. The guy was a lone wolf, and he wouldn't have agreed to a meeting if he'd been suspicious. And Nick had been up against some serious thugs in the past. He didn't think this guy was in the same league.

'Don't worry. I can handle myself,' he said. Toby, the sad sack, nodded approvingly as he picked up his leather jacket and strolled out the door.

They'd agreed an open-air meeting beside the Regent's Canal at Kings Cross. 'Time we had a drink together,' Rintrah had written. 'This one's on me.'

Nick checked his phone; he had plenty of time. Outside, the narrow streets of Soho were busy with early-evening drinkers enjoying the sunshine, spilling out of bars, standing around with pints and wine glasses. Nick moved through the crowd, aware of the recorder snug in the small of his back. He allowed himself a smile of satisfaction. He was a national journalist, working undercover, on his way to a secret rendezvous. What could be cooler than that?

# Chapter 53

He checked his watch. Half an hour before they were due to meet. He pulled on a pair of latex gloves and weighed out two grams of gamma-hydroxybutyric acid from a small tub he kept in the refrigerator. He slid it into a paper envelope, folded it and slipped it into his wallet. It would be enough for the first of his assignations. He had a challenging night ahead.

The caravan was ready. He'd taken the opportunity to go down and make his final preparations the day before, arriving back in the early hours of the morning. He liked driving at night, moving through the darkness sealed in his private capsule, his chosen music blasting through the speakers. It might be a cliché, but he still loved The Doors, still felt the exhilaration of opening up the throttle as the swirl of keyboards and thunder of drums conjured up the storm. He was seventeen again, escaping the stifling suburbs and all they represented. Only this time, he knew where he was going.

He'd awoken to find a new message from the journalist. At first he'd worried that another meeting would mess up his schedule. But the man knew about Oona. Via Helen Oddfellow, Rintrah supposed. Which meant he had to be disposed of, before he could tell anyone else about the connection. It made sense to do it tonight. In fact, it was a good opportunity. Two birds with one stone.

His contact from Manchester had tipped him off that the Oddfellow woman had found something in the library there, although he'd been unsure of its significance. He'd gone to the church in London, tried to intercept her, but lost her. Rintrah was exasperated. People were so incompetent. This was why it was best to act alone. There was no time to visit her flat again. And anyway, she'd be there tomorrow. In the spotlight, ready to be picked off, when he needed her. She could wait. Nick Wilson could not.

He had suggested to the journalist that they meet at the canal basin, newly smartened-up and popular with students, especially in the summer. The informal atmosphere, with plenty of people around, might promote a false sense of security.

His car was in the underground car park. He descended to the garage. There were too many cameras keeping watch over the Porches and Mercedes to risk being seen with Wilson here. He slipped into the anonymous-looking hire car he'd been using for the past week, drove up the ramp and circled the area a couple of times. Finally he found a parking spot on the Kings Cross side of the canal, not far from where he'd rented the car.

He parked and walked to the tow path, sat on a bench and observed the scene opposite. The area was busy with students from the nearby art school, sitting on the deck drinking beer. Wilson had arrived early to their encounter the week before. Was he there already? As he watched, he saw a black guy in a leather jacket walk down to the railing on the opposite bank, turn his back and lean against it, surveying the crowd. He wanted to laugh. Over here, Mister Journalist. I'm behind you.

He strolled over the bridge and went into the canal-side bar. There was a crowd, and he began to worry that it would take too long, that his quarry would give up and leave. But eventually he managed to get served and walked out on to the square with a pint in each hand. The journalist was sitting now, fiddling with his phone. He felt the phone in his own pocket vibrate. He ignored it.

He stood for a moment behind the man, then sat beside him, putting down the drinks.

'Flea. This one's on me,' he said.

The guy jumped, then gave a cocky grin. 'Rintrah the Reprobate, I presume? Good to finally meet you.'

# Chapter 54

The man looked... ordinary. Clean-shaven, white teeth, mousy brown hair in a nondescript style. He was younger than Nick had been expecting: mid-twenties, perhaps. His clothes were ordinary: white T-shirt over blue jeans. He didn't look like a tortured artist, or someone obsessed with William Blake. He looked like an IT support worker from one of the dozens of technology firms that had moved their headquarters to the new office buildings of Kings Cross. His voice was soft, the American accent understated.

'You're from the States?' Nick asked. He was surprised; he'd kind of thought that Blake was a British obsession.

'California. What about you?'

'Liverpool. But I've lived in London for the last five years.'

'Yeah, but...'

Nick sighed. 'Where am I from really? My mum's from the north of Ireland. My dad's from Trinidad. I was born here.' Now was not the time to point out that there had been black people in the UK for centuries, and he was as British as any white person.

'How did you get into Blake?'

Nick remembered what Barbara had told him. 'I liked the

old Marvel comics, when I was a kid. And then I got into Alan Moore's stuff – *Watchmen*, and *From Hell*. Which was pretty freaky. So I started to find out about Blake through that. And found out he's even more freaky.' He grinned. 'How about you?'

The man picked up his pint. 'Yeah, similar trajectory. He's the man.'

Nick raised his glass. 'To William Blake.'

The guy chinked glasses. 'To revolution.'

Nick needed to get him on to the blog, and his plans.

'So, I went along to the feminist writers' conference this morning. You know, to check it out. You said you had something planned? All the feminazis in one place, like you said.'

Rintrah looked sideways at him. 'You went along? And they just let you in?'

Nick shrugged, realised it probably wasn't a good idea to admit he'd had a press pass.

'Yeah. I pretended I was a student.'

'Right. And what are you really, Flea? What's your real name?'

Nick was starting to feel uncomfortable in the heat, a little nauseous. He wished he could take off his leather jacket. He took another gulp of cold beer.

'I'm Nick,' he said. He'd decided to stick with the same first name – common enough not to identify him and easier to remember. 'I work in IT. What about you?'

'Nick from IT.' The man's voice was slightly mocking. 'Welcome to the revolution. What part do you think you'd like to play in it?'

Nick really didn't feel good. He wasn't a big drinker,

certainly not in the daytime. The combination of the sun beating down and the beer was making his head fuzzy.

'I'm up for anything,' he said, his voice coming out a little louder than he'd intended. 'I do kickboxing. I can handle myself all right. Just tell me what you want me to do.'

The man laughed. He still hadn't told him his name, Nick remembered.

'Who are you, anyway?' It came out a bit aggressive. He tried to rein it back in. 'I mean, you know my name. I can't just call you Rintrah.'

'All in good time.' He was smiling, leaning back on the deck as if something had greatly amused him. 'You look hot, Nick. Why don't you take off your jacket?'

He really wanted to. He started to shrug it off, then remembered. 'Nah, I'm all right. Don't want to lose it.' He could feel sweat trickling down his back, the recording device clammy against his skin. His throat felt dry and he took another swig of beer.

'I could do with some water,' he said.

'Of course.' The guy was on his feet, helping Nick up. 'Let's go over the bridge, under the trees. You'll feel better in the shade. I've got a bottle of water in my car over there.'

Nick's feet wouldn't work properly. He was confused. This wasn't meant to be happening. He stumbled over the bridge, leaning on the guy's shoulder. People were staring at him, laughing.

'Too much beer and sun,' the guy told them. 'He'll be fine. Let's get you home, shall we?'

Nick swivelled his head and tried to focus. The man's eyes shone brightly, unnatural in the blurred facial features. Shit. The beer, he realised. There was something in the beer.

'Stop it,' he slurred. 'Help me.' He tried to raise his voice, but found he could not.

'I am helping you, Nick Wilson,' said a soft Californian voice. 'Here, let's get you in the car. I'll take you somewhere nice and quiet, where you can lie down. Wouldn't you like that? Would that be something you could write about in *Noize*?'

# Chapter 55

Helen was at her desk, trying to push aside all the confusion in her head so she could think about the draft of *Infant Joy* and all that it implied.

Tomorrow, she and Barbara were due to take to the stage, in front of hundreds of students, dozens of academics and – if Caroline had her way – a sprinkling of heavyweight arts journalists. She was under no illusions that they would get an easy ride. And they had less than a day to incorporate this major new find into their presentation.

Her previous experience of unveiling a literary discovery told her to expect scepticism, at best. People who had studied a writer their whole lives were not, as one might naïvely expect, delighted to be presented with a surprise new finding. The reactions varied from polite disbelief to outrage, especially when the person doing the discovering was not a bearded professor of many years' standing, but young and female. They would need to be meticulous in not over-stating any of their facts, but also bold in outlining the potential implications.

She looked again at her transcription of the lines. 'I am not yet born.' So it had been written before the baby's birth – if indeed Catherine's pregnancy had lasted that long. That tied

271

in with Christina Rossetti's poem, the infant who never lived to see the light. She remembered the drawing of the babe in arms and her throat tightened.

Helen had privately doubted Barbara's theory that Catherine might have written poetry herself. But the two sets of handwriting, the lines alternating, told its own story. Catherine could have been writing at her husband's dictation, she supposed. But the intimacy of the words suggested a closer collaboration.

She would leave it up to Barbara to decide how much of her theory to advance. The discovery of a new poem by Christina Rossetti and an early draft of a poem by William Blake was more than enough to be getting on with.

She'd left the document with Barbara, who was jittery with nerves about how to keep the precious page safe. They could take it to the British Library after the presentation, Helen suggested, enlist expert help to preserve it, study it and authenticate it as William Blake.

When she got home, she'd called Father John. To her relief, he had not reported her to the police for the theft of the book. He'd sounded bemused, but accepted her embarrassed promise to return it the next day.

'I trust you. And I'm sorry. The man – he got away. Although he might have taken a few bruises home with him,' he admitted. 'Your friend who sleeps in the church was quite enthusiastic in coming to my aid.'

'Is that how a priest is meant to behave?' asked Helen, laughing.

'Not really,' he admitted. 'Is that how a researcher is meant to behave?'

'I suppose we're quits,' Helen had agreed.

She picked up her phone again. It was gone ten. Was it too late to call Barbara? She guessed her friend would still be working on the presentation.

She noticed a text message from Rose, which had been sent half an hour earlier. Swiftly she clicked it open.

'I've got one of those letters,' the message read. 'Like the one Oona had. I'm scared.'

Helen had not told her of her own letter. She opened the image attached to the message.

At first she thought it was beautiful. It was a painting of a rose, petals delicately tinted in pinks and greens, violet and apricot. In the centre, a woman's body. Opened up, like the rose petals, her knees and arms spread wide, displaying her breasts, her arse. Her head, flung back as if in ecstasy, her mouth open wide. Her hair, with its rainbow colours, spread around her head like a halo. It was, without doubt, a portrait of Rose.

She looked more closely at the intricate drawing. Crawling into the corner of the girl's mouth, a pale worm. Another, making its way around the mound of a breast, latching on to the nipple. Shuddering, she saw more worms, crawling into the vagina, the anus. Thorns twined around the figure's wrists and ankles, tethering her in place, the vegetation questing up her limbs, scrolling into the margins.

Christ, thought Helen. This is the worst yet.

She read the inscription at the top of the page, in black ink script: 'O Rose thou art sick.' She knew the poem well: Blake's sinister lines about 'the invisible worm that flies in the night' and how 'his dark secret love does thy life destroy'.

She'd seen enough. She called Rose's number, remembering with fear how she'd ignored Oona's email just days earlier.

She prayed it would be answered.

'Hi, Helen.'

'Thank goodness.' Helen had never been so pleased to hear her voice. 'Rose, are you OK? What a horrible thing.'

'Yeah, it freaked me out a bit.'

'Do you want to come over?'

'No, I'm fine now. Honestly. It just scared me a bit.'

'Where was the letter?'

'In my pigeonhole. There was no stamp or anything, so someone must have put it in by hand,' she said.

'OK.' Same as her own letter, then. Helen was thinking. 'There must be CCTV in the student residences, right? Or at least someone on the reception desk. So we must be able to find out who put it there. Maybe I should come over. We could talk to the security people together.'

'Yeah, maybe tomorrow?' Rose's voice was sheepish. 'I'm a bit tired now. I thought I'd get an early night.'

Was there someone with her? Helen wondered. Perhaps she'd called a friend, or a boyfriend. Deepak, she supposed.

'All right. Let me know if you change your mind. Sleep well.'

She clicked her phone off. Maybe she should take Rose's advice, get an early night too. She could get up early and work on the presentation. Tomorrow was going to be a tough day.

# Chapter 56

Helen flashed her staff card at the man on the security desk.

Half an hour after speaking to Rose, she'd called her again, troubled by the gruesome image of the letter. The call went straight to voicemail.

She tried to keep calm. Rose had said she was going to sleep. Maybe it would be better to wait until the morning. But Helen was rubbish at waiting around. The text messages, the horrible letter, made her think of Oona's death. She'd arrived too late that morning. Perhaps, she thought, this was a second chance.

The security guard raised an eyebrow. 'Bit late for visitors,' he remarked.

'I'm her tutor. I had a message from her... she was worried about something. I wanted to check that she's all right.'

He sighed and waved her through. Helen ran up the stairs, trying to push away her memories of finding Oona. She marched along the corridor, hoping Rose wouldn't be too annoyed at being woken up.

There was no answer to her knock.

'Rose? Can you hear me?' she called. 'It's Helen. I wanted to check you're OK.'

The door next to Rose's opened. A tousle-haired girl looked out.

'What's happening?'

'I'm looking for Rose,' said Helen. 'Have you seen her?'

The girl shook her head. 'I heard water running, though. Maybe she's in the bath.'

She retreated into her room.

Helen knelt, looking for light. Water soaked through her jeans. The carpet was wet, water oozing out from under the pale wooden door.

She ran down the stairs to the security guard. 'Quick. There's no answer, but there's water coming from under the door. We need to get in and see if she's OK.'

Sighing, the man followed her.

'These girls. No sense of responsibility.'

Helen hurried him along the corridor. He held an electronic fob against the door, and the lock clicked.

Rose's bedroom was chaotically messy. The door to the bathroom was open, the bath overflowing, water seeping across the floor. But the bath was mercifully empty of Rose. The security guard rushed to turn off the taps.

'That's a new carpet, you know.' He disappeared, muttering about getting a mop.

Helen slowly let out her breath. The image that had flashed through her mind was still vivid. Rose, her wrists slashed, blood pouring into the water. The sick panic that she might have come too late, again.

Still shaking, she sat on the edge of the bed. Where was Rose? Had she simply gone out, left the bath running and forgotten about it? The room was damp and warm, steam rising from the sodden carpet. Helen could smell the over-sweet scent of Rose's perfume. The room felt freshly vacated, the girl's presence still strong.

Brightly coloured clothes were piled high on the armchair. The bed was stripped bare, with a pile of fresh bedding laid out as if Rose had been about to make it up. On the desk were a few used mugs, a handful of crumpled tissues. Above it, a collage of printed-out photographs, mainly Rose with her arms around her friends, their goofy smiles breaking Helen's heart with their innocence. One showed Rose cheek to cheek with Deepak. She'd scribbled biro all over his face.

Bloody Deepak. Helen wondered if he had anything to do with Rose's disappearance.

The security man came back with a mop. He looked over Helen's shoulders at the photographs.

'That one!' he exclaimed. 'She's been in and out all evening. Ants in her pants. She must have forgotten she'd turned on the taps.'

'Rose went out? What time? Did she say where she was going?'

He sucked his teeth. 'Let me see. She came in, and then she came back down again five minutes later, asking about who had been in and out, and whether anyone had left a note in her pigeonhole. Which I couldn't tell her, because of data protection.' He meditated a moment. 'Then she went back up again.'

'And?'

'Then she came down again, not ten minutes after that. She said she was meeting a friend. Not seen her since.'

'And when was that?' Helen asked, trying not to scream with impatience.

He shook his head. 'Dunno. Maybe… half an hour ago?

About half ten, I reckon.' He finished mopping the floor. 'I'll have to report this. It could have been a lot worse.'

He took himself off. You're right, thought Helen. It could have been. But where was Rose now, and why wasn't she answering her phone? She tried it again, with the same result.

Feeling guilty, Helen started to look around the room. On the bedside table she saw a thick cream-coloured envelope, like the one that had been delivered to her door. Rose had texted her the photograph, so perhaps she wouldn't mind if she looked at it. She opened it, found the obscene image, carefully drawn in pen and ink, washed with watercolour. And the sinister words from Blake's poem.

'Join with me and you will be cured of sickness,' read a message at the bottom of the page. But who was me? And which friend would Rose have gone to meet? she wondered. Outside of the tutorial group, Helen didn't know Rose's friends. Not Liz, presumably. Habib, perhaps. Deepak was most likely, she supposed. She knew they'd split up, but Rose had been very keen on him. Would Rose go to meet him late at night, if he called?

She would, Helen suspected. She'd drop everything. Helen pulled out her phone and rang his number. It rang for a long time, with no reply. Maybe the phone was switched to silent. Maybe he was with Rose, and didn't want to be interrupted, especially by his bossy old tutor. Maybe that's why Rose wasn't answering, either.

She stared again at the letter. The artist had Blake's facility with the human figure, the musculature delineated with sure lines, the colours delicate. She thought of the Blake drawing that accompanied his poem *The Sick Rose*. Little white worms, she remembered, crawling along the thorns, disappearing into the heart of the bloom.

The letter decided her. She dialled the number of the officer who had taken her statement after Oona's death. He'd been sceptical, but at least he would understand what had happened. The phone went to voicemail. Helen left a brief message and wondered if that was enough. Rose had gone to meet a friend, barely half an hour previously. And now she and the friend she had presumably gone to meet weren't answering their phones. Helen could imagine the police response.

She could go to Deepak's flat, she supposed. See if Rose was there with him. But then they might have gone out, and anyway, it would seem very creepy for her to turn up on his doorstep. She called both their numbers again, then sent text messages asking them to call her. That, she supposed, was the most she could do. Wearily, she headed home.

# Chapter 57

Petrarch poured himself another whisky. He was drinking the good stuff, now that he knew they could afford it. He'd opened his favourite single malt and worked his way halfway down the bottle. It was almost midnight; he should probably go to bed.

He hadn't confronted Veronica about the money. After her outburst the day before, he'd been avoiding her. But he'd told Brett not to bother coming in. What was the point? Why flog himself to death trying to write the stupid book, when they had enough money for him to retire whenever he wanted?

Retirement. He'd been brooding on that possibility since his discovery of the money. Why not? He was over sixty; many of his peers had taken early retirement years ago. And he'd been shaken by this business with Oona; badly so.

Maybe it was time to admit defeat. He couldn't kid himself that he was a young man anymore; his academic triumphs were clearly behind him. He could no longer see the big picture when he shuffled through his index cards. He lacked the energy, the belief that had driven him fearlessly through Blake's majestic late works, their complex and dense imagery. Now all he could see was confusion.

He'd visited a few of his former colleagues in recent years, scattered among small cathedral cities or quiet seaside resorts. Stacked up in retirement flats with family photos and books they didn't read anymore lining the walls of the little rooms. Sit there and you can look at the sea, one had told him when he'd visited Eastbourne or Bexhill or wherever the hell it was. Sit and look at the sea. You'll be dead soon, Petrarch had thought. The man had been, too; six months later, he'd been diagnosed with prostate cancer, and a year after that he'd died.

Petrarch didn't want to die. He didn't want to sit and look at the sea, or stroll around the cathedral close, listening to the bells of evensong, raising his hat to elderly spinsters. He wanted to wander through London's carnival streets, a peacock attracting admiring glances. He wanted the possibility, intrigue and promise of a Soho night, seeing all the girls and boys dressed in their mating finery, burning brightly. He wanted sex, dammit, and adventure, excitement, love. But he was getting tired. He wasn't sure he was up to another fight with the university authorities.

He'd tried to call Caroline, to explain about the visit from the police. Her assistant, sounding wildly excited, had taken a message. Caroline herself had rung back a few minutes later.

'There's a letter in the post,' she'd said, without preliminary greeting. 'You're suspended, pending a disciplinary investigation into your relationship with Oona Sinclair.'

He'd stammered and blustered, of course. Plausible deniability, unsubstantiated gossip, jealous students with grudges. But he knew the game was up. Once Caroline had decided to cut someone off, they stayed cut off.

'Get yourself a lawyer, Petrarch,' she'd advised. 'Don't think I'll let our friendship influence the outcome.' It would be far easier for everyone, she'd intimated, if he retired promptly, without bringing any more scandal to the department.

The front door opened. Damn it; he'd planned to be in bed before Veronica got home. He heard her kick off her heels, then the door to the study opened.

'Still awake?' She looked animated, her colour higher than usual. She must be having an affair, he thought. He couldn't remember how many years it had been since he'd last seen that look on her face. Perhaps when she went to the Palace to receive her MBE.

'Still awake,' he confirmed. 'Want a drink?' He waved the whisky bottle, hoped he wasn't slurring his words.

She hesitated, then sat down. 'Why not?' She took the bottle from him. 'My, my. Are we celebrating?'

'Should we be?' Maybe now was the time to broach the question of the money. 'How are our shares doing?'

She smiled, a bland smile like a nurse might give to a confused patient. 'We're managing,' she said.

'I'm not going to finish the book,' he said. He hadn't intended to say it; had hardly known he was going to say it until the words were out of his mouth. He felt a huge relief, a burden falling from his back. He leaned back in his chair, flexed his shoulders.

'What?' Her eyes opened wide. Even now, he noticed, her forehead did not crease.

'It's not working, Ronnie. It'll be a dud, even if I kill myself to get it finished. I'll call the publisher in the morning and tell them. And the Beeb, of course.' There was mild regret in that thought. He'd always liked doing telly. He enjoyed all the young people fussing around, making him feel important. But he supposed they wouldn't do it anyway now, not with the suspension and the scandal and everything.

'But you can't.' She sounded petulant, like a child. 'We need the money.'

'Don't be ridiculous,' he said. 'I know, Ron. I've seen the statements in your bureau. And anyway, you'll save on Brett's salary, if I don't need him anymore.'

He caught a flash of guilt in her eyes. Ah, he thought. That's the one, then.

'Nonsense, darling. I have a little money in funds, you know that. But it's not enough for us to live on.'

He sighed. 'Don't treat me like a fool. It's enough for a small army to live on. It's certainly enough for the two of us.'

'But it's not just us!' She pouted like a spoilt child. 'You can never have too much security. And what about David? There will be grandchildren, one day. I want to leave a legacy. What about my charity work?'

He put an arm around her shoulders. 'Don't fret. There's plenty for everyone.'

She wriggled out of his grasp and got to her feet. 'It's my money, Petrarch. Not yours. Don't think you can just take it, like you've taken everything else.'

'Sweetheart, we're married. We share things. Remember?'

'Oh, I remember. I share everything. I share my husband with other women – and men, don't think I don't know about that. And I share my money, my family's money. I share the humiliation when the police come round to ask about dead students, and when your little girls come here begging to see you, and when your colleagues look at me with pity. Maybe I've had enough of sharing.'

'Maybe you should consider sharing your bed more often,' he called to her retreating back. 'Maybe then I wouldn't need to look elsewhere.'

She froze in the doorway and whipped around. 'Screw you, Petrarch. You've been shagging around since the day we met. Why would I want you in my bed, grubby and diseased from all those students you've coerced into yours? Look at yourself. A fat old man, useless and disgraced. A has-been. And I hear you're about to be sacked. Give me one good reason why I should stay with you.' She held his shocked gaze for a moment, then smiled her thin, contemptuous smile. 'No, I can't think of one, either.' She closed the door behind her.

Petrarch was sweating. Fat old man. Grubby and diseased. She hated him, he realised. Real deep-down loathing. This wasn't the accumulated irritation of a long marriage, where you reached a point of acceptance of each other's differences and simply rubbed along. This was visceral.

Would she leave him? The way she'd put it, there was precious little reason why not. She didn't need him for money. The prestige his position had once offered had gone. He'd just admitted to her that his grand project, the book that would cement his academic reputation and make a star of him for a new generation, was doomed.

And if she did leave, what would he do? He couldn't afford to live in this place on his own. The bank statements had made that clear – Veronica hadn't been lying about the astronomical service charge. But he couldn't bear the thought of living anywhere else, of moving away from this sumptuous palace, right in the heart of the city. A little flat in a dreary seaside town, he thought. He shuddered, imagining Veronica settling him in a chair, a blanket over his knees, by a window. Sit there and look at the sea.

He poured himself another whisky. Over my dead body, he

swore.

# Chapter 58

J ust after three o'clock, Helen stopped trying to sleep. Whenever she slipped into unconsciousness, the dream came for her again. Each time, she woke in a clutch of panic.

The dream always followed the same pattern, although the faces changed. The hand reaching for hers, desperate for help. For half a second she was paralysed, unable to grasp it. Then the scream, and the fall. Often, the face was Richard's. Sometimes, weirdly, the face belonged to her father, or her sister. Tonight, she saw Rose's face, turned to her in terror. And yet again, she was too late to prevent disaster.

She sat up in bed, switched on the light and waited for her panicky heartbeat to slow. Tea, she decided. And once she'd got up and made a cup, she knew she wouldn't get back to sleep. She saw again Rose's overflowing bath; relived the awful moment when she expected to see another dead girl, arms floating in the water. She checked her phone again; no message from Rose, or Deepak. But why would there be, at this time of the night?

Trying to distract herself, she sat at her desk and reviewed the slides that Barbara had sent over for the presentation. It was good: a careful balance of newly discovered facts, bold theory and academic caution. She hoped it would be well-received by the audience.

Too restless to concentrate, she shut down the computer and focused on the noises of the house. Since the arrival of the letter, she'd become more nervous, listening for footsteps on the communal stairs, keys in locks.

She stood at the window and scanned the street outside. Was there someone out there, watching her flat? She saw the cars passing to and fro, into and out of the city. The noise of the traffic was so familiar she barely noticed it anymore. A fox was nosing about the pile of bin-bags outside the chicken shop across the road. It seized something in its jaws and trotted away, taking fried chicken back to a family of cubs.

She opened the window. The air was warm and still, almost windless. Helen thought again of Rose, out there somewhere in the London night. With Deepak, perhaps. Or back in her room, asleep. She'd call her first thing in the morning. And if she couldn't get hold of her then, she'd call the police.

Helen pulled on jeans, jersey and walking boots. There was only one cure for insomnia. She grabbed a jacket and let herself out of the flat. If someone was watching, let them show themselves.

Outside, the night was as quiet as it got in London. Cars swished past, food deliveries and taxicabs servicing the nighttime needs of the city. She paused on the pavement, looking for the fox. She caught a glimpse of a ragged tail, whisking around the corner of the building, and followed.

The animal led her towards the river, past the fancy new apartment blocks that had been built on Deptford's waterfront. She breathed in the river's dank exudation, listened to the slap of the water against the embankment wall. It was high tide. The river swirled uncertainly in eddies, troubled as it tried to decide which way to go. Helen sympathised.

She turned left, heading upstream towards the city. The fox disappeared, finding more pressing business in a small children's playground slotted between the housing blocks.

Helen swung along easily, her shoulders relaxing as she got into her stride. She felt safe on the move, out in the open. Only in confined spaces did the claustrophobia know where to find her. She thought again about moving. She loved the area, the historical heart of Greenwich and the remains of the Deptford dockyards, and she'd always loved her little flat. During the day, when she could see the treetops and the sky, it was fine. But at night, the walls started to close in and she heard footsteps in the creaking of the old house.

'Why not move back to Bromley?' her sister had asked. 'You could get a decent two-bed flat, or even a semi-detached house. It's much better value for money.' Helen grimaced. They'd grown up in the dormitory town, with its identikit high street and uninspiring rows of 1930s-built houses. Her sister was queen of the suburbs, with her immaculate four-bedroom house and two children. It was fine, but it was everything Helen had tried to escape. One thing was certain: if she did move, it would not be to live closer to her sister.

If her contract was renewed, maybe she could afford to move somewhere near the university. She thought for a moment of Petrarch's opulent apartment in Bloomsbury; Deepak's palatial residence where she hoped Rose was tucked up, asleep. But there were smaller flats among the mansion blocks of Euston Road and the converted warehouses of Kings Cross. Further north, maybe, up to Camden and Somerstown.

She frowned. She was a south London girl. Moving to north London would feel like a betrayal. And who would look after Crispin, if she moved?

She paused and gazed north across the river. The tide had turned now, the flow moving smoothly downstream. Both sides of the great waterway were lined with expensive housing, the richer citizens of London clamouring to live next to the Thames, where they had once shunned its stink and the dirty trades that fed it. Helen would be loath to live too far from the river. Where would she go, when the walls closed in and she couldn't sleep at night?

She moved on, passing like a ghost among the converted warehouses of Rotherhithe with its ancient church, along the riverside path to Bermondsey. Her feet ached and she was thirsty. As Tower Bridge loomed into sight, lit up like a funfair, she turned inland towards the all-night café on Tooley Street, a familiar haunt that had offered shelter to her night-wanderings before.

It was an old-fashioned greasy spoon servicing taxi drivers and delivery guys, early-starting labourers and night shift workers on their way home. She smiled at the heavy-eyed Turkish owner as he wiped down the Formica tables and set out condiments, then took her mug of brick-red tea to a seat in the window. The sky was pearl-grey above the street lamps. At half-past five, the city was waking up.

She checked her phone. No message from Rose, nothing from Deepak. One email from Nick, sent the previous afternoon. He'd set up another meeting with the man who wrote the Rintrah blog. Helen wondered if he'd showed up this time. Presumably, if there was news, Nick would have called her afterwards.

There was an email from a university in Ontario wanting her to speak at its Elizabethan Drama festival. The Blake Study Group newsletter, which announced a competition for a frontispiece design to accompany a new edition of *Songs of Innocence and Experience*. She thought of the Rintrah images, and shuddered.

She'd told the police about the letters, and their similarity to the comic strip posted on the Rintrah blog. Maybe she should take another look at the blog. Carefully she navigated her way to the page that Nick had shown them.

To her alarm, her phone started playing music at her. She recognised it – The Doors' gloomy anthem, *The End*. She rolled her eyes, remembered Barbara telling her that the sixties rock band was one of many in the counterculture influenced by William Blake. So far, so adolescent. She slotted in her headphones, to avoid disturbing the other customers.

There was a new post, a comic strip, dated the previous day. 'The End,' said the ornate capitals at the top. Below, a Blake-like serpent coiled across the page, children seated on its back, one holding a set of reins attached to the monster's jaws. Riding the snake, she thought, as Jim Morrison's hypnotic voice urged his audience to do exactly that.

The first image underneath the title scroll seized her attention. It was from the poem Barbara had shown her, *Visions of the Daughters of Albion*. A man and a woman, bound back to back. They were sitting on a rocky beach, with the sea behind them. Looming over them was the monstrous figure of Rintrah the Reprobate, head thrown back, laughing.

The woman's hair was tinted in soft rainbow colours, and her body was gently pink. His skin was dark, black hair cropped close to his head. Helen felt sick. The woman in the image, bound and weeping, was Rose. And the male figure was Nick.

She scrolled through the rest of the images. The picture of the bound couple was the first of four. In the second, the figures of Rose and Nick were positioned on their knees, hands clasped as they begged for forgiveness before the scaly creature.

'The children of Albion bewail their transgressions,' read the text beneath it. 'They offer themselves to Rintrah to purge the world of sin, which is energy.'

In the third, the monster whipped the man, who was tied to a tree. The woman tore her hair and wept. In the background, incongruous, was a sketch of a picture-book cottage, complete with thatched roof and tiny windows.

'Rintrah roars and shakes his fires in the burdened air,' the text read.

The final picture was stranger still. The woman and the monster appeared together, surrounded by flames that radiated from them as in a sunburst. At the margins, faces of women emerged from dark clouds, contorted with fear or pain, their mouths open and shrieking. Four words appeared beneath the drawing:

'We shall build Jerusalem.'

The music drew to a close. 'That's all, folks!' said a jaunty voice, seemingly lifted from a cartoon network. 'Tune back in for the grand finale, streaming live at fourteen-hundred hours on Friday May twenty-second.'

Helen set the phone down on the table, trembling. What in God's name was this? And where the hell were Rose and Nick?

She took a gulp of cold tea, mind racing through the

possibilities. She had to go to the police. But would they understand the threat, would they believe her? She could at least report them missing. She checked the time: six o'clock.

She snatched up her phone and called first Rose, then Nick, hoping against hope that they would reply, that the blog images were just an idle threat, a nasty fantasy. Both phones went straight to voicemail. She left a message on each, trying to keep her voice calm. She rang Deepak's number, then suddenly remembered him telling her the previous day that he'd lost his phone. In which case, how could he have called Rose?

Damn. If Rose was not with Deepak, where was she? Definitely time for the police. She began with the number of the officer she'd called the previous night. Again, it went to voicemail. She left another message, then searched in her wallet for the card of PC Maggie Lambert, the woman who'd looked after them when she and Rose had found Oona's body. Mercifully, she picked up.

'Hi. Yes, of course I remember,' she said. Helen was relieved not to have to explain who she was from the beginning.

'I can't find Rose. She left her room last night, about ten-thirty. And I'm worried that something has happened to her.'

Helen outlined the circumstances as well as she could. She tried to describe the letter Rose had been sent, similar to the one that Oona had received days before her death.

'I've got a photo of it. I can send it over.'

'So what was it – some kind of poison-pen letter?'

'Sort of. But the blog – I told your colleague about it, a sort of comic-book thing? I've just looked and there's another series of pictures on it, and they suggest Rose is being imprisoned somewhere,' said Helen. She was trying to keep her voice low, knowing how mad she sounded. And how did she begin to explain Nick and his potential involvement?

She shot a glance at the café owner, propped up on the counter immersed in his own phone. He didn't seem to be taking any notice.

'Can you send me a link to the website? And forward me the photo of the letter sent to Rose?' The woman's voice was polite, but Helen wondered if she either believed her or understood what she was talking about. 'I'll put in a missing person report about Rose. I'm about to go off shift, but I'll make sure this gets to the people who need it. To be honest, though, Dr Oddfellow, if she was last seen going to meet a friend – and you think it might be this Deepak Sinha – then that is the most likely explanation.'

Helen sighed. 'I know. But he told me he'd lost his phone. It doesn't feel right to me.' How to explain the dread that came over her when she looked at the images on her phone, the fear of what they might represent?

'Tell you what, I'll swing by Mr Sinha's apartment on my way home, to check whether she's there,' the woman offered. 'And if she's still AWOL, we'll know to start looking.'

Helen thanked her and ended the call. What now? She felt a wave of tiredness. She could go home and grab an hour's sleep, she supposed, but it barely seemed worth it. She'd have to fight her way through the gathering commuter crowds, try to sleep over the noise from the morning lorries, then turn around for the journey back to work.

She checked the time again. There was one person who would understand the images on Rintrah's blog, she thought. And she wasn't far away.

# Chapter 59

Barbara buzzed Helen into the Hercules Road flat, bleary-eyed without her make-up.

'I couldn't sleep,' she said. 'Not until after three, anyway. I can't believe it's today. I can't believe I'm doing it at all. You're going to have to carry me on to the stage. I don't think my legs will hold me up.'

She poured Helen a coffee and lit herself a cigarette.

'It'll be all right,' said Helen, automatically. The presentation seemed almost irrelevant, a whole world away from the nightmares she had uncovered.

She pulled out her phone. 'I need to show you something. I can't find Rose. She'd had one of those letters, like the ones Oona and I were sent. And then I looked on the Rintrah blog, and found this.' She held out the little screen to Barbara.

'Wait. I can't see properly. I haven't got my contact lenses in.' Barbara opened her battered laptop and navigated to the website. 'Jesus.' She peered at the images through heavy black-framed glasses. 'What the hell is all this about?' She turned off the sound.

Helen sighed and sat down, warming her hands on the coffee mug. 'I hoped you might be able to tell me. I've talked to the police. I'm worried that Rose has been kidnapped or something. That she's being imprisoned somewhere, like in the drawings. And look. Isn't that meant to be Nick?'

Just saying the words out loud made them sound ridiculous. She waited for Barbara to tell her so.

'God, Helen.' Barbara was scrolling through the images. 'These are sick. Is this what Rose was sent?'

'No. Although that was bad enough. Rintrah doesn't seem to have posted it, but Rose sent me a photo. Here.' She showed Barbara the image on her phone.

Barbara looked. '*The Sick Rose*. This is crazy. Really nasty stuff. Whoever is doing this is really twisted.' She read the text. '"Join me and you will be cured of sickness." What's he planning?'

Helen shook her head. 'I know. I'm scared. He says at the end of the music to tune back in this afternoon.' She looked more closely at the images, easier to see on Barbara's laptop than her phone. 'I was hoping we could work out where they were. The policewoman I spoke to said she'd check out Deepak's flat, in case Rose was there. But I've got a nasty feeling about it. I don't think this is just some sick fantasy in his imagination, do you?'

Barbara stubbed out her cigarette, grabbed her book of Blake's illustrated poems, and sat next to Helen.

'Let's take a proper look, then.' She enlarged the image on the screen and zoomed in on the first frame. 'OK. This is fairly familiar. It's the second plate from *Visions of the Daughters of Albion*. We looked at it before, remember? Bromion and Oothoon bound back to back, with the jealous Theotorman weeping next to them. But the rainbow hair suggests Oothoon is Rose, and we think Nick could be Bromion? Why Nick, by the way? I didn't think they'd met.'

Helen sighed. 'He was setting up another meeting. Yesterday evening. And now I can't get hold of him.'

Barbara looked more closely at the first image. 'The background is the sea, with a blood-red sun or moon, similar to Blake's image. But Rintrah is not in despair, as Theotorman was; he's looming over them, laughing. He's not jealous of them, he's rejoicing in their captivity.'

She looked at the second image. 'The man and woman pleading look like they are taken from Blake's image of Adam and Eve discovering the corpse of Abel. Then Rintrah again – and this time he has the sword.' She looked more closely. 'Also the bowl, from the *Ghost of a Flea* painting. Suggesting he is ready to shed blood and collect it.'

She turned to the next image, the man suspended from a tree while Rintrah whipped him.

'God! Look at that, Helen!'

Helen wrinkled her nose. 'I know, it's horrible. Do you know where it comes from?'

'Not the whipping. I don't remember anything in Blake about people being whipped.' Barbara thought for a minute. 'Maybe one. From illustrations to a book about a slave colony. But look at the background. The cottage?' She grabbed the book again and started flipping through the pages.

Helen stared at the sketch of the cottage by the sea, behind the contorted figures.

'This? Is this a real place, then?'

'Look.' Barbara heaved the book on to her friend's lap. 'Here it is. Halfway through *Jerusalem*, for no reason I can fathom, and I've seen no-one come up with a reason for why it should be here.'

Helen looked. The exact same cottage, with a broad lawn

before it and the sea behind, little windows and a thatched roof. An angel hovered over it. Underneath, in Blake's neat writing: 'Blake's cottage at Felpham.'

'Where's Felpham?' she asked.

Ten minutes later, she was looking up trains from Waterloo to Chichester. Felpham was the seaside village where Blake and his wife had lived for two years. Some of his most eccentric works, including his epic poem *Jerusalem*, were written at Felpham. The cottage they had rented still stood, Barbara said, and had been bought by the Blake Society, who were in the process of renovating it. The once-isolated village was now a suburb of Bognor Regis, popular with holidaying families and retired couples.

'He's taken them there,' said Helen. 'Why else would the cottage be in that picture? And the sea is the background of the first picture. They must be in the cottage.'

'They can't be,' insisted Barbara. 'It's not rented out, or open to the public. And he might just have thrown that in as a random image, like Blake did in *Jerusalem*.'

Helen pointed to the text under the final image. '"We shall build Jerusalem". And Blake did build Jerusalem there, didn't he? He wrote it in Felpham. It's all pointing the same way. I need to go there.'

'But you can't go!' wailed Barbara. 'There isn't time. Tell the police, for goodness' sake. You can't go yourself. We're on at two. You'll never get back in time.'

Helen looked up from her phone. 'Yes, I will. There's a train at ten past seven. It gets in at nine. I can get a cab to Felpham from Chichester Station. Plenty of time to look around and get the train back at quarter to twelve. You won't know I'm gone.' She laced her walking boots back on and reached for her jacket.

'I bloody well will.' Barbara grabbed her wrist. 'Please. Helen, I'm only doing this because you talked me into it. I can't do it on my own. I need you to go through the slides with me again. I can't...' she tailed off, her face raw with distress. 'Please.'

Helen paused, realising the depth of her friend's fear. But she couldn't let Rose down. She couldn't arrive too late, yet again, allow whatever horrible thing Rintrah had planned to go ahead.

'Come on, Barbara,' she said. 'You've been through scarier things than this. You've faced down classes of hostile school kids intent on making the supply teacher cry. You've survived Petrarch Greenwood. You can talk to a few tame academics. And I'll be with you, right by your side.'

Barbara rose silently and went to the window. She blew her nose and stood with her back to the room.

'I'm not like you,' she said. Her voice was harsh. 'I don't bounce back. I'm not brave or heroic. But I am loyal. I look after my friends; I stick by them. I expect the same in return. Maybe that's stupid of me.'

Helen felt wretched. 'I will stick by you. I'll be there, I promise. But I need to do this. The police...' She had already imagined the phone call. The off-duty PC, promising to pass on Helen's suspicions about the Felpham cottage. The air of polite disbelief. And nothing happening, unless someone bothered to prod an under-worked beat officer in Bognor to take a stroll into Felpham and knock on the door. As if that would have Rintrah coming out with his hands up.

'I'll call the police,' she said. 'From the train. But I need to get going. I'll ring and let you know if I find anything.' She put a hand on Barbara's shoulder. The woman stood rigid, unyielding. 'I'll meet you at the conference,' Helen said. 'I'll call from the train on the way back, let you know what time it gets in.'

The woman glanced at her, nodded. Helen realised she was trying hard to keep her emotions under control.

'Right,' she said. 'I'll see you soon. Don't worry.'

Helen took the stairs to the ground floor two at a time and hurried through the railway arches, past the Blake mosaics to Waterloo Station.

# Chapter 60

Nick awoke from a nightmare of suffocation. He gasped, gulped at air. There was something over his face, hot and itchy. It smelled of old sweat and petrol. His throat was sore and he swallowed, licked dry lips. He wanted fresh air, a drink of cold water.

He tried to throw off whatever was draped over him and realised with a clutch of panic that he could not move his arms. He was shackled, his wrists tied behind his back and his ankles bound together. His arms hurt. And he was naked, he realised, under some sort of blanket or rug.

Christ. What had happened to him?

He tried to remember. He'd gone to meet Rintrah at Kings Cross, by the canal. They'd had a drink, then... Then nothing. A blank. His head hurt all over, like his brain was too big for his skull. Shit, he realised, he'd been drugged. Rintrah must have put something into his drink.

He groaned. What an idiot he'd been, preening himself about his kickboxing and his undercover skills. And all it had taken was a couple of mouthfuls of beer.

He remembered the hidden voice recorder and felt for it behind his back. It was gone. Well, he told himself, of course it was. Rintrah had obviously seen through him from the start; had been ready for him. And he'd walked straight into the trap.

Whatever came next was unlikely to be good, he thought, fear cramping his stomach. From what he could remember of Rintrah, he'd not looked physically intimidating. Average height, average build. A bit nervy, neat and tidy in his ironed white T-shirt and clean jeans. Not someone who looked like he would relish a fight. But then he hadn't needed to be strong. Just cleverer than Nick.

He swore aloud and tried to twist his fingers to reach the tie around his wrists. Whatever Rintrah had planned, it might go better for him if his hands were free.

'Are you awake?' A girl's voice, a croaky whisper, not far away.

'Yes! Who are you?'

'Shh. He'll hear us.'

He dropped his voice. 'Sorry.'

'I'm Rose.' The girl's voice, with its attractive Irish accent, was familiar.

'Rose? Rose from Helen's class? I'm Nick. We met. I came on the Blake walk?'

'Really?' She sounded excited, as if that was a good thing. Nick remembered her well, a pretty girl who was clearly in love with the Indian guy who'd been acting like an idiot. And she'd been with Helen when they found the body of the student who'd died. What on earth was she doing here?

Nick thought of the depraved images of women on Rintrah's blog and feared for Rose even more than he feared for himself.

'Are you OK? Do you know where we are? Can you see anything?'

She sucked in her breath. When she spoke, her voice was serious, as if she was answering an exam question.

'So, we're in a small room. There are yellow curtains, closed. Narrow beds on either side. You're on one bed and I'm on the other. There's a blanket over you.'

'Can you get it off my face? I'm tied up.'

'I'm scared to do that,' she whispered. 'I don't want to piss him off. He's got a gun.'

Great, thought Nick. I'm tied up and he has a gun.

'OK, don't worry. Do you know where we are?'

Nick's mind was trying to tell him things. He had a vague memory of an earlier awakening, thirsty and confused. He'd been bundled into a car and given water to drink. Then nothing. Then waking again, stumbling over gravel, the crunch of it beneath his feet.

'Not really. Listen, though.'

He listened, heard nothing. A few birds squawked. No, scrap that. The sound was more distinctive, a mournful call that made him think of a baby crying.

'Seagulls!'

'Yeah. And when we got here last night, I could hear the sea. Waves on a shingle beach.' She sounded triumphant. 'We're by the sea.'

'We arrived together?'

'Yeah. Late. I don't know what time.'

'What happened? Do you know who this guy is?' Nick had located the ligature around his wrists: a plastic cable tie. It bit hard into his flesh as he flexed his arms apart, trying to stretch the plastic.

'No.' She sounded frightened. 'He wore this horrible mask. I got a text, about half-past ten last night, from one of my friends. Deepak. You met him, on the walk. He said to meet him in Gordon Square, under the tree where we have our tutorials. But he wasn't there. And this guy... he jumped out in the dark. I started to scream, but he pointed the gun at me.'

She stopped.

'What...'

'Shh.'

Nick heard the door being opened.

'Good morning, Rose.' The voice was the same as yesterday, a soft Californian drawl.

'What's going on?' she demanded. 'What do you want?'

He laughed, his voice low. 'I thought you'd like a cup of tea. Isn't that what you British people like? A nice cup of tea?'

'I'm Irish,' said Rose, belligerently.

'I'll take it away, then,' he said. 'But you won't get another one.'

There was a pause. 'I would like it,' she said, her voice reluctant. Nick understood. He'd kill for a cup of tea, himself. 'But I don't want to go back to sleep.'

So she'd been drugged too, he realised. He lay still, breathing as quietly as possible, working on the cable tie, trying to put the pieces of the situation together. Why had the man kidnapped Rose? Was it something to do with Oona's death?

The man laughed. Nick heard the bed creak as he sat down. 'Here. No more time for sleeping. I need your help, Rose. There is so much to do today. But you will be by my side. Our own private revolution, you and me. We're going to change the world, Rosie.'

'Don't call me that,' she snapped.

Nick heard a slap, and a shriek.

'I'll call you what I want. And you will answer. You have

to do what I tell you. Don't spoil it, Rosie. This needs to go exactly right. Now, take off your top.'

'I don't want to.'

Nick heard the sound of a gun being loaded.

Shit. He couldn't lie here and let this happen.

'What's happening?' he yelled, thrashing under his blanket. 'Leave her alone!'

There was silence for a moment, then the blanket was plucked off. Nick looked up into a terrifying face, white as paper with a red smirking mouth framed with a curly moustache. It took him a second to realise this was a mask, the Guy Fawkes mask that had been adopted by protestors all over the world.

'Awake, then?'

Nick gasped as the man threw the remains of a hot mug of tea over him, the liquid scalding his naked skin.

'No!' shouted Rose, her face distraught. 'You'll burn him.'

The man laughed. 'Yes, I might,' he said. He raised the gun, pointed it straight at Nick's head. 'You actually thought you were cleverer than me, didn't you?' he said, softly. 'You're really not.'

Nick's breath stuck in his throat as he watched the finger on the trigger. The man wore latex gloves. No fingerprints, then, no evidence. Despairing, Nick tried to remember if he'd promised to call the *Noize* news desk when he got back from the meeting. Had they sprung into action, called the police when they couldn't contact him? Were they tracking his mobile phone? Would someone break down the door of the little room, grab the gun in the next millisecond before Rintrah could fire straight into Nick's brain?

He thought of Toby, the lazy git, and knew that he was

doomed.

# Chapter 61

'Wait.'

Rose put a hand on the man's arm. She'd pulled off her T-shirt.

'Don't hurt him. I'll do what you say,' she said.

Nick tried to speak, but fear had closed his throat. He met Rose's eyes for a second, then she looked away, her cheeks flushing pink.

The man turned slowly to look at her, expression hidden behind the ridiculous mask. Nick let his breath out, a long quavering stream. Now would be the time, he thought. Jump him, grab the gun, overpower the man with Rose's help. But his wrists and ankles remained bound, and anyway, the gun was still pointing at his head, its force pinning him to the bed. It would take no more than a twitch of that gloved finger.

'Sit down.'

Rose sat obediently on the opposite bunk.

'And you, get up. Stand over there.'

With one hand, the man cut the ties on Nick's ankles, and then pulled him up by his shoulder. Nick stumbled, his recently immobilised feet unwilling to take his weight. He leaned against a built-in wardrobe in the corner of the room.

The man waved the gun at Rose. 'Pull up the mattress.'

She knelt before the bed, tugged at the upholstered fabric. It lifted up on a hardwood base, revealed storage space underneath. Oh no, thought Nick. Not that. He could handle a fight. He could handle spiders, or snakes, or heights. Pain, even. He'd been through that: three operations to fix his broken wrist. Small spaces, though. Being trapped. Not good.

The man leaned into the box, placed a small device in the bottom. 'It's attached to a pressure pad,' he said. 'It creates a very small explosion.' His voice was gleeful. 'More of a spark, really. Amazing what you can learn to do on the internet.'

He gestured to Nick with the gun.

'Get in.'

Nick began to shake. 'No, come on, man. Please. That's horrible.'

'Rose?'

'Yeah?'

'Come here.' The girl stood next to him, vulnerable in her bra and miniskirt. 'Open your mouth.' Shooting a terrified glance at Nick, she complied. The man put the tip of the gun between her teeth, his finger once more on the trigger.

'Your choice, Nick. Get in the box, or let Rosie taste that bullet.'

Nick locked eyes with Rose. You tried to save me, he thought. I'll try to save you.

He stepped into the box.

'Lie down.'

Carefully he unfolded himself on the hardboard floor. Rintrah took the gun out of Rose's mouth and pointed it again at Nick.

'That's better.'

307

He threw the blanket in after Nick, over his head. Smelling the petrol and sweat, Nick shuddered again and screwed his eyes shut.

'It's soaked in gasoline,' said the man, conversationally. 'If you move and trigger that device, you'll burn to death inside your box. I'll douse the rest of the caravan before we go.' He laughed. 'Your choice, really. You could just lie nice and still, and starve to death.'

'Please don't do this,' he heard Rose whisper.

The man laughed again. 'Well, if you do exactly what you're told, Rosie – who knows? We might come back and rescue him. Would you like that?'

Lying as still as he could, Nick heard the base being lowered back down. He opened his eyes to complete darkness and fought the urge to scream. Breathe, he told himself. All you can do right now is breathe.

# Chapter 62

Finding Blake's cottage had been the easy part. The taxi driver from Chichester had known it immediately, dropped her right outside the high flint wall in what was now called Blakes Road. The cottage was hemmed in by other houses and bigger than she'd expected, although the windows and thatched roof looked the same as in the drawing.

Helen stepped warily through the gate. On the train coming down, she'd begun to question her hasty assumption that Nick and Rose were being held in the cottage. But her many calls to their phones had gone unanswered. Wherever they were, they weren't at home.

She'd called the police again, but Maggie Lambert was off shift. She spoke instead to the sceptical policeman, who confirmed that he'd had the report from PC Lambert and said he'd pass the information on. Helen didn't want it passed on. She wanted someone to go and find Rose, right now.

The front door was heavy dark oak, studded with iron. A notice pinned to it explained that William Blake's cottage was currently closed for renovation. She peered through the narrow windows. The low-ceilinged room was piled with furniture draped with dust sheets. A pair of stepladders leaned against the chimney breast, a black plastic bucket to one side.

The other ground-floor window was boarded up. Helen followed the wall around to the back of the house, into a big garden with a lawn and vegetable patch. Scaffolding was erected this side, and some of the thatch had been removed. Underneath it was blackened, rotting. The windows showed large, pleasant rooms with fireplaces and oak beams. This wasn't how she'd pictured the Blakes, imagining them crammed into a tiny peasant's hovel. They seemed to have inhabited a big, airy house that would keep any modern-day stockbroker happy.

She'd read about the cottage on her journey. It had been bought by the Blake Society a few years back, after many years in private hands. The society wanted it to become accommodation for struggling artists. From what she could see, work appeared to have stalled. For long enough for someone to make it into a prison? she wondered. Were Rose and Nick inside?

She'd called Nick's office just after nine and spoken to an overly familiar man who claimed to be Nick's boss. He'd said that Nick hadn't yet arrived in the news room.

'Can't get the staff,' he'd laughed. 'Lazy sods.' Helen, knowing that Nick was tenacity itself on the trail of the story, was even more alarmed. She'd tried to persuade the man to tell her when Nick had last been seen, and where he was going.

'Sorry, love. Confidential.'

'I think he could be in danger,' she'd said, trying to get him to take her seriously. 'If you know where he was going, you should really tell the police.'

She needed a way into the cottage. The hefty oak doors and windows on the ground floor looked impenetrable. She stepped back into the garden and gazed up at the top floor. There was one window quite close to the scaffolding, which didn't look flush. It might be worth a try, she supposed. People were less careful about upper windows.

She scanned the surrounding houses, feeling exposed. Any one of them could contain a conscientious neighbour, getting ready to call the police about the strange woman trespassing in the garden of Blake's Cottage.

Oh well, she thought. No sense in coming all this way and then just going home again. The only way was up.

She braced her foot against a diagonal scaffolding pole, grasped the upright and hauled herself up to the first horizontal. The structure seemed firm enough, but the gaps between footholds were wide. She paused to assess her next move. From her perch, she could see the seashore: a whole sweep of coastline beyond the trees of the village. She climbed further, trying not to think about the drop opening up beneath her, focusing on keeping her hands and boots glued to the scaffolding. So long as she didn't look down, she was all right.

She reached for the next pole, swung her legs over so she could get to the section closest to the house. Wrapping an arm around a diagonal, she leaned as far as she could towards the window and peered in.

An angry face glared back. Helen jumped, losing her grip. For a sickening moment, she swayed backwards and thought she would fall. Then her back struck the scaffolding board and she managed to grab hold of the structure again, pressing her face against the cold metal. Her heart hammered painfully in her chest.

God, she thought. That had been close.

She looked back at the window, but the face was gone. It had been a man, his face surrounded by scarecrow hair and beard, rimed in dirt. Had she seen Rintrah? She thought of the blog with its violence and hatred, and shivered. Somehow, even as she'd started to climb the scaffolding, she'd not really expected him to be here.

She moved back to the window, more cautiously this time. It was ajar by an inch or so. She saw a nest of bedclothes on the bare boards of the floor. Someone, then, had been sleeping here. Apart from the bedding, the room was empty. The door stood open. Whoever she'd seen had gone.

Helen wavered. Had he gone downstairs? This might be her chance to search the house for Rose and Nick. Or he might be waiting behind the door, ready to cosh you over the head, she reminded herself. And then he'll have you as well.

She sighed. She already knew what she was going to do.

She sat for a moment on the horizontal pole, one arm looped around a vertical. The window was stiff, but with a bit of jiggling, it came loose. The casement was small, but not too small when she'd flung the window wide.

She leaned forward as far as she could, clutched the window frame in one hand and thrust her head and shoulders through. Flailing with her feet, holding her weight with one leg as she gained purchase, she pushed her torso through the gap. She wriggled, trying to get enough momentum to drag her legs through.

'What are you doing?'

'Shit!' The man was still there, huddled against the wall next to the window. He looked very young and almost as scared as she was.

'I'm stuck.'

'Wait.'

The man took her hands, hauled her in with surprising strength. She somersaulted on to the floor, landing on his sleeping bag. The smell suggested he'd been using it for a while, and didn't often get the chance to wash it. He crouched back against the wall, watching.

'Sorry,' she gasped. She sat for a moment, trying to get her breath back, eying him as warily as he was watching her.

'Who are you?' His accent was eastern European of some sort, Polish or Romanian. He had dark eyes, a bushy untrimmed beard and curly hair to his shoulders.

'I'm Helen. Who are you?'

He shook his head. 'Not important. What are you doing?'

'I'm looking for someone. My friends.'

He shrugged. 'There's no-one here. Only me.'

'And who are you?' she asked again.

He laughed as if she'd made a joke. 'Oh no. You don't get me like that.'

Helen shrugged. 'Can I have a look around? My friends – I think someone might have brought them here.'

'OK.'

She scrambled to her feet, then tensed as he stood by the door, waiting for her to go through.

'You go first,' she said, unable to shake the fear she was walking into a trap. She followed him from one empty room to another, checking cupboards and trunks as she went. Nothing, and no sign that anyone else had been here.

'See? I told you,' he said. 'I've been here for weeks. No-one else comes.'

313

'What are you doing here?' she asked.

He walked to the window, with its view of the sea. 'I read about this place, William Blake cottage. They said it was going to be a place for artists, for poets. That people could work and live where he worked. So I came. All the way from Bucharest. And it was empty. So I came in, the same way as you.'

'You're a William Blake fan?' she asked, starting to feel sorry for this young man, so far from home.

'I'm not a fan,' he said, spitting the words. 'I'm a follower. A disciple. An artist.'

Fear bloomed again in Helen's stomach. 'An artist? Have you been working here?' She thought of the blog posts, the horrible but skilful drawings.

'I'm always working,' he said, his voice sulky. 'Look.'

He gestured her to a door at the end of the corridor. Cautiously, Helen walked ahead of him, braced for attack any moment. Was Rose in that room, bound and gagged? And who was he – a student, someone she had somehow overlooked at college?

'Open it.'

She swung the door open.

# Chapter 63

The room was beautiful. It was painted a delicate egg-shell blue, with Blakean angels flying around the walls and foliage creeping from the corners. Rainbows spanned the ceiling; pink cherubs sat in golden clouds. Children danced in circles, holding hands, beneath trees whose leaves danced in the light. It could not be more different from the hellish visions of Rintrah's blog.

'I have made a heaven in hell's despite,' he said.

She turned to him, delighted. 'You really have,' she said. 'It's brilliant.' She hoped the Blake Society would think it was brilliant, too. Would they overlook his breaking and entering to impose his vision on the room? Maybe she could talk to someone – Barbara, Petrarch. Perhaps they could put in a word.

The thought of her colleagues reminded her of the urgency of her quest. She checked her watch. Shit. Almost ten o'clock, already. And she was no closer to finding Rose and Nick.

'I don't suppose you've seen any other artists since you've been here?' she asked, trying to keep her voice casual. 'People interested in Blake, I mean. Maybe people who came to look at the cottage.'

He shook his head. 'Most people come and look at the

notice on the door, then go away. They don't climb up the scaffolding.'

'No, I suppose not.' Helen joined him at the window. 'You have a great view of the sea from up here. I can see why Blake found it so inspiring. I don't think he'd seen the sea before.'

'I hadn't seen the sea before,' he admitted. 'Until I got off the coach and on to the ferry from France. It was horrible. I was so sick.' He laughed. 'I like to look at it from up here, or from the beach. Not on a boat with the sea all around, so your stomach doesn't know which way is up.'

'I sympathise.' Together they surveyed the shore, the sea sparkling beyond the garden trees.

'Holiday camp up that way,' he said, pointing. 'I work in the kitchens, sometimes. I need food, you know. As well as money for paint.'

Helen saw a row of run-down caravans. 'Up there? Where those caravans are?'

He shook his head. 'Nah. Big place, further along the coast. Very good. Butlin's Holiday Resort.' He enunciated the words with pride. 'Those caravans – they're shit. I tried to get work there, from the woman who owns the stables. She's a bitch.' Beetch, he pronounced it. 'She said I could stay in one of the caravans, if I looked after the horses. But then she said some guy had offered to pay more than double the price, so long as she left him alone. So I came here.'

Why would someone with money pay over the odds for an old caravan? 'Did you see the guy?' asked Helen.

'Yeah. Ordinary looking, nothing special. He walked over to look at the cottage. Sat in the garden for half the morning, drawing. I wanted to walk on the beach, but I had to stay inside until he'd gone. He's not there much, though.' He shaded his eyes against the sun as he looked through the window. 'He came down last night, after midnight. But I can't see his car now.'

Helen shivered. 'I think... I wonder. Could you see if he had anyone with him? A girl, or maybe a girl and a man?'

He shook his head. 'Nah. It was dark; I just saw the headlights, then the lights come on in the caravan.'

'I think I should go over and say hello,' said Helen. She smiled, trying to hide her nerves. 'Which one is it?'

He showed her. 'Last one along. But you should be careful. He's got a gun.'

Helen stopped. 'A gun?'

'He lines up targets on the beach, sometimes, at the weekends. Shoots them all to bits. He's good. Very quick.' The man grinned, showing even white teeth. 'Do you want to go back out the window, or through the door downstairs? I'd come with you, but I don't like guns.'

# Chapter 64

The woman at the stables wasn't hard to find. She was hosing down the yard when Helen approached, khaki combat pants tucked into rubber boots and her hair pulled tightly into an unflattering ponytail. Two big German shepherds jumped around her, playing in the spray from the hose. Helen paused. She wasn't keen on big dogs. They set up a cacophony of barking as she reached the yard.

'Sorry to disturb you,' she called, over the noise. 'I'm looking for a guy who rents one of your caravans. A man on his own. Can you help?'

The woman pointed the hose down, shooed the dogs back. 'Friend of yours?' she asked.

Helen shook her head. 'No, but I'm trying to find a friend. I think he might know where she is.'

The woman's eyes were hard, smoker's lines around her mouth. She looked down the line of caravans.

'He's not here. Car's gone.' She picked up the hose again.

Helen hesitated. She was running out of time. 'Look, I know this is a bit out of order. But I'm worried about my friend. She's young, only eighteen. And she's gone missing. I don't suppose you could let me check? Make sure she's not in the caravan? She might be being held against her will.'

The woman lit a cigarette, looked Helen up and down, from her walking boots to her cropped blonde hair.

'Are you police?'

'No. Just her friend.'

'Yeah, right. She's one of those eastern European tarts, I suppose. It'll cost you.'

Helen swallowed. 'I'll give you a tenner. It's all I've got on me.'

She held out her hand, and Helen drew the note from her wallet.

'It's the last one along, by the wall.' Unsmiling, the woman dug in her pocket for a bunch of keys. She pulled one off and gave it to Helen, then turned the hose back on to the dogs, who jumped up in delight. 'He's a dirty sod. If he's in, tell him I want him out. I'm not having him bringing tarts here.'

The campsite was not particularly attractive, despite the location next to the beach. The sea wall cut off the view, a concrete barrier running the length of the shore. A row of dilapidated trailers were hooked up to a big generator. Cars were parked alongside the trailers, on the dirt track that ran parallel to the sea wall. Outside one, a woman and two kids sat on folding chairs, each immersed in their mobile phone and apparently uninterested in the beach that lay just the other side of the wall.

The final caravan was set back a bit from the others. Helen circled it. All the windows were shut, faded yellow curtains pulled closed. She could see no lights, no sign of life. There were tyre tracks in the dust next to the trailer, but no car.

Helen rapped on the front door. No answer.

She fitted the key into the lock and turned the handle. It opened easily, the door swinging back. She stood on the step, letting her eyes adjust to the low light.

The room was empty. It smelled strongly of petrol, as if someone had been using it to work on a car engine. Couches with dingy yellow upholstery, worn thin and greasy with use, surrounded a table covered with a plastic sheet. Detritus was scattered around the table: bits of wire; lengths of insulating tape; an empty bottle of hand sanitiser.

She stepped inside.

The walls of the caravan were covered with taped-up sheets of paper. Some displayed hand-written lists, timetables, neatly drawn diagrams. Others showed sketches and drawings. With a shock, she began to see images she recognised. A pen-and-ink sketch of Blake's *The Ghost of a Flea*. A despairing face, shrieking into the void. Pencil sketches of the illustrations from Blake's *Visions of the Daughters of Albion*. Opening a cupboard door, she was confronted with the painting she'd seen on the blog that morning: Rose and Nick bound back to back, Rintrah laughing above them.

She'd found it. This was Rintrah's lair. But how long would he be absent?

She flung open doors throughout the van. A tiny, very clean bathroom with a bottle of antiseptic hand wash next to the basin. A bigger room with a double bed, neatly made with expensive-looking navy striped bed linen, incongruous in the cheap caravan. For a moment, she thought she could smell a whiff of Rose's cheap perfume. She sniffed the air again, wondered if she'd imagined it.

She checked the wardrobe. Empty, except for a few hangers and a bag from a smart London dry-cleaner. She pulled out drawers from under the bed – spare sheets, clean and neatly folded.

The next room had two bunks either side of a narrow aisle. It too smelled of petrol. The bare mattresses were stained, yellowing. The curtains were closed. She looked around, checked the wardrobe. A clutter of cleaning equipment – brooms, mops and buckets – fell out. Shoved in the top of the wardrobe was a brown leather jacket, black jeans and a white T-shirt. She held the jacket a moment. It looked a lot like the one Nick had worn when he'd come to visit her and Crispin.

She returned to the main room. If Rose and Nick had been here earlier, they weren't here now. She looked again at the paper taped to the walls, hoping to find a clue to where they'd gone.

'Manifesto,' read one heading. 'To be enacted on the day of my death.'

The text was accompanied by drawings of Rintrah with his sword, striding through a sea of bodies pleading for mercy. Helen read the text, wondering about the mind that had written it.

'Sooner strangle an infant in its cradle than nurse unacted desires,' read the first item on the list. 'Better to live an hour as a man than a year as a slave,' read the next. The motivational mottoes were interspersed with a list of targets – feminists, liberals, journalists – the familiar enemies of the far right. Teachers, for some reason. 'Heap their bodies high,' the list concluded. 'Build Jerusalem over the bones of the dead.'

Helen shivered. This man must be found, and soon.

Another paper showed a diagram, which looked to be the floor plan of a building. Entrances and exits were marked, blocks of seating, a stage. She frowned. A theatre? Was he planning to stage some kind of event – a rally, perhaps?

She couldn't imagine many theatres welcoming that sort of custom.

She opened doors at random in the kitchenette. The cupboards were stacked with protein shakes and energy bars. Rintrah was clearly not big on cooking. Taped to the inside of one cupboard, a familiar flyer. Her heart thumped. *Out of the Silence*. The conference that was already underway, at which she and Barbara were due to speak in – she checked her watch – three hours' time.

She gazed at the flyer, then around the room. He has a gun, the man at the cottage had said. Her eye went back to the floor plan. She looked more closely. It was the theatre where the conference was taking place, she realised.

Christ. She remembered the words on the Rintrah Roars blog, threatening to pay the conference a visit, all his enemies in one room. He was planning to stage an event, all right. She stepped to the open door and called Barbara.

'Where the hell are you?' The woman's voice was frantic. 'Are you back yet?'

'I'm in Felpham. I've found where he was staying. Listen, Barbara, he's going to target the conference today. He's got a gun. Have you been to the university yet?'

Quickly Helen described what she'd found, over Barbara's squawks of alarm.

'I'm coming back as soon as I can. But I need to get the police over to see this. And you need to warn Caroline. She has to get the police in London involved. Evacuate the hall, cancel the rest of the conference. You have to tell her to get them out.'

Helen was about to call the police when she heard a thump from the bunk room behind her. She paused, returned to the tiny room. She could see nothing, two empty bunks either side of the aisle. The noise came again. It was low down, near the floor. She knelt and lifted the mattress on one of the bunks. There was a plywood board beneath it; storage space, she realised. The thumping came again, more clearly. Dear God. There was someone in there, and she'd almost missed them.

'I'm here, Rose,' she called. 'I'll get you out.'

She folded back the plywood base, fumbling in her haste.

'Help.' It was a man's voice. Quiet, almost impossible to hear, as if he had been shouting for a long time.

A grey blanket, stinking of petrol, a figure beneath it. Helen uncovered the man's face. A terrified pair of eyes peered out, screwed up against the light. He was stuffed into the bunk like a corpse in a coffin.

'Christ! Nick. Oh my God. Are you all right?'

He shook his head, the movement seeming almost too much for him. He looked terrible. He tried and failed to speak, managing only a ragged croak. She brought a glass of water, held it for him to sip.

'Where's Rose?' were his first words.

'I don't know. I came here to look for her. Nick, who did this?'

He shook his head again. 'Get out of here,' he said.

'As soon as I can get you out,' she said. 'Here, let me help you.' She put her arm under his bare shoulders to help him into a sitting position. His hands were tied and he was naked beneath the blanket.

'No!'

Too late, Helen saw the mechanism spark beneath him.

'Get out!' he croaked. 'This whole place is soaked in petrol.'

# Chapter 65

Helen grabbed Nick's arm, pulled him out of the box. 'Come on! You can do it.' He fell to his knees, unable to stand.

The flames took hold of the blanket. The curtains disappeared in a flash of fire.

'Go,' he pleaded.

'Get up. I'm not leaving you.' Helen heaved him to his feet and wrapped her arms around his shoulders. Lucky he's small, she thought, blessing her own height and strength. 'Stay with me,' she told him. She dragged him to the door. The nylon carpet was alight, blue flames sending up clouds of black smoke. She stamped out the embers as well as she could. The air itself was alight now, petrol fumes taking the flames higher, licking greedily at the flimsy walls.

Helen shoved Nick through the door and pulled it shut behind them. But the flames had already spread through the carpet and on to the floral upholstery. The foam cushions were ablaze in seconds. The smoke was choking, foul-smelling. Helen lunged for the front door, half-dragging Nick behind her.

'Almost there,' she yelled. 'Don't stop now.'

They fell out of the caravan, Helen skinning her palms

against the gravel as Nick landed on top of her. She gulped at the fresh air, thankful to be out of the smoke. But there was no time to rest; they needed to get away from the van.

'Get up.' She scrambled to her feet. He stumbled up, swaying. 'Quickly!'

They ran to the sea wall and threw themselves over it. The caravan behind them exploded in a ball of blue and orange fire, the whoosh of heat searing Helen's hands and face.

She lay on the pebbles and sucked in the sea air, coughing out the choking smoke. Her heart thumped hard. She rolled on to her back, stared up at the blue sky, listened to the regular hiss of the waves. She could smell burned hair; felt a patch at the back of her head that had been singed.

'Are you all right?' she asked, after a second.

'Yeah. You?'

'Yeah.'

She sat up, took in the state of her friend.

'Nick, what the hell's been happening? Where's Rose? Was she here?' She took off her jacket and draped it around his shoulders.

'I don't know. She was here earlier.' He began to cough.

Helen stood and looked back over the wall. The caravan was burning fiercely, but the other vans were far enough away to be safe. The family she'd seen earlier were still in their folding chairs, staring slack-jawed at the burning van. Helen saw the woman from the stables march down the track, dogs trotting ahead of her.

She crouched down. 'I think we should get out of here,' she said. 'The woman who owns the place is bound to think I started the fire. We need to get back to London and find Rose. I think he's heading for the conference. Maybe he's taken her with him.'

There would be nothing left of what she'd seen in the caravan, she realised. No maps of the lecture theatre; no mad manifesto; no flyer from the *Celebration of Women's Words*. Nothing to show the police.

'Are you OK?' It was the guy from Blake's Cottage, crunching up the beach. 'I saw the fire.'

Helen was relieved to see him. 'Yeah, but we need to get away from here. My friend is hurt, and he's lost his clothes. Can you help?'

They tied the man's ragged shirt around Nick's waist and hobbled along the beach, then up the lane towards Blake's cottage, supporting Nick between them. In the kitchen of the cottage, the man produced a knife to cut Nick's wrists free. There were bloodied wheals around them. They'd leave a scar, Helen knew, a thin white line like a bracelet.

'We need to find him something to wear,' said Helen.

The man shrugged. 'I don't have many clothes. But I will find you something.' He disappeared upstairs.

Helen called a taxi to take them to Chichester, watching out the window, half-expecting the woman from the stables to appear with the local constabulary.

'Nick, who is he? What happened to you?'

Nick shook his head. 'I don't know. I mean, he's Rintrah, obviously. But I didn't find out who he really is. I'd arranged to meet him by the canal in Kings Cross. We talked a bit. But he must have spiked my beer. The next thing I remember is waking up in the caravan. Rose was there.

'He put a gun to my head. I thought he'd kill me then, but Rose tried to help me.' He looked as angry as Helen had ever seen him. 'He made her take off her T-shirt. Then he put the gun in her mouth and forced me to get into that horrible box.'

He stopped for a minute, breathed deeply and looked away.

'Then he put the lid on. I didn't see or hear anything else, till you came. I don't know what he did to Rose.' He put his head in his hands. Helen watched his shoulders heave.

'It must have been awful,' she ventured, putting a hand on his shoulder.

'Yeah,' he whispered. He reached for her hand. 'I thought I was going to die in there.'

She squeezed his hand, breathed in the sour smell of sweat and fear.

'You're safe now. Nobody's going to die.' She hoped to hell she was right.

The young man came back into the kitchen with a pair of faded old cut-off jeans and a dirty pair of trainers.

'I don't have anything else,' he said.

Helen turned aside as Nick pulled them on, then handed over her denim jacket. He might look like a scarecrow, but at least he wouldn't be arrested.

'Thank you so much for your help,' she told the Romanian artist. 'Won't you let me have your name? I'll make sure we replace the clothes.' And I'll talk to the Blake Society about getting you some proper help, she thought.

He shrugged. 'Gabriel. People call me Gabi.'

'Like the angel,' said Helen, smiling.

He laughed. 'Yeah. Like the angel.' He looked out the window into the garden. 'Shit. There's some police coming up the path. You better go upstairs.'

'What about you?' Helen asked.

'I'm OK,' he said. 'Go on, quick.'

Helen and Nick climbed the bare-boarded stairs. Helen

led him into the room that overlooked the garden. A loud peremptory knocking on the front door rang through the empty house.

'Police!' shouted a voice.

She heard the door creak open. 'We're closed to visitors,' she heard Gabi say. 'Opening again in a month. Come back then.'

She opened the window and gestured to the scaffolding. Nick went first, cautiously grabbing the scaffolding poles and swinging himself out on to the structure.

Helen heard heavy footsteps coming up the stairs. 'I'm an artist,' Gabi said. 'Not an intruder. I'm working on a mural. Here, I'll show you.' She sat on the windowsill and quickly clambered down the scaffolding into the garden.

Outside in the lane, they were almost mown down by a taxi, pulling up alongside the empty police car. It was the same driver as she'd had three hours earlier. A lifetime ago.

'Find what you were looking for?' he asked.

'Some of it,' she said. 'Can you get us to the station in time for the next London train?'

He looked at his watch. 'If I step on it. Jump in.'

# Chapter 66

Petrarch's hangover was one of the worst he'd had for years. He'd finished the good whisky after Veronica flounced out, then moved on to the everyday stuff. His mouth was sour and his stomach roiled. His head – the less said about his head, the better. It hurt. That was enough.

At least the flat was empty. He couldn't face Ronnie this morning, much less the ruins of his marriage. His marriage, his career, his whole life. He'd been sick in the middle of the night; retching in the bathroom like a student. Bringing up the dregs, the poison of the years with Veronica. She'd had him fooled, all this time. He tried to feel angry, and failed. He'd given her precious little reason to be loyal to him, he knew. All he'd wanted was to be loved, he thought. By everyone. Was that too much to ask?

His stomach craved something hot and greasy, a decent fry-up. No chance of that, he knew. Ronnie had been on a healthy eating drive for the last few years; the fridge held nothing more exciting than rocket leaves and protein shakes. He'd refused to try them, even when she'd read out the list of vitamins and minerals.

He drank tea and ate some toast. He didn't feel like getting dressed. But he did feel like sausages and bacon and fried bread. There was a café in Museum Street that hadn't been gentrified yet and would happily provide the works. But even the friendly Italian staff might raise an eyebrow at the professor in his pyjamas.

He dragged himself to the bathroom and stood under a long, hot shower. He felt a little better. If he was going down, he thought morosely, he might as well do it in style. He waxed his moustache, trimmed his beard, brushed and flossed his teeth. In the bedroom, he selected his favourite teal silk shirt, topping it with a brocade waistcoat. The weather was too warm for a jacket. His hand-made chestnut leather shoes gleamed. When he looked in the mirror in the hall, only his eyes gave away the pain.

He stepped on to the street, wincing in the bright sunshine, and made his way to the café. It was decorated with Arts and Crafts style tiles in a William Morris design; rather elegant for a greasy spoon. He used to come here every day when he first moved into the flat, relishing his status as a Bloomsbury local.

'*Buon giorno, Professore!*' Stefan, the owner, claimed to be Sicilian and in hiding from the Mafia. Petrarch thought this unlikely, given the readiness with which he volunteered this information to complete strangers. He looked genuinely pleased to see him. 'It has been too long. What can I get you?'

Petrarch sat and ordered, holding nothing back. Stefan beamed and fetched a big cappuccino, its frothy head dusted with chocolate. The sweetness soothed Petrarch's mood. Maybe things would work out in the end.

A woman came into the café, looking harassed, talking on her mobile phone. She was attractive, with black bobbed hair and cropped cigarette trousers, a crisp white shirt skimming the outline of her breasts. A bit outside his usual age range, though. She sat in the window and ordered black coffee.

Something about her was familiar. With the sideways light on her face, he saw she was older than he'd realised at first. In her forties, maybe even more than that. Black cat-eye make-up didn't hide the laughter lines around her eyes. She wore bright red lipstick, silver hoops in her ears. Was she a former student? he wondered. Maybe one of his girls? He felt a sentimental blooming of affection. So many of them, so pretty. He'd loved them all, in his way.

She turned her head, still talking on the phone, and met his gaze. She froze, her mouth open mid-sentence, a look of horror on her face. In the same second he knew her. Not her name, but he remembered the girl. God. It must have been Cambridge days. There was something – a pregnancy, was that it? And she'd been so sweet, so trusting. He'd paid; or at least as far as he could remember, he had.

'Here we are, *Professore*,' said Stefan, putting a huge plate before him. 'Enjoy!'

The woman was still staring at him. She finished her call. The smell of bacon rose to his nostrils, salty and tempting. He started to eat, but she was distracting him.

He tried a smile. 'I know you from somewhere, don't I?' Defuse it, acknowledge the connection but keep it firmly in the past.

She pocketed her phone, picked up her coffee and moved to his table. Damn. That wasn't what he'd meant to happen.

'You should do, Petrarch,' she said, crisply. 'You fucked me often enough.'

He choked on a mouthful of sausage. 'I'm sorry, I don't...'

331

'Yes, you do. I saw you recognise me. Barbara, in case the name escapes you. Barbara Jackson, Trinity College, 1988.'

That was the one. Barbara. North London accent, quiet and bookish on the outside. Gratifyingly eager to learn, and not at all quiet in the sack.

'I do remember,' he said. He hoped she wasn't going to bring up the pregnancy. Such a long time ago.

'You taught me Blake,' she said. 'In one way and another.'

He thought she might smile, acknowledge the naughtiness of their youth. She didn't.

'Which is why I'm speaking at your university, in two hours' time,' she said. 'At the *Celebration of Women's Words*. Are you involved?'

God, Caroline's wretched feminist conference. He was supposed to put in an appearance. The staff had all been urged to make sure they turned up, show their support. But since he'd been suspended, he didn't think he needed to go.

'Well, not really. I'm a man, you see,' he said, trying to make a joke of it. She didn't respond. 'What are you talking about?'

'Thing is,' she said, taking a swig of coffee, 'I need to talk to someone in charge. I've tried phoning Caroline Winter, but she's not taking any calls. I suspect she thinks I might pull out, so she's refusing to talk to me. But there's a possibility someone is going to attack the conference.'

'Really?' Oh Lord, was she some kind of conspiracy theorist? 'You'd better talk to the police.'

'I have,' she said. 'They said they'll pass it on. They say the university already has security in place. Apparently there have been some threats from anti-feminist groups online.'

'Well, that's all right, then,' he said. He shovelled down a forkful of bacon and egg, feeling his hangover ease.

'Not really.' She was staring at him again; most off-putting. 'Petrarch, I never wanted to see you again after the abortion.' Shit. They always had to bring it up, every time. 'And I don't particularly want to see you now. But I need help. This is serious. My friend Helen...'

'Helen Oddfellow?' God, the wretched woman got everywhere. He remembered now: she had organised some mad presentation about Catherine Blake. What rotten luck to run into her partner here.

'She says one of the students is missing. Rose O'Dowd. She's been working with us on the presentation. And Helen went off looking for her, and found her friend. He'd been tied up and left for dead.'

'What?'

'In a caravan, in Felpham. Near Blake's cottage.'

Petrarch's brain, sluggish still from the hangover, couldn't keep up. 'Felpham? What the hell was she doing there?'

Barbara was showing him something on her phone. He peered, then gave up and got out his reading glasses.

'Look. Do you know who made these drawings?'

He took the phone, and almost dropped it. The same delicate style with the horrific content; the same Blakean imagery as in the letter that Oona had been sent.

'You've seen it before,' said Barbara.

'No! No, just that the style... it's familiar. As you'll know, if you remember your Blake.' He looked again. The image was clearly of Rose, the little Irish student, and a black man. Tied back to back, like the second page from *Visions of the Daughters of Albion*. It was rather delicious.

'Where did you get this?' he asked.

'It's from a blog. A sort of online comic that references

333

William Blake. The guy who posted them – he says something is happening today. An uprising, a jihad against feminism.'

Petrarch's head hurt. The woman was deluded.

'Why do you think he's going to attack the conference?' he asked. He wished she would go away and leave him to finish his breakfast.

Barbara sighed. 'I don't know. Because he hates women? Maybe because I'm going to tell everyone that Catherine Blake wrote at least one of the *Songs of Innocence.*'

He burst out laughing. 'That's preposterous. Catherine was illiterate.' He stared at the woman. 'You are joking, right?'

'Certainly not. We have evidence. I'll be presenting it later. Assuming nothing happens to prevent me.'

Stefan took away the empty plate. 'Anything else, *Professore? Signora?*'

'I'll have a couple of those cannoli,' he said. He was craving something sweet to round off the meal. 'Pistachio and chocolate. Barbara?'

She sighed. 'Oh, go on then. I'll have a couple too,' she said. 'And another coffee.'

She'd always had a good appetite, he remembered. Not like some of the skinny ones who nibbled on salad leaves. Not like Ronnie, with her protein shakes. He was feeling sentimental. Maybe he should have married this one instead, back when she'd been a pretty little girl, fresh and enthusiastic. Before she got hung up on this feminism business, wasted her life chasing implausible theories about Catherine Blake. Maybe she would have produced a child he could actually be interested in: a bonny baby with its mother's wit and liveliness. They might even have been happy.

'Tell me about this evidence,' he said, leaning over the table.

'Only if you promise to come and help me talk to Caroline,' she said. She smiled, for the first time. 'You were always very persuasive. Let's see if you can persuade her to listen to sense.'

# Chapter 67

I f there was security, thought Petrarch, it didn't seem particularly tight. A bored-looking guy with a clipboard and a high-vis jacket waved them through the doors as soon as Petrarch showed his university staff pass. At least he hadn't been put on some sort of blacklist. He'd had visions of an alarm being triggered by his presence, guards coming to haul him away.

The Bloomsbury Theatre was a massive building, its brutalist architecture making it feel even bigger. Inside, it was cold, the air conditioning combining with the thick concrete walls to keep out any hint of early summer warmth. Petrarch was glad he'd worn his waistcoat.

'We're looking for Caroline Winter,' he told a girl putting out programmes. 'I have one of this afternoon's speakers with me. She needs to talk to her.'

'Right-oh,' said the girl, a hearty type in jeans and sweatshirt. 'Stop Looking At My Tits,' read the legend across the front of her shirt. He frowned and looked away. 'She's in the office, up the stairs and to the right.'

Caroline was sitting at a tiny desk overflowing with paper, her curly hair escaping from an unflattering hairband. An open packet of biscuits was at her elbow and she was munching on a lunchtime sandwich. On the wall, a big print-out of a spreadsheet showed the events from the conference, the ones that had already taken place crossed out in heavy black ink. She looked up, wearily, at Petrarch's knock.

'Petrarch. What a surprise.' Not a particularly welcome one, by the look of irritation that crossed her face. She switched her gaze to the woman at his side. 'Are you Barbara Jackson? I'm glad to meet you at last. I was just going over my notes for your introduction. You studied at Cambridge, yes? Was that under Professor Greenwood?'

'Partly,' said Barbara, her voice dry.

'Good, good. I have some media interviews lined up for you afterwards. The *Times Literary Supplement* and the *London Review of Books*. I've given them your slides, so they should be well-briefed. Perhaps we could do a video clip, too, for the website? We're filming the whole thing, of course. It's being live-streamed. Great viewing figures so far.'

Barbara closed the door. 'Professor Winter, we need to talk about this afternoon. It's urgent.'

Caroline looked wary. 'Take a seat.' She sat with her pen poised. Petrarch recognised that look. It was determination not to be deflected from her course under any circumstances. Whatever obstacles were put in her way, she would bulldoze straight through them. Alarming as Barbara's story had been, he didn't hold out much hope of success.

But there was a determined set to Barbara's jaw, too. She pulled up a hard plastic chair, the only other one in the room, leaving Petrarch standing awkwardly by the door.

'I think there is a credible threat that someone plans to attack the conference this afternoon,' she said. 'Whoever is behind this has kidnapped one of the students. Another man was drugged and left for dead.'

Caroline pushed back her papers. 'I don't believe it. Why have the police not been in touch?'

'They told me they would be talking to you,' said Barbara, a touch of panic in her voice. 'They said they'd review your security. Look. Look at these threats, posted online just last night.' She shoved her mobile phone across the desk, showed Caroline the blog post of Rintrah and Rose, surrounded by flames.

Caroline perched her reading glasses on her nose and peered at the images. 'Nasty. But not direct, are they? We don't know this conference is the target.'

'Except we do. Rose O'Dowd – you know her? A first-year student. She's helped me with the research.'

'One of my tutor group,' put in Petrarch. 'She was with Helen Oddfellow when they found Oona.'

Caroline glanced at him, then switched her attention back to Barbara. 'Where is Helen? She left a message with my secretary, but I haven't had time to call her.'

'Rose went missing last night.' Barbara pushed on. 'She had been sent a letter with this type of image. Delivered into her pigeonhole at the halls of residence. The same style as the letter sent to Oona, before she died.'

Rose had been sent a letter too? Petrarch felt sick. These horrible letters, the horrible pictures.

'Was… was anyone else pictured?' he asked, remembering the grotesque way he'd been drawn in the images of Oona.

The women ignored him.

'What letter to Oona?' Caroline was looking bewildered. 'I don't know anything about this.'

Perhaps because you didn't care to find out too much,

thought Petrarch.

Barbara stared at her. 'Really? Anyway, that's not the point. Helen was worried. We looked together at the blog and spotted that one of the images included Blake's cottage at Felpham. So Helen went to Felpham this morning, to try to find Rose. And she found a caravan, with a plan of the conference hall and a flyer for this afternoon's lecture. And her friend, Nick, who had been investigating the blog. She's on her way back.' Barbara checked her watch. 'I hope. She promised she'd be here by two. But the point is, you have to call off the conference. Cancel the rest of the talks, get everyone out. It's not safe to go ahead.'

'Wait!' Caroline held up her hand for a moment. She took off her glasses, massaged her eye sockets. It was a gesture Petrarch knew from many a faculty meeting. When she opened her eyes, he could see she had made up her mind.

'Firstly, Rose O'Dowd is not missing,' she said, firmly. 'I saw her about ten minutes ago, passing through the foyer carrying some boxes. Barbara, I don't know what all this is about, but if you have genuine information then pass it to the police. I do not have time for this wild speculation.' She replaced her spectacles. 'I do hope your talk this afternoon is based on something a little more credible. I would be most embarrassed if I'd brought the *TLS* over here for nothing.'

The meeting was over, but Barbara didn't know that yet.

'It's dangerous to go ahead,' she said. 'Surely you can see that? And whoever you saw, it can't have been Rose. She was in Felpham.'

Caroline glanced up briefly. 'I can assure you it was Rose. Why don't you go and find her, reassure yourself that this is all nonsense? We'll deal with whatever escapade Helen has got herself into later.'

She threw a scorching look at Petrarch.

'Perhaps you could take Barbara to the speakers' room, Petrarch? She can check over her slides and prepare for the presentation. She'll need to be ready to go in half an hour.'

Petrarch took Barbara's arm. 'Come on. Let's see if we can find Rose.' He tugged her out of the room.

# Chapter 68

The train journey to London seemed interminable.

Nick had refused to go to hospital, despite his ordeal. 'We've got to find Rose,' he insisted. 'I'm coming with you.'

Helen had called everyone she could think of. Jessica said Caroline was refusing to take any calls, but that she'd tell her that it was urgent. PC Lambert was off shift, but had left a message on Helen's voicemail to say she'd called in at Deepak's flat and found him alone. He said he'd not spoken to Rose for days. The male officer who'd interviewed Rose confirmed that PC Lambert had reported the girl missing. He said he'd circulate Nick's report of a 'possible sighting' in Sussex.

'But she's not there now,' Helen said. 'That's the point. She was kidnapped, and we don't know where he's taken her.'

'I'll contact the Sussex force,' he'd told her. 'They'll send a team to the site. If that checks out, we can widen the search.'

Desperate now, Helen escalated her calls, trying to explain to politely incredulous call handlers about the caravan in Felpham, the online blog, the man with the gun. The more she talked, she thought, the madder she sounded. No-one seemed to take her fears seriously.

Nick slept, woke ravenous and ate both the sandwiches Helen had bought at the buffet car, then slept again. She was far too wired to eat or sleep. She went online, scanning the Rintrah Roars blog for clues, going back through the posts. The blog had started in September of the previous year. *Same time I started at Russell,* Helen thought, *the beginning of the academic year.* Was Rintrah a student? It seemed the most likely explanation. The comic strips, despite the skill of the execution, had the puerile obsessions of the adolescent male – naked women, guns, revenge. But Nick had said the man was older, mid-twenties. A Californian accent. She frowned. There were plenty of American students at the university, although none on the Blake course. Plenty of mature students, too.

Scrolling through the posts, she noticed a shift from a fairly innocent hedonism in the earlier comics, to a much darker, angrier tone from January onwards. One in particular caught her eye. Rintrah, the scaly monster, sat with his chin in his hand, gazing at the ground. Behind him was a sketch of the London skyline at night – Saint Paul's Cathedral, Big Ben, Tower Bridge. Underneath, the legend read: 'I expected more of you, London. With your deep history, your great poets and playwrights. But you are the same as cities everywhere, merely seeing the surface of things, obsessed with trivia, valuing only money.'

There was something poignant about the image, the monster brooding on disappointment that the city did not live up to his dreams. What had happened? Helen imagined a troubled young man, away from home for the first time, eager to make friends and find the exciting city life he'd dreamed of. Finding, perhaps, that London was not the easiest city in which to make friends. That changing your location was not the same as changing your life.

'What are you looking at?' Nick was awake again. She showed him.

'The Rintrah blog. There were images from it pinned up in the caravan.' She scrolled through to the final post. 'That went up last night. I think it's meant to be Rose. And that's you, isn't it? Tied back to back with her. Did he tie you up like that?'

'Nope. I was out cold for most of the journey. I guess he stripped me and tied me up when we arrived in the caravan. Rose was on the other bed. I don't think she was tied up. She was very scared.' He glanced at Helen. 'Bloody brave, though. She's a hell of a girl.'

Helen smiled. 'Yeah, she is. We're going to find her, Nick. We've got to.'

Nick was frowning. 'She said she didn't know who he was. But then – right at the end, just before he put the lid on me, I think she might have realised. Maybe she recognised his voice. Did I say he'd put a mask on? Really freaky. It scared the shit out of me when I first saw it.'

If Rintrah put a mask on when Rose was there, but not when he met Nick, did that mean he was someone Rose knew? From the university, then? Or maybe, Helen thought, from Petrarch's party. She'd said it was mainly older students. Helen tried to think of second- and third-year undergraduates from the US. She could think of one or two: a much older guy who'd been in the military and a skinny kid from New York.

'Did he have a crew-cut? Big guy with heavy muscles?'

'Nah.' Nick grinned, rueful. 'I might have been more careful if he had been.'

The green countryside had given way to suburbs, chains of houses and railway junctions, warehouses and car parks. The urban mass became denser and the streets narrowed. Helen checked her phone.

'God. We've got barely half an hour. I'd better call Barbara again.'

She came off the phone grim-faced. 'It's going ahead. Caroline refused to cancel. And – weird thing – Caroline told Barbara she'd seen Rose this morning, in the conference centre.'

'Really? That's good news, isn't it? He must have taken her there.'

'Come on.' The train was slowing, weaving its way on a mass of interlinked rails into Waterloo Station. Helen jumped out as soon as the doors opened, headed out of the station at a furious pace, trusting Nick to keep up with her. She made it to the head of the taxi queue before anyone else.

'Bloomsbury Theatre. It's an emergency, so please go as fast as you can.'

The taxi driver eyed Helen in the mirror. 'Better get out my blue lights and sirens,' she said. 'Can't have you arriving late for the theatre, can we?' She pulled away from the kerb with exaggerated care and manoeuvred into the traffic. Three minutes later they were crawling across Waterloo Bridge, the wide expanse of the river stretching the sky. Up-river, the Houses of Parliament glittered in the sunshine.

Remember, remember, thought Helen. Nick had described the man's Guy Fawkes mask. Guy Fawkes had been found in the cellars of the Houses of Parliament with his barrels of gunpowder, the plot averted. Would she be in time to thwart whatever Rintrah, the spirit of rebellion, had planned? She checked her watch again. Seventeen minutes to two. The cab swerved into the underpass, emerged on to the busy thoroughfare of Kingsway. The taxi got caught by traffic lights at Holborn, then they were away, speeding up and around Russell Square. At eight minutes to two, they arrived at the Bloomsbury Theatre. Helen paid and sprinted to the entrance, to be met by a broad-chested security guard.

'I'm staff. I'm supposed to be giving a lecture in five minutes,' she said, unearthing her university ID card from her wallet. 'And he's a student.' She saw the guard look dubiously at Nick's ragged clothes. 'He's helping me.'

'All right, Miss. We've been put on top alert, you see. I've had to search everyone's bags. But as you haven't got any...'

'Thanks.' Well, that was something, she thought. Perhaps Rintrah would have been prevented from entering with his gun.

She ran up the stairs to the main auditorium, Nick at her heels. A young woman in a sweatshirt stood by the entrance, giving out flyers for the talk.

'I'm supposed to be speaking next,' Helen gasped, breathless from the stairs. She could hear a hum of conversation from the auditorium. Barbara hadn't started their talk yet.

'Blimey, you're cutting it fine,' said the girl. 'It'll take you ages to go round the back. Why don't you take the entrance down there? It brings you out at the front of the auditorium, and you can go up the stairs when they announce you. Does Caroline Winter know you've arrived?'

Without waiting to answer, Helen dashed for the door. She emerged into the auditorium just as the house lights went down. Anxiously, she scanned the darkened room. The auditorium was almost full. Caroline had done her publicity work well. Helen couldn't see Barbara, but supposed she was back-stage. Should she try to get back and find her?

'There!' whispered Nick.

Helen followed his pointing finger. Sitting in the front row of the theatre was Rose.

# Chapter 69

T hank God, thought Helen, passionate with relief. She had not been too late; Rose was alive. She squeezed Nick's hand.

'That's good.'

The stage lights went up and Caroline walked into the spotlight, screwing her eyes up against the glare. Too late to join her, thought Helen. She'd better go and sit down. She hoped Barbara would forgive her.

'Welcome back for this final session of this *Celebration of Women's Words*,' she said. '*Out of the Silence* highlights the work of women writers who went unrecognised, unheard and unpublished during their lives. And,' she paused and raised an eyebrow, 'the women whose work was credited to men. I'm pleased to say this afternoon's session is being filmed and live-streamed around the world. Because this is going to be explosive.

'I'm delighted to welcome our first speaker this afternoon, Barbara Jackson. Barbara is going to talk about one of the unknown poets of the eighteenth century, Catherine Blake. But although you may not know her name, you will undoubtedly know one of her poems – and I am sure you will have heard of her husband, William Blake. Barbara also has a surprise for us – a newly discovered poem by a much better-known woman poet, Christina Rossetti.'

She paused, clearly enjoying the buzz of surprise. Helen looked around the hall and noticed Petrarch Greenwood sitting halfway back, watching with interest. She hadn't expected him to attend.

'Let's sit with Rose,' Helen whispered.

She and Nick squeezed down the row towards the vacant seats to Rose's left. They were the only seats remaining. Lucky that no-one ever wants to sit in the front row at lectures, Helen thought.

'Barbara, who has dedicated her life to researching William Blake since she began her career at Cambridge University, has come to believe that Catherine was more than Blake's helper, companion and domestic worker. She will present evidence that Catherine herself had a hand in composing at least one of the *Songs of Innocence*, attributed solely to her husband. Ladies and gentlemen, please welcome Barbara Jackson.'

Helen flopped down in the seat beside Rose, while tentative applause rippled through the audience. Rose turned in her seat, startled. Her face crumpled when she saw Helen.

'Rose, are you OK?'

Barbara, pale under the lights in her white shirt, black trousers and red lipstick, came on to the stage, clutching a pile of index cards. She looked terrified. Helen felt a pang of guilt that she wasn't by her side, as promised.

'Oh God, Helen.'

'What is it?'

Rose was shaking, tears spilling out from swollen eyelids. 'Keep looking ahead,' she murmured, her neck rigid. 'Don't say anything. Don't move, or call out.'

'All right,' Helen whispered. 'Just tell me what's going on.'

'Keep looking ahead,' Rose said, her voice cracking.

Helen watched the stage, where Caroline was leading Barbara to the podium and showing her the remote control for her slides.

'There's a bomb taped to my chest,' said Rose, so quietly that only Helen could hear. 'I can't control it. He'll set it off if I do anything. Or if you do anything. So don't.'

Helen drew in her breath, a long inhale, absorbing the implications. Rose continued.

'His phone controls the bomb. And he's got a gun. He's going to shoot Barbara. But if I try to stop him or warn her, he'll detonate the bomb and kill us all. If you were on stage, he'd shoot you too.' She flicked her eyes sideways. 'I'm sorry, Helen. I didn't know he was going to do this, I promise.'

Helen placed her hand gently on Rose's arm. Keep breathing, keep still, she told herself. She wished to hell she'd not brought Nick with her. She wondered if it would be safe for him to get out without the gunman noticing.

'All right. We're going to work this out. Where is he?'

'Don't look at him. He's halfway back, in the central aisle, operating the camera. He brought in the gun in the boxes of video equipment. He'd told Caroline he would live-stream the session.'

Helen kept her eyes rigidly to the front, where Barbara was taking her place behind the podium, Caroline standing beside her. The urge to turn and look at the gunman was strong. Rose groped for her hand and took it, squeezing hard. Her fingers were cold, but slippery with sweat.

'Nick,' Helen murmured, leaning slightly towards him. 'Stay very still, until I tell you to get out. Then run.'

'What?'

'Hush. Listen to me. I need you to get a message out, to the security guards and the police. Rintrah is behind the camera, in the middle of the hall. He's got the gun.'

She felt him start to turn, and grabbed his arm with her other hand. 'No! Don't look. Drop down in your seat. You need to get out without him seeing.'

A woman in the seat behind leaned forward and tapped Helen on the shoulder. She jumped.

'Shh!'

'Sorry,' whispered Helen. The last thing she wanted was to spark a mass panic. Maybe Nick could go once the lecture had started. But would that be too late?

On stage, Barbara thanked Caroline for the introduction and picked up the remote control. The screen behind her illuminated.

Helen had been through the slide set the night before. Their first slide had been Blake's tender portrait of Catherine, eyes cast down and her hair softly curling against her white cap. But that wasn't what was displayed. Instead, Blake's figure of Rintrah, the scaly green monster holding a sword, appeared on the huge screen. There was a murmur around the hall.

Barbara turned her head, saw the image and froze.

'That's not...' she began.

There was a popping sound, like fireworks going off.

Red bloomed across Barbara's white shirt. As she stood, frozen, Caroline launched herself across the stage and pushed her to the ground. The gun cracked again as the women fell to the floor.

# Chapter 70

I t took Petrarch a second to understand what had happened.

He'd noticed Brett fiddling about with the camera equipment as he'd taken his aisle seat a few rows behind. Petrarch had assumed that his research assistant was currying favour from Caroline by offering to film the conference, probably looking for a permanent post on staff, now that Petrarch himself was all washed up. Maybe he had ideas of replacing Petrarch in the department, as he appeared to be replacing him in his marriage. He observed the young man with loathing.

Then, when the image of Rintrah appeared on the screen, Petrarch had a moment of revelation. Who had been at the parties, but not taken part in the sexual play? Who'd stood on the sidelines, awkward and nervous? He'd been sulky afterwards, claimed the girls had been avoiding him and Petrarch should have done more to encourage them to partner with him. Petrarch remembered how harsh he'd been with Oona when she tried to visit, after the last party. Oona, he remembered, had refused to go with him, had told Petrarch there was 'something creepy' about the assistant.

When the first shot was fired, Petrarch saw the flash from

where the camera was stationed. And then Barbara – pretty, fierce, funny Barbara – fell to the ground, blood all over her shirt, Caroline pushing her out of the line of fire. All his fury, all the protective instincts that had failed him thirty years previously, propelled Petrarch to his feet. He saw Brett steady his gun, line up the sights and aim it at the two women.

No. He would stop this.

Petrarch launched himself from his seat, threw himself down the steps at the man's back as the gun cracked again. Before half the audience had even realised where the shots were coming from, he'd knocked Brett to the ground, flattened him with his weight. I might not be good for much, he thought grimly. But I'm bloody heavy.

Brett was young, though, and stronger than he looked. As the house lights came up and horrified screams tore through the air, Petrarch felt him twist around. Something stuck into his stomach, hard and cold. He knew what it was.

'Get off me, you disgusting old goat.' Petrarch looked down. A fixed cynical smile, surmounted by a moustache and stripe of beard, stared blankly back. He doesn't look human, was his first thought. But his brain rearranged the image. A mask. The boy had put on a mask, like the coward he was.

'I know it's you. Stop this. You don't have to do it,' Petrarch said. Wasn't that what they said in the films? 'There's always a choice.' God, he sounded like some clichéd Sunday night police drama. Couldn't he do better than this?

The man was going to kill him, he realised. A rising panic in his gut, where the gun stuck into his flesh. This was it. He began to shake. But he would not give way. He'd messed up his career, he'd messed up his marriage. He would damn well die with some dignity. And if he died saving the lives of some of the young women in the hall, it wouldn't be a complete waste.

I have tried, he thought. I've lived my one and only beautiful life, caught the joy as it flies. I have seen the world in a grain of sand, held infinity in my hand. I have blazed bright. He thought of William Blake, singing joyful songs as Catherine ministered to him on his death bed.

It wasn't enough. He wanted more.

'We'll sort it out. Let go of the gun.'

The boy laughed. 'Too late, old man. Too fucking late.'

A sudden numbness spread through Petrarch's body, followed by a crack so loud it hurt his ears. He felt winded, as if he'd been pushed hard against a wall. He counted one heartbeat, two. Then pain bloomed hot, searing through his thoughts, all-encompassing.

Faintly, a long way above his head, he heard a familiar voice.

'His phone, Petrarch! Where's his phone?'

# Chapter 71

H elen raced up the steps to where the gunman lay pinned under Petrarch's body. She heard the shot, saw Petrarch convulse, then lie still. The gunman was struggling out from under his weight, trying to get to his knees.

'His phone, Petrarch!' she yelled. 'Where's his phone?'

The man looked up at her, his blank Guy Fawkes mask slipping sideways. He pulled it off, and she saw his face. Christ. It was Brett, Petrarch's research assistant. He twisted his arm behind him, trying to reach his back pocket.

Taking a deep breath, Helen launched herself on to Petrarch's back, forcing his weight back down and trapping Brett's gun arm. Brett screamed. His other arm lay awkwardly behind him at an impossible angle.

'I'm so sorry, Petrarch,' she said, wondering if he could hear her still. 'Hang on there. Help's on its way.' She certainly hoped it was; the hall was pandemonium with people screaming and clambering over seats to get out. She glanced up, saw Rose still sitting like a statue at the front of the auditorium, Nick beside her. Damn it, she needed him to get out, get help.

And Barbara, where was Barbara? Helen's first instinct had

been to run to her friend, but she knew how many people in the hall were in danger if Brett detonated his bomb. She craned her neck, but could see nothing.

Helen forced herself to focus. His phone, that was the important thing. She shifted her weight, ran a hand up a jeans-clad leg. The phone was in the back pocket. Gingerly, she extracted it, just as two security guys finally thundered down the stairs.

'Don't move!' one yelled. 'The police are on their way.'

Brett was cursing, a sheen of sweat on his face.

'He's got a gun,' Helen called to the security men. 'In his right hand. It's pinned under him at the moment. Can you get it?'

The guy closest to her took a step back. 'No way, man. We don't have authority to deal with firearms.'

If he fires it again, thought Helen, the bullet could go straight through Petrarch and into my body.

'Clear the hall,' she called to the security guards. 'Everyone except the girl in the front row. Leave her where she is. But get everyone else out.'

They bounded away. How long before the police get here? wondered Helen. And how long could she keep Brett pinned down like this? He was shouting, calling her all the vicious names under the sun.

She glanced at the phone.

The screen showed a set of numbers inside a circle. The circle was disappearing, as the numbers changed. Helen stared for a moment before she realised.

00:03:42. And then 00:03:41, 40, 39. He had the bomb on a timer. And in less than four minutes, it would explode.

# Chapter 72

This wasn't how he'd wanted it to end. He'd wanted to be in control, watching the fleeing students, picking them off as they screamed and cried, knowing that after five minutes of carnage, the whole hall would be blown sky-high. He'd imagined himself in the centre of the mayhem, standing tall, laughing as he waited for the end.

Instead he was trapped under bloody Petrarch Greenwood, the great walrus of a man, unable to see what was happening. And now the unbearable Helen Oddfellow had broken his arm, trapped his gun, and taken his phone. Which meant he could not short-cut the whole thing and blow the hall up now, while it was still full of panicking women.

The timer was underway, the seconds ticking past. He didn't want to die like this, trapped and in pain. But at least they would die with him. Helen, with her privilege and her high-mindedness, filling Rosie's head with crap about feminism. And Rosie, his chosen one, his sacrifice. He wanted her alongside him, completing him with her death. Where was she? He'd told her to stay in the front row, to keep still. She'd done it, too. She'd obeyed him.

Except... Except how did Helen know to get his phone? Rose must have told her. He felt a rush of fury at her betrayal.

'You evil witch,' he yelled, screaming at Helen. 'Women like you should be raped to death.' He saw shock in her eyes, thought for a moment she was reacting to his threats. Then he realised she had seen the countdown on the phone. He'd set it just before the first shot.

No. No, he wanted her to be there when the explosion came. And now she had seen the timer, she'd get out. She'd run for it, and save herself. He wanted her to die, for her body to be torn to pieces. It wasn't fair. Nothing was going to plan.

But she didn't run. She looked at him, her eyes steady.

'Tell me how to stop it,' she said.

He smiled, incredulous. 'Really? You think so?'

'If we don't stop it, you will die with me,' she said. 'You, me, Petrarch and Rose.'

God, she was stupid. Didn't she realise? That's what he wanted. And the longer he could keep her talking, the more likely she was to die with him.

'Greenwood's dead meat already,' he said, contemptuously.

'But you don't have to die,' she continued in her maddening, reasonable voice. 'You can save yourself. It's not too late.'

Tick, tick, tick. 'And why would I want to do that?' he asked. 'What would make it worth my while living? The pleasure of your company?' He sniggered. He'd always liked baiting women.

'You're young, Brett. No matter how bad things seem today, you have years ahead in which things can get better. You won't always feel like this. And what about Rose? I thought you liked Rose?'

He felt himself flush. Was she taunting him? 'What's she said to you?' he asked. 'The duplicitous little bitch.'

He saw uncertainty flicker in her eyes as she realised she'd

357

misjudged him. Go on, Helen. Think again. Tick, tick, tick.

'Rose,' she called, 'can you come here? I've got the phone.'

So Rose was still in the building, a walking bomb. Well, that meant she'd be nice and close when it exploded. He closed his eyes. Their flesh would meld, vaporise as one spirit. All he had to do was wait.

# Chapter 73

H elen watched the timer tick lower: 00:02:58, 57, 56. Could she just cancel it? There were two options: cancel or reset. But what if one of them set off the bomb immediately? She glanced around the hall. Most people were gone.

Rose stood and walked towards her. Helen saw she was not alone. Nick was on one side of her, Habib on the other. They were both holding her hands. Helen swallowed, moved by their show of solidarity.

'Boys, it's time to go,' she said. 'Rose and I will work this out. But there's no need for you to put yourselves in danger. Make sure everyone else is out of the hall, and get out yourselves.'

Habib looked around. 'I can't see anyone else,' he said. 'I'm staying with Rose. She's my friend.'

'Me too,' said Nick. 'She saved my life. I'm not going anywhere.'

'Barbara!' called Helen.

'I'm here.' Barbara's voice, weak, from behind the podium. Helen felt a wash of relief.

'Are you OK?'

'Not really,' said Barbara. 'There's quite a lot of blood. My shoulder hurts. I'm afraid... I think Caroline is dead. Are you all right?'

'Yes.' Helen really wasn't. She was terrified. Knowing that would not help Barbara, though.

'Habib, can you get Barbara out? It'll be quicker to get her medical help that way,' she said. She knew that paramedics would not be allowed to go into a room with a gunman until armed police had resolved the situation. And she wanted as few people in the building as possible. Her eyes were glued to the timer: 00:02:21, 20, 19.

'I could walk,' called Barbara. 'If someone can help me.' Her voice shook. 'I'm bleeding quite a lot.'

'Habib?'

He nodded. 'I will help.' He touched Rose on the forehead. 'Have courage in your heart,' he said.

And then there were just three of them: Rose, Nick and Helen. And Brett, of course. The countdown was below two minutes.

Nick crouched down beside them. He stared into Brett's face, as if searching for something. Don't do anything, thought Helen. Don't provoke him. He still had the gun, although she wasn't sure if he could use it.

'You were going to burn me to death,' said Nick, softly. 'You shut me in that box, left me to die in the most horrible way I can think of. What did I ever do to you?'

Brett's eyes flickered. 'Poor little black boy. You're no good, your sort. You never will be.'

'Stop it, Nick,' snapped Helen. 'There's no time for this.'

Brett shoved her shoulder, taking her off-guard. Before she could react, she was thrown to the ground, her body slamming awkwardly against the audience seats. She felt a sharp pain in her ribs. Rose screamed.

Helen scrambled to her knees, still clutching the phone. Brett and Nick grappled on the ground. Petrarch's body lay on its side, his beautiful waistcoat soaked in blood. Brett was covered in it, his grey T-shirt almost black as he struggled. The gun was lying next to them.

Helen gripped her side with one hand, struggled to her feet. Every time she breathed in, it hurt. Before she could get there, Rose had grabbed the weapon. She pointed it at Brett.

'Stop it! Leave him alone!'

Brett looked around in surprise.

'Rosie! You wouldn't shoot me, would you?'

Nick took the chance to grab Brett's broken arm and twist it behind him. He screamed with pain.

'Lie still,' commanded Nick. 'Or I'll do it again.'

'Stop it!' shouted Helen. 'Everyone calm down. We need to cancel this timer. Rose, did he tell you how to stop it? Which do I use, reset or cancel?'

'I think...' Rose looked uncertainly from the gun to the phone. 'He said there was no going back. That it couldn't be cancelled.'

If it can't be cancelled, thought Helen, maybe it can be reset? She could hear sirens from outside the building, but there was no time to wait. They were down to the last seconds. She glanced up at the camera. Was it still running? she wondered. Caroline had said they were live-streaming the conference. Were there people watching this from around the world? She hoped someone had thought to stop the feed.

Hands slipping with sweat on the glass screen, Helen pressed 'reset' and closed her eyes.

# Chapter 74

Nothing happened. It was the best nothing that Helen had heard in her life. She opened her eyes, dizzy with relief.

'Timer paused,' said flashing text on the phone. 'Enter the password. Timer will resume in 60 seconds.'

Oh, Christ.

'Password,' she said to Rose. 'Come on, any ideas?'

Brett lay on his back, bathed in blood, a big smile on his face.

'Shall I twist his arm again?' asked Nick. He sat on Brett's chest, king of the castle. 'I'll make him tell us.'

She saw a flicker of fear pass over Brett's face. Helen was transported back to her own ordeal at the hands of an inquisitor who'd held burning cigarettes to her skin. The experience would never leave her. She felt again the hot wash of shame, the humiliation of being powerless. The desperation to do anything, anything at all, to make the pain stop. She'd have said anything, lied, invented what she thought he wanted to hear. That was no way to get to the truth.

'No,' she said. 'No-one is going to do that.' She held Nick's gaze, saw his frustration. 'We will find a way out of this,' she said. 'But not like that.'

She turned to Rose. 'Think. What would he use as the password?'

'His name?' said Rose, her voice uncertain. 'He said it a few times; that everyone would remember our names.'

Brett. Really? Helen looked at the front of the hall, saw the image of Blake's monster projected on the screen at the front. Rintrah? Maybe that was more likely. Quickly, she typed the letters into the phone. Nothing happened; the message continued to flash. Fingers sweating, she tried Brett. Nothing.

'What's his second name?' she asked, trying to remember. She must have been introduced to him properly when they first met.

'Albion,' said Rose. She started to laugh, a little hysterical. 'Like England, he said.'

'Please,' said Nick. 'Let me twist his arm a bit.'

'Wait.' Helen typed in the letters. Nothing. God. Maybe she'd better let Nick do what he said. She felt sick.

'Brett.' She crouched beside him. 'Please. This has gone far enough. Let me stop it.' His smile was mocking, but his eye twitched. 'You don't really want to die like this, do you? Why not give yourself a second chance?'

She saw him shift focus, look beyond her. He took a deep breath and closed his eyes. He was expecting the end, had accepted his death. She turned her head, looked to the front of the hall.

The projection had changed. This must be the image he'd planned to be showing when the bomb went off, she realised. As it would in about ten seconds' time, unless she could somehow guess the password.

It was magnificent, uplifting. A young man stood on rocks, his arms outstretched, his hands wide in welcome. He was a figure of harmony and beauty to match Da Vinci's *Vitruvian Man*, every muscle delineated with grace. Around him was a starburst, a rainbow of colours that seemed to emanate from his own body, as if he was shining, a sun. It was the image Petrarch had over his desk.

'What's that called?' she asked, urgently. 'The painting?'

'Albion!' shouted Rose. 'Albion...*Albion Rose*.' She turned to Helen, her eyes gleaming. 'Our names. Me and him. There's a poem; Barbara showed me.'

Brett roared with anger and struggled to throw Nick off. Quickly, Helen typed the letters into the phone. The little box stopped flashing and disappeared. The timer stopped. Four seconds remained on the screen.

Rose stared at Helen. 'That was it.' She sat down abruptly, and started to cry.

Brett lay down again, closed his eyes. '"Albion Rose from where He Laboured at the Mill with Slaves,"' he recited, his voice far-away. '"Giving himself for the Nations he danced the Dance of Eternal Death."'

At the back of the hall, Helen heard shouting, and armed police burst through the doors.

# Epilogue: one month later

An impeccably dressed woman with perfectly arranged hair walked with confidence to the microphone at the front of the hall. They were in University House, the grand Art Deco building where Russell University graduation ceremonies were held. It had been thought inappropriate to present the lecture in the same theatre where Brett's murderous spree had unfolded.

The woman smiled, a sterile, smooth smile.

'Welcome to the inaugural Petrarch Greenwood Memorial Lecture,' she said. There was a ripple of applause. Helen watched from the back of the hall, next to the exit. Her claustrophobia had worsened; she always needed to see a clear way out. Nick sat beside her, his usual bounce and chatter stilled. Like her, he now found enclosed spaces and crowds difficult to handle.

'As you know,' said the woman, her voice containing just the right amount of tremolo, 'my late husband Petrarch was Professor of Poetry at Russell University for many years. He was also a world-renowned expert on the work of William Blake. His tragic death last month robbed the world not just of his presence, but of the work he was destined to do. His final book was unfinished. But I can tell you, it would have been a masterpiece.' She paused and dabbed her eyes. Helen could see no glint of tears.

'So I thought it fitting that I should set up a memorial lecture in Petrarch's name, linked to a Russell University fellowship to be funded from the Greenwood Foundation. And I am delighted to welcome now the first Greenwood Fellow, Barbara Jackson. I think it is very fitting that Ms Jackson, a former student of my husband, will deliver the inaugural Petrarch Greenwood Memorial Lecture.'

Veronica paused. Barbara, chalk white but smiling, walked on to the stage. Her arm was still in a sling, her shoulder wound healing. Helen shuddered, half-expecting to hear again the sound of gunshots, see the burst of scarlet across Barbara's white shirt. She wasn't sure if she herself could have delivered this lecture. But Barbara's voice was steady as she thanked Veronica Greenwood and turned to the audience.

'They say that every great man is backed by a great woman. I'd like to thank Mrs Greenwood for her generosity and support in giving me the time and resources to continue my academic research into Catherine Blake. As I hope I will show, Catherine was far more than a help-meet and supporter of her husband. And I'm sure that Mrs Greenwood's contribution to Professor Greenwood's work was also far greater than many people know.

'I would also like us to take a moment to remember Professor Caroline Winter, head of English at Russell, who died in the same tragic incident. And who by her courage saved my life.'

There was a moment of silence. The lights dimmed and the slide of Catherine Blake's portrait appeared on the screen.

'I have no name,' read Barbara, softly. 'I am but two days

old. What shall I call thee?'

The slide changed to the tender image familiar from *Songs of Innocence*, a woman with a new-born baby on her lap, enclosed in the bloom of a flower.

'Pregnant women talk to their babies all the time,' said Barbara. 'And to their new-born infants, of course. What is your name? What shall I call you? I hope you'll be happy, I hope you'll be healthy. That dialogue, simple and tender, is what we see recorded in *Infant Joy*. And although it's possible, I accept, that a man might imagine that conversation between a woman and her unborn child, I'm going to suggest that at least some of these are Catherine Blake's words we are reading here.'

Barbara continued to build her case, calm and certain. She showed them the Rossetti poem, and explained how it had led Helen to All Saints church and the missing pages from *An Island in the Moon*.

'And what a treasure we found there.' She projected a slide of the first draft of *Infant Joy*, the two hands of Catherine and William Blake interspersed.

Helen watched with admiration. Barbara's confidence had grown enormously since the disastrous first attempt to give the presentation. They'd sat up late the night before, drinking wine and eating pasta, while Barbara tried to explain.

'Two things,' she'd said. 'I had a chance to say what I needed to say to Petrarch before he died. And just about the worst thing that could possibly happen to me on stage actually happened. I survived. So who cares if people think I'm nuts? So long as they don't shoot me, I'll be happy.'

Helen surveyed the auditorium. The audience was rapt; even those of her colleagues who had expressed scepticism were watching with respect. She spotted Father John, the vicar of All Saints, near the front of the hall. He'd come to visit Helen in hospital, where she'd been treated for her broken ribs, and had kept his promise to say nothing about the purloined prayer book, which Helen had returned.

Rose was sitting in the middle of a group of women students halfway back, all leaning forward and taking notes. Liz sat next to her, scribbling diligently. Helen worried about Rose. She'd spent a week at home with her family in Ireland, then returned, insisting she was well enough to take her exams.

Attempted rape and kidnap had been added to Brett's charge sheet. Rose had told Helen and Barbara about it, shaking as she recounted how he'd tried to force himself on her in the caravan.

'He couldn't do it,' she'd said. 'He got upset. I had to comfort him. I thought, if I was nice to him, he might let Nick go. But he didn't.'

The armed police who'd burst into the theatre hadn't planned to be nice to Brett. Had Helen herself not blocked their line of fire, she had no doubt they would have killed him on sight. The thought that she had somehow managed to keep at least one person alive gave her a sort of comfort. The deaths of Caroline and Petrarch, which she had been unable to prevent, weighed heavily.

On stage, Barbara had moved on to the evidence she'd uncovered of Catherine Blake's pregnancy, during the early years of the Blakes' marriage, when they lived in Poland Street with Robert, William's brother, as their lodger and colleague.

'There's one possibility I can't quite exclude,' she said, arching an eyebrow. 'Catherine Blake was pregnant only once in their long marriage, as far as we know. And that was when Robert was living with the Blakes. Before that time, and for the long years after Robert's death, the Blakes seem to have been unable to conceive. It does rather make you wonder who fathered the child so celebrated in *Infant Joy*?'

Helen smiled. She herself had pointed that out to Barbara, as they mused over the poem found in Christina Rossetti's prayer book. Given Blake's views on the communality of love, and his devotion to his brother, she wondered whether he had even encouraged such a liaison. And Catherine herself – did she have much say in the arrangement? Was it her choice, or was she again acting as an obedient wife, her only wish to please her husband?

Helen couldn't imagine being so in thrall to a man that she would sleep with whoever he wanted, and allow him to do the same. Perhaps it was as well that she was single, she thought. Better a steady solitude than the loneliness of two people failing to harmonise.

As usual, she tried and failed to suppress the thought of Richard. With him, she had glimpsed the possibility of two lives entwining, without one strangling the vitality out of the other. She thought of the two hands, alternating lines, in the first draft of *Infant Joy*. Two minds, working together. But Richard had been a rare man, and she didn't expect to find another like him. She felt herself too on-edge, too odd and solitary and impatient, to make a comfortable companion.

She glanced at Nick, jiggling his knees up and down. He too was restless, independent. He'd been difficult to be with since Felpham, prone to angry outbursts and fits of depression. She got the feeling he resented her for having seen him helpless, scared and vulnerable. Nick didn't like being rescued. He wanted to be the hero, not the victim.

369

She pulled her thoughts back to the present. Her gaze rested again on the heads of the students in front of her. Habib was missing. He'd had problems with his visa, he'd told her; had been accused of cheating in his English language test. Which was ridiculous; his written English was excellent, even if he occasionally made mistakes in speech when agitated. He was frightened of being deported, scared that word would somehow get back to Iran about his attendance at Petrarch Greenwood's party. Helen had promised to help however she could.

A thunderous burst of applause greeted the end of the lecture. Helen rose to her feet with the rest of the audience and cheered as Barbara, her cheeks now pink, smiled and bowed. As the noise continued, Helen and Nick slipped quietly out of the auditorium.

She breathed more freely in the daylight. She'd promised to catch up with Barbara later that evening, after she'd been congratulated by everyone and done her press interviews. They headed for Gordon Square.

June had brought with it rainclouds and cooler weather, after the heatwave of May. The grass was green and lush, the paths damp. Helen didn't mind the change in weather. They sat on a wet bench and she drew a letter from her jacket pocket.

'I'm delighted to offer you a permanent post as senior lecturer in poetry and drama at Russell University,' she read. With Petrarch and Caroline gone, the university was moving fast to attract or retain staff in the English department, which had been gripped by panic after their deaths.

The students were in the middle of examinations, the staff struggling to cope with the additional work and lack of leadership caused by Caroline's sudden death. The situation was compounded by the discovery on Brett's phone of dozens of messages from Jessica, who seemed to have been feeding him a constant stream of gossip and inside information about departmental business. She'd been suspended while her role in the atrocity was investigated. The university's vice chancellor was keen to lock staff into firm contracts. But Helen was unsure whether she wanted to be locked in.

'Will you take it?' asked Nick. He'd resigned his job at *Noize* and moved back to his brother's house in Lewisham. He planned to go freelance, specialise in investigative reporting. He'd already been asked to work on a documentary about the far right and the Dark Web for an independent production company.

'Don't know.'

The offer was generous. But it would mean more time in her cubbyhole of an office, more time tied up with administration and marking and exam preparation. Helen was impatient to be outside, to go back to her walking and her writing, alone in her flat. She'd almost made up her mind to decline. Maybe the university would accept her for a part-time role, a couple of lectures and tutorials a week. Maybe they wouldn't. Either way, Helen thought, she would find her own path.

She shoved the letter back into her pocket, got to her feet and stretched. She felt like a walk, a good, long walk through Holborn, down to the river and along the Thames at Bankside. If the tide was out, she'd go down the slippery steps to the foreshore, walk on the silt and see what the river had left behind, the tides forever turning over the detritus of London's history.

'I'm going walking. Take care of yourself, Nick. See you again soon.'

He rose and hugged her. 'See you. And do some writing!'

She smiled. She'd unearthed her poetry notebook from its drawer the night before. It would be waiting, when she got back.

She thrust her hands into her trouser pockets and felt for the short length of clay pipe that she kept there, rolled it between finger and thumb. Richard had retrieved it from the Thames silt, rubbing it clean and handing it to her, the first day they had met. It was her talisman, a memory of him and a reminder of all the lives that had come before their own: dockers and sailors and ferrymen, filling their tobacco pipes as they plied their trade. Hidden stories, ripe for discovery. She felt the tug of the river, the excitement of a blank page.

She began to walk.

# Notes

The historical background to *The Peacock Room*, including what is known of the life of William Blake and Catherine Blake and the interest in Blake of the Rossetti family, is based on real events. As usual, I have taken what is known and asked 'what if..?'

Russell University and its staff is entirely fictional, despite sharing its location with a well-known central London university. Having lived and worked in Bloomsbury, I couldn't resist using its literary squares and circles as a backdrop.

I researched *The Peacock Room* in the British Library and the Lambeth Palace Library in London, the John Rylands Library in Manchester, and the Fitzwilliam Museum in Cambridge, all of which are well worth a visit. My thanks to the staff at these institutions for their assistance.

My reading for *The Peacock Room* included two excellent biographies of William Blake, Peter Ackroyd's *Blake* and Richard Holmes' edition of Alexander Gilchrist's biography, *Life of William Blake*. Notes about the Gilchrist biography alerted me to the connection with the Rossetti family.

My bible for the works of Blake was Thames and Hudson's beautiful facsimile *William Blake: The Complete Illuminated Books*. I was fortunate enough to visit the Tate Britain's 2019 William Blake exhibition multiple times.

If you enjoyed *The Peacock Room* and would like to keep in touch, sign up to my newsletter at my website, annasayburn-lane.com and please consider leaving a review on Amazon or Goodreads. Your reviews really help me to reach new readers.

# About the Author

Anna Sayburn Lane is a novelist, short story writer and journalist, inspired by the history and contemporary life of London.

Anna has published award-winning short stories and was picked as a "Crime in the Spotlight" new author at the 2019 Bloody Scotland International Crime Writing Festival.

She lives on the Kent coast.

**You can connect with me on:**
- http://annasayburnlane.com
- https://twitter.com/BloomsburyBlue
- https://www.facebook.com/annasayburnlane

**Subscribe to my newsletter:**
- http://eepurl.com/dyUtmX

# Also by Anna Sayburn Lane

The Peacock Room is the second Helen Oddfellow mystery. Have you read the first one in the series? Start reading here.

**Unlawful Things**
**A hidden masterpiece. A deadly secret buried for 500 years. And one woman determined to uncover the truth.**

When London tour guide Helen Oddfellow meets a historian on the trail of a lost manuscript, she's intrigued by the mystery – and the man.   But the pair are not the only ones desperate to find the missing final play by sixteenth century playwright Christopher Marlowe. What starts as a literary puzzle quickly becomes a quest with deadly consequences, unfolding along the pilgrim road from Southwark to Canterbury.

When Helen realises the play hides an explosive religious secret, she begins to understand how much is at stake. Relying on her quick wits, she battles far-right thugs, eccentric aristocrats and an ancient religious foundation.  There is a price to pay for secret knowledge, but how high is too high?